W9-BVW-290

THE WORLD GIVES WAY

THE WORLD GIVES WAY

A NOVEL

MARISSA LEVIEN

This book is a work of fiction. Names, characters, places, and incidents are the product of the author's imagination or are used fictitiously. Any resemblance to actual events, locales, or persons, living or dead, is coincidental.

Cover design by Lisa Marie Pompilio
Cover illustrations by Arcangel and Shutterstock

Redhook Books/Orbit
Hachette Book Group
1290 Avenue of the Americas
New York, NY 10104
hachettebookgroup.com

First Edition: June 2021

Redhook is an imprint of Orbit, a division of Hachette Book Group.
The Redhook name and logo are trademarks of Hachette Book Group, Inc.

Quote on p. ix excerpted from Italo Calvino, *Invisible Cities*, trans. William Weaver. Orlando: Harcourt, Inc., 1974.
Quotes on pp. 6, 84, and 337 excerpted from Gertrude Stein, *The World Is Round*. New York: Young Scott Books, 1939.

Library of Congress Cataloging-in-Publication Data
Names: Levien, Marissa, author.
Title: The world gives way : a novel / Marissa Levien.
Description: First edition. | New York, NY : Redhook, 2021.
Identifiers: LCCN 2020046202 | ISBN 9780316592413 (hardcover) | ISBN 9780316592420
Subjects: GSAFD: Science fiction.
Classification: LCC PS3612.E92354 W67 2021 | DDC 813/.6—dc23
LC record available at https://lccn.loc.gov/2020046202

ISBNs: 978-0-316-59241-3 (hardcover), 978-0-316-59239-0 (ebook)

Printed in the United States of America

LSC-W

Printing 1, 2021

For my parents.
For Michael.

THE WORLD GIVES WAY

At times I feel your voice is reaching me from far away, while I am prisoner of a gaudy and unlivable present, where all forms of human society have reached an extreme of their cycle and there is no imagining what new forms they may assume. And I hear, from your voice, the invisible reasons which make cities live, through which perhaps, once dead, they will come to life again.

—*Invisible Cities*, by Italo Calvino

Geoffrey: Why, you chivalric fool—as if the way one fell down mattered.

Richard: When the fall is all there is, it matters.

—*The Lion in Winter*, by James Goldman

1

MYRRA

Myrra smashed a roach with her bare hand as it crawled along the wall, then recited a small eulogy for the deceased in her head. Perpetual survivors, the roaches had managed to sneak a ride on this world to the next, even when every other bit of cargo had been bleached and catalogued over a century ago. Myrra admired their pluck, but Imogene would hate the sight of an insect, and where there was one, there were always more. It was late, nearly three a.m. The roaches liked to explore at night, and Myrra's room was close to the kitchen.

Myrra retrieved an old rag from her stock of cleaning supplies and wiped off her palm. Then she sat back down on her cot, a lumpy pillow propped behind her back, and resumed writing her letter.

It was strange to be writing with paper and pen, but since Imogene had found Myrra's tablet last month, Myrra had needed to improvise with other methods of communication. What a row that had been. Myrra had been so careful hiding the tablet, taping it behind the mirror in her room. But there'd been a bad spate of earthquakes lately, and it had fallen out at an ill-timed moment when Imogene was inspecting the room. Marcus never bothered enough to care about that sort of thing, but Imogene was livid. She'd only grown tenser and madder and more controlling in the past year, and as she'd screamed at Myrra, she'd framed the tablet as the ultimate transgression. For her part, Myrra had tried her best not to show her contempt. She still winced thinking of the sound the tablet made when Imogene smashed it against the side of a table, the glass cracking, the screen going irreparably black. Just a thin, flat piece of silicon and metal, but it had been a door to the world for a while. And it had proved so useful when it came to Jake.

Jake had given her the tablet six months ago. She remembered him pressing it into her palm in the alley behind his father's store. He was so happy to be helping the cause of the contract workers. His hands lingered against hers, and his forefinger stroked her wrist. Light, like a stolen kiss. That was when she knew she had a shot. They'd gotten good use out of that tablet.

Still, no point mourning something that was already gone. There was always another way through a problem. At least a pen was something easy to steal. Paper even easier. Marcus had boxes and boxes of the stuff, and he was terrible at keeping track of everything in his collections. He relied on Myrra for that.

What was important was that Jake liked writing this way. Paper was unique. Antique. Romantic.

Myrra inspected the red welt on her knuckle where the pen pressed against her finger. A pen was such an unfamiliar thing to hold. The first few letters she'd written to Jake had been disastrous to look at: violent slashes of ink darted across the paper, interrupting the shaky letters she tried to form. The pen spun out of her hand every time she thought she had a grip. Eventually she learned to hold it like chopsticks, and things improved from there. The lines of ink were still more jittery than she wanted; nothing compared to the smooth looping cursive she'd seen on some of Marcus's antique letters and papers.

Myrra wrote with slow care, frequently checking her spelling in one of Marcus's dictionaries. It was maddening, how long it took. And there was no backspace. Just an ugly scratch to black out the word if you got it wrong. Jake would want her simple, but just simple enough. Misspelled words and bad handwriting would send the wrong message.

Dear Jake. Start slow and familiar, not too mushy. Apologize for not writing sooner. Myrra decided to throw in as many *sorrys* as she could, to make him feel a little loftier. Tell him you miss him. Ask to see him. Don't say why. Don't say I love you, yet.

You have to tease these things out. Add spice to the sauce a little at a time, let it simmer. Patience. Do this right, and where might you be in a year? The first thing Myrra pictured was diamond earrings, long and dangling like exquisite icicles. Imogene had a pair like that. She'd worn them with her blue silk gown at the last state dinner. Myrra pictured a vast bed as wide as it was long with soft mussed sheets. She pictured gold around her finger.

That was Imogene's world she was seeing. Jake was a grocer's son. Myrra would get a gold ring, but not the diamonds. At least not right away.

In fifty years, Myrra would be free. The work contract her great-grandmother had signed would finally be fulfilled, and she was meant to be satisfied with that. Hard to imagine how it would feel, really, to be free. In fact, most other contract workers in her generation considered themselves lucky; her mother and her mother's mother had not lived with that luxury. It was a frequent topic of conversation among her compatriots; everyone had different plans for what they'd do with their futures once their contracts ended. Most were unimaginative. Women she'd worked with in the laundry had talked about opening their own wash-and-fold service shops. Hahn, a boy she ran into now and then at the grocery store, was endlessly talking about the bar he'd open someday. He had it planned down to the prices of the drinks and the music on the stereo. Some who were employed as maids or handymen were planning on keeping the same positions with their host families; all they were looking forward to was a future where they got paid and had proper drinking money.

But Myrra refused to buy into this kind of talk—in fact, she took pride in her dissatisfaction. A butcher she'd once worked for had told her that the good meat farms knew how to keep their animals fat and happy, trusting enough that they'd cheerfully trot toward the slaughterhouse. The law said that in fifty years she'd be free; well, in fifty years she would be dry and creaky with baggy skin and sagging breasts, looking like the old retired whores off Dell Street who still powdered rouge over their spotted faces. She'd have five good years, ten at most, before her body gave out. Five years after a long trudging lifetime of labor. What kind of life was that? She refused to wait and only get what she was given. Not when she was young and Jake was there for the taking.

She continued the letter for a few paragraphs more, keeping the anecdotes light and quick, asking plenty of questions in between. Jake liked it when she was inquisitive. She mentioned a particularly successful dinner party that Imogene had thrown for her political wives' club. Imogene had been drunker than usual, and the result was that she forgot to critique Myrra on the details of the meal. It was a nice change—lately the household had felt tense, and Myrra wasn't quite sure why. Both Imogene and Marcus would frequently sink into spells of silence; they'd snap at Myrra unpredictably for any old thing.

But Myrra didn't want to think about that. She certainly didn't feel like writing it down in a letter. Instead she described the food. Jake liked that she knew how to cook. She mentioned that Charlotte had been sleeping better—it was a relief, after the latest bout of colic. Myrra wasn't sure how much Jake cared about Charlotte, but she couldn't help writing about her. Charlotte was the only good part of her days.

It was a miracle that Charlotte was here at all for Myrra to fawn over. Marcus hated babies—he hated anything messy. There had been months of guilting from Imogene before he finally agreed. It was elegantly done, Myrra had to admit. If Marcus hadn't gone into the business himself, Imogene could have made a great politician.

"I'm getting older now." Myrra remembered holding a china tray and watching as Imogene passively yet artfully batted her words over the coffee cups, over the breakfast table, arcing them right over the top of Marcus's wall-like news tablet barrier so they'd fall right in his lap. "If we don't try soon, we might never be able to have one." He would volley back a grunt, or mumble something about stress at work. Finally, after many mornings of similar repetitive banter, Imogene found her kill shot, something to fire straight through the tablet, hammer through his mustache, and knock out his teeth: "Don't you want to make something that will outlive us? What about your legacy?"

Talk of his manly legacy, his ego, and he was cowed. Imogene won the match.

But once born, Charlotte was treated as an investment by Marcus, and Imogene mostly ignored her in favor of getting her figure back. Myrra knew Charlotte better than anyone, what songs she liked, which cries went with which problem, what you could do to make her giggle.

Maybe this could also be the type of thing Jake liked. Jake seemed like the kind of guy who wanted kids someday.

Myrra ended the letter with a genuine note of thanks for the book that Jake had given her. Another object secretly given in the alley behind the shop, but at this point they'd moved past the quaint brushing of hands. Myrra had shown her appreciation in the most intimate of ways. She knew just how to touch him now.

Myrra mostly stole books from Marcus's library, but this one was hers to keep. Just as long as Imogene didn't find it. On reflex, Myrra reached down and let her fingers slip through the slit she'd cut into her mattress. She felt around through the foam batting until she found the rough spine of the book. She pulled it out and cradled it in her palms. It was an old one, with tanned pages and a faded orange cover. But then again, they were all old. Books, like paper, were rare. Marcus had one of the largest collections in New London, but most people only had tablets. It was truly a beautiful, meaningful gift. Jake's family was well-off, but this was something else. This was an I-love-you gift. An investment gift. *The World Is Round*, by Gertrude Stein. Myrra had taken to reading five or ten pages each night. It was fun—bouncier than the books she'd swiped from Marcus. Some of those had been terrible slogs, pushing through only a word or a sentence at a time. Tolstoy, Balzac, Joyce. The writing was dense and impossible, and mostly it made her feel stupid. But she kept at it, powered by spite and stubborn force of will. People who got paid read books, so she would read books too.

She opened the book and found the page where she'd left off. "The teachers taught her / That the world was round / That the sun was round / That the moon was round / That the stars were round / And that they were all going around and around / And not a sound."

One section in, the words began to rearrange and swim. Myrra's eyes were heavy.

Myrra squinted to see the wooden clock under the amber lamplight. Imogene, with her shrewd touch, had snagged the clock along with forty other pieces in a wholesale antiques buy, but it broke in half after a bad fall from a tall shelf. Imogene let her keep the pieces, and with a little glue, pliers, and wire, Myrra had managed to get it ticking again. Myrra liked analog clocks—reading their faces felt like deciphering code. Little hand pointing to the right, and long one pointing straight down: three thirty now. Too late (too early?) to be fighting sleep.

Fluffing out the pillow lumps, she closed her eyes and curled up on her side. She was just starting to feel warm under the blankets when she heard the comm box ring out. Myrra sat up with a shock, looking at the speaker on the wall near the door. Imogene was calling. Probably the baby was fussing. Poor little Charlotte, stuck with such a cold mother. Maybe her colic hadn't gone away after all. Myrra groaned as she slid her arms into a nubbly blue robe and her feet found slippers. She walked over and pressed the red button on the comm box.

"Should I heat up a bottle?" Myrra asked.

"No—no, Charlotte's fine. I just need your help with . . . something. Could you just—could you come to the terrace, please?" Imogene's voice sounded high and frail—as if she had spontaneously reverted to being five years old. Had she been sleepwalking again? She'd gone through a good bout of ghostly hallway strolls when she was pregnant, but all that went away when Charlotte was born.

"Ma'am, can I ask if you took your sleeping pill this evening?" Myrra tried to keep her tone measured—not good to shock a person who was still asleep.

"Jesus Christ, I'm lucid, I'm awake. Can you just get up here, please?" That sounded more like Imogene.

"Yes, ma'am."

Myrra considered rifling through the mound of laundry in the corner to find the cleanest dress in the bunch, but the snap of Imogene's voice still reverberated through the room. Go for speed over presentability at this point, and stick to the robe and slippers. Myrra tucked the nubbled folds higher and closer around her neck. Fifty floors up at this time of the morning, the terrace was bound to be damp.

Myrra slipped out of her room, pushing open the door and easing it closed behind her. The door was an intricate and beautiful object, carved and inlaid walnut with a sculpted brass handle. The rest of her room was simple and bare, but the door had to present itself on the exterior side as well as the interior. Myrra's room was on the bottom floor, in a dark corner behind the main staircase. It wasn't likely a guest would find their way back there, but just in case, she still got a good door.

Imogene and Marcus Carlyle's penthouse was a three-story feat of opulence, with sweeping staircases, vaulted ceilings, marble floors, and antique lead-glass skylights. This amount of living space in a city as packed as New London was exceedingly rare, and by showing the penthouse off as often as possible, the Carlyles were able to provide an easy, nonverbal reminder that they had secured a permanent place at the top of the food chain.

Rushing away from her room, Myrra paused for a moment at the bottom of the stairs, and her face fell briefly in anticipation of the climb. The master bedroom was on the top floor. Most people would have put in an elevator, but Marcus loved antiques, and he demanded authenticity.

But Imogene was waiting. Myrra took another breath, shook

some energy into her body, and headed up. Her hand slid along the polished wood of the banister. Before coming to the Carlyle house, Myrra had never encountered real wood, but here it was all over. This had been poached from an English estate in the old world. Other woodwork on other floors was made from a darker wood, almost black, and full of labyrinth-like geometric knots that made Myrra's eyes cross. Marcus had told her once that these came from Morocco. England. Morocco. New York. Art Deco. Bozart. These names never meant anything to Myrra, but she usually just let him talk, trying to absorb what she could. Knowledge was useful, even if it was snippets of antiquarian trivia. Marcus was apt to brag about origins and provenances given the slightest provocation.

As she passed by a row of bedrooms between staircases, she lightened her step and slowed down just a touch, avoiding any creak in the floorboards. Lately Imogene and Marcus had been sleeping in separate bedrooms, with Marcus taking up residence on the second floor. Myrra wasn't sure if this was a cause of all the tension she'd felt between them or just another symptom of it. The whole thing filled Myrra with worry, though she couldn't pinpoint any real reason for it. Why should she care if Marcus and Imogene had marital problems? They'd never been a happy couple, exactly. This latest separation meant nothing. Myrra didn't see a light on behind any of the bedroom doors, but that didn't mean Marcus was sleeping. Marcus was an insomniac at the best of times. Over this period he'd barely slept at all.

Marcus's behavior had become increasingly erratic and mercurial, with him breaking into frantic bouts of chittering laughter in silent rooms, then suddenly throwing objects against the ornately papered walls in a screaming rage. More than once in the past month, he'd reached out to Myrra in an abrupt motion while she was cleaning or setting down a plate, gripping her wrist or arm a little too tight, jerking her closer to his face. Then he would come back to himself and let her go, usually with an offhand comment: she hadn't dusted something right, or the meal was undercooked. His eyes were wild and bloodshot, their focus imprecise.

Marcus had never been all that intimidating to Myrra before. Despite his insistence on stairs, he had never developed much in the way of muscle mass. Neither fat nor thin, Marcus had skin with the pale, yeasty quality of raw dough and babyish fine hair that pasted itself to his head. But lately he'd lost weight, and his body was becoming what could best be described as wiry—not just for his sudden thinness, but because now Marcus seemed constantly, electrically tense and poised to spark at any moment.

Over this time, Myrra had frequently looked to Imogene to see if she noticed the change, but Imogene never commented. Mostly she stared off into space, lost in her own thoughts. Thank God Myrra had Charlotte to pay attention to. The rest of the family belonged in a madhouse.

Just at the top of the third-floor staircase was Marcus's study. There was an amber light emanating from the crack under the door. She could smell his cigar smoke. Myrra could feel the pressure of Imogene waiting for her, but she eased her pace further, keeping her footfalls as slow and dull as drips in a sink. She imagined him in there, poring over parliamentary strategy, or perhaps already spinning it for the morning broadcast. From observing Marcus, Myrra had learned that news from the government never came in blunt, clear bursts; there were stairsteps to the truth.

From behind the door, she could hear him pacing. Myrra held her breath.

When she'd gone in there yesterday with Marcus's afternoon tea ("It's still important to observe English customs," he often said), his desk had been riddled with stacks of tablets, some depicting charts with plummeting downward curves, others with tightly regimented words darkly marching across each screen. Myrra secretly practiced her reading while pouring him tea; there were lots of good complex phrases to untangle, like *Yearly Decline Tracking* and *Integrity and Stability Projections*. Marcus was standing over them, huffing, with sweat stains murking out from the creases in his arms. Myrra had gambled on his patience and asked about the charts. Sometimes Marcus liked to play paternal and explain things to her.

"Oh, it's just our downfall," he said with a thin giggle, but then his eyes began to well up, even as he was still forcing out laughter. His hand twitched and he spilled tea all over the tablets. Without reacting, he walked out of the room in a trance, leaving Myrra to clean up the mess. Myrra hadn't known how to react, but it had left her uneasy.

Once she was out of earshot of the study, Myrra rushed the rest of the way to the master bedroom. When there was no one to entertain, Imogene would often spend days in here, avoiding the endless stairs by having things brought to her in bed. Now the bed was empty, as was Charlotte's bassinet. Maybe Charlotte needed feeding after all. Myrra couldn't understand why Imogene would behave so strangely about it. Nobody in this house was sleeping, apparently.

The terrace was adjacent to the master suite of the penthouse. She looked around at the chairs, chaises, and tables. It was large enough for Imogene to throw the occasional rooftop party. The floor was laid out in stunning patterned tiles that retained heat when the sun shone on it, but now, in the dark, they were cold enough that Myrra felt it through her slippers. The damp of early morning seeped in through her robe, through her skin, into her bones.

Myrra didn't see Imogene at first. She raised her head to look at the city skyline, and that was when she spotted her. The terrace was bordered by a cement wall a little over a meter high that acted as a railing to keep people safe from the drop below. Imogene was standing on top of that wall, with Charlotte in her arms.

Adrenaline flooded Myrra's system, lasered her thoughts into focus. Charlotte. What was she doing holding Charlotte up there? Charlotte looked cold—Imogene didn't seem cold at all. Imogene didn't seem to care much about where she was standing. She hadn't seen Myrra yet. Myrra hung back and tried to think what to do.

Imogene paced with bare feet along the top of the wall. It was wide enough for her to walk comfortably, wide enough that people frequently set their plates down on it during rooftop parties. Imogene seemed in control of her body, aware of her surroundings. But Myrra wished she would stop moving around, wished she would sit, give herself a lower center of gravity. The wind picked up at this high an altitude.

Imogene should have been shivering. All she had on was a filmy nightgown and her favorite velvet shawl. Though she hadn't really dressed, not properly, she was fully done up. Dark-red lipstick. Hair curled and pinned in a wave. Myrra was momentarily impressed that Imogene had managed to do her hair at all without assistance. She really was very beautiful, Myrra thought. Sour, but beautiful. The whole situation felt staged, more like a movie scene than the real thing. But then, that figured. Marcus had met Imogene when she was working as an actress, and doing quite well, to hear Imogene talk of it. But that was all before they'd purchased Myrra's maid contract. She had been Imogene's honeymoon present. Myrra wondered why Marcus bothered chasing other women at all. They'd been together for so many years before the baby, and Imogene was still radiant. Myrra wondered if money bought beauty.

Imogene leaned outward to look down at the street below. It threw her body into an impossible angle. Myrra gasped. Imogene turned at the sound and noticed her. She was wearing the smile that she dusted off whenever Marcus brought over his Parliament friends.

"Good morning," Imogene said.

"Good morning," Myrra croaked out.

It was hard to breathe. She calculated her odds of being able to run forward and grab Charlotte if Imogene tried to jump. Was she going to jump? Or was this just another strange mood?

Imogene bounced the baby absentmindedly. A high-altitude breeze caught the edges of her skirt, and it danced buoyantly up and down. Myrra stared at Charlotte, asleep and unaware; she took a slow, fluid step toward them. If she could just get close enough—

"Do you think this is real wind, or do you think they manufacture it?" Imogene tossed off. She watched the fabric bob up and down against her body.

"I don't know, ma'am. How does real wind work?" Myrra asked. This wasn't what they were supposed to be talking about right now. Imogene's voice didn't sound like she was sleepwalking, but could she be sleepwalking?

"I don't know, actually." Strange, to hear Imogene say, "I don't know."

"Something to do with changes in air pressure," she continued. "Maybe the world is big enough to create wind on its own." She let out a single short laugh. "But that's the problem, isn't it? We all call this a world. It's a ship."

"There's lots of ways to make a world. This is a world," Myrra replied. Don't contradict her, she thought. No telling what might set her off. Just get Charlotte.

Imogene rolled her eyes skyward. "Fine, it's a world. You know it was Marcus's firm that came up with the terminology, back when our ancestors boarded? There was a whole PR campaign. As per usual, it was the workforce that really took the bait."

Bitch. Myrra couldn't help the word popping into her head. Imogene tossed out small insulting barbs to Myrra out of habit, but now was not the time.

"I would have liked to feel real earth under my feet," Imogene said.

"We will."

"No, we won't."

Myrra didn't know what that meant or why Imogene would insinuate such a thing. At the mention of it, Myrra felt a different kind of fear, something larger and vaguer than the fear she had for Charlotte. Maybe Imogene was trying to belittle her again. She just wanted to frighten her. Only Imogene would have the balls to talk like this while also threatening to throw herself off a building. If that was what she was doing. Myrra was usually able to navigate tense situations, but here she was at a loss.

"I hate to involve you in this at all, really, but...well, I know I'm making the right decision here, I really do. I feel at peace with the whole thing." With one hand, Imogene briefly touched the side of her head to check that her hair was in place. Her calm was slipping; her eyes kept darting between Myrra, Charlotte, and the drop. She might actually jump, Myrra realized. Imogene was afraid. Myrra dared a few more steps forward.

"But when I came up here, I—well, it's the baby...I can't do this with the baby. It's stupid, really, but I don't think I have the stomach for it."

"Not stupid," Myrra said. She inched closer to Imogene, close enough to brush her skirt. "Can I...can I hold Charlotte for you?"

She stretched her arms up. Imogene pulled Charlotte away

reflexively, and Myrra flinched at how close she was to the edge. She froze, kept her arms aloft, and prayed that Imogene would meet her halfway. Imogene let out a small sigh, and her shoulders slumped.

"Yes, yes, you see, that's why I called you up here. I need someone to take the baby. I'm so glad you took my meaning—I know it's hard for you sometimes." Myrra clenched her teeth, resisted the urge to snap something at her. She was about to throw herself off a building, for God's sake.

Uncharacteristically, one of Imogene's manicured hands flew to her mouth, and her eyes widened with guilt. She stood silent for a second. Myrra could tell she was choosing her next words with care.

"I apologize," Imogene said. Unheard of, to hear Imogene say, "I apologize." Myrra fought the urge to empathize with Imogene. She'd been burned by that feeling before.

"Will you please take Charlotte for me? I can't jump if I'm holding her, and I don't want to leave her out here in the cold—" Imogene crouched on the balls of her feet, lowering Charlotte. Without another word Myrra closed the gap between them, and gathered the baby in her arms. Imogene let out a small animal-like cry upon releasing her.

A wave of relief engulfed Myrra. Charlotte was safe, still sleeping, nuzzling her head against Myrra's chest, completely unaware of the peril she'd been in. Myrra turned her energy back to Imogene. Now to get Charlotte's mother down, if she could.

"Ma'am," Myrra ventured, "maybe if you came down and talked about it, we could figure something out—"

"Stop playing therapist, Myrra, you're not at all subtle," Imogene snapped, then looked guilty again. Myrra wasn't used to Imogene looking so regretful.

"Look, Myrra—I'm sorry. I know I've put you in a terrible position. I just—I don't know how to handle this," Imogene continued, changing her tone. "You're probably smarter than I give you credit for. You must know—you must have sensed that something is going wrong."

"I know you and Mr. Carlyle have been having some trouble—"

Imogene cut her off. "It's nothing to do with that. My God, the idea that Marcus would ever drive me to—" Imogene let out a short laugh, then her face crumpled. She was crying. It was hard to track her ping-ponging emotions. "Honestly, if I were less of a coward, I'd take Charlotte with me. It's cruel, leaving her to suffer."

Myrra didn't know what to say to her. She felt small and insignificant and confused. Something was happening here that she wasn't grasping. She clutched Charlotte tighter, as though she would anchor Myrra in some way.

"Please come down," Myrra said, her voice sounding higher than she wanted it to. A cold wind streamed up Myrra's robe, flowing between her legs and around her belly.

"I can't," Imogene said through tears. She was still crouched, her eyes drilling into Myrra's. "I don't have it in me, to see what comes next. If we're going to die, I want to go out on my own terms."

Myrra stared back at her, uncomprehending. These are ravings, she thought; she's snapped, we need to get Imogene to a hospital. And then, one horrible, insidious idea: What if something terrible was coming? What if Imogene was talking sense?

"Surely you must have noticed something's wrong," Imogene repeated. Her voice sounded distant.

A slideshow flitted through Myrra's unwilling brain: the past twelve months, men from Parliament rushing in and out late at night. Every time they'd handed their coats and hats into Myrra's waiting arms, she could smell the flop sweat and fear on them. She'd talked herself into thinking that it was all to do with the next election, but now that she thought about it again, that didn't make much sense. They'd never looked that scared before.

"What's wrong?" Myrra asked, almost to herself.

Meetings at all hours, shouting through the wall, then whispers so soft that Myrra couldn't make out a syllable even with her head flush against the crack in the door. Scientists and physicists over for tea, with red puffy eyes and wheezing breaths behind loosened ties. Marcus's desperate clutching, the violent downward-sloping charts littering his desk. What Myrra read when she practiced her reading: "Surface Stability." "Hull Integrity Patterns." "Oxygen Depletion Reports."

There had been another earthquake last week. Myrra had panicked at the time, not over the shaking but because she had been cleaning crystal stemware; she'd desperately dashed around the table, arms and fingers splaying out in all directions like a juggler's, trying to catch each piece before it fell and shattered. It was the third earthquake in a month. The seismic reports said that they were only supposed to happen when the world passed certain gas pockets in space or came too close to a star. Something had changed.

The wind's icy fingers slid across her skin again. She started shaking. It was so cold. She wanted to believe that she was scared because of Imogene standing on the wall, scared because she'd almost taken Charlotte with her, but there was another reason to be scared.

Something was wrong with the world. The ship. The world.

Myrra wanted to stop thinking. She wanted Imogene to climb down from the wall. I am not standing here on the roof, she thought. I am sleeping in my bare little room, condensed in a cocoon of blankets. Tomorrow is laundry day. I am hiding books under my pillow. I am growing ever smaller.

"Oh, here—" Imogene noticed her shivering, slid the shawl off her shoulders, and wrapped it around Myrra. "I don't need it anyway. I'm hot all over."

Myrra let her finger trace the curled patterns embossed on the velvet of the shawl. It was blue, a blue so deep you could dive in and swim. She glanced down at her pilled knit slippers. Her toes were going numb. How was Imogene so warm?

"What's wrong with the ship?"

"There's a crack in the hull," Imogene said. "It's growing. There is no way to fix it."

2

THE SHIP

There is a ship gliding through the endless black of space, the bottomless topless boundless void of space. It drifts past galaxies, past planets, past novae and asteroids and red dwarfs and black holes, past moons and minerals, fire and ice. But mostly it drifts past nothingness. It defies the natural order and exists, a minuscule speck of something in a wide swath of nothing.

Size is a relative concept. In the vastness of space, the ship is small, a sliver of a quark in the mass of the expanding universe. But to the people inside it, it is the whole world. If one were to estimate its size based on comparison, we could say it is roughly the size of what once was Switzerland.

When it launched off the planet generations ago, its destination was so far away that the distance was measured in years rather than in miles or kilometers. It would take roughly two centuries for it to get where it was going.

Parents told their children where they came from, and most children did what was normal and only half listened to the story. When the time came to explain to their children how the world worked, the next generation provided them a diluted version of their origins, and as the decades marched on, people began to take their surroundings for granted. The world is a relative concept.

There are manuals and books publicly available delineating how the ship runs, who commissioned it, who built it, who financed it, who pilots it, and so on, but not many people bother to look up those books. Inside the ship (the world) there is a sky, there are cities and landscapes immaculately designed. Nobody remembers that someone once designed them.

Even if people bothered to question their surroundings, the mechanics of the ship don't matter, not when everything is running smoothly. What matters is when the mechanics stop working the way they should. It matters when the world (the ship) breaks down.

There's a crack in the side of the ship. The majority of the population does not know that it is there. The crack is growing, too large now to fix or patch. It is irreversible. It may have been an engineering error, something unforeseen when the craft was built 150 years ago. It may have been a collision with a bit of something in the blackness, an asteroid or even something small. A mineral particle the size of a walnut can still cause damage if it hits just the right spot going forty thousand kilometers per hour. The source of the damage doesn't matter. What matters is that the damage is there.

As a result of this crack, every person on this ship, this world, will perish. It is worth considering whether even this really matters. Will it make a difference to the red dwarfs and novae and moons if the tiny speck of life gives in and assimilates with the lifelessness around it? Probably not. The universe will swallow up the speck and continue its own expansion, until the eventual moment when it too will collapse.

MYRRA

Imogene's fingers were still bunched around the shawl, and all her energy and tension seemed focused on pulling it tighter around Myrra's arms. The shawl was becoming a straitjacket. Myrra tried to pull away, but Imogene held on.

That wasn't right, what Imogene was saying. That couldn't be right. Something that catastrophic couldn't just—

"No," she heard herself say. "How can there be no way to fix it? We have a whole world of people here. There has to be someone with a plan—"

Myrra thought of her tablet, the one that Imogene had smashed, how it lit up, connected you to anyone you wanted to talk to, retrieved any piece of information you asked for. A world that produced technology like that couldn't just end with no reason.

"Parliament's pulled every scientist, physicist, philosopher, and carpenter in to work on the problem. They've been at it for a year with no solutions. We'll reach the deadline soon."

This was absurd. There were a million possible solutions.

"But isn't there someone we can contact outside—"

Imogene scoffed. "Where outside? We've traveled a long time. There's no one in any direction for a hundred years."

"No," Myrra said again, louder, a little more forcefully, enough to cause Imogene to rear her head back in surprise. "There's always something you can do."

Myrra finally wrenched herself free, then gasped as Imogene stumbled back—a little too far. As Imogene waved her arms wildly in an attempt to regain her balance, Myrra reached out and grabbed her wrist, pulling her in just in time.

"Thank you," Imogene said, sitting down on the wall to steady herself. "If I'm going to do this, I want it to be on purpose."

Myrra still held on to her, a little too tight. She couldn't feel relief. Too many thoughts were spinning in her head; she needed a way to stop them. Imogene looked down at Myrra's hand gripping her.

"Are you thinking of pulling me down, or pushing me off the building?" Imogene asked her, reading Myrra's thoughts before Myrra even realized she'd been thinking them. "Pushing me won't fix what you're feeling," she added.

Myrra couldn't think of anything to say to that. She let go of Imogene and sat down on the terrace floor, gently setting the bundled Charlotte down next to her. Her hands were shaking, so she balled them into fists, and then she closed her eyes and put her head between her knees. Don't think. Just breathe. Even as she consciously kept her mind empty, she could feel her heart careening against her rib cage. She just had to get her head together.

No one for a distance of a hundred years. Myrra was always about five seconds away from someone at any given time. The colors of the New London Market blossomed out in her mind, like the pigments of Imogene's watercolors pooling out over absorbent paper. The New London Market, with its stalls of patterned cloth slung over metal piping, with steam and smoke billowing out from the shouting food vendors, the cacophony of questions, sales, haggles, and bargains, was beloved by Myrra. Working for the Carlyles, she had more freedom than she'd had in the laundry or in factories. But there was still always the invisible leash, and the market was the farthest point on her tether.

Myrra tried to concoct an errand every week that would require the journey, though it didn't always fly with Imogene. The market was twenty blocks from the penthouse. Take a right out of the tall glass lobby door, then walk down Capital Boulevard for five blocks, make a left on Revenue Street and walk among the slick steel skyscrapers for another five blocks. Cut the diagonal through Sakura Park, with its lovely twisting pink trees in the springtime and its steadfast stone bridge over the canal. Then the long tangle of King Street in Chinatown, where the heady smells of yeasty boiling dumplings, steaming vegetables, and roasting meat would start to swirl around your head and cloud your nostrils. Finally, at the end of King Street, just near the border of the Turkish district, the narrow path would widen and expand like a folding paper fan into the wide steps of the plaza and into New London Market.

This was Myrra's world, a world that was ending. It struck Myrra like a clap on the ear exactly how small a scope it was. A heat pressed behind her eyes, and she felt the sting of her own cowardice and complacency. How stupid she was.

It took her roughly half an hour to walk to the market. What did one hundred years of space look like?

Myrra inhaled the damp morning air and straightened up, looking above her at Imogene. She was sitting facing out now, with her nightgown carefully smoothed underneath her. Myrra laid a hand lightly on Charlotte sleeping next to her, feeling her tiny chest rise and fall.

"Are you all right?" Imogene asked from her perch.

"No," Myrra replied with a little growl. She could smell Imogene's hibiscus perfume wafting down. Of course Imogene had put on perfume.

"When did you learn about this, this crack?" Myrra asked. *Crack* made it sound so insignificant, like a broken mirror or a chipped mug. It was hard to believe Imogene when they were using words like *crack*.

"Marcus told me six months ago. Even then, he was sure they'd find some way to fix it," Imogene replied. "Idiot.

"Marcus is probably downstairs killing himself right now," she tossed off. "We agreed to do it tonight." The calm with which she said it made the words all the more chilling. Myrra couldn't think of a way to respond. How would a man like Marcus kill himself? Don't—don't think of that. Myrra fixed her eyes on Charlotte, on her hand on Charlotte's chest. Repeated to herself, Charlotte is safe. Charlotte is safe. If nothing else, there's that.

They sat in silence for a minute or two, Myrra couldn't tell how long. Eventually, if only because she had the urge to move again, Myrra stood and leaned her elbows against the wall, looking out on the panoramic skyline. Imogene looked at her suspiciously, and when it became clear that Myrra wasn't going to try to pull her down, she followed Myrra's gaze, staring out at the buildings and the gray-blue light at the horizon. New London was a beautiful city, and this was one of the best views you could get. Beautiful and monstrous. Myrra pictured the black silhouettes of buildings, the towers and spires, as black bejeweled teeth winking in the mouth of a monster.

"I think it's wrong to call it a sky if it's made with paint, metal, and lights. It's not the same thing," Imogene said out of nowhere.

"What does it matter, if we've never known any different? This is what sky is to us," Myrra contradicted. "I don't go in on nostalgia for something I've never even experienced. Everyone holds up the old world as this amazing thing, but you were born here, same as me. Our mothers were born here. What could we possibly know about it?"

This was a suspicious sort of freedom, talking with Imogene like this. Myrra caught herself glancing sideways every time she spoke, to check if she'd crossed a line. Imogene just shrugged.

"I suppose you're right, but there's nothing wrong in dreaming about the other kind of sky."

"I never thought about it," Myrra said with all honesty. She hadn't the space or time to spend philosophizing about real versus manufactured. Too many other worries took priority.

She had to get a handle on this situation. Worst-case scenario: What do I do if Imogene is right? Myrra balked at the idea, then rallied again. It was important to anticipate the worst so you'd be ready for it. In Myrra's experience, the worst happened more often than not. So: What's to be done if the world is ending? It might not be, she thought, to comfort herself. But just in case.

"If I believe you—" she started. Imogene looked at her and rolled her eyes at the *if.* "Then how long do we have before the world breaks apart?"

"Marcus told me it would be about two months. But it depends—if the wrong gas pocket hits us, it could happen tomorrow."

She didn't want to believe Imogene. "If the world breaks apart" was almost too big to comprehend. But then the next thoughts hit: I'm never going to marry Jake. Hahn is never going to get that bar. And I am never going to grow old.

Then she started thinking of all the ways she might get out of New London while avoiding surveillance cameras. Her expression must have darkened, or maybe Imogene was just following a similar thought pattern, because the next thing Imogene said was, "There's a safe embedded in Marcus's bookshelf, behind the Mark Twains."

"I know."

Imogene let out a surprised laugh.

"Yes, you would." She paused. "You know how to access it?"

"Palm scan." Myrra smiled. It was a good distraction, seeing the shock on her face.

Imogene smiled back, but it was a sad smile. "Do what you have to do," she said.

A plan was already whirring into motion. She'd knock Marcus out if he was still alive, or, if it was as Imogene thought and he was already dead, she'd have to take his hand.

Down at Myrra's feet, Charlotte whimpered. The cold must finally be getting through her blankets. Myrra bent down and picked her up, tucking her halfway inside her robe. Charlotte wriggled around a little, but eventually her face relaxed and her eyelids stopped twitching. Myrra looked up and saw Imogene watching her daughter with a look of bone-deep grief. It surprised Myrra. This was the most care Imogene had shown Charlotte in the total of her young life. At the very end, she proved herself to be a mother after all.

Imogene reached out and touched Charlotte's cheek. "Will you take care of Charlotte?"

It was a harsh reminder that soon Myrra and Charlotte would be alone on the terrace, that there would be an empty spot on top of the wall where Imogene had once stood. Myrra pushed away the thought.

"Of course," she said, and meant it. She could feel Charlotte's breath against her skin.

Imogene leaned closer to Myrra, inspecting her face. Myrra

could see the ivory powder of Imogene's foundation clinging to the soft downy hairs on the sides of her cheeks. What must she see in my face, when she looks this close?

"I'm so sorry," she said. It was hard to tell whether she meant that she was sorry for the way she'd treated Myrra all these years or for telling her it was all ending. In a rare positive moment, Myrra decided to think the best of her and assumed she was sorry for all of it.

Myrra could feel the warmth radiating off Imogene's skin. Imogene leaned closer to her face, impossibly close, and kissed her.

Then she pulled back, stood, and kicked her body out past the wall and into the stillness of the air.

It felt to Myrra as though Imogene's body hovered there in front of her for an unbearable length of time, so long that she worried something had happened to the gravity. Her nightgown and stray wisps of hair pooled out around her body as though in water. Her skirts hovered up around her shoulders and Myrra saw her pale nakedness, her immaculate vulnerable flesh. Imogene had her eyes squeezed shut and her mouth open wide enough to swallow the world.

Then the moment passed, and Imogene dropped like a sickened, ungraceful lump. Myrra leaned over to watch her descend, so far down that she couldn't see or hear the body's impact when it finally struck the sidewalk.

4

MYRRA

Myrra's life contained a multitude of tangent universes, now all collapsed to nothingness like matter in a black hole.

When Myrra was five, she was first employed in a bakery. Every night she would kick up clouds of flour and sugar with her microfiber broom, then watch the clouds dissipate while she mopped. For Myrra, this was a temporary situation. Her mother would be coming for her once she was out of the hospital, and she would be granted release from her contract. Together they'd find a cozy room somewhere, with flowered curtains and maybe a dog.

When Myrra was eight, her contract was sold to a butcher shop. She was still cleaning, but instead of sugar, her skin was now coated with the smell of fat and blood. It clung to her like grease to an oven. She didn't know where her mother had gone, but she no longer expected her return. Now she pictured a woman coming upon her one day in the street, a woman with long silk skirts, shiny shoes, and a kind face. She would be rich, would have an important job where she traveled, a diplomat or an entertainer. This woman would have a need in her eyes that would match the need in Myrra's, would buy her contract and adopt her, and together they would hop around the world. The rest of her life would be spent comparing the softness of hotel pillows.

When Myrra was twelve, she worked in a laundry. It was harder to remember her mother's face, but she knew she'd inherited her curly black hair. The damp heat of the washing machines caused it to coarsen and frizz. An assembly line of workers crowded the laundry space and slept on top of each other in adjoining dorms at night. Everything smelled of sweat. The next time her contract was sold, she figured, she would be able to calm her hair down, comb it out, maybe swipe a lipstick from somewhere. Then she would catch the eye of some boy, preferably a tall one with really, really blue eyes. Chest bursting with love, he would buy her contract and free her. Maybe they'd get married later, when they were older.

When Myrra was thirteen, Marcus and Imogene bought her contract, and Myrra saw real wealth for the first time. Imogene looked especially young then. She was the most beautiful woman Myrra had ever seen. Myrra beamed with thoughts of her and Imogene becoming friends, of traveling with the family on important parliamentary errands, becoming an indispensable aide in the government. One day she would save a particularly wealthy committee member from scandal, and out of gratitude they would release Myrra from her contract.

When Myrra was sixteen, she dreamed of blackmailing her way out of servitude. If she just kept her ears open long enough, one day Marcus would mistakenly let a secret drop out of his mouth, something salacious, and Myrra could threaten to sell it to the press. Humbled and ashamed, Marcus would make the arrangements to terminate her contract and would pay her a tidy sum, enough to buy a little house somewhere far away, preferably near water.

When Myrra was nineteen, she briefly considered poisoning Imogene and Marcus, running away with the cash and the jewelry, and living the colorful vagabond life of an outlaw.

When Myrra was twenty-three, she met Jake when he took her order at the grocery counter. He was not especially tall, and he did not have blue eyes. In fact, he wasn't very interesting at all, and mainly talked about food supply deficits. But Myrra could tell that he was aching to prove himself to someone. She could work with that.

Once, among all these other possibilities, when Myrra was in a mood of particular bitter anger, she had fantasized about total destruction: ground and sky being rent to pieces, the entire population screaming and collapsing, and then nothingness.

Myrra felt her life flashing before her as she stared at the empty spot on the terrace wall. She imagined Imogene's body smashing to the ground, then forced the image out of her head. Nothing good would come of that. Trying to keep her mind blank, she turned and slowly walked back through the master bedroom. She thought vaguely that she needed to act, to do something, but it was hard to focus.

This might be shock, she thought, and recognized in a detached sort of way that this kind of detachment wasn't a good sign. She kept Charlotte tucked inside her robes and wandered over to the espresso maker that Imogene kept on the shelf near her vanity. Coffee. Coffee might help. At the very least it would warm her up. There was something about shock and cold, something Myrra remembered an EMT telling her once when there was an accident at the laundry. Something about blood flow, she couldn't remember, but she thought she remembered that it was a good idea to keep moving. She walked in circles around the room while she waited for the tiny white cup to fill with coffee.

One double espresso later, Myrra was starting to feel more like herself. She was still walking in circles, but now she felt her feet on the ground and could recognize her arms connected to her body. It came to her again: she needed to act now. Imogene's body would be discovered soon, if it hadn't been already.

She needed to leave. Her old survival instincts sprang into action. Walking into Imogene's gigantic closet, she grabbed the largest bag she could find that was still a backpack. She'd have to be able to walk with their belongings; public transit would be out of the question. With her employers dead—was Marcus dead?—Security agents would be looking for her if she disappeared. With the free hand that wasn't holding Charlotte, Myrra filled the backpack with all the warm, practical clothes in Imogene's closet. Imogene was taller than she, but they were roughly the same size. She'd hit the kitchen too, before she left. But money. Money would be most important.

Myrra sighed. This was going to be the hard part. She had to access the safe, and for that she had to find Marcus. Which in all likelihood would mean finding a dead body.

Shake it off. Don't think too hard about the future, just think about the next minute. One foot in front of the other. Myrra deposited Charlotte in her bassinet for now and made her way down the stairs, all the way downstairs, to the kitchen. A knife would be helpful, either for threatening a still-alive Marcus or for— Don't think about that. She chose a good-size cleaver out of the drawer.

The light was still on in Marcus's study. The door looked larger, heavier, than it had before. Myrra let her hand hover over the antique bronze doorknob; she had the illogical sensation that if she touched it, it might bite her. Before she could think further, she grabbed the knob, turned it, and threw the door open with more force than was probably necessary. The study was empty, but the side door was open, the door to Marcus's adjoining bathroom, and the lights were lit. Myrra heard a distant dripping. Tap. Tap.

She forced herself to enter the study, forced herself through the side door. Tap. Tap.

Marcus was submerged in his claw-foot bathtub, lying up to his neck in red water, his face as white as the porcelain. One of his arms jutted out of the bathtub with the wrist facing up, a long gash carved into the inside of his arm. There was a huge pool of blood on the white tile underneath, and what blood was left in his body streamed down in tiny rivulets and dripped slowly off the tips of his fingers. Tap. Tap. His head flopped toward the arm, as though in his last moments he'd watched the blood gushing out of his body.

Myrra froze for a moment in the doorway. The panic inside her was rising, tightening her throat and filling her brain with a buzz like swarming insects, the panic wanted to erupt, to shake her body, to paralyze her from further action. But she didn't have the luxury of dwelling on this; she needed to move. What time was it? Four? Five? Myrra tried to calculate the likelihood that someone had already seen Imogene's body. Which side of the building had she jumped from? The boulevard or a side street? Myrra couldn't remember. If agents got here, they might assume murder over suicide; she could end up a scapegoat. She'd seen it happen before when things got messy and they wanted to clean up in a hurry. It was always easiest to blame the help.

No time. Myrra approached Marcus's body, careful to sidestep the pool of blood. She knelt down near his face and pressed two fingers to his neck, waited. No pulse. His eyes looked hazy and gray, as if a film was starting to form. He really was dead; there was no saving him. She wouldn't have to feel guilty about taking his hand.

She adjusted his outstretched arm so that it flopped against the bathtub; his arms weren't stiff yet, she noticed. He must have died less than an hour ago. He and Imogene really had synchronized things, whether they knew it or not. Myrra wondered why they hadn't killed themselves together, but then answered her own question when she remembered Imogene's contemptuous looks over the dinner table and Marcus's many, many affairs.

Could she cut off his hand while pinning it sideways against the tub? It would be better if she didn't have to drag Marcus's entire corpse out of the bath. She tried once, twice, to get a good angle, switching hands and altering her footing. Finally she had it, standing with her feet planted straddling the pool of blood, bent over, holding his wrist tight with her right hand and the cleaver in her left.

She took a deep breath and tried to remember what it was like when she was young and working in a butcher shop. The butcher had always cut the meat with very strong, certain strokes. One good chop should do it, if you aim right.

It will be fine, she reassured herself. Just think of it like osso buco.

Myrra raised the cleaver behind her in a wide arc and swung it forward, hard and decisively. It hit his wrist at just the right spot, cut through, and clanged harshly against the porcelain on the other side. The blow reverberated and vibrated in her bones, and it hurt to keep a grip; Myrra dropped the cleaver, and at the same time, Marcus's hand fell away and plopped on the floor.

A sharp knife, a single stroke. She'd done it. The hand lay a few inches away on the white tile. Myrra didn't know whether to be relieved or disgusted.

The safe opened easily enough. Pressing his palm against the sensor, Myrra tried to pretend it wasn't a real hand at all, that it was some sort of grotesque prop from a movie. It helped that at this point Marcus's skin felt like rubber.

There was the usual inside: boxes of Imogene's more expensive jewelry, ID cards, credit cards, and account cards. She took the IDs, but Myrra left the jewelry alone; even if she had time to pawn it, there were probably tracking chips embedded in the most valuable pieces. Likewise, she left most of the credit cards and account cards alone; agents would be watching those accounts soon. She was looking for one card in particular.

There were benefits to being ignored; when Marcus was working, he often forgot that Myrra was in the room. Over time she had seen things when Marcus thought she wasn't looking. Like most people at his level, Marcus had not made all his money legitimately. Moreover, when it came to taxes, Marcus had followed in the footsteps of his wealthy predecessors and hidden copious sums in undisclosed accounts. Where there was an account, there was bound to be an account card—very few people worked in cash nowadays.

There was a slim black wallet in the back of the safe, containing only a few stray key cards from old hotels and one account card in the mix—the only one she'd seen without Marcus's name on it. There was just the name of a vague-sounding corporation that Myrra had never heard of. Certainly not one of Marcus's public companies. This was it.

There was no time to spare, but Myrra had a nagging feeling; she couldn't leave yet. What Imogene had told her, what she'd just witnessed, the entire thing felt absurd. Especially absurd was the idea that she might believe Imogene. This was an extreme situation; she couldn't trust her own mind, and she certainly couldn't take Imogene's word. If this was true, there would be evidence of it in Marcus's office. Not just stolen glances at structural reports, as she'd seen before, but real proof.

Marcus's tablet was left out on his desk, unlocked, as though he wanted the information inside to escape. A blue light on the corner of the screen pulsed, indicating sleep mode. Myrra brushed her fingers across it, as though she were gently waking a child. The screen lit up, displaying his latest messages, and Myrra scanned the subject lines: in between the multitude of advertisements, political punditry, and *Financial Times* newsletters, there was a group mail chain that seemed relevant. Myrra recognized several of the names in the message stream: Liu. Swardson. Kerchek. Mallory. Novak. Three were scientists, two were in Parliament; she'd taken their coats and served them tea. Mallory had grabbed her ass once while she was serving drinks at a fundraising reception.

She swept across the screen with her fingers, scrolling through their dialogue, going back over a year. The early messages had a professional and polite tone: one of the scientists, Dr. Liu, kept referring to "our hull problem"; lots of conjecture as to whether this was really a long-term issue. A few months later, references to fatalities with workers in the outer hull—Myrra hadn't even conceived that there would be a workforce in the hull of the ship. From there it looked as if the group had started taking the problem more seriously.

Then came the many projected solutions, posited by the scientists and discussed by the politicians. Everything was still professional and orderly; different ideas for fixing the hull were labeled and rigorously tested: Solution 1, Solution 1a, Solution 2, Solution 3, Solution 3a (with reverse flux), Solution 12, 13, and so on. Nothing had worked.

The conversations between the men got shorter, and the tone got darker. There was a brief discussion of informing the public, an idea that was unanimously quashed for fear of widespread panic. Talk turned to plans for death.

Some of the messages had attachments. Myrra clicked on one: exterior drone shots of the tear in the hull, which looked more like the torn fabric of an overcoat than layers of supposedly impenetrable metal. Another attachment showed blueprints of the ship. The world. She couldn't think of what to call it. Her brain switched back and forth, as it did when she wasn't quite sure of the pronunciation of a word.

The blueprint showed a distant exterior view; Myrra had never seen what the outside of the world looked like. It wasn't at all how she'd pictured it; the world was a cylinder. It looked like a tin can, like one of the cans of diced tomatoes Myrra kept in the kitchen. She looked closer. On the interior, one flat circle showed topography: rivers, mountains, cities, and seas. The other flat circle was the sky. Two rods were attached to the outside of the cylinder, halfway up the curved sides, halfway between the ground and the sky. These rods (labeled axles, Myrra noticed—they must spin) extended and attached themselves to a wide, thin, C-shaped piece of metal. Large billowing shapes were attached to the sides of the C—the diagram labeled them "solar sails." Myrra had seen pictures and paintings of sailboats before. This was like no sailboat she'd ever seen.

The diagram was unsettling to see, it made it difficult to trust the ground under her feet. She suddenly felt as though she could feel the world spinning, end over end, and the feeling made her nauseous. Logically, she realized that the entire piece of machinery (no longer a world in her eyes, but machinery) must be massive, but it looked so delicate, the axles thinner than filament, the solar sails lighter than silk. How had they ever made it this far?

One last label pointed to a tiny squiggle drawn on the side of the cylinder, so small it was possible to think it was simply an error in the pixelation. The text on the label simply read: "Hull Breach." It's real, Myrra thought.

Downstairs, in another room, Myrra heard one of Marcus's antique clocks chime. It was five a.m. She needed to leave.

5

NEW LONDON

When the city of New London was conceived, it was meant to be a bit of everything to everyone in the old world. The British won the right to name it in a lottery draw, though other countries heavily contested the results. The word *colonizers* was bandied about, but the decision stuck.

One by one, cities from all regions of the old world added features to this new metropolis, as if stitching increasingly incongruous patterns into a quilt. The Chinese commissioned brilliant jade gates to serve as portals to all major entrances of the city, teeming with carvings of curled clouds and tigers and trees and flowers, accented with Cambodian rubies and Peruvian silver. Kenya donated the majority of its wildlife preserves to a zoo of unprecedented size; the menagerie also contained pandas, penguins, narwhals, jaguars, capybaras, koalas, and myriad other animals, too many to name. Turkey insisted on a market bazaar full of snaking lanes and stairs and stalls, originally filled with Turkish spices and Turkish textiles; however, over time jars of Vegemite and kimchi popped up on the shelves next to the more traditional spices. Stars of David and Diné Spider Woman Crosses were woven into the wool of the Turkish carpets. Sweden and Norway envisioned the new city as an architectural apex, with sleek metal buildings rising to great heights, whose clean lines and vistas would inspire calm and efficiency. Korea cared less about its aesthetics and more about the technology that would run the city, outfitting the Nordic architecture with proactive computer systems to anticipate every need, from the running of the trains to the requests of the customers at tiny coffee kiosks. Food, too, became an amalgam of different regions and different tastes; Ethiopian stew swirled in dark mole sauces, dal found its way into Creole jambalaya, Nepalese momo could be deep-fried in a Kentucky buttermilk batter, and pizza could still have pepperoni, but could also be topped with cassava, plantains, or pickled herring.

Even the streets began to embody the spirit of this collaboration (some would say argument): instead of a grid, New London's network of streets could best be described as forming a tense knot, as if a large circle of people had each grabbed a strand from an especially tangled ball of string and all pulled outward at once. This went on and on, with different cultures adding different flavors and blocks and layers onto the already immense city, until it was the largest populated area on the new ship. Each country added its dreams to this new city, hoping to re-create its own vision of home. The result of the mix was something entirely new and not familiar to anyone at all.

The crack in the world, the rift that is growing, is nearest to New London. Though the death of the population will happen relatively quickly, New London will be the first to see the destruction. In three months' time, the wide expanse that people think of as the sky will break open. There will be an ear-piercing crack, then a deafening whoosh as air rushes past the people and trains and towers, upward into this new violent tear in the sky. Then the people themselves will rise and be sucked away from what they thought was solid ground. Vehicles, dumpsters, animals, and smaller structures not affixed to the pavement will also be suctioned out of the rift with horrible force.

The population will then become debris drifting in the dark, dead within fifteen seconds once they're blown out into the blackness of space. Their positions and expressions will be fixed in their last moments, like those of the citizens of Pompeii. Some people will be frozen with outstretched arms, reaching for a handhold to keep them attached to the ground, or maybe reaching for a loved one, a last warm touch from a fellow living being. Others will have screams permanently etched on their faces, that last look of panic and fight from the moment they saw the imposing vastness that awaited them. Still others will see that same formidable darkness, and, upon their reaching it and having the breath sucked from their lungs, their expressions will be frozen not in a moment of terror but in one of wonder.

6

TOBIAS

The New London Security Bureau was an office full of the clicking of shoes on cement and the ambient humming of technology. The air-filtration systems assured that every brushed-steel surface was dust-free, every pop-up screen was lined up in the exact same spot on each desk, which were positioned apart from each other at a length of seventy-five centimeters (Tobias had measured). From his spot on the second-floor balcony, Tobias could see down into the atrium where the spread of desks looked like cubes in a great silver grid. He loved it.

Tobias didn't dislike disorder per se—he always felt a little misunderstood when his coworkers made fun of the satisfied smile that crossed his lips as he observed a well-ordered chart or a detailed filing system. He had occasional moments of chaos, just like anyone else. He just liked the balance that order gave to chaos—the presence of efficiency and stability made one appreciate chaos more when one came across it in the wild. Like seeing a red fedora in a sea of black bowler hats. Tobias appreciated disarray in short, colorful bursts.

Tobias crunched into his kimchi-and-tomato sandwich, feeling the vegetal juices burst over his tongue with an acidic tang. He adjusted his seat on the hard stone bench, leaned over to let his elbows rest on his knees, and felt his spine pop. It had been a long shift, midnight to eight. He could hear the percolation of Agent Simpson's coffee maker in the break room and resisted the urge to go beg for a cup. After his sandwich he would go back to his apartment, crawl into bed, nuzzle himself between the pillows and the wall, and drown himself in sleep under his duvet.

It was only his second year as a desk tech on the Security Bureau; he was still at a low rung on the ladder, still prone to receiving graveyard shifts. As a rite of passage, the older agents habitually sent him their forms and evidence tallies at the close of a case, endless reams of bureaucracy scrolling across his screen, each with a different stamp and signature required. Tobias took his hazing in good humor and kept his work immaculate. Carr and Davies were retiring soon—there would be spaces to fill.

Simpson popped his head out from the break room, a cup of coffee in hand. His mustache needed a trim, Tobias noted. Wiry, rebellious hairs were sticking out from his lip at all angles.

"Hey, Bendel." He nodded. "You look tired."

Simpson had a knack for stating the obvious.

"I am."

Simpson leaned against the doorframe and took a sip, seemingly satisfied with the conversation. He craned his neck to peer over the rail and down into the atrium. From above, Tobias could see the frenetic energy that was building among the hive of desks. Workers poured in from the brass double doors of the lobby. Shift change.

Simpson's eyes widened for a moment, as though a new thought had just dropped into his head from a higher, divine plane.

"Hey," he said, waving his espresso cup in Tobias's general direction, "Barnes was looking for you."

"Barnes? When?" Tobias sat up straighter.

"I dunno, like a half hour ago...I ran into him down by the desks." Simpson had produced a croissant, seemingly from nowhere, and was now holding it in his left hand, gesticulating with both pastry and coffee in an attempt to paint the picture.

Tobias shot up from the bench, brushing the crumbs off his slacks, his hands moving in sharp, jerking motions. What was it about adrenaline? The more tired you were, the more potent it felt. Tobias's synapses fired off like signal flares.

"You could've mentioned that sooner," Tobias tossed off as he gathered his bag. He saw Simpson take another languid bite of pastry.

"Sorry," he called out as Tobias rushed down the stairs.

Tobias knocked lightly on the polished wood of Director Barnes's office door. He let his hand rest on the cool ridged surface a moment. Tobias had an appreciation for fine things, and wood was hard to come by, in abundance only in the homes of the super-rich. As head of the New London Security Bureau, Barnes had an office with a polished wood door and a large wood desk to match. Tobias wouldn't say that he coveted these objects exactly, but he did linger over them. At eye level on the door, Barnes's name had been set in gold leaf, the letters outlined neatly in black.

"Come in," he heard Barnes grunt in the interior.

Tobias crossed the threshold. There was the desk, with its precisely carved angles and beveled feet. Barnes was seated behind it, staring at the screen that had been retrofitted to its surface. He looked up.

"Oh, Toby—come in."

Barnes was still allowed to call him Toby. When Tobias had first entered the bureau, there had been a lot of murmurs. Talk of his mother and father, talk of whether Tobias was fit for such a career. But more than anything there had been talk of nepotism on Barnes's part, of the director playing favorites with his adopted son.

But in these past two years Tobias had won them over. He took every brain-eroding office assignment, and he worked every late shift until the veins popped in his eyes. It gave him an immense sense of triumph to note that there were plenty of people in the bureau now who had forgotten his history, who were surprised to learn that he had any connection to the director at all. Now he was Bendel, but to Barnes he would always be Toby.

Barnes gestured to a chair in front of the desk, and Tobias sat.

"Simpson said you were looking for me?"

Barnes grunted an affirmative. He began scrolling through his screen.

"Just a minute," he said. "Have to find the file heading—"

Tobias waited patiently. They'd recently adjusted the filing system for accuracy, going by the victim ID number instead of the surname. But Tobias knew better than to speak up—Barnes wouldn't appreciate the correction.

Barnes's skin reflected the blue of the screen. It was not a flattering light—its sharp brightness cast into relief every wrinkle and crease around his eyes and mouth. Papery folds echoing his many frowns and furrows of brow. It hit Tobias more and more frequently that this solid pillar of a man was aging. The white strands in his salt-and-pepper beard (much more fastidiously trimmed than Simpson's mustache) glowed in the light of the screen.

Tobias tried to crane his neck to see Barnes's screen. For the past two years Tobias had basically served as a dignified file clerk, but nobody went to the director's office to go over filing. Adrenaline coursed through him, he felt the familiar pricking under his skin. His hands shook. This could be a new case, his first case. He sat on his hands in an attempt to still his body.

"Here it is," Barnes said after a few minutes. "Early this morning, a disturbance was reported at Atlas Tower."

Barnes threw the screen up on the projector, and the wall of the office was engulfed in the image of a shattered body on cement. Tobias tightened his lips, taking great care to keep a stoic expression for Barnes's benefit. This could simply be some sort of consultation, but if it wasn't, Tobias wanted to embark on his first case with a heavy dose of worldliness and professionalism.

The photograph was arresting. There was very little to discern in the shrapnel of white flesh, the shards of bone, and the gelatinous red viscera, but Tobias surmised a woman based on the delicate lacy fabric that was muddled in with the carnage.

"Imogene Carlyle. Thirty-nine," Barnes said, by way of explanation. "Mrs. Carlyle lived in the penthouse suite of Atlas Tower with her husband, Marcus Carlyle, forty-eight." Barnes tapped a button on the screen, and the image changed to a pale man half-submerged in an antique claw-foot bathtub, the liquid inside a disturbingly deep red. One of his arms flopped haphazardly over the rim of the tub, and Tobias could see the slashes on the inside of his forearm where he'd opened his veins. His hand was severed at the wrist. Tobias concentrated on keeping his face serene and leaned closer. The amputation was clean. No blood. On second glance, he could see chips and cracks in the porcelain on the side of the tub, near Carlyle's arm.

"His hand was chopped off postmortem, against the side of the tub," he said, and then looked to Barnes for confirmation. He nodded.

"Were there prints on the hand?" he asked.

"Yes."

Barnes tapped the button again, and the image changed to a registration portrait of some kind. The girl looked young.

"Myrra Dal. Twenty-five."

Tobias surveyed the face now projected on the white wall. A dark, tangled billow of hair, dark complexion. Underfed. Her skin and face showed signs of fatigue and long labor, but her eyes were still very sharp and very black.

"Myrra Dal is under contract with the Carlyles. Mrs. Carlyle's body was discovered at five thirty this morning, and by that point Myrra Dal had already left. It's likely she chopped off Mr. Carlyle's hand to get access to the family safe. Jewelry and account cards were undisturbed, but it looks like she stole the Carlyles' ID docs. If there was cash in the safe, she might have made off with that as well."

Smart. Account cards could be tracked. Some jewelry too. She'd probably try to get one of the IDs altered, sell off the others. Tobias cleared his throat and tried to avoid the black eyes of Myrra Dal, who seemed to be taking on a three-dimensional shape as she stared down from her photo.

"The deaths seem like suicide, but—" Tobias said.

"But she cut off a man's hand," Barnes finished for him. "And two suicides at the same time?"

Tobias agreed it was suspicious, but privately he thought it almost seemed too simple an explanation, that Dal had killed her employers and made off with the money. There was something about the timing, the way the actions came together, that felt off. Why take the time to fake suicides but do something as obvious as cut off a hand? Why have the wife fall onto the sidewalk, where the body was sure to be found quickly? There was something more going on, but he didn't yet know enough to try to argue the point.

"We're looking at suspicion of murder, theft for sure," Barnes said. "And for breaking her contract, obviously. But also kidnapping—" Barnes tapped the button on-screen again, shifting the image from Myrra Dal to a posed family portrait of Mrs. Carlyle, reassembled, and Mr. Carlyle with clearer eyes and rosier cheeks. Between them was a smiling blonde baby.

"The child, Charlotte Carlyle, is currently missing."

Tobias peered at the picture. It was always unnerving to see images of people alive after having seen pictures of the bodies. It seemed a rude defiance of entropy.

Mrs. Carlyle's expression seemed screwed tightly into place. She had matched her lipstick to her husband's tie. Mr. Carlyle was smiling and holding his wife's hand, but his grip on her fingers was a little too tense. Tobias could see the whites of Marcus Carlyle's knuckles bulging against his skin. Even baby Charlotte's eyes seemed puffed and bloodshot. This must have been the tenth or fifteenth take of this picture, of them holding this pose. These were the type of people who projected happiness and endured the burden of that projection.

Barnes was talking again. Tobias refocused.

"—and anyway, there's still a heavy suspicion of foul play. They certainly look like suicides—but Dal had motive to kill them. It takes a certain something, to butcher a corpse. Someone who's capable of cutting off a dead man's hand is capable of having killed him in the first place." Barnes leaned back in his chair and stared at the family portrait on the wall. Tobias stayed silent, watched him think.

"Whereas, if they did kill themselves, why run? Her running doesn't make sense. Why break contract? She'd likely get reassigned to someplace just as ritzy. Her work contract will end in her lifetime, why would she risk incarceration?"

To Tobias this felt like an obtuse argument. There were plenty of reasons why someone would risk it, Barnes had to know this. Tobias eyed Barnes in his chair; he was staring up at Tobias, almost puckish. Barnes was testing him—he wanted to see Tobias think, to see him run.

"That's only if she's thinking long term," Tobias said. "There's still another fifty years or so before we reach Telos. That's a long time to wait."

Barnes was nodding along with him. "So Imogene and Marcus Carlyle kill themselves, and Myrra Dal takes the opportunity, runs off before they're discovered."

"Yes."

"It's shortsighted of her. It never takes long to catch up to them... It's a small world. Only so many places to run."

"Sometimes people just snap," Tobias countered. He glanced again at the family picture and at Mr. Carlyle's protruding knuckles. "Especially in a heightened emotional state. I mean, imagine—she wakes up, finds both of her employers dead, she goes into panic mode. She's not thinking logically."

Barnes let that sit for a moment, mulled it over in his chair.

"Why steal the baby, then?" he asked. "Ransom?"

"The ransom wouldn't be worth the trouble," Tobias said. He still hadn't puzzled out why Myrra Dal would take Charlotte. There was no reason for it. Except maybe—he didn't even want to think it, it seemed too sentimental, made him look too green.

He said it anyway.

"Maybe Dal just didn't want to leave her behind."

Barnes looked down at the surface of his desk and gave a small smile.

"That's the reasoning of someone who wants to live in a kind world," Barnes said. Tobias blushed. He felt stupid.

Barnes turned to him and looked suddenly sad, more emotion than Tobias usually saw from him.

"Let's hope that's the reason," he said. Tobias wanted to respond, but was so surprised by Barnes's sincerity that he couldn't find anything to say. All at once he was filled with worry for the man who had raised him. Something in Barnes felt small and hollowed out.

Barnes looked away and gave a cough, as if dislodging any further mawkishness that might be stuck in his throat. He pulled a small memory stick out of a drawer and handed it to Tobias. Tobias held it between his thumb and forefinger, feeling the charge of anticipation in the pads of his fingers. This was his shot, his case. He felt it.

"That'll have any other relevant details," Barnes said, gesturing to the small piece of plastic and silicon in Tobias's hand. For such a small object, it held weight.

"Who should this go to?" Tobias ventured, weary of assumption. Barnes let out a short exhalation that could have been a laugh. His lips turned upward in a rare grin. Definitely a laugh.

"Are you kidding?" he asked. "This one's yours, kid."

Tobias felt a thrumming warmth rise through his body. "You sure?"

Barnes waved a hand between them, swiping the air. "Ah, you've been ready to get out there for the past eight months. I just didn't want to make it look like I did you any favors."

Tobias wanted to leap straight over that antique wood desk and hug Barnes around the neck. Instead he settled for a handshake. Barnes held his hand an extra second, warm and firm. He looked at Tobias with bright pride in his eyes.

"You're gonna do great," he said. He paused for a moment. "And, Toby—"

Tobias knew what was coming. It was their own private joke. His face opened up in a smile.

"Your parents would be very disappointed in you."

7

MYRRA

Now that they were outside with the noises of traffic and people, Charlotte was unhappy, and Charlotte was crying. Myrra was trying to stick to the alleyways—the smell from the dumpsters didn't make things better, but there were no traffic cameras, and fewer people to slow them down. It was rush hour now; the sidewalks were packed. They needed to cover as much distance as possible before Security agents could catch up.

Charlotte let out another wail; she kept vacillating between screaming and occasionally needing to breathe. Myrra didn't quite know why she was still holding Charlotte. The baby should have stayed back in the penthouse—no reason why Myrra should take her along. It was going to be next to impossible to stay ahead of Security if she was also carrying a baby. Myrra looked down at Charlotte, who let out another scream and beat her tiny fists against Myrra's chest. Her face was contorting, turning deeper and deeper shades of red.

She would let go of Charlotte. She would drop her off at the doors of a hospital; maybe that beautiful church on the corner of

Grand Street and Samcheongdong, she could lay Charlotte at the feet of one of the statues. Borrow or steal a tablet, place a quick anonymous call, and Security would come. She could be gone before they got there. Surely the Security Bureau would find a family willing to take her in (they were bound to be swarming the penthouse by now; it wouldn't have taken long for someone to discover Imogene's mangled remains on the sidewalk). Probably a fairly well-to-do family, considering the status of the Carlyles. A new set of adoptive parents would crane their necks over her crib, babbling baby talk. And Charlotte could be happy like that for the next month or two. However long they had.

Myrra still had plenty of options, even if she wanted to hold on to Charlotte for just a little longer. It was just too much change at once, to learn that her bosses were dead and her job was gone and her life would soon be gone and the world would soon be gone. She could hardly be blamed for holding on to the one good thing she had left, even if it was a terrifically inconvenient thing.

"Please stop crying," Myrra said to Charlotte's shrieking tomato of a face. She bounced her as she walked, taking hairpin turns down narrower and narrower routes and alleys. Myrra's cheeks felt wet, and she realized she was crying too, though she couldn't pinpoint exactly why.

Since leaving the penthouse, Myrra hadn't thought much about where she would go, only that she needed to keep moving. No problem there. It felt impossible to stand still without her body shaking apart. It was hard to think straight, or think about anything past the next few minutes. She needed to leave the city; with this level of infrastructure and surveillance, they wouldn't stay hidden for long. But she didn't know much about places outside of New London.

Just before ducking into the alleyways, she'd found a transit kiosk with a map of the ferry and train lines. There was no real way to gauge distance or landscape, just colored lines stretching out like strands in a spiderweb away from the large central dot marked "New London." She traced one blue line left to right, a ferry line, leading away from the city. If this was to scale, the closest large city was Palmer—Myrra had heard about Palmer, knew that it was rich and big. That alone told her that Palmer would have just as much surveillance as New London, if not more. But there was another, smaller dot just before Palmer (a smaller dot meant a smaller town, Myrra guessed), a ferry stop labeled "Nabat." Myrra barely knew anything about Nabat, had just heard the name once or twice, as if it were a ghost of a town rather than a place anyone actually visited. She took that as a good sign. Nabat would be her destination, just as soon as she dropped off Charlotte. It would be too dangerous to actually ride on the ferry, but she could follow the line on foot, camp if she needed to, stay off the grid. Whatever it took to keep agents away.

Skyscrapers loomed over the street on both sides, casting the alleys in shadow. They were still in the finance district—finance had the tallest buildings, higher than Atlas Tower, rising so high that Myrra wondered if they actually did graze the sky above them. Elevated train tracks wove between the buildings, impossibly high above the ground. Today the sky was a cheerful blue, bright even in the early morning, due to the summer season. Myrra considered the sky, really considered it for the first time. Someone must program the seasons. Was it just atmosphere above them? Someone—who?—had designed that trick visual... the clouds, the blue, the sun, the stars. Where was the operating center? She wondered about the small moving parts, now that it was all breaking down. Don't think about that.

Maybe it wasn't breaking down, maybe it was all just a terrible prank that Imogene and Marcus were playing on her. Maybe Marcus's body was a dummy, maybe Imogene had jumped into a net hanging below the balcony, maybe they'd planted all those diagrams and schematics on Marcus's computer, they'd planned it all just to be horrible; never in her life had Myrra wished so hard for their cruelty. Maybe she could go back and her life could continue with the tentative plans and machinations she'd kept hidden in her pocket. Maybe this was all a big hoax.

Myrra's gut told her different.

Stop thinking about it. Stop thinking about it. Think about how to keep moving.

The back ways were quieter, but they still passed the occasional contract worker out on morning errands. New London was a city that liked to show a good face—polished metal, fresh paint, sidewalks pressure-washed so strenuously that they had to be resurfaced twice a year. Curated shop windows with charming lettered signs and matching brightly colored awnings. Myrra walked where the rats and the roaches and the trash cans were. This particular neighborhood was affluent enough; quite a few families employed maids and valets. Contract workers tended to take the alleys, knew how to get where they were going faster than the average commuter. They all rushed their way to the markets and shops, just as Myrra had done most days, their heads filled with shopping lists for dinners, tailoring and dry-cleaning orders, lists of supplies for the odd home repair. Myrra met their eyes, and on every face she saw death.

Myrra laid out a map of the blocks in her head. If she remembered the layout of streets correctly, it was possible to get to the back entrance of McCann's Grocers without ever hitting a major thoroughfare.

Another gentleman passed by, probably a butler judging by his outfit. He tipped his black bowler hat at her and smiled at Charlotte. They wouldn't be suspicious. The odd nanny carrying a baby wouldn't look out of place, even if the baby was crying. Though agents would definitely be at the penthouse by now. They would know that she'd abandoned her post and run.

When Myrra worked at the laundry, one of the workers broke contract. Myrra had worked next to her in an assembly line, pressing clothes. Cora. She was older, too old for the work they were doing. They should have placed her in a house or as a nanny, something less physical. Maybe she'd had bad behavior on her record prior to that point, Myrra didn't know.

The laundry was a massive establishment, one large cavernous space comprised of cement, metal, and machinery, full to the ceilings with hot air and steam. Myrra couldn't breathe in there. She would go to bed each night in the adjoining dorms and lie down on her thin foam bed, her arms and hands streaked with red burns from the irons. She didn't judge Cora for trying to break out. On the contrary, Myrra had predicted it; she would catch her staring blankly at the gray cement wall in front of them while folding clothes. She didn't seem to be looking at anything in particular, but Myrra got the sense that in those moments Cora was staring down her whole life.

She remembered the night Cora tried to make her escape. It was a spontaneous, stupid attempt. Myrra woke one night to see Cora's legs poking out of a high, small window as she struggled to push herself through. She remembered seeing Cora's feet disappear through the window, the shouts outside. Then the crack of a gunshot. Myrra had been nauseous, had assumed they'd killed her, but the next day another girl told her that the guards only used tranquilizer darts. "The Contract Workers Rights Alliance pushed through legislation," she said. "They only use darts now."

No telling where Cora was now, if she was even still alive. She had been old when Myrra knew her, and that was so many years ago. Myrra didn't know exactly what happened to people when they broke contract. There were the whispers the kids used to tell each other in the dorm bunks at night.

Like: If they catch you and bring you back, they feed you to a great big machine that grinds you up into pulp and repurposes you into dog food for the rich.

Or: When they catch you, they bring you to a laboratory where they take out parts of your brain. Not your whole brain, just the parts that make you *you*, so that for the rest of your life you'll be a zombie drone who never thinks of running away. Then they put you to work in the sewers and chain you to the walls at night. Every contract kid had a fear of the New London sewer drains thanks to that one.

Myrra wondered, not for the first time, if that was what had happened to her mother. It was a stupid, hopeful thought—her mother was most likely dead, and any other possibility, even if it meant she was chained alive in a sewer somewhere, denoted hope. Then a truly insidious notion slithered through Myrra—maybe, now that she was free to go where she pleased, she might find her mother again, see her one last time before everything came crashing down. It was dangerous, Myrra knew, because there was no way that a quest like that ended well. And yet the thought was in her head now, like a melody playing on repeat.

The only real things Myrra knew about penalties for breaking contract were that the people who tried it disappeared, but they (probably) weren't killed. The CWRA had lobbied against the death penalty and won, years ago, before Myrra was born. They were also the ones who'd allowed for the marriage loopholes—if you could find someone to marry you, someone who could buy out your contract, you could be free. Heavily restricted, but it was a way out. All that work with Jake, it all felt moot now. He was nice enough, but she couldn't fathom spending the remaining months with him.

Still, he might yet be useful. Once, during a rendezvous in the grocery stockroom, he'd told her the story of him and his school buddies getting their IDs altered to get into bars. She had Imogene's ID now, but they'd flag it immediately if it stayed in her name. Jake was bound to know someone. He was bound to help her, if she could phrase it right...but how to explain the baby? She'd have to figure it out.

Myrra was well acquainted with this route. She passed the place where you could get a few free croissants or laddu if you knew the assistant cook at the bakery, or leftover dumplings from Jorge's Dim Sum if you'd done a few select favors for the dishwasher. She took in the smells coming from the back kitchen doors: she was hungry. The smells hit Charlotte at the same time, made her pause midshriek, then cry out even louder. She must be hungry too. Myrra made a right turn after passing the dumpsters for the Kurry 'n Kebab House, taking in smells of cumin and coriander and rotting onions, then wound her way behind a block-long line of garment shops. Myrra could see through the open back doors, bolts of fabric rolled around long cylinders, standing in rows against the workshop walls: silk and wool, satin and burlap. Five more blocks, another right turn, and she'd be behind McCann's.

There were mounds of plastic crates stacked near the back door, waiting for recycling pickup. It must be a stock day, she thought. Myrra waited for her moment—she needed to catch Jake alone. He usually ended up by the dumpsters once every few hours, for a smoke break. She was very familiar with this alcove by now.

Recessed from the alley, it had just enough space for the dumpsters and an occasional delivery truck, but the layout of the buildings also allowed for a few darker out-of-the-way corners, pockets of privacy that Myrra had taken advantage of time and again with Jake.

She didn't want to stay with him, she couldn't fathom settling in such a way anymore, but there were some fond memories here. He had always been very tender with her, had always looked at her as if she was some wonderful glowing discovery. It would be wrong to take that kind of devotion for granted.

She shoved some debris off a crate lying next to a wall and sat down with Charlotte on her knee. Charlotte balled her fingers into fists and rubbed them against her squinched-up eyes. She was still crying, a hungry cry. The noise was starting to give Myrra a headache.

There was a banana in her bag; that would be soft enough for Charlotte to eat. The cries quieted the second she pulled it out of her pack. She peeled it and broke it into small chunks, raising each to Charlotte's open and expectant mouth. Charlotte mashed her face against the food in Myrra's hands, smearing mush across her cheeks and onto Myrra's fingers. Myrra wiped the slime onto her skirt and stared at the messy carnage of saliva and fruit splattered around Charlotte's mouth. Had she actually eaten any of the banana, or just painted her face with it? Gnats hovered around her cheeks, already attracted to the scent. She should have left her behind before coming to Jake; things would be easier that way. But not yet; she wasn't ready yet. Instead she propped Charlotte against her shoulder, patting her back lightly until she heard a burp.

Ten minutes later Jake appeared at the back door, and without even looking up at his surroundings, he immediately produced a lighter and a small metal cigarette case. The spring-loaded door slammed behind him. Myrra waited to catch his attention until he'd had a drag. She lifted a hand to her mess of hair—after the insanity of the last few hours, she couldn't be sure what she looked like. But then, she figured, looking a little bedraggled might help her cause.

"Jake—" Myrra called out, trying to keep her voice more on the side of timid.

Jake looked up and smiled in surprise. A clean, sunshine smile. He didn't seem to register that she was holding a baby.

"Myrra, what are you doing here? It's not Sunday, is it—?" He raised his cigarette case to offer her a smoke. Genuinely happy to see her, as always.

"No thanks," she said, and he lowered the case, looking a little confused. Under most circumstances, if there was something that Myrra could have for free, she took it. But right now, she didn't want anything slowing down her words. She struggled with how to begin.

"It's good to see you," she said, and smiled back at him. He still looked confused. "It's not Sunday," she continued. "I came early."

Jake tilted his head and looked at her with affection. "Aw," he said, "I missed you too."

He lowered his cigarette and bent his face closer to hers for a kiss, but then noticed Charlotte and paused.

"Is that—?"

"This is Charlotte." Myrra bounced her on her hip. Over the past year, she'd told Jake many stories about Charlotte, but she wondered how much he actually remembered.

"What's she doing here?" Jake reached a finger out toward the baby, and Charlotte grabbed on with both hands, pulling Jake's knuckle into her mouth, covering it with drool and banana bits.

He pulled back and wiped his fingers on his shirt. He kept his eyes on Myrra, questioning. She took a breath.

"Jake, something's happened—" Myrra said.

"Do the Carlyles know you've got her?" Jake asked. He took another drag, looking again at the baby. His voice held the weight of suspicion now. Maybe this had been a bad idea. Myrra needed to turn this back in her favor. She needed pity.

"They're dead," Myrra blurted. Maybe just the truth was best.

The cigarette nearly dropped out of Jake's mouth.

"Dead?" he asked. "What happened?"

Myrra stared at Jake's wide, square face. He'd had a haircut since she saw him last; neatly combed, cut close on the sides. His face was a mess of shattered confusion. Myrra didn't think he'd ever really experienced death in his life.

"I watched Imogene jump off a building. Marcus slit his wrists in the bath."

"Why?"

"I don't know," she said. Truth was good, but not the whole truth. Jake wouldn't believe it anyway.

"This is insane."

Jake paced. He snubbed out his cigarette and discarded it, even though it was only half-finished, and immediately lit a second one.

"I didn't know what to do—I couldn't stay in there with the bodies, I couldn't leave Charlotte..."

"Why didn't you call Security?"

"Can't trust them—"

"That doesn't make any sense." Jake walked back and forth, back and forth. He stared at the ground, his brow furrowed.

Myrra didn't want to have to explain herself any further. With her free hand, she reached out and touched his elbow. He stopped and looked up at her.

"Listen," she said, looking deeply at him with what she hoped was a needful expression. "I am asking for your help."

Jake's face softened. Good.

"I know I didn't handle this the way I should," she said. "But you've shown me so many wonderful things these past few months: the book you bought me, the stories you've told me, a life full of good memories and good people..."

Jake took her free hand in his. Myrra readjusted Charlotte on her hip and took a step closer to him.

"You taught me to want more from life—so when I saw the opportunity to leave, I took it." She looked down, took a breath. Give him the choice. Don't rush it.

"I don't know what I've been to you, and it doesn't matter. I haven't had that many people care about me in my life, and I just wanted to say that you've meant more to me than anyone." She looked up at his face again. His eyes were glistening. Good.

"I have to leave now, and I really don't want to put you in the middle of this or get you involved in any way, but you're the only person I can go to." She meant this.

He leaned into her. He was very close now. Charlotte squirmed a little—Myrra had a feeling she didn't like the smell of the cigarette.

Jake bent down and kissed her, and she leaned into him sideways, keeping Charlotte at bay on her other side. It seemed that Jake had forgotten about Charlotte again, and that worked fine for Myrra's purposes. He parted his lips and the kiss deepened, with Myrra following his lead. For a moment she felt the shock of sense memory, of Imogene kissing her just hours before. Imogene had been softer, much less insistent. Jake pulled back and looked at her, put his hand on her cheek.

"What do you need?" he asked. He gave her a small smile.

"Do you still know someone who can alter IDs?" she asked. "I need to get out of New London. I have Imogene's card, but I need to change the name."

Jake's expression faltered as he ran a hand through his hair. She knew what he must be thinking—teenage high jinks were one thing, but aiding and abetting a fugitive was a different matter entirely.

"You don't have to come along... you don't have to be a part of it at all. I just need a name and a phone number. I don't want to get you in any trouble."

Jake took a step back and dropped another cigarette butt, grinding it beneath his heel. He stayed silent, staring off toward the dumpsters. Myrra watched him. It was hard to tell what he was thinking, but she sensed that if she pleaded her case any further, it would start to feel forced. Jake had a simple view of the world, but he wasn't altogether stupid.

After another moment he gave a slight decisive nod with his chin, as though ending a conversation.

"The truth," he said. "Imogene and Marcus really killed themselves? I know you were in a desperate situation..." His voice trailed off. He was skeptical enough to ask the question, but too nice to come right out and accuse her of anything.

"I watched Imogene jump off a roof. I saw Marcus dead in his bathtub," she repeated. She couldn't help feeling a little frustrated, but she kept it in.

He gave another nod. He believed her.

"Then what kind of person would I be," he started, "if I didn't help you?" He broke into another grin. She smiled back at him, relieved.

His smile grew wider and his eyes lit up with inspiration.

"What if I came with you?" He turned fully back to her,

propelled by the confidence of his convictions. Oh no. Myrra kept the smile screwed onto her face. "I mean, we were headed this direction anyway. I want to marry you. I've said as much almost a dozen times. The only thing stopping me was my dad, I know he wouldn't—" Jake fell silent, but Myrra finished the thought in her head. Approve. Allow. Always needing permission. Still a boy.

"Anyway, we wouldn't need to worry about that if we started over together, somewhere new. You're important to me too. I love you, and I want to make you a part of my life." His face was lit up like a light bulb. There was no way he would help her if she refused him now.

In her stress Myrra squeezed Charlotte a little too hard, and she started crying. No. Not now. Myrra switched her to the other arm, bouncing her again. She was used to carrying Charlotte for long stretches, but even her arms were aching at this point.

Jake's smile faded a little as he was reminded of the baby, but he soldiered on.

"First thing we have to do is drop her off at a hospital or something. I know you love her, and she's really sweet, but I don't think we'll be able to take her with us." He spoke in a firm tone, as a father would to a child. Though she had been thinking the same thing just minutes ago, it sounded repugnant coming from him.

"If you think it's best," she said, keeping her voice sweet.

Jake went on, his grand plan coming together piece by piece. "When we got our IDs changed last time, we went to this guy named Boots. He moves around a lot, but I've got his number." Myrra nodded along with him. "We can drop off Charlotte, head over there, get your ID changed, and catch a train out. Could head to Troy. Or Palmer would be cool…"

The fool. He didn't even know to avoid trains. She kept nodding at each aural cue, tuning him out. Still, he had good intentions.

Her brain had trouble holding on to the idea of the finite amount of time before her, but she could focus enough to know that she didn't want Jake dictating the time that was left. Her bag was sitting on the ground by the plastic crate. Opening the zipper, she made a nest in the clothes and nestled Charlotte in the bag.

Jake was talking, thinking out the particulars of their escape. She walked back to him, keeping the bag in her sight line. She could see one of their favorite dark nooks behind Jake's shoulder. This next part would go better with her hands free.

8

TOBIAS

"We wouldn't have to deal with this shit if they'd followed through on tagging." Simpson tapped through the crime scene images at such lightning speed, Tobias was unsure if he was absorbing any information at all. They were on a metro line suspended high above the city, zooming so fast that the trains emitted a moaning whirr as the cars displaced the air. Tobias always enjoyed watching these trains from the ground, not so much riding on them. From so far below, the heavy steel tracks became thin gossamer, the trains blinking across at such speeds they looked like a bright electric ping traveling down a wire.

"Courts said it wasn't ethical," Tobias replied. Simpson was slouched in one of the green plastic benches, but Tobias had to stand. He'd been allowed a few hours' sleep before heading out, but his body had rejected such stillness, nervous energy frequently jolting him awake. Tobias took a few deep barrel-chest breaths in an attempt to slow his heart rate. When that didn't work, he began tapping his foot against the hard floor to give his muscles an outlet for their freneticism.

"What's unethical about it? She chose to go under contract."

"Well, technically, her great-grandmother chose."

Tobias watched as Simpson cycled through the pictures again. Myrra Dal's sharp face flashed across the screen in the carousel of interior shots, bodies, blood, and wounds. There was an optical trick to the photograph; every time Tobias saw the frame of her face, it felt as if she were looking directly at him. Her eyes burrowed into his like needles, injecting judgment and anger. He recognized that Barnes was trying to start him out with an easy one—this girl barely topped fifty kilograms, and, despite the bodies, she wasn't especially threatening on paper. But something in her photograph made Tobias recoil.

"Please." Simpson rolled his eyes at Tobias's argument. "All I know is seventy percent of our cases would be solved a lot quicker if we tagged these people. Do you know how much time I've spent chasing down runaways?"

"Well, hopefully, with your experience, this one won't take too long," Tobias said, trying to stay pragmatic. He couldn't deny that the gleaming newness of his first case had been tarnished a little once he realized he was partnered with Simpson. He couldn't fault Barnes for the choice; Ray Simpson had years of built-up practical knowledge and well-honed instincts. Unfortunately, this left him with a personality that vehemently rejected nuance.

When Simpson had knocked on Tobias's door earlier that day to go over the case, he'd barged in past Tobias without a word, helped himself to the fruit salad lying out on Tobias's kitchen counter, and told his new partner to pack a bag.

"Where are we going?" Tobias had asked as he watched his lunch steadily disappear, forkful by forkful, down Simpson's gullet.

"Palmer," Simpson grunted out between bites.

"Why?"

"Because they always end up in Palmer." Another forkful.

"Why?"

This second *why* had especially offended Simpson, who started to wave the fork around for emphasis.

"Why? I don't know why—because it's the opposite of here, probably."

That was the extent of the details offered. Now they were on a metro train headed toward the edge of New London, where a canal shuttle waited to take them to Palmer. Simpson looked up from the revolving sequence of pictures on his tablet and stared at Tobias.

"Will you stop tapping your goddamn foot?" Each word shot out of his mouth like a dart. Tobias looked down at the linoleum floor and willed his shoe to be still. Funny, he thought. A city as advanced as New London, and they still designed it so the metro would have linoleum floors. They felt strangely out of place. Maybe there was just something about public transit that demanded cheap, replaceable materials.

More as an excuse to move than anything else, Tobias closed the gap between himself and Simpson and sat down next to him. He pulled out his tablet and woke up the screen, tilting it toward Simpson's face.

"I wired us into the canal shuttle feed at Palmer. She hasn't shown up yet." He brought video up on the screen: hundreds of commuters with backpacks, purses, and rolling suitcases wove through. Facial-recognition software framed each person's face in turn with a little green box, stalling the video for a millisecond each time as it ran a new facial scan, relegating the motion on camera to unnerving stop-start jerks.

Simpson moved the tablet away from his face and put his own back in his bag.

"Look, Bendel, I know you're super-duper excited to finally be going on a field trip, but I'm missing my kid's birthday for this. Can you just dial it back a little bit for me?"

He sighed and took a second look at the feed. "This is helpful, though. Good job."

Tobias wasn't proud of it, but he felt a rush of pleasure at receiving Simpson's approval.

"You ever been to Palmer?" Tobias asked, trying to follow Simpson's request and ease up.

"A few times," Simpson said. "Took Ruth there for her birthday last year."

Tobias raised his eyes to the status screens on the wall. Four stops to go. Simpson grunted.

"What about you?"

"Just once, with Barnes. But all we did was get off the ferry, pick up some evidence, and get right back on the ferry again." Tobias didn't mention it, but he knew Palmer quite well, from his life before Barnes. Though Tobias tended to view his criminal parentage as a circumstance out of his control, the agents of the New London Security Bureau looked on it as a genetic deficiency. Instead of constantly explaining himself, he found that omission worked best. If he didn't mention his mother and father in conversation, there was a certain level of forgetting on the part of his colleagues.

Before they were incarcerated, his parents had shuttled him around to all the grand locales. Palmer, of course, and New London, but also the Kittimer Mountains for vacations, and Troy's tropical resorts. Tobias kept fragments of memories of this time that he never talked about. Golden spigots in hotel en suites. Heavy velvet curtains with tassel pulls to block out all manner of light and noise. Dinners that seemed more sculpture than food, though his father still always found error with something on his plate. Deep cushioned mattresses. Tiny ornamental boxes that seemed too small to hold anything at all.

"Palmer's nice and all, but I couldn't understand living there," Simpson was saying. Once, Tobias and his mother had stayed in an apartment in Palmer for six months, waiting for his father. Tobias remembered his stay feeling pretty normal, but then anything felt normal in repetition, especially when you were a child. Flexible bodies, flexible brains, at that age.

With the clarity of years, Tobias could now see the faults in his upbringing, like the answer to a puzzle that, once pointed out, is so obvious it makes you smack your palm to your forehead. Ingrid had spent the months pacing a little too quickly back and forth across the rug in front of the apartment's bay window, had swung a little too hard from bright conversation to sudden gasping sobs. There were pills she popped lightly into her mouth, throwing her son a playful eyebrow waggle and a smile. He'd assumed they were mints. There were nights when she rushed him into the closet, saying, "Hide and seek, hide and seek!" when a hard rapping sound surprised them at the front door, and he would just hear snippets of conversation, muffled and echoey through the door like a distant radio—"He's not here right now," "Haven't heard from him," "Will give him your message"—all the while tucked up between an unopened box of highball glasses and a never-used vacuum cleaner. After the thud of the front door closing, and the shunting sound of the dead bolt, Ingrid would pop open the closet door with a whoosh, eyes wide and smile severe, shouting, "Found you!"

Such a strange, put-upon life they led. Tobias's thoughts strayed back to the portrait of the Carlyles, all tense smiles and tight grips. There was something there too.

"Why would the Carlyles kill themselves?" Tobias wondered aloud. Simpson looked sideways at him.

"A family that rich, there's bound to be some terrible things going on behind closed doors," he said.

Tobias agreed with the sentiment, but couldn't see the specifics. He voiced possibilities aloud, hoping Simpson would catch something he hadn't. "Techs swept their accounts. They weren't having money trouble. No history of mental illness in the family..."

"Husband had a few mistresses, but he didn't seem the type to get bothered over that," Simpson added.

"Were any of the women blackmailing him?" Tobias asked.

"Maybe. No evidence of it yet, though. And anyway, that might be a reason for Marcus to kill himself, but I don't think Imogene would be especially sad about it. Their marriage seemed pretty cold already. She'd stay alive for life insurance alone, and the chance to wear the latest designer black dress."

That all tracked with how Tobias read their case file. They didn't seem like people who allowed themselves to get flustered over much.

"So why?" Tobias asked again. Simpson leaned forward, propping his elbows on his lap, and gave a noncommittal wag of his head.

"Dunno," he said. "But the case is Myrra Dal. Let's stick on her."

Tobias must have looked disappointed in his answer, because Simpson added, "Look, if we catch Myrra Dal, she's probably the best lead to finding out why. She'll know more about them than anyone else."

Tobias's tablet emitted a pinging sound. Simpson leaned in to look. "You've got a message."

Tobias looked at his mail folder and jumped to see it was from the station. He read it immediately, eager for more information.

"We have to head back," he told Simpson. He stood up and grabbed his bag, readying himself to exit at the next stop. "The techs found some letters under a floorboard when they did a second sweep of the penthouse. A possible accomplice."

Simpson's face shifted from irritation to engagement. He stood up as well.

"Where?" he asked.

"She didn't really tell me where she was headed." Jake McCann was seated in front of them, looking nervous.

Tobias looked the witness up and down. He was trying hard not to judge Jake and failing. He kept looking at the ground instead of at their faces. He had a grocer's apron on, but it was so freshly white that Tobias doubted it had ever come into contact with hard labor. Joseph McCann, the owner of the store, hovered over his son's shoulder.

Joseph had set up a few chairs in one of the back stockrooms. Simpson was seated directly in front of Jake, while Tobias stood behind him, leaning against the wall, watching. The whole room smelled like vegetables.

Simpson had taken the lead in questioning Jake. Tobias couldn't get a read on what Simpson thought of the kid, but he could tell that Simpson was getting increasingly annoyed at Jake's father, who kept interjecting, "Now, you're not implying—" or "None of this is Jake's fault—" every time he thought Simpson took his line of questioning too far.

The kid. Tobias kept thinking of him that way, even though he knew they were the same age. It was all relative; compared to the guys at the station, he still felt like a boy, but standing next to Jake, he felt a boost of superiority. Between the odd fly-by-night life with his parents and the stern upbringing with Barnes, he'd never felt especially coddled. Something to be thankful for, he thought, if this is the way you turn out.

"So she didn't tell you where she was headed—but you guys wrote to each other a lot. Did you get any ideas as to where she might like to go? Places she might like to see? Or even any friends that she had, in other towns?" Tobias noticed that Simpson was keeping his voice unnaturally gentle, as if to not aggravate Jake's excitable father.

"Umm...no. Not really. I think I was her only friend." Tobias detected the slightest hint of wistfulness in Jake's voice as he said this. Whether or not his observation was true, Jake certainly wanted to be her only friend.

"It seems like you were a pretty good friend to her," Simpson observed, and Jake nodded.

It hadn't taken much to get Jake to admit that he'd had a friendship with Myrra Dal, and that he'd seen her that morning. But he claimed that Myrra Dal had simply met him to say goodbye and that there hadn't been any further details exchanged. Jake was a terrible liar, pausing to think in all the wrong places, looking anywhere but in the agents' eyes, practically sweating in puddles. Tobias could tell that Jake's story wasn't true, and he could tell that Simpson could tell. Simpson was amping up his questioning, starting out gentle and leading up to attack Jake's story from a different side. Despite himself, Tobias was gaining a grudging respect for Simpson's technique.

"Meeting with her, tutoring her, buying her presents, that's a really good friend," Simpson continued.

Jake nodded again. "Well, like I said, I felt bad for her, she didn't have anybody. I've donated to the CWRA a few times, I think it's terrible how workers are treated."

A grumble from Joseph behind them, and Jake tensed his shoulders slightly at his dad's disapproval.

Simpson nodded sympathetically. "It is, just awful. And I want you to know, she's not in any trouble, not yet. We just need to find her so we can figure out what happened."

While Simpson carried on his line of questioning, Tobias skimmed through the scans of the letters that had been sent to his tablet. There weren't many; from what Tobias could gather, the two had been communicating electronically, but at some recent point Myrra Dal's tablet had been confiscated. Dal had stolen antique paper out of Marcus Carlyle's office, and they'd kept up communications from there. In Jake's letters—they only had his, with his heavy, blocklike handwriting—he'd expressed that he found writing on paper to be very romantic, but there was nothing more explicit than that regarding their relationship, at least nothing that Tobias could find. But still.

Simpson was still questioning Jake, taking him through the beginnings of his friendship with Dal. Jake was just explaining how he'd helped her with some particularly large grocery runs when Simpson interjected.

"And when did you become romantically involved with Myrra Dal?" Simpson kept his face open and innocent. Joseph McCann, however, was staring daggers at his son. Jake blushed so hard his skin practically glowed. He stared up at his father, then back to Simpson.

"I—I didn't." He spoke with a weak voice. "We were just friends."

Joseph smacked Jake in the back of the head, his face as red as his son's. "You complete asshole! Did you even use protection, or do your mother and I have to get you tested for diseases?"

Joseph was about to go in for another smack, but Tobias stepped in to block him. Jake was cowering in his chair, and Simpson motioned for his attention, held his gaze.

"Listen, Jake," Simpson started, "you didn't do anything wrong here. We're not after you. We just need to know what she said before she left. The whole story."

Jake took a breath. All people wanted was to be told that it wasn't their fault.

Tobias had held back the father long enough for him to calm down. Joseph was now fuming in the corner of the stockroom. Tobias turned his attention back to the interrogation. Jake explained how Myrra Dal had come to him for help, Charlotte in her arms. He explained how he'd offered to help her alter the documents, volunteered to go with her. That led to another moment of pulling Joseph off his son.

"But ultimately, she convinced me that I should stay behind, that she should go forward on her own." Jake blinked one too many times, and Tobias heard the change in his voice. He cut into the conversation while still holding a warning arm up to Joseph's chest.

"How did she convince you of that?" Tobias asked. Jake looked at Tobias but didn't say anything. Tobias waited, knew to wait, stared him down. Simpson leaned back, allowing Tobias his turn. Tobias shot a barely perceptible glance his way, hoping it was enough for Simpson to glean his appreciation.

Another bout of silence.

"You both seem pretty deep in love, why wouldn't you go with her?" Tobias asked. Jake's mouth was crumpling into a frown. It wouldn't take much for him to fold.

"Didn't she want you to go with her?"

Tobias leaned in a little closer to Jake, noticed his eyes welling up. He'd never gotten to question anyone before. He felt bad for the kid, but he had to admit he enjoyed the rush, the tension of the situation.

"I thought she did." A small voice. A tear popped out of Jake's eye. Tobias nodded, invited him to continue.

"I told her I'd go with her, and she seemed really happy about it, and she kissed me, and we . . ." Jake trailed off for a second, blushed. Simpson and Tobias exchanged a look. Myrra Dal was much savvier than Jake gave her credit for. Not that that was a surprise. Before Jake's father could pick up on the direction of the conversation, Tobias jumped in.

"And what happened—after?" Tobias asked.

"Well, then she said it would be better if she went alone to get the IDs changed, safer for me—it made sense when she said it." Jake sighed. "We picked a place to meet up later, but she never showed."

"You idiot," Joseph said, from where he was stewing in the corner.

"I'm sorry, Dad," Jake said, staring at his feet. A tear dropped down onto the top of his shoe. Jake sniffed. "But maybe something happened to her—maybe she was detained or something—" Tobias rolled his eyes out of Jake's line of vision, and Simpson glared at him.

Simpson stood and put a hand on Jake's other shoulder and said gently, "Maybe so. In any case, why don't you give us the name of the ID guy that you recommended? And if you have any of Myrra's letters stowed, we'll take those too."

Jake looked up at Simpson, unsure. Simpson smiled at him, a rare thing to Tobias's recollection.

"Listen—you help us out with this, and we'll call it square. You had good intentions. You don't have to get into trouble over all this." Simpson flashed his eyes over to Tobias again. The look said, Don't challenge this. The information is more important than a citation.

"Don't judge that kid too harshly," Simpson said on the way out. "Love will kill every last brain cell you have."

Tobias was tucking a bundle of Myrra Dal's letters into the pocket of his bag. Paper. It felt rough and delicate.

"Still, there's something to be said for basic human judgment," Tobias countered. They walked down the sidewalk back the way they had come. The elevator onto the train platform was the next block over.

"How do you figure that?" Simpson asked.

"People choose who they pursue. It's not like he fell in love with her overnight. He let her take advantage."

"Sometimes it's a roll of the dice. When I first met Ruth, I totally let her take advantage—she read off my chemistry tests every week for the entire fall semester. But in the end, I got the date."

"Sorry, I didn't mean it like that," Tobias said. He'd never met Simpson's wife. First day, and he was alienating his partner. But Simpson still seemed good-natured, more at ease now than he had been with Tobias's foot-tapping. He walked lightly over the threshold of the elevator and pressed the door-close button.

"No offense taken," he said. The elevator shut behind them, and the two of them sped upward, fast enough for Tobias to feel his insides shift. He stared fixedly at the elevator button and tried his best to ignore the speed. "Joke was on her, anyway. I got a D in chemistry."

Tobias laughed, happy to still be in Simpson's good graces.

"We gonna go check out Boots?" he asked.

Simpson shrugged and watched out the glass walls as the streets shrank below them. "We'll send some guys to follow up on the phone number, but that'll take a while. I've had to track down that guy before. He never stays in the same spot, can sniff out agents a mile away. We'll stick around the city one more night, sift through the evidence, and if the uniforms haven't found Boots by then, we move forward."

Tobias didn't follow. "Move forward where? That's our only lead."

"Palmer."

Tobias felt a wave of exasperation for Simpson. "Really?"

The elevator dinged and the doors parted. They were back on the metro platform. Tobias allowed himself to be swallowed up by the sea of people surrounding them, dared to stand close enough to the edge of the platform that he could picture himself falling onto the tracks. A brief image of Imogene Carlyle's corpse flashed through his mind. There was an odd burning smell coming off the tracks. After scanning for a few minutes he spotted the source: a dead pigeon lay contorted near the electrified rail. Nobody else seemed to notice the smell, but it was making Tobias nauseous. He did not want to go to Palmer.

Simpson walked ahead of him, looked back through the veil of people passing, and shouted, "Come on."

Tobias pushed through the crowd to catch up.

"Nothing that kid told me leads me to believe otherwise," Simpson said. "They always go to Palmer."

Tobias felt better later that evening once he was back in his apartment, just him alone with a tablet full of evidence, letters to sort through, and a puzzle to solve.

Tobias had read through the letters a couple of times already, handling them delicately, the oils of his fingers barriered by standard-issue white evidence gloves. Even then, touching the antique paper felt like an indiscretion. He was astonished that she'd been ballsy enough to steal it. He sat at his tiny foldout table and spread the letters out as far as the surface would allow. Tobias's apartment was an economical space, so every fork and plate and corner drawer had its purpose. New London didn't allow for much living space unless you were as rich as the Carlyles. Barnes's apartment had been similar when Tobias had moved in with him; he had taught Tobias to only hold on to the things he needed. Comfort could be found in people, in life, in a job well done, not in objects. David and Ingrid, by contrast, had been magpies, constantly collecting little baubles that they would eventually abandon in an escape when the inevitable landlord or loan shark came calling. Tobias looked around his apartment, its orderliness and calm, and felt mostly satisfied, though his thoughts strayed to Barnes's warm wooden desk. He would get there someday.

With the letters spread out as far as they were able to be on the small tabletop, Tobias tried to get a better sense of Myrra Dal, of the why of her. Something more than Simpson's reductive reasoning. There had to be more than "She'll go to Palmer." He arranged the letters in order of date, lightly handling Jake's papers at the corners and keeping scanned letters from Dal's quarters up on his tablet screen. The content of their correspondence was actually fairly tame, nothing too salacious. Myrra Dal had kept it tame, knowing Jake was after something purer than just sex. He was looking for someone to save.

The letters started halfway through their courtship, presumably after Myrra Dal's tablet had been confiscated by Imogene. At the start the letters were mostly inquisitive, and they operated under the guise of friendship. She asked Jake about his family, his job, what books he liked. She made sure to remain constantly thankful for his attention and correspondence: "My world is so small...it's so nice to be able to just talk to somebody, and not have it be about laundry or cleaning skedules."

Another letter, about a month in: "Your professer sounds like a pain in the ass. But you're smart—if you do the work and do it well, in the end she'll have to give you an A, right? I wouldn't worry too much. Honestly, I'm just jealous of all the stuff you get to learn! I'm just happy that I learned to read...though you've been very kind to ignore my horrible spelling."

Tobias couldn't quite tell if the misspelled words were honest errors or strategic. Always there was a hint of her less-than life, but blended with humor, to keep from alienating Jake.

Shortly after that, Jake volunteered to tutor her. The letters got a little shorter—they were able to talk more in person. Snippets and references here and there to stolen conversations. They met before or after grocery runs, for short enough bursts that the Carlyles seemingly hadn't noticed. It wasn't long after that that the relationship shifted. There were three letters in a row from Jake, with no responses from Myrra Dal.

Jake maintained some level of poise in the first letter: "Dear Myrra, I really apologize for what happened last week. I'm so sorry if I offended you. You ran off so quick, it's hard to tell if I misread the moment...we didn't really get a chance to talk. Will you be coming by the store this week? Maybe we can clear the air."

The next letter got a little more inquisitive: "Dear Myrra, You missed your usual Thursday grocery run. Is everything okay?"

Then, "I'm getting worried—are you avoiding me, or did Imogene find out about us? I just wish you'd talk to me. Should I not have kissed you? Is it what you want?"

Finally a response from Dal—"I'm so sorry, Jake. I should have written to you sooner... you're safe, Imogene doesn't know anything. I just needed some time to get my head around my feelings for you. I don't want you to think I'm using you or anything like that. I know some contract workers will do some pretty awful, desparate things to move up in the world, I just don't want you to think of me like that. The truth is, I like you a lot, more than I should, and it worries me. I could get us in a lot of trouble, and I don't want that for you. I think it's probably best if we stop seeing each other. I think I like you too much, and it's going to get us hurt. Maybe this will just be better if it stays something wonderful and perfect in my memory. Thank you for everything you've done. Sorry this is such a short goodbye, but I think it's best—Myrra."

Jake chased her, didn't take no for an answer, something Dal had undoubtedly counted on. It was a gamble, but it had paid off. The whole thing felt like a classic romance, hit all the right beats. From there the letters grew longer again, more romantic. Keepsakes of lovers instead of notes from friends.

Tobias had to give her credit. Myrra Dal's letters to Jake felt very sincere, from the first to the last. He felt his sympathy for Jake grow, just a little bit. If Tobias hadn't known how the affair had ended, he wasn't sure he would have seen it coming. There were a lot of personal things that she wrote to him, things that Tobias knew to be true from her files. Like how the smell of raw meat made her gag, ever since that stint working in a butcher shop. The horrid conditions she'd lived in while working for the laundry. She confessed that she still had a habit of sewing valuables into her mattress, after having so much stolen from her when she lived in the laundry dorms. Tobias made a mental note to go back and check Dal's mattress one more time before leaving for Palmer. She likely had the skills to hide the stitching—it was possible that the techs hadn't noticed anything in their initial sweep of the house.

She wrote often to Jake about Charlotte, updating him on how she was growing, what toys she preferred, the little sounds she would make and what each sound meant. This, too, felt honest, though Tobias had to grant that it was hard to tell. But there was such an incongruity in taking an infant on the run—Myrra Dal had sense, she should have left Charlotte behind. The only conclusion Tobias could reach was that Dal loved her.

It was fascinating to think of Myrra Dal holding a pen, pressing down with her other palm on this very piece of paper to steady it against the writing instrument. He was touching the same piece of paper she had touched. He placed his palm on top of one of the paper letters, as if to mirror the motions he imagined, pushing down as if he could push through his glove, through the paper, and touch her hand on the other side. His fingerprints overlaid with hers.

There was one glaring omission in her letters to Jake, one bit of herself that she held back, and that was her mother. When Jake, in a later letter, asked about her family, she said she didn't remember her mother at all. Tobias doubted that.

He flipped through file pages in his tablet until he got to Dal's family records. Ami Dal, removed from work orders at age thirty, the authorities citing mental instability. Myrra Dal would have been five. Young enough to forget, maybe. But her mother had been her only caretaker. Dal's father had never been in the picture. Security had his name on the birth record, but he'd been transferred out of New London to a metalworking operation in Troy months before Dal was born. Tobias wondered if Myrra Dal knew anything about him at all.

Myrra Dal, Myrra Dal. Whenever Tobias thought about criminals, he always referred to them by last name or full name. It was a convenient way to keep them distanced, to separate them in his head from friends, lovers, family, whoever else. Though to be fair, he never referred to his parents as Mom or Dad either. Always Ingrid and David. It was for the best.

Without his meaning them to, they flashed through his mind—frequently drunk, frequently absent, now residing somewhere in a New London jail, someplace he never cared to check on or visit. The impermanence of too many hotel rooms, meals of restaurant leftovers. The sweet rotten smell of stale champagne and hangover sweat. Always some mix of powders and pills near the bathroom sink.

Every action Tobias undertook, every choice and impulse, was weighed down by David and Ingrid. He knew, self-consciously, that he had fashioned most of his identity in direct rebellion against theirs. There was no escaping your upbringing, one way or the other. Tobias thought again of Myrra Dal's childhood, different from his, and more terrible. How much could she remember about her mother, and how much did she let in? Then he wondered what was worse, to remember too little or to remember too much.

Hours later, around dawn the following morning, Tobias cut through the crime scene tape on the door to the Carlyle penthouse. The rookie in him bristled at this. Was he allowed here? Of course he was. He was one of the lead agents on the case. Barnes or Simpson wouldn't hesitate. They'd take ownership of the whole thing.

He'd leave a note for the techs, just in case. He put on his gloves and disposable slippers over his shoes, and, once properly outfitted, he stepped over the threshold.

Even with the fabric of the slippers, every footstep rang out on the marble floor, and the sound reverberated off the walls. He was a trespasser here. The air was heavy, it was so quiet. There was something about crime scenes after the fact, they tended to absorb the horror and come alive. Tobias felt as though there were silent guardians in the air watching him from all sides, upset that he had come.

He pushed past the feeling and made his way through the cavernous foyer. He had to pause and appreciate it. So much space, so much light, so much wood. Framed artwork hung tastefully along the walls. Tobias couldn't help but stop to check and see if any were from his family's collection.

No go. The Bendel collection had been mostly work from the modern period. He recognized a few Turners and an early Matisse. No artists from the new world, no work from the modern period. Nothing under three hundred years old. The Carlyles liked everything old, very old. Classical.

Tobias made his way down a hall behind the stairs to Myrra Dal's room. It was hidden behind another elegant wooden door, but inside it was much more bare than the rest of the house, little more than a closet. A mattress and blankets on the floor, a plastic crate with clothes and rags folded inside, a broken clock and a lamp on top. There was one small window high on the wall, near the ceiling.

There were very few signs of Myrra Dal trying to personalize the space. It was possible that the Carlyles had forbidden any extra decorating, but Tobias suspected it had been Dal's choice. She had lived here for years. He pictured her sleeping on this bed, a tiny mass with thick black hair, curled up on the floor. He pictured her waking up for Charlotte's feedings, rising early to make breakfast, and cleaning when she'd be most out of sight. Heading back to this tiny box late at night, maybe stealing a few minutes of alone time here in between errands in the afternoon.

There were those who would have tried to make the best of it, add mementos to the room, a picture, what have you. But Dal had refused to do so; she wouldn't do anything that would suggest she was putting down roots in such a place. To do so would mean succumbing to the lie that this was a home and this was a life. Dal seemed smart enough to know better. Maybe she had killed them, after all.

He pulled the mattress back from the wall. There were no slits or tears. With a gloved hand, he felt along the bottom seam. Near the top corner of the mattress he felt it. The seams had been cut discreetly, a small incision maybe twenty centimeters wide, enough to hide a tablet or a rolled sheaf of paper. The techs had missed this. He pushed his fingers inside, feeling through the batting and padding of the mattress, and grasped something hard and square. It wasn't a tablet, but it was a similar shape. He pulled it out and immediately experienced the same admiration and covetousness he'd felt for the inlaid wood doors and the artwork in the halls.

It was a book. On the cover it read: "The World Is Round." He opened the cover with care, worried about cracking the spine. It looked very, very old. Had she stolen it? Marcus Carlyle had an enviable antique library. The pages made a whispering, shushing noise as they brushed against each other. Tobias savored the irony that Myrra Dal, a contract worker, lived a life that allowed her ready access to such luxury, whereas he, who had freedom and a steady job, was toiling away in a studio apartment with collapsible furniture. It wasn't the same, he knew. But still.

He read the first line: "Once upon a time the world was round and you could go on it around and around."

Beautifully put, and not true nowadays. The world now was flat. But, Tobias mused, it did still spin around and around. Our feet stay on the ground now thanks to centrifugal force, he remembered learning in school. On the ground, around and around, he thought. But once, in another time and another place, people had stayed where they were due to gravity. Gravity was a force that Tobias understood on an academic level, but he had never really been able to fully grasp it.

Tobias closed the book, almost sorry to have to deposit it in a plastic evidence bag. It ought to go to the lab, he thought, or be stowed in an evidence locker. He decided to take it with him to Palmer instead. It merited further study.

He fished around inside the mattress again, eager to see if any further treasures could be discovered. He pulled out a rolled sheaf of paper and an ink pen, her stash for writing to Jake, no doubt. There were also a couple of coins, and, buried deepest in the batting, a small religious icon made of faded blue plastic. It was a figure of a man with many arms. This surprised Tobias even more than the book. He didn't imagine Myrra Dal to be a religious person, though he knew religion was encouraged among contract workers. All employers were required to allow workers one morning off once a week so they would have time for religious observance in whatever faith they chose. This was always advertised as benevolence on the part of the government, an affirmation of certain inalienable rights, but Tobias thought with skepticism that it was more of a carrot-and-stick trick than anything else. And anyway, it ensured that most people behaved themselves.

He popped the icon into a smaller evidence bag and stowed it in his satchel along with the book. Best to keep this on him as well.

⋆ ⋆ ⋆

The other rooms in the house were exactly as they'd been described in the bureau report. The only other room Tobias was curious about was the study.

He'd examined the evidence very carefully. Imogene Carlyle had had very little need to keep personal records, but Marcus's records were prolific. The techs had run through multiple hard drives: there were notes on the family's finances, business logs, emails, diaries, shopping lists, invitations, blackmail threats, news articles, PR files, recipes, receipts, market research, bills, tax returns, tax evasion plans, and more. Tobias had read it all. Having been on the lowest rung on the bureau ladder for so long, he had learned how to review stacks and stacks of paperwork as efficiently as possible. He had read through every mundane detail. He read fast and he read thoroughly. And he had noticed that there was a gap.

It was hard to see—it wasn't as though there were any one significant thing missing in the time line of Marcus's records. His tax information was all present and accounted for, his accounting books were all intact. But when it came to the last year, there just seemed to be less of everything than in previous years. In previous years he'd been engaged in campaigns for multiple congressmen, had been seated on multiple advisory boards for various state issues, had been consulted on a wide range of laws and federal measures. But in the past eighteen months, it looked as though every large corporate and government contract had vanished overnight. It didn't seem feasible. The techs must have missed a file somewhere. He'd seen it happen before. Over the past two years Tobias had evolved into the techs' number one fact-checker, constantly pointing out tiny gaps in the information, regularly requesting that they take a second look at the scene. People rolled their eyes when they saw him coming.

Tobias entered the wood-paneled room and felt the quiet intensify. If the penthouse was now a guarded tomb, this was the heart of it. Tobias slid his gaze over to a side door just to the right of the desk. It was ajar, and through the gap in the doorway, Tobias could see into a white-tiled bathroom, part of Marcus Carlyle's master suite. There was a white claw-foot tub resting on the white tile—Tobias could just make out one of the curved feet from where he stood. Tellingly, there were streaks of pink along the white sides of the tub, and a wider patch of tiles stained slightly pink just below. The new owners, whoever they were, would have to replace that tile.

He took a few steps closer to the door and felt the air grow denser. He stepped back again, decided not to go in. That would be a morbid indulgence. He needed to focus on Marcus's records.

Tobias sank into the smooth leather of Marcus Carlyle's desk chair—soft and smooth and rich—and sifted through every file he could find on Marcus's tablet and on all supplemental hard drives.

Something had to be missing, but nothing was missing. After an hour of searching, Tobias had found nothing that the IT guys hadn't already dug up. He searched for other possibilities. Maybe Marcus Carlyle had deleted files before he died. He'd have to talk to Barnes. Maybe they could get an IT guy to come in and retrieve something.

His hands lingered on the wood of the stair rail as he made his way back down to the entrance of the penthouse. The polished banister was cool and smooth but grew warm under the heat of his hand. Everything in the New London Security Bureau was metal and plastic. Someday, he thought again, and then wondered if Barnes would approve.

A soft tinkling noise sounded above him. The chandelier was

slowly spinning on its chain, the individual bits of crystal knocking against each other. Somehow his body cutting through the stillness, his footfalls on the floor, had been enough to cause such a disturbance, like the epicenter of an earthquake.

As his feet hit the last step, he craned his neck around to the hallway behind the stairs. He could just make out Myrra Dal's wooden door, the entrance to her tiny cell. Did he know her better now? It felt as though he did. At least a part of her.

9

NABAT

Nabat is a city of artificial history. It was built directly into the side of a cliff, with atria, arches, and columns carved into the stone. The city embeds itself deeper and deeper into the rock in a fractal of caves and tunnels. It is built this way because that is the way that ancient cliff dwellers would have built it, but the city itself is not ancient.

When the ship, the world, first began traveling, people would flock to Nabat. They would run their hands over the carved-out columns, flit through the stone doorways into small lit shops where they would buy tiny glass bottles, leather bags, smithed metal. Wares that looked old but were not. After days of taking in a traditional culture that was not traditional at all, visitors would stay in hotel rooms placed against the cliff face, with balconies and windows sliced out of the stone, providing beautiful views of the tranquil sea below and the mountains far beyond on the horizon.

As generations cycled and trends changed, however, Nabat eventually fell out of style. The flow of tourism dwindled. Then Palmer came along, causing the sea level to rise drastically, and one of Nabat's main access points—the beach below—disappeared. Now small handfuls of tourists still visit each year, but only the die-hard fans looking for a history fix or older nostalgic generations who remember visiting Nabat at the height of its influence.

The people who live in Nabat will mostly be dead by the time the world breaks apart. A series of earthquakes (that is an inaccurate word, but nobody is calling them shipquakes when the ground starts shaking) will occur near the end as the crack in the world widens. One of these earthquakes, of a particularly large magnitude, will cause the cave city of Nabat to collapse in on itself. Parents will order their children to take shelter under doorframes or huddle under tables, but there really is no shelter to be had with destruction of this scale. All structures in the city will collapse. People will either die instantly from the stones falling on their heads, or, worse, end up trapped under rubble and die a more lingering death from dehydration or blood loss.

So even later, at the very end, while others are exploded out into the dark airlessness of space, the people of Nabat will have already experienced a different kind of darkness, the kind that implodes around them.

10

MYRRA

The sun was high and hot, and Myrra felt dirt scratching her skin, pressed in with sweat under the straps of her knapsack. Myrra had improvised a sling out of one of Imogene's scarves and tucked Charlotte against the front of her body. Charlotte was fussy, letting out small moans and scratching her cheeks with her stubby little fingers. The skin on her face was pink from sunburn.

Somehow Charlotte was still in her arms. She'd stood across the street from the hospital, holding her, just outside the reach of Security cameras, fully prepared to stroll over and leave her tucked in blankets next to the door. She waited and watched emergency shuttles come and go, some with patients, some coming in for an engine recharge. She stood and watched the hospital doors for much longer than was prudent. And all that time, she felt Charlotte grow warmer and warmer, tucked in against her chest. And in the end she'd left, still holding Charlotte, swearing all the way.

And of course, you can't just *take* a baby; babies require supplies.

Not long after Myrra left New London, Charlotte started to smell. The sour scent of stale urine wafted up from her diaper. Then the smell of shit was added to the mix, and then, like clockwork, Charlotte started to cry again. Myrra knew her well—she wouldn't be used to getting stuck in a dirty diaper for long periods. Even still, Myrra waited until they were a few hours outside town before stopping at a small roadside market for a pack of diapers and baby food. Charlotte cried the whole way, and Myrra felt her headache worsen, a mixture of noise and dehydration. Even entering the shop was a huge risk; New London was infested with surveillance, she wasn't sure about its suburbs. She tried to keep her head down the entire time she was in the store, but who knew where cameras could hide. Charlotte was a liability. She needed to leave her behind; apparently just not yet. Maybe she could leave her behind in Nabat and take off for other towns from there. It was still hard to keep track of her own thoughts.

They'd walked for a day and a half, stopping only to sleep. As time passed the buildings got smaller and less densely packed, shifting from suburbs to smaller towns and finally to open fields with occasional houses dotting the horizon. Never in her life had Myrra felt so much space around her.

The transit map hadn't given a good sense of distance, so she just had to keep walking and hope that they stumbled on Nabat soon. Myrra kept close to the ferry canals to keep track of their direction, but every time a boat neared she hid behind the ridge. They couldn't risk being seen. Agents must be looking for her by now.

Imogene's warning flashed in her mind: she had two months of life left to live. Maybe. Imogene had also said the ship could break apart at any time, if things were jostled wrong. On instinct

Myrra looked up at the sky to see if it was tearing apart, if a great big hole would open up above her. Who knew if the crack would come from the sky? Myrra checked the ground under her feet, suddenly certain it would break apart and swallow her up. She wondered what would reach her first, Security or the end of the world.

On the shore next to the canal, Myrra noticed clusters of dead fish rotting in the sun. As she stared, another one flopped out of the water onto the sand, its eyes looking surprised, mouth agape and gills straining. Last week, this would have struck her as strange behavior, but she wouldn't have thought about it too hard. Now all nature was ominous—the course of the fish, flight paths of birds, the wind, the weather, everything felt off. Myrra rushed down toward the shore, grabbed the fish by the fin, and flung it back into the water.

She should have a plan. This was one of the great hypothetical questions in life: What would you do if the world were ending tomorrow? What did people usually say? Myrra rifled through common answers in her head. Often people tried to fix past regrets: If I only had one day to live, I'd call my sister and tell her I'm sorry, I'd finally spend all that money I've been saving, I'd tell Jenny I love her... that kind of thing. Myrra couldn't think of any regrets. To regret your actions, you had to have been allowed to act. Regret required choice. Or maybe it was that her whole life was one big regret.

In an emergency people seek out their families. Myrra thought of her mother. She might still be alive, she might be confined somewhere. That was a long shot. Or maybe she'd escaped. Even more improbable. Maybe she'd done the same thing Myrra was doing now, taking the back roads, hiding from the authorities. That almost seemed sadder, as Myrra thought about it. If her mother had escaped, why had she not taken Myrra along? Why hadn't she tried to find her? Thinking about it put her at odds with her own mind—she wanted desperately to have a reason to run toward something, not just away from something else. But Myrra also saw the futility of it: her mother was most likely dead, and if she wasn't, she was too broken to want her.

Ahead the canal dipped underground into a tunnel, leaving Myrra at a loss. A narrow dirt road continued where it left off, following what she hoped was the same general direction. It wasn't long before Myrra understood why the water had changed course. The path fell away, revealing a series of white stone cliffs in its wake, which curved around a massive sea. Myrra had never seen so much water. It didn't even look like water from up here—from her vantage point, the waves texturing the surface looked like crinkles in aluminum foil. She didn't know water could look like that, had only ever seen it in a glass or a washtub or the ponds in Sakura Park. It felt like a solid, silvery thing. A cool salt breeze wafted up to meet her, making tendrils of hair dance around her face. Myrra suddenly felt very, very small.

There was a staircase in front of her leading down the cliff face. From her vantage point, she could see a webwork of staircases etched along the cliffs, interlocking like lines in a fishing net. Off in the distance, halfway down, she could make out a large hole in the rock—a cave? Most of the staircases seemed to lead there. It was impossible to tell the exact size from up here, but it had to be huge. She took another look along the cliffs. She couldn't see another road, not even a hiking trail. Nowhere to go but down.

There was no railing and the drop was perilously long, but somehow the path still felt solid. Everything felt sturdy—each stone step proceeded ahead of the previous one like a soldier on a march, each with smoothly sanded surfaces and precise right angles. There were landings farther down, with windows and doorways etched directly into the rock, some bordered with ornately carved moldings and embossed with gold and silver metalwork. Some of the inhabitants had flung open the iron casements of their windows, and clean linen curtains billowed out with the sea winds, caressing Myrra's face as she walked by. Charlotte tried to catch the corners of the curtains as they danced in the air.

When they finally reached it, the main cave turned out to be even larger than she'd imagined, going too far back for Myrra to comprehend its full size. A row of towering columns stood sentry along the threshold of the cave, carved directly into the stone, linking the ceiling to the floor. The columns were elaborately carved with leaves and geometric knots at the cornices and pedestals. They weren't as tall as Atlas Tower, but they were high enough to still leave Myrra feeling insignificant. High above, in an arched cornice between the two center pillars, a sign was etched into the white stone with the words "Nabat Welcomes You."

Behind the columns Myrra discovered a network of tunnels and grottoes burrowing deeper and deeper into the rock past the grandiose entrance. Iron chandeliers hung down from the stone ceilings all the way back into the farthest nooks, illuminating multiple levels of shops and stairs stacking upward along the cave walls, vertical scrolls of etched stone doorways, shop fronts and signs describing wares for sale. No cameras visible, at least none that she could see. A proper out-of-the-way town.

A flurry of people ascended and descended the stairs and traversed ledges inside, gripping handrails and staring ahead as if such extraordinary architecture were normal. Larger crowds converged on the cavern floor, which formed a sort of town square—determined mothers tugging their children behind them by one hand, harried businessmen pressing phones to their cheeks, workers rolling food carts, battalions of teenagers giggling, delivery boys running or pedaling on bikes with bulging white plastic sacks attached to their backs, and a few elderly men and women walking at a more careful pace, all weaving among each other. Not as many as she encountered in New London, but it was still a familiar dance.

A few meters off, Myrra spotted a simple block bench rising up from the stone floor. She collapsed and shrugged off her knapsack, feeling a buoyancy in her body as she did so. She sat on the bench for hours with Charlotte on her lap, trying not to think about agents or death or the end of the world. Instead she watched the swirling tidal patterns of people mingling and going about their day, content to be outside it.

Myrra tried to get a sense of her location, visualizing a map in her head, where New London was compared to where she was now, trying to picture Nabat and the water and the mountains beyond it, the canals and the train lines. The world might be easier to traverse if she could see it clearly from an overhead vantage point, like the borders laid out on Marcus's antique maps. She remembered them furled out on his dark wood desk with spherical glass paperweights, giant marbles, delicately holding down the corners. Marcus playing the professor, full to the brim with ego.

"These here are the continental borders," he said, and traced his finger down a jagged line of thick, solid black. Myrra's finger lightly tracked the thinner dotted lines, much more common on the map, and much harder to follow.

"Those are the borders for countries," he said, following her finger with his own.

"What's the difference?" Myrra asked, and Marcus grunted and fumbled with one of the paperweights before responding.

"Well, it's a bit complicated, all tangled up with politics," he said, "but they're sort of different regions within the continents. Like how New London has different neighborhoods."

She could tell by Marcus's tone of voice that he was glossing over the full definition, that maybe this was something he'd memorized out of a book. He didn't have any more context than she did, but he preferred the simplicity of being right to a longer explanation.

"You see, this here is Turkey, where this rug comes from. And now in New London, we have a Turkish district." He pointed to a pinkish shape with the same twitchy border lines, next to the larger blue blob that was the sea.

Myrra remembered looking down at the interlocking twirls in the rug beneath her feet. She had witnessed Marcus haggling for it in person, assisting him in the basement of a smoke shop. The broker spun him tales about the rug's old-world authenticity, its origins in a region called Anatolia, and the spices and perfumes woven into its fibers. Myrra didn't tell him that she'd seen the man before, by the back door of a local factory, seen rugs like that being woven with imitation wool through the dusty windows of the warehouse. It was still a fine piece of work.

Turkey had dotted borders too, and thicker black borders against the blue paper sea. The thicker black lines worked better to keep the water out, Myrra imagined. Maybe in the old world there were walls built there.

The town of Nabat felt a lot like New London's Turkish district. The same smell of spices, meat, and smoke came wafting out of metal food carts, and the same tiled patterns adorned the floors of the shops. And there were rugs everywhere, with twisting designs that would have made Marcus rush for his wallet.

Even if they died tomorrow, Myrra still needed a place to sleep tonight. The best hotel in town, she learned, was a few stories down, nearer to the foot of the cliffs and the sea. The Nabat Rafia Hotel had a relatively small entrance, but inside, the ceilings of the lobby bloomed and bowed upward multiple stories, cathedral-like, enough so that Myrra's every footfall echoed on the marble floor. Happy to be indoors, Charlotte let out a shrill squeal that rang out across the arches. Myrra usually loved Charlotte's laugh, but right now it just made her head pound.

As one of the few hotels in Nabat, it was considerably grand. Myrra worried briefly about surveillance, but as she looked up over the arches and stone walls, she couldn't spot any cameras. She'd just have to hope that there weren't any other sensors she couldn't see.

"Do you have any vacancies?" she asked as she approached the counter.

"Of course. Most of the hotel, in fact," the concierge replied. He was a bored-looking young man with dark hair, olive skin, and sullen, half-closed eyes. The name embossed on his gold name tag, pinned crookedly on the breast of his blazer, was Sem. Sem slouched in a red leather chair behind the reservation counter, so Myrra had to crane her neck over the top to see him.

She must have given him a surprised look, because he explained—"Most tourism dried up about thirty years ago, once construction finished up on Palmer." At the mention of Palmer, Sem the concierge gestured out the window next to the counter, down to the bottom of the cliff. Myrra looked out and down, following his gesture, but all she could see was the flat metallic pan of the sea glistening against the sun.

A few well-traveled valets had spun her stories of Palmer, the glamorous underwater city. She'd only half believed them—men are prone to exaggeration when they're trying to impress. But now she looked down at the sea, full of curiosity. All she really knew about it was that whenever Imogene had returned from Palmer, she was always dewy and pink-faced from some sort of spa treatment, and Marcus always looked a little sheepish, having lost a small fortune at a gambling table. She almost wished she'd risked it and gone to Palmer after all, just to see it from the inside. That would be a place to see before you died.

"Suddenly people were more interested in casinos and less interested in cliffside hiking. There was no competing, really. Palmer's on a whole other level." Sem sounded simultaneously bitter and wistful.

Charlotte made a fussing noise. Myrra crooked a finger in front of her face, and Charlotte hooked a tiny hand around it, dragging Myrra's finger into her mouth and sucking on it. Exhausted as she was, Myrra couldn't help smiling a little.

"I think it's beautiful here," Myrra said. The concierge gave her a dubious look.

"It's fine, I guess. I wanted to try and get a job at a resort down in Palmer, or even New London, but Dad says he needs me here. Like there's really a whole lot to do." He slouched farther and rolled his eyes.

"Don't bother with New London. It's not worth the trouble." Even as she said it, Myrra understood the irony of her opinion. Everyone wanted to be where they weren't.

"Maybe. I still want to see it, though. There's not a whole lot to do in Nabat, if you're from here," the concierge explained. "I've been saving up to move out there for a while."

He was saving up his money for nothing. She pictured their bodies frozen solid in the cold of space. She pictured no air. Don't think about that. Any day now. Don't think about that.

"Hey, are you OK?"

In a mirror reaction to her own imagination, Myrra had stopped breathing. She shook the images to the back of her brain and tried to swallow down the bile rising in her throat.

"Yes. Sorry, yes. My mind wandered." Myrra smiled at Sem. She had the sudden impulse to tell him, to shout the truth in his face. But in this case the truth was an impossible thing to believe.

"What sort of room would you like? Single?" Sem the concierge was talking to her again.

She tried to get herself back into the conversation.

"Just go ahead and give me your best room. Biggest bed, fluffiest pillows, the works," Myrra replied. She could take the longest bath imaginable, then sink down into the softest mattress. That was how to live out the end of the world.

The concierge looked her up and down. She must have looked like the bad end of a broom—both she and Charlotte were coated in sweat and dust from the road. He paused another moment, then calmly started typing on his touch screen. He lifted it in his hands to show her. The screen displayed images of what looked like a truly breathtaking hotel suite, with prices and specs outlined below.

"This," he said, pointing to one of the numbers that accompanied the pictures, "is the cost per night for our finest suite." He gave her a meaningful look. "Is that price satisfactory?"

"Absolutely," she said, a smile starting to grow on the corners of her lips. She kept forgetting, and then remembering with great wonder, that she had money. She handed over the card to Sem, who inspected the name.

"Apex Unlimited?" Sem looked at her. "Never heard of it."

"It's a real estate firm," Myrra said. "I'm here on business, figured I'd take advantage of the expense account." These were all words she'd heard Marcus's colleagues use, laughing to each other over liquor and cigars. She was trying to keep the business vague, but Sem still looked skeptical.

"This is a city built into a cliff. We don't exactly have an excess of real estate," he said.

"No, I know, but you mentioned that Nabat's in a downturn... I'm basically a middleman." Another word Marcus's friends used with frequency. Myrra spit out the lies as fast as her brain spun them. "If a corporation is looking to relocate, they hire me to scout areas with unused or redundant business space, places where they can get property cheap."

This seemed to satisfy Sem. He went from skeptical to very interested. Probably looking for a job, Myrra thought. "Well, if that's the case, we've got redundant everything. We could use new business... aside from tourism, the only revenue we've got is data mining—the hard drives stay cooler underground, so there's huge caverns of them deeper in the cliffs, past the main town. Any of your clients work in data mining?"

"Communications, mostly." Again, a word she'd picked up at one of the Carlyles' parties, a word that felt vague and all-encompassing. It seemed to do the job. Sem nodded knowingly but didn't ask any further questions.

"Well, let me know how it goes, or if there's any way I can help."

"Sure thing."

Sem typed the information in on his tablet. "And can I get your ID for the room?"

Myrra held out Imogene's ID with a smile, but she tensed inside. This was her first time using the altered ID. It had looked legit once Boots had finished with it, but there was no way to tell without running it through the system. If the card didn't work, one swipe would send everything crashing down. She pictured Charlotte being wrenched from her arms, a boot on her back pressing her against the floor while someone wrestled her into handcuffs. She wouldn't go quietly. They'd have to tranq her.

Sem took the card.

"Emily Stein," he read aloud, and smiled. "Nice to meet you, Emily."

"Nice to meet you too." She kept her smile fixed, tried to seem relaxed.

Boots had allowed her to choose her own name. Emily was a random choice—one of the characters on Imogene's favorite soap opera was named Emily. Stein was for Gertrude. She felt a pang of sadness—in the rush to leave New London, she'd left the book tucked in her mattress, along with a few other precious objects.

She repeated in her mind: Emily Stein, Emily Stein. Easy to remember, and it sounded common enough to not be too memorable to anyone else. Or at least she hoped.

He swiped the card in and out of a slot on the side of his tablet. Myrra held her breath. After a few seconds, the tablet let out a familiar digital ascending tone and Myrra let herself relax. The ID was good.

"Great. You're all set." Sem handed her a room card and walked around the desk. With him standing up, Myrra was suddenly aware of how much taller Sem was than she. But then again, most people were taller than she. Sem looked down at her dusty backpack and paused a moment.

"Shall I—?" he asked, gesturing to the bag. Myrra had been dreading lifting it again—it hadn't even occurred to her that someone else might carry it. She smiled. This was new.

"If you wouldn't mind," she said, and followed him down the hall to her room.

11

PALMER

Palmer is one of the rare cities that was built after the world the ship had already taken flight. Humanity is not content standing still. Humans are only content when they are conquering the next impossible thing. So even though the world's landscape was designed to meet every need, over a century into the ship's journey, humanity decided to build Palmer.

There is no space left to build in a world with regions and civilizations ready-made, so the city sits at the bottom of the Palmer Sea. That is how Palmer was christened—it was named after the body of water above it. No one really remembers what the Palmer Sea is named after.

Palmer is encased in a series of humongous plexiglass domes that sit on the seafloor. People can access the city through a ferry that descends underground in a tunnel and emerges again inside the domed city. It took teams of scientists and architects months to figure out how to pressurize it just so, so that the glass didn't break, so that the water didn't rush into the tunnel, so that the glass was thick enough to be stable but clear enough to show the beauty of the surrounding ocean. When the city was finally open for business, all the world's press called it a feat of engineering.

Since every section of the world was assembled together with a purpose, and since Palmer came after the world was built, Palmer is a place not of necessity but of distraction. Palmer is where a person goes to find the deepest hotel mattresses, the most delicate cuisine, the headiest cocktails, the most exotic spas, and the most beautiful people. It is also where one goes to find crystal-studded casinos, top-ranked plastic surgeons, clubs to satisfy the rarest sexual proclivities, and chemicals stronger than your average cocktail. Those who reside in Palmer know it is a place to visit but not a place to live. The spectacle fades as one stays there, and that spectacle is replaced with a feeling of decay.

Nobody dies in Palmer when the world ends. The glass domes of Palmer will cave in months before the true destruction occurs. The city will be evacuated, leaving only empty structures and streets. By the time the world is torn apart, Palmer will exist as a broken snow globe under the water. Algae will coat the buildings. Schools of fish will maneuver their way down the avenues where posh bespoke men and women once walked, eels will have found homes under submerged roulette tables, and the first sprouts of seaweed will be growing on the marquee signs, once brightly lit and now gone dark.

12

TOBIAS

That's where Ingrid had me try foie gras for the first time. Tobias stared at a spindly little white-painted chair on the corner of a café sidewalk across the plaza.

Tobias turned his head to another table at the same café. And that's where David sat hunched with his head between his legs for forty-five minutes, sick after too much single malt. Tobias remembered propping David up to get him into a taxi, even though he was barely higher than his father's armpit.

Tobias was sitting with Simpson on a bench in the center of one of Palmer's outer domed plazas, within view of the ferry terminal exit. In an effort to keep his head in the present, Tobias peeled his eyes away from the café and instead looked around at the walls and ceiling of the plaza, trying to count the fish swimming past. Half the dome was made of reinforced plexiglass, to better filter in the light through the sea above them. The Palmer Sea, with water so clear it barely dimmed the sun as it cast its rays down to the city below. Tobias counted a shark, three mackerel, two groupers, and a swordfish, but when a school of tuna swam past the apex of the dome, massive enough to function as a cloud in the watery Palmer sky, he gave up and lost count. The other half of the plaza's dome was encased in polished blue stone riddled with tunnel exits and entrances along the bottom. Ferries ambled out of the tunnels with regularity, entering the biosphere through the lazy, meandering canal waters, dropping off their human cargo at the platform, and then looping back through the exit portals.

The glassy dome was tall and wide enough that it encompassed multiple blocks of buildings in addition to the plaza and ferry terminal, its transparent walls arcing effortlessly above the city's architectural peaks and girders. The dome itself then connected to dozens of other, larger ones via vast interior arches, so that from the outside the city looked like a collection of impermeable soap bubbles clustered on the seafloor.

Myrra Dal was still absent from the ferry's camera feeds. It had been days now, but Simpson didn't look worried.

"Maybe she decided to hide out in New London for a few days, maybe she went for a walk to pick some daisies, but trust me—she'll head here eventually." Simpson took an appreciative bite of a muffin half-wrapped in a waxy bag.

Simpson's laid-back attitude toward detecting was frustrating—Tobias was itching for something to happen. He couldn't sit still, picking up his tablet, putting it down. Pulling up Myrra Dal's file again, coursing his eyes through her life history over and over. He kept tapping again and again on the surveillance footage, refreshing it.

"Would you calm down?" Simpson snapped, looking exasperated for what must have been the hundredth time in two days.

Simpson finished the last chunk of the muffin and wadded up the bag into a tight ball. There was a public trash bin a couple meters off—one of the new ones with a compactor attached to the bottom. Palmer always had the newest of everything. Simpson held the ball in his hand aloft over his head, took aim, then let it go in an elegant arcing trajectory that hit straight in the center of the bin.

"You have no patience," Simpson said, "and I hate to tell you this, since you seem so determined toward a career in Security, but ninety-nine percent of this job is waiting. You need long-term mental stamina. You are going to burn out fast unless you learn how to pace yourself."

"I don't like it here," Tobias said, realized it sounded juvenile, then said, "I'm sorry," almost immediately after.

From the moment Tobias and Simpson stepped off the ferry in Palmer, Tobias had viewed the city as if someone were holding a grease-streaked pane of glass up in front of his vision. Everything came to him in double. When he bought a cup of coffee it wasn't just a cup of coffee, it was overlaid with a cup of coffee he'd bought David after an especially late night, when Ingrid and he, still prostrate in a mussed bed, had flung money at him and slurred the words "Coffee. No lights" before passing out again. Or Tobias would bump into a well-dressed man on the sidewalk, and in his ear he would hear the ghost of David whisper, instructing him on how to slip his hand through to the pocket in the lining of the man's suit, quick and soft like a puff of air. The back of every female brunette head with an expensive haircut was Ingrid; every gray-haired man in a navy silk suit was David.

"It's not my favorite place, sure, but it's not so bad—the food's good here," Simpson said.

Another woman passed by them in a filmy blue dress, a dress that looked exactly like the one Ingrid would wear when David took her out with him on a gambling binge, for good luck. Tobias stood abruptly.

"I think I need to go for a walk," he said.

"Sure," Simpson said, "I can hold down the fort here." He let slip an expression of worry. Tobias knew that Simpson was already annoyed at being paired up with someone so green. Surely this wasn't helping matters. Tobias chastised himself inwardly. Wasn't he the one to be depended on, a force of stability? He could get himself together, he just needed to readjust his focus, to get used to this place as an adult, under a new set of circumstances. Just distract yourself and think about the case. Get out of your own head, get into Myrra Dal's.

"I won't be long," Tobias told Simpson. "Just need to stretch my legs." Already his voice was sounding a little calmer. Good.

He took off down a sidewalk on the main avenue opposite the terminal, which led directly away from the plaza. Looking around at eye level, he continued to see reminders everywhere, in gilt letters on shop windows, in the warm smell of baguettes, olive oil, and exotic flavored vinegars all laid out on pristine white café tablecloths, or in the way the cement of the sidewalk glistened with some sort of ground-up crystalline stone—Tobias wouldn't be surprised if they'd used a low-grade diamond to achieve the effect. The glittering surface danced and flashed with light, shimmering and changing its perspective with every step he took. Since he felt familiarity at eye level, he forced his gaze up again, trying to appreciate the city with new eyes. He was approaching a giant vaulting archway that connected this plexiglass dome to the next.

It really was a remarkable feat, what these city planners had managed to achieve. Tobias had read that it took six thousand contract workers five years to finish the job. When you thought about the scale of the project, that amount of time was practically a blink, though he supposed it helped that they'd used unpaid labor.

It left an enormous budget for everything else. Tobias blinked in sudden recognition as he remembered a detail from Myrra Dal's file: her father had been part of the Palmer work crew. He pictured the men working in dark makeshift air chambers, laying down stone. When Tobias was feeling idealistic, he called Palmer the height of human achievement. When he was feeling less so, he called it money.

Tobias passed under the archway now, into the next plexiglass dome. It dwarfed him and swallowed him, the size of the architecture, the people weaving around him on all sides without thought. He was a tiny screw embedded in a massive clockwork. Whatever his agitation, whatever problems complicated his mind, it was good to remember that they were small, existentially speaking. Tobias took comfort in recognizing his insignificance among this wide scatter plot of people, a tiny nanosecond blip in the endless stretch of time.

"Toby, never forget that we came from a very prominent family," David Bendel used to say, trying to drum his son's legacy into his head, as it had been drummed into his by Tobias's grandfather. "Your great-grandfather was the toast of New York. We had a penthouse on Central Park West, a summer home on Cape Cod. We hosted politicians, magnates, artists, all the important people." The phrases *Central Park West* and *Cape Cod* were evoked frequently, to the point where Tobias imagined them as places bathed in gold. His bubble burst when his father excitedly showed him a picture of Cape Cod he'd found in a history book.

"It's a beach," Tobias said, with little enthusiasm. David gave him a look and shoved the picture closer to his face.

"Yes, but it's the right beach," he responded, exasperated.

Then the tablet would come out, shoved under Tobias's nose like desperate documented proof in a trial. *You see, Counselors, considering the evidence, it is irrefutable that we were important once.*

Images of his great-grandfather Alan Bendel, a white-haired specter of a man, usually in a blue suit shaking hands with various other white-haired men, sometimes in front of flags, sometimes at podiums behind paintings. Interspersed were images of Tobias's grandfather, younger, with dark-brown hair, a similar face, similarly clad in a suit, though these images were usually candid, his grandfather at an art opening, laughing amid giraffe-like women with glittering dresses and shiny straight hair, or in a club toasting with whiskey with a crowd of other suit-bedecked men, the flat whiteness of the flashbulb causing flares against their glass tumblers, illuminating their faces against bluish darkness. These family images failed to elicit any sort of emotional response from young Toby, though he tried his best to nod along as David regaled him with his ancestors' exploits. Mostly he would just stare for long periods at the photographed faces, as if they contained in their expressions some sort of uncrackable code.

Much more interesting were the examples that David would show of their former art collection.

"Alan Bendel loaned this one to the Met—you remember I told you about the Met, didn't I, Toby?" David would wait for a nod from his son. "Anyway, this one was loaned to the Met a record number of times. They showed this one at the Tate for a Freud retrospective—they used it for the poster—"

Tobias would tune out his father's voice like a radio and take in the artworks instead as David swiped through to one and then the next. The smudged, thickly globbed faces of Lucian Freud and the confrontational expressions of Frida Kahlo, the twisting bodies of Egon Schiele, the symphonic swatches of Alma Thomas, the patchwork color of Paul Klee, followed by the engulfing pigments of Mark Rothko, so deep they sucked the air out of your lungs. His favorite, a painting by Roman Opałka, who painted steadily increasing numbers in neat little rows across large swaths of canvas. Tobias absorbed and obsessed over the details of these artworks with the same sort of fervor he held for Barnes's antique wood desk. He ached to touch them, to see the real paintings in front of him, but the collection was long gone. It was the only thing Tobias mourned from his father's stories. Tobias thought again of the Carlyle penthouse, with so many paintings and drawings on the walls. He'd cycled through every room in the photographs on his tablet. None were from his family's collection, though he'd wished it to be so. He had the thought that if he stood in front of one, in the place where the painter had painted, in the spot where his great-great-grandfather must have taken it in, he might at that point understand a little more about himself, how his genetics had decayed from great art collectors to con artists.

This world was much more unforgiving than the last when it came to status—half the Bendel collection was liquidated before boarding just to pay for the passage, and the rest had been sold off one at a time over the years to pay for the right domiciles, the right vacation spots, the right friends. Eventually even those faded away, through indulgence and bad money strategy.

"It's appalling, the lack of respect," David would often mutter when no one pledged fealty upon the utterance of his surname. Ingrid would huff in agreement, usually while grasping the neck of a martini glass. The only person he ever hooked with stories of his lineage was Ingrid, who was also the last declension of a so-called great family. She would readjust herself to sit up straighter on whatever velvet cushion in whatever hotel lobby they happened to be occupying and say, "Grandpa Radcliffe was in oil," as if that meant anything to Tobias. He grasped what they seemed unable to acknowledge, which was that this new world was entirely populated by the wealthy families of the previous one, old and new money, but all varying degrees of rich (aside from the contract workers, but they didn't count). What use was it to be a giant among a multitude of other giants?

Regardless, David and Ingrid had clung to whatever legacy and prestige they could, and when the last remnants were wiped away by debt, they stole and conned their way into the lifestyle they thought they were owed.

Stopped at a crosswalk just past the archway, Tobias picked up pieces of litter that clouded like a low fog around the base of a trash bin. He pictured commuters, men in power suits, women chatting on phones, tossing off crumpled wrappers without a look back to see if they landed on their mark. Tobias disdained that sort of lazy obliviousness, whereby people tunneled through life without seeing a thing around them. There are consequences to actions.

"Appalling," he muttered to himself, and realized he sounded just like his father.

The crowds helped his mood, at least enough for him to rejoin Simpson and keep working. Tobias didn't want to leave Simpson alone for too long, partially because he didn't trust Simpson to be thorough, and partially because he didn't want to be seen as lazy.

Back at the ferry terminal, boats cycled through. Simpson sipped coffee, occasionally glancing at the surveillance feeds. Tobias was staring at Myrra Dal's picture on his tablet.

"I don't think she killed them," Tobias admitted to Simpson. He almost wished it would start an argument.

Simpson sat quietly and didn't take the bait. Tobias continued, as though he had.

"Look at her life right before this. She's making all these long-term plans, conning Jake. Why would she go and kill the Carlyles? Seems way too impetuous for someone thinking that far ahead."

Simpson set down his coffee and leaned over the table.

"It's very likely she didn't," he said calmly. "But she broke contract, kidnapped a baby, and cut off a dead man's hand, so I think it's probably fine we're chasing her."

"I just think there's something we're missing. She had an out. Why did she leave? Why did she take the baby?"

"You're new at this," Simpson said with a tilt of the head. Tobias resented the patronizing tone. "You haven't had a chance to see yet, the weird things people will do when they're in a state of panic. If Myrra Dal came across the Carlyles' bodies, or, worse, if she actually witnessed the suicides"—Simpson paused for effect—"then yeah, I can absolutely see her doing everything she did. She probably did it without thinking."

It wasn't the worst logic, but Tobias pushed back anyway.

"It just feels like there's some large piece of information we're missing," he said.

Simpson shook his head.

"No, no, you're overthinking this. You know how many skips we get a year from contract workers? I handled dozens of them in my first couple years on the force. It's the work we always give to the new recruits." Simpson made a gesture to Tobias across the table. "Truth is, I was promoted out of doing this crap years ago, but I'm stuck on this case now because a very, very rich family is involved, and also because you're Barnes's favorite pet, and he wanted someone good working the case with you."

Simpson stopped for a sip of coffee but continued before Tobias could get angry or object. "And all these skip cases are a little funny. People get weird when they snap. It's actually been better, the last ten years or so. You should hear some of the senior agents talking about how bad it used to be."

Tobias had heard the stories. Barnes had explained once that about a generation ago, Security saw a lot more of these cases, contract workers losing their heads. A lot of poisonings and intentional gas leaks. Occasionally more violent and bloody confrontations—kitchen knives if they were domestics, or perhaps a foreman flung into the machinery if they were factory workers. More often than not, the workers killed themselves along with their host employers.

"It's easier to get lost when there's no light at the end of the tunnel, no focused goal to strive for," Barnes had said. "We're a few generations in now, in this world... The first generation, they were the ones who signed contracts in the first place. They had ownership over their decision. And now this generation, they know they'll be freed in their lifetime, they've got a fixed point to concentrate on. But those middle generations—boy, I don't know. Maybe it helped if you had a kid right away, were reminded of what you were working for..."

But Myrra Dal belonged to that blessed generation—the generation that would see freedom. What was the point in tossing her employer off a roof?

Whenever Barnes discussed the contract arrangement, he did so with a shake of his head. It never really sat right with him, he often said, but then again, with the economy and the cost, he didn't know if he could come up with a better solution. Tobias had taken on Barnes's opinion regarding the politics of this, and, like his mentor, he still did his best to uphold the law. The system was flawed, but it was the system they had, and it would mean complete chaos if anyone were to try to change it at this stage.

It stung to think that Barnes might have brought Simpson on as a babysitter. The hurt must have shown on Tobias's face, because Simpson was looking a bit contrite.

"Look," he said, "it's not that you aren't a good agent. I think you actually have the makings to be a pretty great investigator, once some of the newness wears off of you. And I'm pretty sure Barnes thinks so too. You just mean a lot to him, that's all. Even someone as gruff as Barnes is bound to be a little protective, you know?"

Simpson gave Tobias a small conceding smile, and Tobias relaxed. He wished he didn't need the validation.

"Toby? What is it?" Barnes's voice was a little fuzzy on the tablet speaker, but came through all the same. It was evening, and Tobias was back in his hotel room. He wasn't quite sure why he'd called Barnes in the first place. He wanted to hear his voice, he supposed, and wanted to discern whether Barnes really thought that Tobias was capable at all, or whether this job was just something Barnes was throwing to him as a reward, like a dog treat. He didn't say any of this. Instead he talked about the case.

"Hi, Barnes—I was just wondering—is it possible for us to get an IT guy to take a look at Marcus Carlyle's drives again? It feels like there are some files missing, and I was wondering if we could manage some data retrieval."

Barnes coughed, and Tobias could hear him shuffling around on the other side of the speaker. Barnes would be back in his apartment by now. Tobias wondered briefly what Barnes was having for dinner. He didn't always eat healthy when Tobias wasn't around to check on him.

"Don't worry too much about that," Barnes said finally. "Marcus Carlyle had a lot of access in the government, so some of the higher-ups came in first thing, went through everything in the office, and pulled anything above our security clearance. Any gaps in the information are to do with that."

Tobias was dumbfounded.

"Why didn't I know about this earlier?" he said, not sure if he sounded like a professional agent or a rebellious child.

"They assured me that none of it was relevant to the case," Barnes said, "and they asked that I leave it off the report. Simple as that."

"But you didn't see any of what they took?"

"Toby, security clearance exists for a reason."

"Sure, but there's something here worth questioning—"

"You suddenly think you're above the law? You can't pick and choose the rules, you know better."

Tobias backpedaled. "No, no—I know. It just feels like it might be connected to the case, that's all."

While he talked, Tobias adjusted the tablet so that it was exactly parallel to the edge of the table. Then he adjusted his tablet stylus so it was parallel as well, then he arranged the plastic hotel brochures in order of size. It was as though Barnes could see Tobias's movements through the machine. His voice softened. "What does Simpson think?"

Tobias's heart sank.

"Simpson doesn't think it matters. He thinks Dal just snapped and left."

"Then that's the lead you ought to follow," Barnes said. "Don't get ahead of yourself. All you have to do for now is find her and bring her in. We can get the whys and hows out of her during interrogation."

A low, rough whooshing noise overtook the tablet speakers. Barnes was breathing too close to the microphone.

"You're doing a good job, Toby," he said. "You're just putting too much into this, moving too fast. Just follow your instincts and enjoy the chase."

"Yeah, OK," Tobias replied.

Barnes disconnected the call. Silence. Tobias stared at the objects arranged on the table. He stared at them long enough that the tablet fell asleep and the screen went dark, and all he was looking at was the shiny black reflective surface. Tobias was good about keeping the glass smudge-free, so when the tablet was shut off, it was as good as a mirror. He appreciated the shine off the glass, with a little curve to the light at the corners. From where Tobias was sitting, the surface reflected the hotel ceiling and the edge of the sconce on the wall. There was a small hairline crack forming in the ceiling's drywall. Maybe they could get a discount on the hotel bill.

He was trying not to think too hard. He picked up the tablet, watched the screen light up blue again as his index finger touched the glass, and began a search, also with as little thought as he could muster. He didn't want to consider what it meant to doubt Barnes.

He searched for anyone employed by the government: politicians, independent contractors, economists, scientists, security, military, even the janitors. Then he ranked them by security clearance. It was like shuffling and arranging a deck of cards. David had once taught him how to do that, back when he thought (wrongly) that Tobias might be willing to learn to count cards.

He pored over the files for all people at Marcus Carlyle's level. There weren't many such people—maybe sixty—and, predictably, the information kept on each was minimal. Mostly just a name, date of birth, occupation, and maybe a list of previously held positions. These were people with power who knew how to keep their secrets. Even with that scant information, however, Tobias was able to spot one disturbing coincidence: four people on the list had died within the past year, all under unnatural circumstances.

Four was a small but significant number. Not enough to immediately set off alarm bells, but significant. The deaths had been fairly spaced out over time—one of New London's top structural engineers had fallen in front of a train last December. The following March, the secretary of security had drowned in the Palmer Sea while on vacation. Tobias remembered that one from the news. Four months later, in July, an environmental lobbyist had died of an overdose. Then, a week ago, Marcus Carlyle had slit his wrists. All but the Carlyle deaths had been ruled accidental.

Tobias didn't know what to do with this information, but he knew it was important, and he knew that he was growing afraid. Even as he tried to not think past the present moment, he felt nauseous. Tobias felt the same sensation he'd felt in the crowds of Palmer earlier that day, the feeling of insignificance that at the time had comforted him. Now that feeling turned—instead of a cog in the beautiful machine, he felt like one of a million ants in a colony, all climbing hills of sand, unaware of a thunderstorm about to drown everything. He didn't know what this meant. He had a feeling Myrra Dal knew.

He couldn't tell Barnes about this—Barnes would simply chide him. A foreign voice rang out in his head: There's following the rules, and then there's burying your head in the sand. It didn't sound like something he would think. It sounded like something Myrra Dal would say. After reading her letters over and over, he could hear her voice so clearly. Maybe he could tell Simpson, if he found the right opening. They could follow up once they found Myrra Dal, and ask her for the explanation.

Tobias's wants, in the grand scheme, were small. He didn't want to be a part of something big, didn't want to be the one to expose corruption, usher in change, make his mark on a worldwide scale. He simply wanted to live a stable life, take satisfaction in a job well done and the steady climb of a career, and reside in a nice apartment in a nice part of town.

Whatever this was felt beyond his reach, and he was ashamed to find he had the sudden ignoble impulse to ignore the nauseous feeling in his stomach and stop any further investigations altogether. Maybe he could even drop the Myrra Dal case. Even as he thought the thought, he knew he wouldn't abandon anything. He would continue to do his job and do it well. He didn't quit halfway through. The entire precinct would balk. He was the dependable one, the one to be counted on. That superseded all bouts of anxiety.

He turned off his tablet again, undressed, and climbed into bed. He shut off the light and shut his eyes, but didn't sleep.

MYRRA

Myrra quite literally did not know what to do with herself. The first waves of uncertainty had hit her after Sem left her alone in the hotel suite. The suite was massive: multiple rooms, seating areas, and a huge stone balcony worthy of the Carlyle penthouse. She walked around to take it all in but avoided the balcony door.

Ever since Imogene killed herself, she'd been going and going. Now, in Nabat, well off Security's radar (she'd been looking and looking and had yet to see a single camera), she could finally stand still for a while. But this, in itself, was unexpectedly daunting. Her entire life had been dictated by the people she worked for. Whether she obeyed or rebelled (and she'd done plenty of both), all her actions had been reactions. She didn't know how to just *choose* what to do with her time.

Then there was Charlotte. Myrra regarded the baby in her arms like a small alien thing, a vestigial limb that she couldn't separate from herself. The porters had set up a bassinet near the bed. She unwrapped Charlotte and laid her down, watched her freely wriggling her limbs with a grateful look. She stretched her two pudgy arms in opposite directions to occupy as much space as possible. It was the first time Charlotte had looked calm since they'd left the penthouse. This kid expected luxury.

Whatever freedom Myrra thought she had now, it was hampered by her bringing Charlotte with her. She knew that.

Myrra crouched beside the bassinet and inspected the bottom of Charlotte's foot. Babies' feet were so odd; it was uncanny to see a foot that had yet to walk—no calluses, no worn skin. She brushed a finger along the bottom of Charlotte's foot; Charlotte giggled and twitched in response.

She'd stay for a few days here, then leave Charlotte in the hotel with a note for the maids to contact local authorities. She could steal a boat at the bottom of the cliffs, head to some other small town across the Palmer Sea, someplace just as low-tech as Nabat where she could stay off the radar. She could be long gone before they found Charlotte, and then the both of them would be safe. Safe, but separate.

In just a few days she would do this. But Myrra could have time with her till then.

It wasn't just the choices. Every second held too much weight now that time was limited. Myrra felt an overwhelming pressure to pack each moment with meaning, to act and think profoundly. What she did instead was drink.

She liked all the small bottles that came with the hotel room. Imogene had often chatted about what hotels were good or bad, she'd even gifted Myrra a free robe once, but she'd never explained that everything came in miniature. Tiny bottles of shampoo, small flat cakes of soap. Shot-size bottles of whiskey. She grabbed three from the knee-high fridge and poured them all into a single glass, no ice. She'd never had good whiskey before. At first she sipped it, the way she'd seen Marcus do over cigars with his colleagues. When that didn't relax her, she knocked the whole thing back in one gulp. That was the way workers drank moonshine in the laundry.

Time swam.

That evening, Myrra watched Charlotte roll back and forth in her bassinet, bending her leg up to her face, trying to eat her toes. She seemed unaware of anything past the movement of her own limbs. For Charlotte everything felt new, all the time.

Did she know her mother was gone? There must be some feeling, even with a mother as distant as Imogene. There are things you get used to, a familiar primal scent, a rhythm of breath and heartbeat, a signature warmth in the skin. Even for a baby, there must be a sense of loss when that goes away.

When she was a child, Myrra had slept in the same bed as her mother. It used to annoy her: the intrusion of limbs, the heat, the lack of space. After her mother was gone, it felt impossible to sleep in the absence of it. The bed felt terrifyingly empty and sterile to the point where, all these years later, Myrra would often wake up and find her body had unconsciously pushed itself to the edge of the bed, leaving a gaping space on the other side. Sometimes, just before drifting into sleep, reaching out with intangible senses, Myrra still felt a sunken weight next to her on the mattress.

Maybe Charlotte hadn't sensed this similar absence yet with her mother. Lord knew Imogene hadn't been sleeping in the same bed with her. But eventually some hard feeling would embed itself in her, some deep-down subcutaneous sense that something was missing, something irretrievable. Myrra hoped the world would be gone before Charlotte was able to recognize it.

* * *

That night Myrra woke up suddenly, in that way whereby the eyes stay shut and the body stays still, but consciousness is suddenly alive and whirring. Without willing it, she pictured Imogene jumping off the balcony, her terrified expression. Fear washed over her body. Don't think about this. Don't think about it. But there was nothing else to think about, not while lying awake in the dark.

With her eyes still closed, she started tallying the days that had passed, the days she had left. It reminded her of waking up before her shift started at the laundry, waking up at four, realizing that she had an hour left to sleep. An hour left to sleep, two months left to live. Minus what, two days? How many weeks in a month, how many days, how many minutes? It might not even be two months—it could happen tomorrow. Myrra thought of an egg cracked on the floor, a soufflé deflating. Imogene's shattered skull. The whole world was that fragile. It was difficult to breathe. The blanket was too heavy—there wasn't enough air in the room. Her head hurt—the whiskey.

The body was mostly water. Myrra had learned that somewhere. When her body was frozen in space, would it feel like ice? Eyeballs are especially watery. Would they shatter? Myrra pictured her body floating, frozen shards of her eyeballs floating, drifting slowly away from the rest of her. She turned over in bed and squeezed her eyelids tighter in response to the thought. She pulled her knees in to her chest.

Where was Charlotte? She needed to check on Charlotte. Somehow Myrra never pictured her dying, not the way she pictured herself dying. Maybe that's why she was having so much trouble letting go of her. Myrra walked over to the bassinet. Charlotte must have been kicking in a dream; her legs were snared and tangled in the tiny blanket. Myrra delicately freed her limbs from the fabric, rested her hand on Charlotte's sleeping foot. Every part of her skin radiated heat, practically glowing. Myrra wondered where all that heat went. Everything in the universe was moving steadily from hot to cold, Jake had told her that once.

Charlotte furrowed her brow in her sleep, making Myrra's heart skip. When Imogene and Marcus had first brought Charlotte home from the hospital, her face had been scrunched up just like that. Her face stayed scrunched up and angry long after. She cried constantly. Myrra thought this was an entirely logical response to being ejected from the warmth of a mother's womb, but Imogene was annoyed. She and Marcus hired a photographer to come in a week after the birth, but ultimately the photo session had to be rescheduled because Charlotte wouldn't stop crying. Imogene eventually handed the baby off to Myrra, and she and Marcus took the photographer aside to negotiate a new appointment time.

Myrra had walked Charlotte around the room ten or twelve times, bouncing her and spinning her and singing to her, before she finally stopped wailing. Even then, her face stayed puckered in a grimace. Myrra was still walking her around, cooing to her, when Imogene walked back over.

"I hope her face doesn't stay like that," Imogene had said. "She looks like a tortoise."

With that she waltzed out of the room, off to a gym appointment. Marcus disappeared upstairs into his study. And Myrra and Charlotte were alone again. It was the first time Myrra had been left alone with the baby, the first of many, many times to come.

"You keep that face as long as you want," Myrra had said, and continued bouncing her. "No one asks to be born. I think you're allowed to be a little indignant."

Charlotte had mashed her face into Myrra's shoulder, rubbing her eyes back and forth against the fabric of Myrra's dress. Myrra remembered her chest swelling with love, tears almost immediately welling up in her eyes. You're mine, she had thought.

In the dark of the hotel room, Myrra continued to caress Charlotte's foot. There were deeper reasons why she couldn't let Charlotte go, beyond just the panic of the moment. Charlotte stirred and Myrra pulled her hand away, suddenly anxious that she might wake her.

The room was too cramped, too hot. Myrra looked to the balcony doors. They still scared her, but she needed air. She walked out into the coolness of the night and paced along the stone floor. Tonight the sea was calm. There was a full moon; the sky was riddled with stars. Artificial moon, artificial stars. Were they light bulbs? The water glittered below. This was beautiful, but it wasn't enough to live on. In her plans, Myrra hadn't thought much past getting to Nabat. It was so much harder to know how to live when you knew the immediacy of your death.

Charlotte hadn't wanted to be born. Through the labor of her years Myrra had often felt the same way. She felt another jolt of adrenaline at the thought of her own death, the picture again of her own body frozen and drifting in the dark. She stopped pacing for a moment to grip the rail. Her skin stretched taut over the white bones of her knuckles.

She wondered if this was how Imogene had felt, if she had been alone in the dark on a balcony, thinking just a little too hard. She wondered how a person could both not want to have been born and not want to die at the end.

A flicker of movement caught her eye, a pinprick of orange light in the dull dark glow of the moon. Someone was on the balcony adjacent to hers, smoking a cigarette. She could see their silhouette now that she was looking properly. The small dot of orange glowed brighter as the dark figure brought the cigarette to their lips and drew in the smoke.

"Hello?" she called out. Her greeting echoed over the stone.

"Hello?" a young man's voice replied. She recognized it. Sem, the concierge. The dark figure of Sem moved toward the balcony door, reached out, and fumbled along the wall. The light on his balcony flickered on, and Sem, now fully illuminated, squinted at her.

"Emily?" he called out.

"Hello!" she replied. She was overwhelmingly relieved to have another human being to interact with. Myrra turned and closed the curtains to the room before turning on her own light. The balconies were about six meters apart, but now, with a little illumination, she could see Sem very clearly. She imagined looking back at this spot from some vantage point far out in the middle of the water: two adjacent glowing specks high up on the black cliff.

"Do you live in the hotel as well?" she called out.

"No, my dad and I live down the road there—" He waved his arm vaguely at a cluster of staircases going down the cliff. "But I like to take advantage of empty rooms every now and again. Living with your parents gets cramped."

"How long has your father owned this hotel?" Myrra asked, more as an excuse to keep talking than from actual interest.

"It's been in my family since the start... My great-grandfather commissioned it, I guess, when the world was still being built." Sem looked down idly at the cigarette between his fingers and tapped away the ash. He didn't seem to find his birthright very interesting, and Myrra couldn't help judging him for all that he took for granted. Myrra had no heirlooms or stories of her ancestry.

The only thing she had of her mother's was her cheap little plastic statue. Myrra pictured it tucked away inside her old mattress and regretted again leaving it behind. But maybe that was how life was supposed to go—a person shouldn't have to think about family or future or possessions. They were meant to exist as a given. Maybe being young meant it was OK to ignore these things, indulge in selfishness. This was what allowed for progress and identity. Myrra had been denied this, but that didn't mean it was the wrong way to be.

Sem fidgeted with his nails, cigarette hanging limp from his bottom lip. An awkward silence had taken hold of the conversation. The wind kicked up from the sea below, whooshing around her head and tangling her hair.

Sem said something to her, but the wind made it difficult to hear.

"What?" Myrra shouted at him, then flinched at her own volume. Charlotte could wake up.

Sem smiled and shouted louder. "I'd kill to be doing what you do," he said. "Traveling around—"

Another gust of wind rushed past her ears, and she lost the rest of what he said. But she heard just enough to feel the irony in his words.

Sem waved at her and tried again. "Do you want to just come over here?" Sem called out. "It's hard to hear—"

Myrra looked sideways at the balcony door. She would, if not for Charlotte.

"I can't," she shouted back. "The baby's asleep."

Sem nodded.

"I could come over there," he called out. He had a sort of mischievous look on his face. Myrra hadn't lived much, but she knew when someone was propositioning her.

But maybe that wasn't a bad thing either. Just minutes before, she'd been panicked and gripping the balcony rail. Sem offered mostly empty conversation, but all this nothing had a calming effect. She just needed to get out of her head for a while. And if Charlotte had slept through all this shouting, she'd stay asleep even if Myrra brought in company.

"OK, but don't be too loud when you knock on the door!"

"Got it!" Sem gave her a look as if he'd just won at cards. He stubbed out his cigarette on the stone and disappeared inside. Myrra stayed out for a moment longer, losing feeling of herself as the wind roared louder around her. The sea had been so quiet a second ago.

She stepped inside and closed the balcony door with a quiet click. She could hear Charlotte's heavy breathing, a slight whistle to it. As promised, the knock on the door was so soft that Myrra barely heard it. When she opened the door, Sem held up a few miniature bottles of whiskey and waved them in the air.

"Just in case you're running low—on the house," he whispered, and walked past her into the dark room. She noticed again how tall he was. Lanky and tall, with limbs that swung around in wide arcs.

The suite had a seating area off the main bedroom with two plush armchairs and a couch, separated by a glass door. Here, just as in the bedroom, there were windows with a sea view. The glass had a warped old-world quality to it that appealed to her. She could still hear the wind distantly outside. Myrra lit a dim lamp and grabbed a couple of glasses off a small corner bar. She sat down in a chair, where she made sure she could see Charlotte's bassinet through the door.

Sem flopped onto the spot on the couch nearest to Myrra's chair. The casualness with which he moved about made her uneasy, as if it were his own living room. Sem poured whiskey into the two glasses and handed one to her.

"So why are you awake right now?" he asked.

"It's been a strange few days for me," she said, not knowing if that was really an answer to his question.

"What's been strange?"

Myrra wanted to really talk to someone, but she had to think about how much to reveal, how much could be couched in a lie. She took a sip of whiskey, a more delicate Marcus-style sip this time. Her head still swam from the drinks she'd had before.

"A lot. A lot of change. A lot of death," she said finally.

"I'm so sorry," Sem said. He paused between words, stumbled over what to say, unable to come up with a better response.

"It's all right. It's hard to tell yet, but I think I might be better off now than I was before." Sem looked confused, but Myrra didn't know how to explain further without going into detail. She looked to her side, through the glass door, to check on Charlotte's bassinet. All was still quiet.

"Your daughter is beautiful," Sem said, following her look.

"Thank you. But she's not my daughter. A friend of mine died and left me to look after her." A convenient narrative, and he seemed to buy it. Charlotte looked nothing like her, after all.

"What about you?" she asked, shifting the conversation away from herself. "What are you doing up this late?"

"My shift at the front desk ended at midnight, but I've always been an insomniac, so I figured I would just hole up in one of the rooms, grab some drinks, and watch the sunrise." He waggled his head a little as he talked, and his lips curled up in a way that Myrra had to admit was charming.

"Alone?"

"Most of my friends left town when we graduated. One of the

reasons why I want to head to New London. But there are still folks I hang out with, mostly hotel employees. René, he's the porter, he gets a bunch of us together on Friday nights to play poker."

"I used to play cards at my old job." In the laundry, in the dorms. "We used to play snap. You ever played snap?"

Sem smiled bigger, a little less suavely and a little more genuinely. "Yeah—I played that with my sister."

"We used to bet on snap," Myrra continued, "and at one point I picked up a duplicate deck and started cheating to win hands. I made some good money for a while."

"Did you ever get caught?" Sem asked.

"Yeah, eventually. We stopped playing after that." This was an understatement. A few of the other women had blackened both her eyes and given her a nasty welt on the side of her rib cage.

Sem looked at her for a long, silent moment. He had such a nervous, adolescent energy. He wants to kiss me, she thought. It was a good thought. Or at least a distracting thought.

Then wind rattled the windows, making Myrra jump up from her chair. For a second she thought maybe the world was finally shaking apart.

Sem stood up alongside her, concerned. "Are you OK?"

She stole a look out the window. A dusting of stars shone through the glass; there were no cracks in the sky that she could see. "Sorry—the wind is just very loud. Is it always this loud?"

"It picks up really suddenly out here, since we're so close to the water," he said, and took a step toward her. "There's nothing to worry about."

He reached out and placed a hand on her arm, left it there and stood quietly, questioningly. She was so amped up that the touch of another person made electrodes crackle and snap on her skin. Not entirely a bad sensation, but a frenzied one.

He was still holding a glass in his other hand, so loose and casual against his hip that Myrra was sure it was going to slip out of his grip and shatter on the floor. She thought of the price of the glass. It looked expensive.

His hand was firm and warm. Myrra tried to imagine: even if all the objects in the room got sucked up into space, somehow this hand might steady them and keep their feet rooted on the ground. He would taste like whiskey and cigarettes. This, at least, would feel familiar; Jake always tasted like cigarettes.

He was so tall he had to bend down to kiss her, a little clumsy at first. Then he threw his arms around her, all limbs, and held her tight to the spot. This suited Myrra fine. She needed the feeling of someone squeezing her, engulfing her. They tripped and stumbled their way to the couch, Sem able to find his way there with his eyes closed. He's done this before, Myrra thought. Well, of course. Tourists must be his main mode of entertainment.

She leaned back on the couch, and Sem pressed on top of her, and it felt good to be compact and small, to have someone's hands trail up her side and push up her dress, someone without a care in the world, someone who expected to have a good fun fuck and then go on living, wave goodbye to her in a couple of days and then eventually move away to chase a new life in a different town. She wished for time for him, time for him to screw around and fail and stay immature and stupid, she wished for time for herself, she wished for ignorance, she wished…

She stared at the ceiling through his hair, imagining the roof ripping away. He would not be enough to keep her anchored to the floor. If the world ended right now, would this be a good last moment? Heat rose in her face. She was all pins and needles, and her breath came fast. He was kissing her neck. It felt hot and wet and good, but without her knowing why, tears were bursting from her eyes, and she cried out—

"Stop—" she said, her voice raw. She sat up, her hair disheveled and her dress bunched halfway up her body. Sem jumped away from her with a worried look.

"I'm sorry, did I—"

"No, no, you didn't do anything," she choked out. The world was spinning around her, around and around. It was making her dizzy. Sem placed a hand on her knee and she jumped, unable to control her own body.

"Would you like some water?" he said, eager to fix the situation. Sem ran to get another glass and fill it up in the bathroom. She listened to the water running out of the tap, the rising noise of the glass filling up. It felt as though the cells in her body were about to shake apart and spin out in all directions.

She took a deep breath. It was hard to hold air in. Her heart was ricocheting off the walls of her rib cage. Sem returned with the water and sat, his face furrowed with worry.

"I'm sorry—it's just I heard some terrible news recently, and I don't know how to handle it..." she said. More vague half-truths, but what else could she do? There was no way to make someone understand.

But would it be so terrible to tell him? she thought suddenly, rebelliously. She was full to the brim with anxiety and confusion. It was going to spill out somewhere.

Maybe this could be good for him, she reasoned. Maybe it would give him the choice of how to live the rest of his life. Maybe he'd get to see New London after all. Maybe it was more cruel to lie. And it would be good for her as well. She recalled a preacher who would come to the laundry when she was a child, handing out rosaries and cheap plastic medallions, trying to convert the workers. "Tell me your sins," he'd said. "Confession is good for the soul."

Myrra took the water from Sem and drank a long gulp. His face was open, inviting her to continue.

"Listen," she said, "this is going to sound crazy."

"OK." Sem let out a small, unsure laugh.

"What if there were something wrong here, with the world—" she started.

"I get it," Sem interjected, nodding and trying to pick up the conversation. "The world is really fucked up. The class system? The government? It's enough to never sleep again..."

"No—no, not like that," Myrra talked over him. "I mean, it is fucked up, but what if something else was broken, something physical? I mean, this whole thing is technically a ship. There are mechanics that can go wrong." Myrra watched him. He wasn't buying it. None of this was coming out right.

Behind Sem's head, near the ceiling, Myrra suddenly noticed a crack in the wall. How had she not noticed it before? This entire city would fall into rubble. Sem followed her eyes and looked back at her with a smile, as if he had finally locked on to her particular brand of paranoia.

"Oh, yeah, I'm sorry about that—there's been a lot of tremors in the region. Have you guys been feeling those in New London?" He was keeping his voice deliberately light. "But we had a structural engineer come through and analyze everything. You don't have to worry.

"I can get you a discount on the room, if it's bothering you," he added, gesturing to the crack.

"No—I don't care about that," she said, shaking her head. "That's not it at all."

She needed to change tactics.

"Just—just think about if the world were ending next week. If there's anything you've been wanting to do—moving to Palmer, New London, anything—don't wait to do it."

Sem shifted uneasily in his seat.

"Um, this is a weird conversation..."

Myrra sighed and buried her face in her hands. This was not going to go the way she wanted it to go. It was too big a concept. She was surprised *she* believed it, even after reading all of Marcus's data spreads.

"Though I guess if I only had a week to *live,* I would stay in Nabat," she heard Sem say through the fog of her own thoughts. "New London's cool, but, I mean, my family's here. Who wants to die surrounded by strangers?"

Myrra didn't know what to say to that, didn't want to think about what that meant for her. Silence settled in like a fog around them, broken only by intermittent gusts of wind outside the window. Sem stood, moving slowly and delicately, as though he were trying not to startle a particularly skittish animal.

"I think I ought to go," he said.

After an awkward goodbye, Myrra lay back down on the bed and waited for the blue light of dawn. It had been a mistake, a selfish one. Telling Sem the truth wouldn't save him from anything. He already had a life, with roots and people who loved him. It was just so lonely, being the only one to know. There were others, she supposed, who knew this secret, but certainly no one she could interact with. And, as it turned out, it was a secret she couldn't divulge even if she tried.

She envied Sem his roots and attachments. She thought again of her mother. Maybe she still had family, somewhere. A picture came to mind: Myrra running into her mother on a crowded city street, completely by chance. It was a small world. These things happened. Or maybe she would rescue her from a cold anesthetized institution, or from some underground prison. Just as quickly, she batted those thoughts away. She wasn't a kid anymore, dreaming of imaginary lives. Don't think about her. Don't think about it.

Myrra could fill up the sea with all the things she refused to think about.

14

TOBIAS

"I was looking through some background information..." Tobias started, trying to sound as casual as possible and failing. Simpson glanced at him from behind a pair of lowered sunglasses. It gave Tobias the unfortunate view of both Simpson's sarcastic look and his own nervous expression in the warped reflection of the mirror lenses. The lens view of himself showed his hair sticking up in places, slouched shoulders. He straightened up to a more confident posture and tried to pat down any cowlicks without looking too obvious about it. He hadn't slept well.

Another twenty-four hours had come and gone with no sign of Myrra Dal. Tobias was appalled to find himself on a pool deck instead of in a precinct office. Simpson, of course, did not seem to mind. He was sunning himself on a chaise longue. Tobias perched on the edge of an adjacent deck chair, thinking about how best to bring up the other deaths he'd discovered.

Tobias had received permission from the Palmer office to set up additional cameras—all access points in and out of the city were now covered by surveillance and facial recognition. If the software caught Dal's face, an alarm would sound on his tablet. With the cameras in place, they were no longer tethered to the area around the ferry terminal, and Simpson had insisted on exploring. They were currently passing the time beside a large kidney-shaped swimming pool in Apogee Park, a green zone located atop Palmer's highest tower, in its largest atrium. The park was furnished with rolling lawns and lush trees, all flourishing from being nearer to the light of the water's surface. All other seats around the pool were occupied by scantily clad women and men teasing their nakedness with all the latest fashions. He and Simpson stood out in their collared shirts and slacks.

"Anything interesting?" Simpson asked, inviting him to continue. Tobias saw an amused twinkle in his eye just before Simpson pushed his sunglasses back up on the bridge of his nose.

Over the past day, as Tobias had set up the cameras, worked with Simpson to connect the feeds, and done half a dozen other tasks for the investigation, all important but all mindless work, the three other deaths had stuck in his mind, coming up again and again, as unwanted as an earworm chorus of a bad song. He had vacillated over and over throughout the day, deciding sometimes that the deaths meant nothing, then deciding that they were related to some monumental conspiracy, then deciding that the whole thing was something his brain had concocted out of boredom. But still, the thoughts persisted. His only hope was to bounce the information off Simpson, sound as nonchalant as possible, and hope that Simpson would be a good barometer for how to react.

He sent out his test balloon.

"I noticed that Marcus Carlyle wasn't the only high-level death we've had this past year. There've been three others who've died that had his level of security clearance."

Simpson's eyebrows rose behind his glasses, but his expression stayed stoic.

"Does Barnes know?" he asked.

"I haven't told him," Tobias said. Simpson didn't reply, just sat silently, waiting for Tobias to give him the rest of the information.

"Last night I asked Barnes about some holes in Marcus Carlyle's hard drive files, and he told me to leave off investigating Marcus. Apparently some government guys came in and removed sensitive data before we got there."

Simpson let out a long stream of air, half a whistle, half a sigh.

"And now you're worried that Dad is going to give you a slap on the wrist for not listening to orders," he said. Tobias didn't really know how to respond. Simpson was right, but Tobias didn't want to give him any more reason to treat him like a kid.

"I've had spooks wipe evidence before," Simpson continued. "It's a pain in the ass. It doesn't happen a lot, but it's more common when you're working with someone as high up as Carlyle."

Tobias sensed a chip on Simpson's shoulder about this. He didn't like being patronized either, at least not by bureaucrats.

"Still," he said, "it was a good instinct to follow up on that. I'm not saying the deaths mean anything, but it would be stupid to rule them out. Barnes gets pressure from a lot of places, from above and below. Sometimes that paralyzes a person."

It was the first time Tobias had ever heard Simpson criticize Barnes, and he almost moved to defend him, out of sheer loyalty. Instead he held back and gave Simpson the space to talk. Simpson was saying things that Tobias had been too afraid to think the night before.

"Keep that in your head. Once we catch Dal, we'll see if she knows anything. Barnes doesn't have to find out about any of this until we know more. It'll be easier for him to see the good decisions from the bad that way." Simpson smiled at him. Tobias smiled back, smiling at himself in the sunglasses.

Tobias turned and grabbed his tablet off the side table. There hadn't been any alerts from the facial recognition, but he glanced over the grid of video feeds all the same. "How much longer, do you suppose, before Myrra Dal shows up here? How long does it usually take to chase someone down?"

Simpson bobbed his head from side to side, noncommittal. "It depends on the case. Sometimes it's really cut-and-dried to find someone, especially if they have friends or family. But aside from the McCann kid, Dal had nobody. Nobody alive, anyway."

Simpson looked down for a moment, his lips drooping into a slight frown. Maybe he pitied her. Tobias didn't pity her per se, but he worried about how much he empathized with her. He wondered if she had ever felt close with the Carlyles—some families often referred to their maids and household staff as "a part of the family." Tobias knew such thinking was common, though he personally assumed it was a psychological out, a way to keep guilt at bay, more than an actual sign of affection. Some even left their servants money or heirlooms when they died, though it was notably rare for an employer to free a contract worker in their will. That would require much more legal work, to bequeath a servant their contract. Most of the time it stretched past the bounds of a boss's generosity. The Carlyles' will, Tobias had noted, did not bequeath any money to Myrra Dal. Imogene and Marcus had maintained a nice professional distance from the help.

"Myrra Dal didn't take any money," Tobias mentioned, almost to himself. He and Simpson had looked over that angle a couple of ways. The safe in the bedroom had been opened, but all cards and jewelry were still inside. The only thing missing was Imogene

Carlyle's ID. Their assumption had been that Myrra Dal was smart enough to know that the card accounts could be traced.

"We've covered the Carlyle accounts—all the money's still there," Simpson said, but he sat up as well and turned to face Tobias.

Tobias could feel an idea assembling at the edge of his brain, but he hadn't quite put it together yet. "How is she getting by right now, if she didn't steal any money?"

Simpson shrugged. "Maybe she's camping. She seems resourceful."

"With a baby, though? Babies are expensive."

Simpson laughed. "That I know."

Simpson looked down at Tobias's tablet, lying faceup on the deck chair. Tobias followed his glance. Still no hits.

"Well, maybe she'd been stealing from the Carlyles a little at a time. Maybe this was a long-term plan. I caught a contract worker once, worked in a house just like Dal, who'd managed to rack up ten thousand in nine months without the family noticing. He doctored shopping orders, swiped change off the dresser, pawned the things he was sure they wouldn't miss." Simpson smiled and shook his head. "I was actually kinda sad I caught that guy. He was smart."

"Marcus Carlyle seemed pretty savvy with money, though." Tobias had looked through his financial portfolio and had found it dense enough that it took a few tries before he'd been able to read through the thing and make sense of it. He had companies within companies, companies that had been sold where he still maintained controlling interest, companies licensed under a variety of false titles. All the financial institutions tangled up with one another in such a way that only after looking at the whole spiderweb long and hard could you tell that there was a sublime organization to the whole thing, organized to maximize profit and minimize taxation. Marcus had known where his money was at all times.

"That's true." Simpson was now leaning forward a little, taking a deeper interest in Tobias's line of thinking. "Marcus Carlyle was rich...that special upper-echelon version of rich."

Everyone here had been rich at one time or another. Tobias remembered a photograph of his great-grandparents that David had shown him, champagne flutes in hand in a magnificently furnished room, dressed in the best finery, clearly indulging in their wealth. But the Carlyles were part of that stratospheric class, the one where you didn't just enjoy your wealth but learned tricks to hide it. He felt light rays filtering through the water and glass, warming his pale skin. He looked up at all the beautiful people surrounding him, golden in the sun's glow, radiant in their idleness and financial comfort. This was the life his parents had been chasing. He looked down at the surface of the pool—the water looked too bright and pigmented, a false blue.

"What if Myrra Dal took advantage of some money we didn't know about?" Tobias asked. They had looked into Marcus merely as the victim of a crime, but they could easily dig deeper into his finances.

"That's something worth looking into." Simpson stood up and stretched. It might have been wishful thinking, but Tobias thought he noticed Simpson looking at him a little differently, more like a peer. Simpson offered him a hand and Tobias stood up as well, happy to have an ally.

"Why don't you call IT, get his corporate account numbers, start pestering the banks? I'll come up with an excuse for Barnes," Simpson added. It felt wrong to keep Barnes on the outside. It shouldn't be so easy to swap Barnes's support for Simpson's. But Tobias knew he was right, and he wanted the win.

"Absolutely," he said.

"All right. But keep watching the feeds. She's still gonna show up here eventually."

The surrounding sea had been pretty clear of fish for the past hour, but as they gathered their things to walk to the elevator, a large shark swam directly overhead, briefly casting a shadow over the pool. Simpson smiled at Tobias, darting his eyes up at the shark.

"That's you," he said. Tobias blushed with pride.

Tobias imagined a dark room, not a menacing dark, but a comforting dark furnished only by a single dim lamp and two plush armchairs. He recognized that this room in his head was a composite of hotels he'd slept in as a child and Barnes's cramped living room, where he'd spent his teenage years obsessively studying. He imagined himself in one of the chairs and he imagined Myrra Dal in the other, as she was in her worker's permit photo, with wild tangled hair and a gray smock.

He imagined what they would say if he was able to have a conversation with her.

"Did you kill the Carlyles?" he would ask.

"No," she would answer. "They killed themselves."

In his head she was not offended by the question. In his head she kept her gaze fixed on him.

"Why would they kill themselves?" he would ask.

"They were afraid," she would say. She would not elaborate further.

"That engineer. The secretary of security. Did they kill themselves too?"

"Probably."

Even in his own mind, he was too afraid to follow that line of inquiry further.

"Why did you steal the baby?" he would ask instead.

"Because I love her," she would say.

In this imagined conversation, Myrra Dal was cryptic, but only because his brain could not create her answers out of anything more than what he already knew or suspected. There were other questions that he didn't ask, questions connected to governments and to breakdown. These questions hovered as unformed thoughts that Tobias was unwilling to acknowledge, outside of a vague feeling of apprehension.

In his head she stood up, walked over to him, and wrapped her hand gently around the side of his neck. It was an oddly tender gesture. She looked down at him with black eyes.

"It's all right," she said. "You'll catch me, and everyone will be so proud."

The earthquake hit at two a.m. Tobias was still awake in his hotel room, triple-checking the tracking requests on all the Carlyle accounts. He'd just stood up, preparing to make another cup of espresso with the hotel's coffee machine, when he felt the room shake.

It was violent enough to knock him off balance. The floor jerked from under him, and he felt his torso veer sideways in the opposing direction. Within seconds his knees buckled and he fell halfway on the hotel bed.

There had been occasional tremors before—their world, after all, was traveling through space at high speed, and he'd been taught growing up that earthquakes were usually the result of a collision with an especially large piece of debris. Tobias remembered being in Troy with his mother when he was five and feeling the ground seize under him. He remembered his mother's annoyance at the spilled wine. But that had been a much smaller, singular motion, over and done with in a matter of seconds. This was lasting much longer and was much harsher. He could hear a screaming in the distance, the squealing sound of tearing metal—Tobias couldn't remember, was that usually the sound an earthquake made? There'd been a lot of earthquakes lately, but this was the biggest.

The floor kept shaking; Tobias turned to lay his body flat on the bed. He could see the ceiling fan above him, attached by a single thick wire, swinging in a wild arc back and forth, the fan blades smacking and scraping against the ceiling. Tobias had the vague thought that the fan was likely to break loose if this shaking kept on much longer; he imagined it crashing down on his head, but he didn't move.

The wall to the side of the bed bowed outward and cracked. The fan continued to sway and jump, but the wire held fast. Tobias wasn't sure if he was able to stand up; he kept waiting in vain for the shaking to stop.

Tobias could not tell if minutes or hours were passing—it was so loud, the world was roaring. Gradually the tremors in the room diminished, as did the shrieking and the noise. When the quake had been reduced to only slight vibrations, Tobias tried to stand. As if to spite him, the floor bucked straight up and down one last time. His back scraped against the corner of a table as he fell, and he screamed out in pain. By the time he landed fully on the floor, the room was still.

Tobias let himself lie where he'd dropped. He wasn't sure how badly he'd hurt himself, but he didn't have the energy yet to investigate. He looked over at the ceiling fan. It continued swaying gently.

Even after the shaking stopped, there was still noise: a deep groaning, coming through the floor and the walls. Likely the building was no longer structurally sound. He ought to get up, but the thought alone was exhausting. Pain pulsed along his back, warning him against movement.

Without sitting up he bent his arm into an awkward position between his back and the floor and tried to feel if any ribs were broken. He pressed his fingers against the most tender areas, wincing at the intense pain that accompanied every touch. It was excruciating, but as he felt around, it seemed as if his bones were intact. He pulled his arm out from under his torso and lay there for another minute, eyes closed.

The building let out longer groans from somewhere deep within its core. It sounded almost musical, like low descending notes reverberating in a closed acoustic chamber. What floor was he on? Fifth, he remembered. In a thirty-story building. So if the building collapsed, he'd most likely die from being buried in the rubble. All this went through his head, but his thoughts felt oddly detached from his body.

A loud knock brought him back to his senses—the sound of knuckles frantically rapping outside his door. He rose immediately, using his arms to gingerly push himself up. It was funny, Tobias thought, that this was what was finally getting him up off the floor. Propriety was priority.

"Bendel! Are you OK?" Simpson.

"Just a minute," Tobias shouted back, and he steadied himself enough to stand up and walk. The room had a vanity mirror positioned adjacent to the door. He paused a moment, turned around, and lifted up the back of his shirt. A large welt-like bruise was blossoming across his back.

"Bendel?" Another insistent knock. Tobias lowered his shirt and opened the door. Simpson looked amped up and wide awake.

"Sorry," he said in reference to his slowness. "I fell against a table—"

"You OK?"

"Yeah, I think so."

Simpson pushed past him into the room. "Get your stuff together—they're evacuating the building."

Simpson moved with jittery energy, and when he saw how slowly Tobias was moving, he started packing for him, throwing his tablet and clothes into a backpack, tossing his wallet and badge at him, ducking into the bathroom to retrieve Tobias's razor and toothbrush from the shower.

The letters. Myrra Dal's letters were laid out on a side table next to the bed. The shaking had scattered some onto the floor. It looked so unprofessional. While Simpson foraged for toiletries, Tobias collected the documents frantically, no time for gloves, his skin was actually touching the paper, everything out of order, but at least they were safe again in an evidence bag. He tucked them into the backpack, along with Dal's book and the blue figurine.

"What are you doing?" Simpson poked his head out of the bathroom door.

"Nothing."

Simpson threw the last of his toiletries into the backpack for him. "Then let's go."

Tobias stared at him, dumbfounded. Simpson snapped his fingers in front of Tobias's face.

"Move!"

"Sorry—I think it was the fall..." Tobias took a deep breath, and his ribs screamed at him in response, but the extra oxygen felt good. "Let's go."

Tobias grabbed the backpack that Simpson had put together and followed his partner out. He forced his body to walk faster than his mind wanted to allow. The groaning of the building was getting louder.

Out on the sidewalk, hotel staff were setting up a perimeter, trying to usher all the hotel guests as far away from the building as possible, but unfortunately all adjacent buildings were also high-rises, each in its own tenuous state of disrepair. Tobias heard a strange crackling noise above him, even louder than the moaning buildings. He looked up and immediately felt another surge of adrenaline course through his system. Tiny fissures were growing and connecting and expanding across the dome, like cracks in an eggshell.

Tobias felt his energy come back and the pain in his body dull. He swung his head around wildly, looking for Simpson. Tobias could see him across the street helping the staff.

"Simpson!" Tobias shouted, and Simpson jerked his head over to Tobias, eyes alert. Tobias pointed upward, toward the dome. "They have to evacuate the city!"

Simpson followed Tobias's gesture, and for a split second, Tobias could see an expression of pure terror wash over his face. Then Simpson pursed his lips, looked back at Tobias, and nodded.

Almost as if Tobias's words had evoked a divine command, the harsh din of static sounded through the streets, coming from small silver speakers that Tobias hadn't previously noticed. They rang with static for a few seconds more, like a digital cough to clear a digital throat, and then an authoritative voice reverberated through the city:

"Attention. Attention. Please stay calm. This is an evacuation. All residents of Palmer, please walk in an orderly manner to the nearest ferry terminal and board the departing boats. Please stay calm." The speakers quieted down for a moment, then repeated the message. "Attention. Attention..."

The announcement was louder than the groan of the buildings, louder than the sharp sound of the plexiglass cracking. When the evacuation message sounded out the first time, the crowds of people seemed not to register it, but by the second cycle everyone had quieted down. By the third cycle, everyone was shouting again, and everyone was dashing to the ferry terminal. No one was calm. No one was orderly.

People became animalistic and stupid in large crowds. He looked over to Simpson, who jerked his head at the legions of hotel guests who were running through the streets toward the boats. It was a wordless gesture, but Tobias understood it: they would have to be Security now and do their best to guide them.

From there, time moved both quickly and slowly. Tobias had never experienced so much noise at once. He could hear metal creaking and the sounds of the cracks advancing in the glass, a low rumble anticipating the weight of water that wanted to bear down on them. And on and on, the din of the droning speakers, whose automated messages had not changed since the start of the chaos. "Attention. Attention. Please stay calm..."

He and Simpson corralled people as they streamed out of the blocks of buildings in waves, shouting the way toward the ferries, and when shouting couldn't be heard, they used hand signals. When it looked as if everyone in their general area had left, they started heading toward the ferries themselves.

Tobias jerked Simpson's sleeve as they made to evacuate and pointed toward the doors of the buildings. He shouted as loud as his lungs would allow, the strain of it ripping through his vocal cords: "Should we do sweeps inside?"

It seemed impossible in a city full of towering high-rises, but it was protocol, and Tobias's brain always jumped to follow protocol. It wasn't clear if Simpson heard him, but he seemed to understand the question. He shook his head: no. There wouldn't be enough time. They had to just hope everyone was out.

Simpson jogged to follow the horde of people, waving his hands and continuing to push them toward the platform, and Tobias followed behind. After about ten blocks they spotted signs for the main ferry terminal behind an impossible sea of heads and bodies pushing forward, smashing each other. Someone's going to get trampled, Tobias thought.

Within minutes Tobias was crushed from all sides in the crowd as more and more people were added to its mass. He could see the corner of Simpson's head, a patch of blond hair and an ear. They were no longer Security or authority—now they were part of the crowd.

There was so much pressure coming from all around him that he was certain he could lift his feet completely off the ground without sinking down, and Tobias felt a resulting panic rise in him, but he forced his mind to beat it back. Other people were stupid, other people lost their heads. Not he.

The noise was deafening.

He moved a few blocks closer to the ferry entrance and could hear, barely, under the din of all the people shouting and the buildings groaning and the ceiling cracking, another loudspeaker sounding out ahead of him. He stood on his toes and willed his body to be a little taller and saw, just over the shoulders and heads, nine or ten men with megaphones, standing on the tops of trash cans above the crowd, trying to direct the flow of traffic. They all wore thick black bulletproof vests with "PSB" printed in large white block letters on the fronts.

Another large clap of noise roared above them, and Tobias looked up, though he was afraid of seeing how the damage had progressed. Cracks and fissures in the dome reached all the way down the sides now; it was getting hard to see through the glass for all the shattered pieces.

Thousands of bodies pushed against him as he moved forward

another couple of inches. He could see the ferry terminal platform now, raised a few feet from the sidewalk—the evacuation route. It won't be long, he chanted to himself. It won't be long. It won't be long.

Palmer Security agents were standing on the platform with tasers and barricades three meters high, forcing the waves of people into funneled lines once they got near.

The barricades towered higher as they neared the evacuation line, and somehow the bodies around him managed to compress even further. Tobias tried to think of Barnes. Barnes would never crumble in a crisis, and Tobias would never disappoint Barnes. He could see the platform. It won't be long. It won't be long.

A Palmer Security agent towered directly over him on a trash can. Even this close, Tobias could hardly make out what was blaring through his megaphone. All was noise. The crowd heaved him forward. Though he felt as though his ribs might snap, he let the bodies carry him.

All he could see now were people's heads and the shattered ceiling above him. Tobias felt a sudden burst of worry for whoever was left and twisted his head to see behind him. There weren't that many people left behind him—enough to crush his body, but he could see where the crowd stopped. He and Simpson had spent enough time guiding everyone out of the hotel that they were in the last wave to board the boats. He looked up at the dome above and thought it would be a cruel cosmic joke if it came down now, just at the end, just when he was so close to being saved.

At the platform a Palmer agent brandished a taser at him, ordering him to stay back and wait his turn. The agent's face was gray and pale, and his collar was ringed with sweat. The glass and metal shrieked overhead. The dome was going to give it was going to give—

"Let us up!" Tobias broke, transformed into that shrill panicked animal he'd sworn he wouldn't become, shouting into the void of noise. "Let us up or we'll die!"

No one heard him, and it didn't make him feel any better to shout it out. They were so close. Tobias spotted Simpson on the platform. Simpson would make it out, and Tobias would die here. Tobias swore he felt a drop of water splash on his head from above. The dome was going to give.

In a frantic gesture, the agent waved him and four other people onto the platform. As Tobias scrambled up the stairs, he took a wide, grateful breath. Hot tears welled in his eyes. With the last shred of cogent thought he had, he checked his torso for his bag—still there. He took a brief moment to lift the flap and look inside. The tablet was still intact, all his data on the case was still safe. And the letters—Dal's letters were still there.

A ferry departed down the canal and disappeared into the dark tunnel. Another emerged from an opening on the other side of the loop, ready to take on new evacuees. People clambered on, rocking the boat violently back and forth.

Tobias saw Simpson board as he himself climbed over a railing, too rushed to find a proper entrance. It was standing room only. Tobias grabbed on to a pole to hold himself steady and waited, praying for the boat to depart, praying to reach safety before a wall of water rushed up behind them.

15

MYRRA

Myrra was shaken awake. The floor was moving. This was it. Her next thought: Charlotte.

Lurching out of her bed, she ran to the bassinet. Fighting the shifting ground beneath her, she scooped up the baby and fell back against the mattress. Whatever else happened, Charlotte would not be alone, she would not be alone.

The room shook. Charlotte struggled and screamed in her ear and Myrra clutched her tighter, this girl who was not her daughter. You are mine.

A minute or two passed. Gradually the shaking ebbed and then ceased entirely. Myrra stared at the dark windows. They were both still breathing.

Charlotte squirmed against Myrra's grip. She was upset by the shaking and the noise, but once everything had gotten quiet again she seemed even more upset by how hard Myrra held on to her. The hours ticked by. Eventually Charlotte cried herself out and drifted off in Myrra's arms. Myrra stayed wide awake.

A soft blue light poured through the cracks in the curtains. In spite of everything, another day dawns. Myrra sat up, depositing Charlotte back in the bassinet with a pacifier. Her head hurt. She'd take the morning to calm down, she decided, then she would steal a boat and leave town. But it was getting harder and harder to picture leaving Charlotte behind.

She took a look out the window to make sure the world was still there. The sea below looked choppier than normal, with all sorts of objects floating on the surface. Myrra thought she saw the arm of a couch pop through the crest of a wave. She wondered where it all had come from—the landscape looked fine from her balcony, but maybe part of Nabat had crumbled into the sea.

Around ten, Sem knocked on her door. She invited him in, but he stayed on the threshold. He wasn't meeting her eyes. Looking down at the doormat, he explained that Palmer had collapsed that morning, a couple of hours after the earthquake.

"I don't know if you felt the shaking this morning, that was when it happened." When she was able to get a proper look at his face, she could see that his eyes were red.

"I felt it."

Myrra couldn't quite fathom what this meant. She tried to picture Palmer through the stories she'd been told—domes of glass on the seafloor. When Sem said "collapsed," had he meant everything? Were there just some buildings wrecked, or had everything imploded? Suddenly it came to her, all the debris she'd seen in the water. A harbinger of things to come.

"They say it's the worst quake we've ever had... Palmer was built to withstand a lot, but this was too much—" His voice cracked as he said it. "The domes cracked under the pressure of the water."

So it was the whole city. Everything—gone.

"How many people were in the city when it collapsed?" she asked. She noticed a tear forcing itself down Sem's cheek. He wiped it away with the back of his hand, self-conscious.

"Um...they evacuated," he said, and she gave him time to steady his voice. "I think most people made it out, but—"

He took a breath and continued. "But they all escaped here. It's the nearest town, so—I guess it makes sense. Sorry—" He wiped another tear. "I have a lot of friends living there, so it's just...it's just kinda weird."

"It's OK." Myrra leaned in and gave him a hug. She wasn't sure if the gesture would be welcome, considering their odd encounter the night before, but Sem wrapped his arms around her and hugged her back. She felt the moisture of his tears and his breath warming her shoulder. After a minute he let go.

"Sorry," he said again. He took another, longer, calmer breath. "What I came here to ask was if you'd take some of the refugees"—he stumbled on the word *refugees*—"into your room. It's your choice, of course, but Palmer was a pretty big city, much bigger than here, and we don't have a lot of space—"

They needed the room. Myrra was reminded of emergency drills in New London—spare cots would be rolled out onto the floor, tired bodies would be ushered in to take up every square bit of space.

"Sure," she said, and reached out to place a hand on his shoulder. He flinched, and his face changed as he looked at her.

"What is it?" Myrra asked.

"That stuff you were talking about last night. Everything breaking down...That was just theoretical, right?"

Myrra didn't know how to respond. She'd tried lying when she arrived, then she'd tried telling the truth, and both options felt somehow manipulative and wrong. Guilt rose in her. She knew what he was thinking about. He was thinking about how many earthquakes they'd had over the past year. Maybe he'd noticed birds flying in odd patterns, the odd shifts in the weather. He had been thinking about what she'd said, and then dismissing it, and then thinking about it again. No matter how implausible, once the thought had settled in it was unshakable.

"I shouldn't have said anything..." she whispered.

"How would you even know, if something like that was happening—?"

"I knew people in the government," she said, hesitating on the word *knew.*

She stopped herself from speaking further. Would it make his life better to know this? Had the damage already been done? Ultimately she gave in. There was no way for him to unknow the things she'd already told him.

She fed him the same line Imogene had given her: "There's a crack in the hull of the ship. It's growing. And there's no way to fix it."

She tried to gauge his reaction, but it was impossible to tell what he was thinking. His expression looked completely vacant. She reached out to him, and he leaned away from her hand. "Sem?"

"I have to go check with the other guests," he said robotically, and walked away.

As far as Myrra could tell, there were only three or four other rooms booked in total in the whole hotel. She retreated into her room and closed the door, feeling disgusted with herself, feeling like the angel of death.

Through the window she could see wide strips of sand at the base of the cliff. That beach had not been there yesterday. Objects littered the shore, though she was too high up to make them out. Beyond the beach the ocean roiled like it was caught in a storm, though the sky was cloudless and blue.

16

TOBIAS

They were in a large cavern that smelled musty and wet. No natural sunlight, just a network of caged bulbs wired to the ceiling. Wherever this ferry station was, it was clearly used only for emergencies. It took a few minutes of searching, but Tobias found Simpson amid the hordes of people standing and shivering on the stone cave floor. He looked much more stable than Tobias felt.

"Where are we?" Tobias asked. He knew there were plenty of smaller towns between Palmer and New London, but he always glossed over their names on the transit lines. Just little blips to mark the time: Bethlehem, Liauso, Ilva, Mbaska, Nabat.

"I don't know," Simpson said. "Probably the closest town to Palmer. Kittimer, maybe?"

Tobias turned his head this way and that in the dim light, trying to assess what was going on, trying to assess how he could be of use. Almost by telepathy, Simpson told him, "We need to keep everybody calm."

With that he strode forward and flipped open his badge wallet in one raised hand, the other hand waving about to make space.

"All right, folks, let's back away from the ferry platform—" he shouted out. Tobias didn't know how he had the strength to do it; his own vocal cords felt stripped.

Without arguing, the crowds immediately followed Simpson's orders. People are willing to listen to any authority in this kind of chaos.

In the dim light on the far side of the cavern, Tobias could make out a number of tunnels labeled with illuminated "Exit" signs, and another, larger sign above, carved into the wall, that read "Welcome to Nabat." Nabat. Tobias remembered seeing that name on a brochure once.

Tobias swallowed down a few drips of saliva in an attempt to soothe his raw throat. Then he followed Simpson's lead and, ignoring the pain, joined in shouting and herding groups toward the exit tunnels.

The actual town of Nabat was breathtaking. The sheer size of the cavern structures was one thing, but Tobias was most impressed by the stonework: the intricate carvings around the pillars, the smooth precision of the building facades. It reminded him of the surviving Italian marble sculptures in New London's Classical Museum.

The Nabat Security Bureau was decidedly smaller than what Tobias was used to in New London, and with the population having essentially tripled overnight, everything in the offices was chaos. He and Simpson were greeted upon their arrival by an Agent Demir, who quickly ushered them down the nearest hallway. Tobias noticed they were following signs labeled "Jail Block."

"The transit tunnels were damaged by the quake, most of the boats are capsized on the beach, we can't get anyone in or out,"

Demir said, waving his hands wildly above his head to emphasize his point. They turned a corner and were met with a corridor of ten barred cells, five on each side, cut into the stone walls. Each was filled with dozing members of the Palmer Security Bureau, its iron door ajar. The lucky ones slept on the one or two metal bunks each cell afforded; others slept on cots laid out on the stone floor.

"Most of the refugees are being taken in by families in the area," Demir continued. "But since you two are Security, we've set aside accommodations for you here in the station." He gestured to two empty cots wedged in the corner of the farthest cell on the left. Demir at least looked apologetic. "It's the best we can do," he said.

"What happened to the prisoners you were housing?" Simpson asked.

"We cut them loose. Nothing to be done, we needed the space." Demir shrugged. "Mostly just drunks, anyway."

Tobias didn't necessarily approve, but he couldn't think of a better way to handle the situation. He and Simpson wandered to their cots, stepping over other sleeping bodies on the floor.

"When you've had some rest, we could certainly use your help," Demir said from outside the cell, leaning against the bars. "Our bureau is not equipped to handle this many people."

"Of course," Tobias replied.

They lay on the floor for hours, mostly staring at the ceiling and sleeping fitfully. Tobias's mind wasn't quite right; when he closed his eyes he could still feel people crushing him from all sides. Every half hour or so, Simpson would try to get a call through to his family, but the tablet signals were all jammed. Tobias thought of New London. Had it been hit as badly as Palmer? He wondered if Barnes was OK, but didn't try to call. Simpson was proving how futile that was.

He was still thinking of Myrra Dal. His brain kept putting pieces in parallel: Marcus Carlyle's suicide, his compatriots' possible suicides, the earthquakes, Myrra Dal. There was no real logical reasoning connecting any of it. Just a feeling. A feeling that Tobias tried to keep at bay—he wanted to look at only one piece of the puzzle at a time, otherwise the sense of foreboding was too great for his mind to take. He needed more sleep. He needed to find Myrra Dal. Somehow, he didn't know how, there were answers there.

Tobias had just started to drift when his tablet sprang to life and started pinging with notifications. Tobias bolted up in surprise and nudged Simpson awake. "Network is up."

Simpson immediately reached for his tablet like a drowning man reaching for a life preserver. He heard a speaker connect on the other end, the small muffled voice of Simpson's wife streaming in through an earbud.

"Ruth?" Simpson spoke softly into the microphone, cupping his hand over the side of his head to better hear. "Baby? Are you there?"

Tobias rolled over on his cot and faced the wall, trying to give them a little privacy. He checked his tablet for messages, holding the screen close to his face. A steady cascade of alert boxes popped up on his screen—audit results on Marcus Carlyle's bank accounts, security alerts from his former creditors, messages his tablet had received postmortem. The IT guys had done an amazing job. Tobias was tapped into all his accounts, all his message feeds.

He scrolled through each window of information diligently. Carlyle had multiple mail feeds, though it was easy to tell which ones were more important; some were obviously more publicly accessible, continuing to receive ad messages and news updates. Nothing important. His other mail feeds, a government feed and a privatized feed that Tobias recognized by name as very expensive and very exclusive, were almost completely devoid of new messages. Everyone who had anything important to say to Marcus Carlyle knew he was dead. The privatized mail feed had only one message unopened, with the subject line "Escape Protocol." Tobias skimmed through.

> Feeling fearful for the future? Don't be. While the path ahead may be difficult to face, it does not have to be uncomfortable or painful. As a member of our Federated Government and key donor to the Unified Science Alliance, we are allowing you exclusive access to our life-planning program, Escape. Simply tap into the uplink below and enter your ID PIN when prompted for further information and instructions.
>
> Please note this is a limited-capacity offer. Your discretion is appreciated.

The message sounded like an odd and somewhat vague ad for life insurance. Tobias tapped the link and tried his ID PIN just to see. Access was, of course, barred. No matter. It didn't have much to do with the whereabouts of Myrra Dal. Tobias made a mental note of it and moved on.

Bank accounts came next. He scrolled through the lines of data greedily, previous activity on the account popping up at the top, mostly Marcus Carlyle moving funds from one account to another. Down at the bottom of the list there they were, a whole block of new transactions, starting three days ago.

He scanned the addresses attached to each transaction; mostly they were attached to shops, but somewhere here there had to be a hotel or home rental. There it was, farther down on the list, early in the timeline.

The Nabat Rafia Hotel.

Vibrating with anticipation, Tobias wanted to shake Simpson, shout at him immediately, We found her! I found her! But Simpson was still deep in conversation with his wife, his face naked and vulnerable as he asked question after question about the house, the kids, the dog.

Another ten minutes (Tobias watched them tick by), and Simpson finally hung up.

"She's here!" Tobias said in an urgent whisper as Simpson pressed the disconnect button on his tablet. "Myrra Dal! She's here, look—"

Tobias shoved his tablet screen in front of Simpson's squinting face.

"You did it. Wow—" His brow furrowed for a moment. "Who the hell goes to Nabat instead of Palmer? This place is barely a town..."

"Who cares why she's here," Tobias said, a little exasperated. "The point is, she's here. We have to go get her." Tobias was already standing up, searching for his shoes. He kicked himself mentally: all this time spent in Palmer, and Myrra Dal was living in the town next door.

"Wait—" Simpson said. Tobias was tying one shoe, looking around for the second.

"Wait," Simpson said again, and he snapped his fingers at Tobias to get his attention. Every time he did that, it made Tobias feel like a dog being trained.

"Wait for what? We can't just—"

"Look around. This town's in the middle of disaster protocol. We can't get out, and we've got nowhere to hold her." Simpson gestured around to all the sleeping Palmer agents blanketing the floors of the jail cells. "It could be like this for days."

"They'll get the tunnels stabilized soon. And there's got to be someplace we can hold her—a closet, or handcuffed to the cell bars, something."

Simpson eyed him. "We can't stuff Myrra Dal in a closet until the transit starts working. The CWRA would have our heads."

Tobias felt sheepish about even suggesting it, but plowed ahead stubbornly. Palmer had been the wrong call. Tobias wanted so to be right, to have the upper hand for once, after following Simpson's lead this long.

"Then what do you want to do?" he shouted. A man two cots down grumbled, and Tobias lowered his voice. "Let her go? Give up?"

"No—we still go after her. Need to get eyes on the kid, at least." Simpson raised his hands, placating. "We just have to be smart about it. Transit's down, boats are capsized. Even if she wanted to get out on foot, most of the staircases are damaged. We can't get out of town, and she can't get out of town. But we still have the element of surprise. So we keep an eye on her. We tail her, we know where she is at all times, and the second a train or a boat or something is back in working order, we arrest her and bring her in."

Simpson paused, waiting for Tobias's reaction.

"That sound good to you? Or are you going to bite my head off again?"

Tobias shrugged. He was still frustrated, but it wouldn't do to channel any anger toward Simpson. Simpson was right. The best course of action required a little patience. Tobias was exhausted, his body was bruised and sore. He felt like a walking raw nerve.

"That sounds good," he said, after too long in silence. Then, to show Simpson there were no hard feelings, "I can take the first stakeout shift, if you want. I think it'd be good, to have just one thing to focus on for a while."

"Sounds good," Simpson said, and crumpled back onto his cot once again. Now that there was no crowd to lead, he looked more empty and shaken.

"How's Ruth?" Tobias asked, keeping his tone soft—trying to apologize, in his own way, for snapping.

"She's fine. Shaken up, but fine. Kids are good." Simpson's eyes welled up a little. "It didn't hit as hard there as it did in Palmer, but there's still damage. Some skyscrapers got evacuated, they're making repairs. And, ah—the Keo Bridge collapsed. But that time of night, almost nobody was on it. Last count the fatalities were twelve injured, two dead."

"The bridge collapsed—wow." Tobias tried to picture the Thamso River without it. Was Barnes's apartment in one of the evacuated buildings? Probably not, but he worried for him nonetheless.

He grabbed his bag, the one Simpson had packed for him back in Palmer, and stood to leave.

"I'm glad everyone's OK."

"Yeah, me too," Simpson said. "You gonna call him?" he added, sensing the gaping hole in the conversation that was Barnes.

"Yeah, I will. On my way over." He didn't want Simpson watching him when he made that call, didn't want him to see too much naked emotion.

"Take care of yourself. Check in once you get to the hotel, once you have eyes on her." Simpson was already horizontal and half-asleep by the time he finished the sentence. For someone who hours ago had led throngs of people away from disaster, he now looked quite small.

Tobias wanted to reach out and touch Simpson's shoulder and somehow through that contact fix everything that was wrong. He wanted to feel Simpson's worry ebb away, along with his own. He wanted to tell Simpson that he was OK, that his family was OK, that it was all going to be OK, whether that was true or not.

Tobias walked through the main square of Nabat, inserting his earpiece and dialing Barnes's number on his tablet. He stopped briefly, looking past the white stone pillars that buttressed the cavern opening and out onto the cliffs and the sea. Boats were piled in shattered mounds at different intervals along the shore, along with the jagged remnants of docks, which looked like snapped twigs at this height. Locals told him the beach had not been there before. Tobias could see, on the pale vertical face of the cliff, deposits of seaweed and silt that showed where the waterline had been before Palmer's collapse, some five meters above the sand. He looked out at the water and imagined the ghost city that remained deep under the waves. He shivered to think of his own decomposed body floating somewhere in one of the thousands of rooms in one of the thousands of buildings. In another universe, with another set of circumstances, that's where he was: dead with vacant eyes, fish nibbling at his fingertips.

The ringtone patched through, a little staticky, but connecting. The thought of conversation made Tobias nervous. He didn't feel like talking about his own experience with the earthquake. Better to ignore those aftershocks of panic, let them slowly dissipate on their own. But he'd worried about Barnes all morning. He both wanted to know how Barnes was doing and didn't want to know, didn't want to confirm anything that would add to the trauma of the moment.

Four rings before Barnes picked up the call. He would be in his office now, hopefully, if the precinct was still in good shape. New London was mostly fine, he reminded himself. Not like Palmer. Barnes would be fine.

"Toby?" Barnes's voice on the other line was gruff and professional as always, but Tobias detected a higher pitch to it, a little strain. Tobias pictured him at his beloved wooden desk.

"Hi, Barnes," Tobias said, swallowing down a lump in his throat before he tried to say more. He rubbed his thumb distractedly over some small spiderweb-like fissures in a pillar, letting his fingers follow one crack, then jump to another.

"Are you OK?" Barnes asked.

"Yeah, yeah, I'm fine," Tobias replied. "I'm sure you got the news…Everybody got out of Palmer OK—so I'm OK."

Barnes coughed, and the high tension in his voice eased a little bit. "OK."

"Are you OK?" Tobias asked, once he was sure he could keep his voice level. It would feel like letting Barnes down, in a way, if his voice were to break.

"Everything's fine here. One of the evidence lockers got a bit banged up—how's the case?" Barnes was talking a little too fast.

"Is your apartment OK, are you getting water? I heard there were some burst pipes—"

"Apartment's fine. Been trying to keep everybody calm. Mrs. Reed keeps going on and on about her canary, says the bird is permanently scarred, won't sleep. Of all the things to worry about at a time like this…"

Tobias laughed. It felt good to laugh. They were in a more comfortable place now, he and Barnes.

"The case is going good. We know where she is now, we're monitoring her. Just can't take her in until trains are running again. But we're tailing her until we can." It felt good to sound so in control.

"That's good—that's great. Well done—" Barnes sounded relieved. Tobias laughed again, at nothing in particular. He heard another cough on the other end of the line. Barnes was clearing his throat. "You're doing good, Toby."

Tobias gripped the side of the pillar hard and squeezed his eyes shut, trying to jam down a wave of feeling that was threatening to rise up. He squeezed his eyes so hard he saw sparks behind his eyelids.

"Toby?"

Tobias punched his own arm in an attempt to distract his body. He took a few breaths through his nose. He allowed his eyes to open.

"Toby, you still there?"

Another breath.

"Yeah—yeah, sorry, the connection's bad. Sorry—I'm just—" If he could just get his voice steady—

"I'm glad you're OK," he said finally.

A pause on the line. Barnes cleared his throat again, and the higher pitch to his voice was back.

"Yes, well—me too." More coughing. It was starting to sound like a tic. "Well, I should—"

"Yes, me too—" Tobias said. "We'll talk soon."

"Yes—"

Then a click, and Tobias was left with the soft roar of the waves below and the hum of the crowd in the square behind him, echoing off the stone walls and the arches of the caverns, a never-ending ambient din.

17

MYRRA

Myrra's room was no longer her own. Now it was full of people lying on rollout mattresses, clutching what belongings they still had. The Nabat Rafia had effectively been converted into a refugee camp. The lobby was especially crowded; it was the best place to get a tablet signal. Everywhere people were sitting up on their beds, hunched over screens, trying to get a message out to loved ones or find information on the state of a distant city. Myrra picked her way around the bodies and rolling luggage, hearing snippets of conversations.

One woman, whispering into a speaker: "This is insane. It's taking me fifteen minutes to upload a single news story. There's too many people on the network—"

Another man, camped under a table: "Have you been able to reach Melanie? She should know if there's damage to the Kittimer house—"

An older woman lying on her side with the tablet in front of her face, speaking slowly and clearly to be understood through the bad signal: "I love you. I miss you. I love you. I love you. Be well."

Myrra hiked down with Charlotte to the newly formed beach, ostensibly with a volunteer cleanup crew, but really hoping she'd spot a boat worth stealing. Charlotte was unhappy to be in the sling again, though Myrra's back had gotten used to it. She was less and less able to envision letting Charlotte go. It was getting to the point where she didn't even mind her crying, so long as this tiny living being was there with her, breathing against her skin, interacting with her.

The sand was littered with objects, so densely it was difficult to walk. She compiled a list of her most interesting finds as she stuffed everything into black plastic bags: one purple high-heeled shoe; a scallop-shaped makeup compact; a brown leather wallet (Myrra pocketed the cash inside); a pack of playing cards that had condensed into a single sodden brick; a pink crystal doorknob; the bottom half of a traffic light; lots and lots of broken glass. There were plenty of boats too, but none that looked as if they'd still float.

Security littered the streets, much more than before thanks to the influx of Palmer SB. Myrra wasn't sure if anyone would still be looking for her in the midst of all this chaos, but she wasn't about to let her guard down. Two days ago, there had been a million ways to get out of town, and now, nothing.

There was always a way out. She just had to find it. Until then she kept off the main streets as much as possible and wore large sunglasses whenever she went out; hats, scarves, anything she could use to hide her face.

A man in a suit who was staying in Myrra's room approached her to complain about the thickness of the mattresses.

"It's my back, you see," he said, giving Myrra a smile that he seemed to think was ingratiating. He reminded her of Marcus. "You wouldn't happen to have any extra bedding or blankets I could use, just to pad things up a bit?"

An older man trailed behind him, holding his luggage with a vacant expression on his face. Contract worker. The man in the suit caught her looking at the bag man. He held out his hand for a handshake.

"My name's Richard, by the way." He gestured with his head to the tired man behind him. "That's Bram, my secretary."

Bram didn't speak or give any expression of greeting. He looked straight ahead, seemed to be looking through her.

Myrra didn't return Richard's handshake but did give him a small false smile to match his own. She repeated what she had been told by emergency personnel: only one mattress per person. Myrra had given up her own bed to a family of five; she saw Richard glance at their pillows with a covetous look.

All transit had stopped. She could leave on foot perhaps, but it was harder to buy food at this point, and she didn't know how far it was to the nearest town. Myrra could go hungry, but Charlotte couldn't. And she couldn't leave Charlotte behind now. Before, there had been a guarantee that she would be noticed, at a hospital, on church steps, or even left behind in the hotel room. But in a sea of refugees, who would notice her or have the resources to take care of her? Myrra wasn't going to let Charlotte go unless she knew the baby would be well cared for, whatever time was left.

She knew how far it was to Kittimer, some volunteers had told her, but getting to Kittimer required a boat. A few men stayed down on the shore, working with hammers and nails, sheets of metal and vinyl, patching together bits of shattered fiberglass, making what repairs they could to the boats that seemed worth repairing. Myrra kept her eye on them, visited often.

Myrra ran into Sem one day while she wove her newly-purchased stroller through the lobby. His eyes were bloodshot, and she smelled liquor on his breath.

"How are you doing?" she asked. He leaned into her and wrapped an arm around her shoulders.

"This is crazy," he said, not responding to her question.

She tried again. "Have you been sleeping?"

Maneuvering him with both shoulders, she lowered him gently into the chair behind the reception desk. Sem's eyes looked a little watery. He wasn't looking directly at her; instead he stared out at the front door.

"I'm so sorry. I shouldn't have told you," she said.

"Told me what? It was just an earthquake." He burrowed his body into the upholstery.

Myrra moved her hand down to his cheek, and Sem leaned into it. His eyes closed.

"I don't know what to do," he said, half mumbling. "What am I supposed to do?"

"I don't know," she said. She stayed until she felt sure that he was asleep.

Birds kept smashing into Nabat's cliffsides, whole flocks sometimes, leaving their corpses with bent necks and broken wings to litter the stairs and walkways. News was trickling through a bit better now. Apparently this was happening all over. They were pelting high-rise windows in New London and the stained glass churches of Kittimer, same as they were pummeling the stone walls of Nabat. Something about the earthquake, the size of it, had displaced landmarks just enough that it was messing with the birds' internal navigation.

At night Myrra slept outside on the balcony, with Charlotte's bassinet right beside her cot. She'd been nervous about the balcony, but now it seemed like the calmest place.

One night a seagull hit a wall and fell on top of her, shocking her awake. The bird's neck was bent at an odd angle, its eyes still open. It moved its beak, working it open and closed, full of confusion. The eyes stared at her as though she were some sort of anchor to life, some way of understanding the circumstances. She sat up and stared back. They stayed like that for another minute or so, hard to tell how long, until the bird stopped moving. Myrra thought she saw, in its eyes, the moment of death.

Myrra visited the train station again and stared up at the black dead screens. Would it be possible to head out using the abandoned tunnels? She rocked Charlotte back and forth in her stroller, her eyes trailing the cracks in the walls.

No, too dangerous.

The station was mostly empty. No trains, no people. A woman with a red bucket was spackling the walls at the end of the platform. She was small, with fine features and fine straight black hair. She didn't seem the type to work construction.

The woman dipped a flat putty knife into the bucket, and it came out covered in gold. She scraped the knife across a crack in the wall, and it left a wide golden swipe across its surface. Myrra walked closer. The woman noticed her curiosity and smiled at her.

"It's not actually gold," she said. "It's gold paint mixed into a construction polymer. Strong stuff." She took out a rag and buffed the wall, wiping away the excess. The splintering cracks transformed into the splitting branches of a golden tree, right in front of Myrra's eyes. "This is a version of a repair technique that my grandmother taught me. If something breaks, you don't hide the damage. Instead you fill it with gold and really let the cracks show. It's part of the new life of the object."

The woman looked down at Charlotte, noticing her for the first time.

"Oh—" she said. "How sweet! Hello!"

She danced her fingers in front of Charlotte's face. They were covered in gold too. Charlotte reached out to try to catch the woman's hands, but she dodged.

"No, no," she cooed. "This stuff isn't good for babies to eat."

The woman went back to her bucket with the putty knife. She reached high above her head to fill in a fissure near the ceiling.

"Do you do construction for Nabat?" Myrra asked. "I haven't seen this anywhere else."

"I'm actually a structural engineer—the local government hires me to check all the buildings, make sure they're up to code. This is just something I wanted to do for the town. Felt like a good way to heal something." She buffed out a stray smear of gold on the wall, bringing her face close to the surface to make sure every last bit was clean.

"This was a good test for us, this earthquake. There've been so many little quakes, and now this big one... We've got cracks, but nothing collapsed. That's good!" she said.

As an engineer, surely she would suspect more, not just take the earthquakes at face value. Myrra ventured another question.

"Why do you think we've had so many earthquakes lately?"

The woman, about to add another layer to the wall, stopped her golden knife in midair. She froze in thought, a crinkle formed between her eyebrows.

"It's hard to say," she said. "My best guess is that the world is just getting old. Engineers designed it to last a long time, but we're reaching the end of the journey. Could be that now the world is just going to shake like this sometimes, until we reach Telos." She tilted her head and looked up, a slight frown playing on the corner of her mouth. "But maybe not. There's a lot of smart people running the world. We are good at fixing things."

She resumed her motion with the knife and swiped more gold onto the wall.

"That's what we do," she said, almost to herself. "We fix what we can, and we move forward."

Late one night, crossing the room to fetch Charlotte a bottle, Myrra came across Richard sleeping soundly on two mattresses, one stacked on top of the other. Bram slept next to him, directly on the stone floor.

A white rage sang in her veins. Myrra despised entitlement. It came from a lifetime of acrobatically manipulating herself to accommodate the whims of other people. Myrra knew she shouldn't do anything that would attract attention, but she couldn't help herself. She yanked hard on his ankle, pulling him halfway off the mattresses until Richard was startled awake. Myrra loomed over him, bending down so her face hovered close to his.

"Give him back his bed," she said, rigid but calm. He looked positively terrified.

"But—my back—" Richard said, somewhat delirious.

"Give him back his bed," she said. "Or I will take you outside right now and shove you over the balcony."

Myrra wasn't sure if she would be physically capable of doing this, but she must have sounded convincing enough. Richard scrambled off and dragged a mattress over to Bram, who awoke and looked utterly confused. But then he looked up at Myrra and seemed to understand. He climbed onto the mattress and was asleep again in thirty seconds. Myrra still hadn't heard him speak a word.

The next day, Myrra went down to the shore. One by one, fishermen disentangled the boats that were piled up against the docks. Some liked to talk to Myrra when she came down to visit. One in particular talked nonstop, like a salesman trying to close a deal, big smile, winks, compliments. He was young, strong, and tall, with dark hair and dark features. In another lifetime, perhaps, she would have flirted back a little. But now all she wanted was information.

"A cyclical engine?"

"Yeah, that's what you want. They cost a little more, but you'll make your money back in energy costs. They barely ever need a recharge."

"So does this boat have a cyclical engine?"

"Of course. But," the man said, brushing sealant on the underside of the hull, "let me give you some advice: if you're looking to buy a boat, this isn't the kind of boat you want. Fishing boats like this are too big, more unruly. What you want is something small and sporty, something fast."

Myrra nodded. That might be true, but this boat was the closest she'd found to something seaworthy. Or at least it would be soon.

He keeps his engine keys in his back right pocket, she noted.

Myrra stumbled on Sem again in the dark early morning, while bouncing a restless Charlotte up and down the hallways. He was half-conscious, half on the floor, and in the dim light of the hall sconces Myrra could see that his skin looked disturbingly gray. She drew closer to him; the smell of liquor was overpowering, and something else. Something chemical.

Charlotte let out a small cry, upset that they'd stopped moving.

"Shhhh..." Myrra said, and smoothed her hair, but didn't take her eyes off Sem.

Was he still breathing?

"Sem? Wake up." She tapped gently at the side of his face. He grunted in response.

She couldn't take him to a hospital, not with all the Security about. She needed to get him somewhere she could look him over. There was a bathroom behind the reception desk—at this time of night there was a chance it wouldn't be occupied.

"Come on," she said, shaking his shoulder and hoisting him up to lean against her. With Sem leaning on one side of her and Charlotte on the other, they only barely made it to the lobby before Myrra's grip weakened and Sem slipped down to the floor again. Even after a lifetime of manual labor, she was simply too small to carry that much weight. Myrra sighed and looked around. The lobby was still very dark, bodies and cots scattered across the floor. Everyone was still asleep. Almost everyone.

In a corner of the lobby, a thin young man was sitting awake in an armchair, writing a message on a lit tablet screen. Strange for anyone else to be up this early. The blue glow of the screen illuminated a pale face, casting odd shadows against his cheekbones. With everyone else collapsed on the floor, he looked like a ghost watching over the dead.

At her feet, Sem heaved as though he might vomit. The young man in the corner perked up and took notice. He kept looking at Sem and then back at Myrra, but he didn't get up from the chair. His mouth puckered into a confused frown. Whatever confusion he was feeling, she was going to have to force him to get over it. She couldn't handle Sem alone.

With silent exaggerated gestures she waved at the young man, beckoning him to join her. He stalled for a few more seconds, looking more at her than at Sem, before he shook it off and walked over.

Myrra whispered to him, "This man is sick. Can you help me get him to the bathroom?"

The young man nodded, looking a little dumbfounded. Myrra bent down to grab one of Sem's arms.

"Here, let me—" He jumped forward to grab Sem's other arm, and rose up to take on the majority of Sem's body weight. Myrra was surprised. The man had a wiry build; it didn't seem as if he'd be able to lift Sem on his own.

Together they delicately picked their way around the sleeping bodies until they reached the reception bathroom and set him down next to the toilet. Sem looked at Myrra through dipped eyelids and for the first time that morning seemed to recognize her. He started to speak, but it came out as unintelligible slurring.

"Shhh, it's OK," she said, and lifted up the toilet seat, propping his head near the bowl. She put Charlotte down on the tile in the far corner of the bathroom, still within her sight but out of reach of Sem. Charlotte fussed, crinkling her brow and staring back at Myrra with outstretched arms. Myrra produced a pacifier from her pocket and popped it into Charlotte's open mouth. Charlotte sat back and folded her arms, still not exactly happy, but quiet. Myrra kissed her on the cheek and turned back to Sem.

The man crouched down next to Sem, pushing a pair of horn-rimmed glasses farther up on his nose. A deep crease appeared in his forehead as he concentrated on the problem at hand, and Myrra was almost amused at the way his expression matched Charlotte's.

"Do you know him?" he asked, looking up at her. There was

something odd in his inflection as he asked the question. It felt like someone practicing small talk, but with a more invested curiosity. Like a journalist interviewing a celebrity.

"I met him about a week ago. He's the concierge."

Sem moaned, and his torso seized. His eyes opened in a sudden shot of adrenaline, his neck went erect, and then he dove face-first into the toilet bowl. Myrra looked away, but she could still hear the sounds of him retching.

"It's good he's throwing up," the young man said. "Do you know what he took?" He spoke with authority. Maybe he'd be useful in a crisis after all.

"Seems like mostly booze. Maybe something stronger." Sem's face emerged from the mouth of the toilet bowl. He looked pale. A little bit of sick dribbled down his cheek. Myrra went searching through cupboards for a rag, and then made do with a sponge. She went over to the sink, wetted it with cool water, then crouched down between the man and Sem and wiped down Sem's face. Her knees knocked against the man's knees, and she put a hand on his shoulder to steady herself.

He jumped and looked up when she touched him, and again Myrra felt something awkward in his response; hesitation, a hint of recognition.

He pulled a small flashlight out of his pocket, pried open Sem's eyelids one by one, and flashed the light at his pupils. "Response looks OK," he said.

"Are you a doctor?" Myrra asked.

"No," he said, keeping his eyes focused on Sem's face. "But I've seen alcohol poisoning before."

Myrra waited, but he didn't elaborate.

"Where?" she couldn't help asking. He looked entirely too young and too clean-cut to have made such a claim.

He paused a half second before speaking, just long enough for Myrra to catch that he was lying, but briefly enough that she could also tell he was good at it.

"I worked at a bar for a while," he said. He kept staring at Sem, checking his eyes and face, but it felt as if he was avoiding looking at her. She looked down at his hands. No calluses. His eyes had that pale bloodshot look that came from staring at screens. Office work? No way he'd worked in a bar, at least not the type of bar where overdoses were common. She felt pricks of suspicion creep slowly up her spine, like the legs of an insect. Without knowing exactly why, she darted her eyes over to Charlotte in the corner, making sure she was still safe.

She inspected the rest of him. There was something boyish about him. The lenses of his glasses were smudged, he had floppy brownish hair that was a little unkempt. His hands and feet were too big for his body, as though he was still growing into himself. But his eyes didn't look as young as she'd thought at first glance. They weren't as bright as they ought to be. There was a light that existed in the eyes when a person was still green and hadn't seen much. Jake was like that. Boyish or not, this man had eyes that were dimmer with knowing, the type of knowing that rests on you when you've come face-to-face with the world and realized that the world owes you nothing. The innocent were never able to pick up on this knowing, but Myrra could recognize her kindred.

Well, if he wanted to lie about his life, he could lie about it. That's what she did, most days. But she would watch him.

The man clicked off his flashlight and put it neatly back in his pocket. "He'll be OK," he said, gesturing to Sem.

"So you just carry a flashlight around everywhere?" she asked.

He smiled a little. "I like to be prepared."

Charlotte flopped over sideways onto the tile floor and wiggled back and forth, trying to roll toward some shelves holding bleach and sponges. She hadn't yet figured out crawling, thankfully, but Myrra still rushed over to grab her before she could get at the chemicals. Once again immobilized, Charlotte fussed in her arms.

"I can watch him till he's sober, if you need to get back to bed."

"Don't you need to sleep too?"

The man laughed, a little mournful. "Me? I haven't slept in days."

He was giving her an odd look again, not the look a stranger would give, the look of someone with a level of investment in her life.

"What's your name?" she asked him, sizing him up. It was a strange combination, to like a person and to also not trust him.

"David," he said, which didn't feel quite right. "What's yours?"

"Emily," she said, though she'd wanted to say, "Myrra." She wanted to be honest, in some way, to counteract his lies.

"Emily," David repeated, and smiled with a hit of irony in his expression that she couldn't comprehend. "It's nice to meet you, Emily."

18

TOBIAS

Tobias waited until Myrra Dal was out of the room, then let his expression crumble into panic and concern. He flipped through each moment of the conversation in his head. Had he given anything away? He didn't think he had. He needed to talk to Simpson. He looked down at his wrist. His watch read five thirty. Was that too early to wake him?

The young man—Sem, apparently—groaned again from his spot next to the toilet. His tan cheek was fused to the white surface of the bowl, and as he slouched farther toward the floor, his mouth and eyelid stretched up a little on one side. First things first. He needed to get this kid some water. Then food. Then coffee.

Myrra Dal seemed familiar with Sem. It would be worth it to have a conversation with him, anyhow. There wasn't much food left in the hotel's storage rooms, but after he talked with one of the hotel's cooks, a man named Georg, they managed to find a box of instant mashed potatoes. Sem would be able to keep that down. Mashed potatoes or porridge had always worked best when he'd needed to get David and Ingrid back on their feet.

When he got back from the kitchen with the heated mixture, Sem was still drifting on some sort of a high, but he at least was able to sit up a little better. Tobias dragged his body a polite distance away from the toilet and spooned him some mashed potatoes. Sem felt the substance on his lips before opening his mouth. His eyes were slits. He chewed the mash needlessly, with slow exaggerated movements, like the sloths Tobias had seen as a kid in the New London Zoo.

Five or six spoonfuls later, Tobias ventured a question.

"So," he said, raising another bite of mashed potatoes to Sem's lips. Sem opened obediently. "Do you know Emily very well?"

He waited for Sem to chew and swallow the bite. He decided he wouldn't tell Sem that he was Security. Not yet. Myrra Dal had a way of drawing people to her side.

"Emily," Sem said slowly. "Emily works in communications."

This wasn't helpful. Sem took another bite. The mashed potatoes were getting lukewarm; they had a more paste-like consistency now, but he was still gulping down each spoonful.

"What about Emily? Did you talk to Emily much?" Sem didn't register the question. Tobias snapped his fingers in front of Sem's eyes. "Hey, Sem, what do you and Emily talk about?"

"Emily—" Sem said, but then failed to finish his sentence. Tobias sat back, giving up for the moment. Maybe he would get more out of him in a few hours. He could check back in the guise of a concerned stranger.

His thoughts drifted back to his conversation with Dal—she was surprising. Most contract workers he'd talked to had a certain built-in submissiveness to them, even if they were finding ways to rebel, even if they'd attempted escape. It was something that was carefully taught to them from birth, and it was hard to shake. Even if your higher brain might question authority, that deep-down conditioning held on.

He'd felt her watching him, sizing him up. After the life she'd led, or, to be more accurate, the life she'd survived, she probably sized up everyone that way upon meeting them, trying to suss out motives, weaknesses. He felt a twinge of worry, hoping he'd passed the test. No. It would be fine. He hadn't given anything away.

It felt good to interact with her. He felt a small pang of guilt just thinking it. *Good* wasn't quite the right word, but it was some kind of a breakthrough to talk to her, even if it was under false pretenses. She had better posture than he'd imagined. Her voice was lower. It was strange to hear such a low voice come out of such a small person.

That first day he'd sat in the corner in the lobby, and seeing Myrra Dal walk by in person, right there in front of him, had been a shock to his system. He had been able to recognize her from the worker's permit photo, but she looked very, very different here. A lot of it seemed to be money—her hair was still wild, but now it was styled in such a way that the wildness looked purposeful. Her stained work clothes had been replaced with a stylish purple day dress and high-heeled boots. Even the baby stroller she pushed looked top of the line.

There was also something in her expression that set her apart from the mob of refugees in the lobby. Everyone here still went about daily tasks: making phone calls, checking in on the state of the trains, running out to find food. But they were operating in a sort of haze, as though only a portion of their brains was devoted to such things and the rest of their thoughts were concerned with figuring out, cosmically, how they'd ended up in the situation they were in. Myrra Dal displayed no such confusion. It was as if she'd expected the earthquake. She seemed very tense, as if her body was always on high alert, waiting for a blow. She held on to

Charlotte with a particular intensity, as if at any moment a bomb might go off and she had to be ready to shield her. And she seemed constantly tired. Deep-in-the-soul tired.

It could have simply been her status as a fugitive, but there was something in the way she looked around at the crowds of people, wary of them and worried for them, that suggested she knew something that she was keeping back. Tobias thought again of Marcus Carlyle's suicide, of the other deaths, and wondered about the connection. He both wanted to know more and was afraid to know.

"Can I have more water?" Sem asked, raising his head to take a look around. His speech was still slurred, but there was at least a little more color to his skin. Tobias went to the tap and refilled the glass.

"Emily," Sem said again, staring at a fixed point on the stone wall as though it were another person engaging in the other half of a conversation.

"Yeah, did Emily and you talk much?" Tobias asked, for what felt like the millionth time, shutting off the tap and bringing the glass over to Sem.

"Emily told me the world was going to end," Sem said, his face twisting up and frowning. "That's a messed-up thing to tell someone. She told me that, and then the earthquake happened, and it's just...it's really messed up."

"Was she joking?" Tobias asked, the question out of his mouth almost before it had entered his head. It seemed the only feasible response.

"No," Sem said, and coughed a little on his own spit. His eyes watered. "She seemed really, really worried about it."

Tobias didn't know how to respond to that. It wasn't the sort of information one received without immediately dismissing it as ridiculous. Myrra Dal believes it's the end of the world. Maybe it was a new religion among the workers. Cults popped up sometimes. But that didn't sound right. Not for Myrra Dal. He tucked the information away in his brain to think about later, but for now it was impossible to dwell on. He lifted the water glass to Sem's mouth and tilted it until the water reached his lips. Sem closed his eyes and swallowed, grateful.

Sem shifted his gaze from the spot on the wall to Tobias.

"The world's not going to end, right?" He was looking at Tobias now as if Tobias were the ultimate authority on such issues.

"No, the world's not going to end," Tobias said, trying his best to reflect that authority. Sem let out a long breath, letting the frown crumble and open up into crying outright. He seemed unburdened, as though he'd just confessed his sins.

"Good," he said. "Good."

He curled up in a ball on the floor, propping his head on his arm. He seemed immediately ready for sleep.

"What a messed-up thing to tell someone," he mumbled, and then, "Don't tell my dad about this." Then he closed his eyes and passed out again. Tobias let him. He had no more questions for now and couldn't quite figure out how to process what he had just heard, or whether such a notion was even worth taking seriously. He sat on the dingy tiles of the bathroom floor next to Sem, watching this man he'd just met recede back to sobriety in slow, steady waves, like an ebbing tide.

As he sat there, he thought distantly about the end of the world, distantly because it wasn't an idea one could ever really get close to or truly inhabit. It was as though the thought were only experienced as a far-off voice on a speaker, half-submerged in radio static, or a muffled argument on the other side of a wall. The world had ended once, generations ago, he'd read all about it in history books. And even then they'd found a way to keep going. Life always finds a way to keep going.

At length, with Sem still unconscious next to him, he dismissed the idea entirely. The world could not end. It could not end because life exists. We have always existed, Tobias thought, and knew at once that that was scientifically untrue. But it felt true. I have always existed and will always exist. I—we—I—exist and stretch in all directions, backward and forward in time, going on and on in the past and in the future. The world cannot end, because I exist. The world could not end, because I survived the collapse of Palmer. The world could not end because I haven't yet filed my latest report with Barnes. The world cannot end because tomorrow I will have granola for breakfast. The world cannot end because. Because. "Because" was all that was needed. Anything else was crazy.

Tobias left the sleeping Sem in the care of his coworker Georg and walked toward the darker streets of Nabat, in the deeper caverns where the streets narrowed and stone arches got lower. He risked getting some distance from the hotel to avoid anyone eavesdropping on the call. One or two people passed him with tired, paranoid faces. It was impossible to be alone anywhere in Nabat right now, but at least here, farther in the caves, he was a little more isolated.

On his first day of the stakeout, he'd placed a couple of hidden cameras in potted plants near the hotel entrance. He checked them now. The feeds were still good. He'd know if Myrra Dal tried to leave.

"What happened?" Simpson asked the second he answered Tobias's call. He must know something was wrong. It was still early in the morning, and they'd mostly been debriefing at night. And Simpson wasn't due to relieve him on the stakeout until noon.

"Myrra Dal approached me last night and I had a conversation with her, but I didn't give anything away," Tobias said, cutting to the chase. Simpson stayed silent on the line for a few seconds, and Tobias pictured him pinching the bridge of his nose the way he did when he got frustrated.

"You've got to be kidding me."

"I swear I didn't do anything to engage her. I kept a good distance, I didn't stare—"

"OK, fine, how did it happen?" Simpson asked, still sounding frustrated.

"There was a medical emergency with the concierge—he was sick on booze or something worse. She singled me out because I was the only one awake."

He heard Simpson sigh through the speaker. "And you couldn't say no..."

"The concierge was collapsing on the floor. It would have looked even weirder if I'd avoided her," Tobias finished.

Simpson stayed quiet on the line for a few seconds. Tobias could practically hear him thinking. In his current state of overwork and agitation, his first bitter instinct would be to place blame. They were both exhausted. When not watching the hotel, they had been taking turns helping Nabat Security with grievances and crowd control. Sleep was a distant memory.

Tobias stopped underneath a streetlamp that was lighting a sharp curve in the corridor. There was a large door carved into the wall with a sign above it advertising raw silicon, wholesale. The streets were much more empty back here—nobody wanted to stand around among mine shafts and warehouses. There were small cracks here and there on the walls—Tobias wondered if they'd been there for years, or if the earthquake had caused them. Someone had taken the time to cover the cracks with gold paint.

It glinted and winked at different angles under the lamplight. It made Tobias smile, to see something beautiful like that, back this far in the dark.

He thought about how many cracks he'd seen in the walls lately and thought of Myrra Dal's prediction. His smile faded. No. It wasn't worth thinking about.

"Is the concierge OK?" Simpson asked finally. Tobias reoriented himself in the conversation. This was Simpson's way of moving past this and absolving him.

"Concierge is fine. I watched him through the worst of it, he's got colleagues looking after him now."

"Good."

Simpson had him go through his entire conversation with Myrra Dal, picking apart every detail of the admittedly short interaction. He seemed suspicious but satisfied by how Tobias had handled himself.

"OK," he said. "Hang back for now. Keep an eye on her, but don't—*don't*—talk to her again." He paused, working something out.

"This'll be over soon," he continued. "Nabat agents told me that the trains should be running again tomorrow morning. The second the trains are back online, we'll grab her. Together. Just hang on till then. Don't talk to her anymore."

The trains would be running soon. The sentence sounded like church bells in Tobias's ears. It was the best news he'd heard in a while.

"Yeah, OK. Good plan," he said, then realized how perfunctory that sounded. "I appreciate you talking through this with me," he said, as a follow-up. "I won't let you down."

"It's OK, kid," Simpson said. "Just a bad coincidence. This shit happens, more often than it should." It was the most warmth that

Tobias had heard from him since the earthquake. It was enough for Tobias to forgive Simpson for calling him "kid."

For his next stakeout shift, Tobias changed location. Instead of a corner chair in the lobby, he was now sitting on a bench across the street from the entrance. Across the street and down the block a little, just close enough that he could still clearly see the door, but farther away, much farther away. Hopefully far enough that Myrra Dal wouldn't see him or try to engage him, but close enough that he could still see her comings and goings. That was the danger, losing her now, when they were so close to being able to take her in.

He rifled through his backpack, disentangling charging cords in an attempt to get to his tablet, which had migrated down to the bottom. He realized with some alarm that his tranq gun and badge were also tangled in wires at the bottom of his bag. He retrieved them as well, holstering his gun under his blazer and placing his badge back in the breast pocket. Tobias chided himself—the safety latch hadn't even been properly secured on the gun. He must have removed the gun while half-asleep. He knew he wasn't at his best.

He kept scanning the length of the block and checking the lobby doors. Too many people in the city. It was a miracle that he'd found a spot on this bench. It was a miracle that he'd been able to keep tabs on Myrra Dal at all.

The hotel's double doors swung open and another group filed out with wrinkled shopping bags. Two families from Palmer (you could tell the people from Palmer, because they all looked a little disoriented) and Sem the concierge, holding the door for them, looking more sober and much more tired. His shoulders slumped, and his eyes had sunken into purplish sacks of skin.

Sem looked up and caught Tobias watching him. He gave a

wan smile. Tobias raised his arm and waved. He sincerely wished Sem well. He had a feeling that he would have judged Sem more if he'd encountered him before the earthquake. What Sem had done was stupid. But Tobias felt a certain camaraderie—they'd all been through something, and they were all looking for ways to keep going, some with work, some with distraction. Sem returned Tobias's wave with a small, sheepish rise of the hand.

Just then, as if conjured by their presence together, Myrra Dal appeared, pushing her stroller out of the second lobby door. She noticed Sem and immediately followed his gaze over to Tobias.

His coat was open. His hand was raised. His gun would be visible. On reflex, Tobias lowered his hand immediately and sat down, but it was too late. He saw her expression change: at first a smile, a recognition, and then, when she looked at Tobias a half second longer, the smile went away. For a blip of a moment her expression turned serious, and then it was replaced by another smile, a different smile. This was a pretend smile, an everything-is-fine smile, an I-didn't-see-anything smile, a smile from a person who knew how to mask emotions for survival's sake.

Stupid, stupid, stupid, Tobias thought. He shoved his tablet back in his bag and rose off the bench. He started toward her—the trains weren't running yet, but they'd just have to find somewhere to hold her.

Myrra kept moving away from the door, but not so fast that a passerby would notice. Tobias pushed through the crowded street toward her, and she looked down briefly at Charlotte and the stroller. Tobias knew what she was doing: she was calculating her odds of outrunning him with the baby. The odds were slim.

In a split second she made her choice and turned the stroller around, sprinting back toward the hotel entrance. Bad move, Tobias thought. The hotel had no back exits. He was almost disappointed.

Myrra Dal passed by Sem at the door, whispering something quickly to him. He looked unnerved—Tobias couldn't tell if it was because she'd just tipped him off or because the last time they'd seen each other, Sem had been vomiting his guts out.

Dal disappeared through the door, Tobias ten steps behind her.

As he pushed through the hotel doors, Sem tried to stop him, physically put a hand on his chest—"Hey, man, I didn't have a chance to thank you earlier—"

Tobias tried to push past Sem's hand and felt Sem push back, trying, as casually as he could, to keep Tobias in place. Tobias glared at him, batted his hand away, and continued inside. He could hear Sem chasing him with conversation: "No—wait—!"

Where was Dal? He spotted her dark tangled hair past the crowd in the lobby, getting inside the elevator, the elevator doors closing. She turned back and met his eyes just before the doors closed, an unreadable expression on her face.

Tobias was in a panic. Simpson was going to be livid. He didn't even want to think about Barnes. Where was she going? He'd reviewed the building schematics days earlier. Outside of jumping into the sea, he couldn't think of a way out.

He thought of all this as he dashed for the stairs, taking them two at a time, trying to beat the elevator and figure out which floor would be her destination.

Floor two. He swung open the stairwell door. No one. Floor three, even faster, leaping over three stairs when he could. He swung open the stairwell door; no one was there.

He kept going to floor four, floor five, getting more and more winded as he went. Was he outpacing the elevator, or worse, was he too late? Dal's room was on the sixth floor; it was the most likely place.

He swung open the door at floor six and came face-to-face with

Myrra Dal, who was standing in front of the door with her arms raised above her head. There was something in her hands—

Tobias felt something metallic and cold smash against the side of his head.

A fire extinguisher. Myrra Dal had been holding a fire extinguisher.

Tobias heard a ringing in his ears, something wet was running down the side of his temple, but he managed to stay upright. Dal raised her arms to hit him again. He looked past her and saw that Charlotte Carlyle was in the stroller a few feet behind her. Tobias sidestepped her as she swung, stumbled into the hall, between Myrra Dal and Charlotte. He whirled his head around in both directions. The hallway was empty. For the first time in days, now, when he needed help, no one else was around. Everyone was in a room.

Tobias reached for Charlotte's stroller and wheeled it back a few paces, out of Dal's reach. Now he had a bargaining chip. Myrra Dal's eyes widened in horror, and she immediately dropped the fire extinguisher.

With one hand Tobias kept a firm grip on the stroller, and with the other he wiped away the blood that was streaming down the side of his head. His sleeve came away with wet streaks of red. How hard had she hit him? He shook the blood off his sleeve as best he could and reached for his gun. He tried to aim at Dal's chest, but his arm was dipping a little.

"Myrra Dal, I am detaining you under suspicion of kidnapping, breaking contract, and for possible involvement in the deaths of Marcus and Imogene Carlyle," he said as authoritatively as possible. He wished Simpson were here. He'd have to wait to call him until Dal was handcuffed.

Myrra Dal raised her hands in the air, looking both terrified and threatening at the same time, like a cornered animal. It was hard to conceive that a person that small could be that intimidating, but here she was. It was something feral in her face, an expression that suggested that she would go for the throat if she needed to. Her eyes kept darting between Tobias and the stroller.

"What's your real name, David?" she asked. She gave no indication that she'd heard his previous statement.

"I need you to lie facedown on the ground with your hands over your head." He tilted his head the wrong way, and blood started pouring into his eyes. Head wounds bled forever, he remembered learning in training. He wiped the blood away with the back of his gun hand, as though he were wiping tears from his cheek. His muscles felt slow, as if he were moving through water.

"I would like to know the name of the agent detaining me," she replied.

It felt dangerous to tell her his name, even though, as he flipped through his memory of *The New London Security Bureau Handbook*, it was actually one of the inherent rights of criminal suspects. He relented.

"My name is Tobias Bendel."

"Now we both have the right names," Myrra said.

"Yes," Tobias said, somewhat needlessly. It was hard to hold the gun up. There were clouds in his head.

"Why did the Carlyles kill themselves?" Tobias heard himself ask. His mind felt distant from his body. He let go of the stroller for a moment, just long enough to slap himself across the face. It brought him back a little. A little more focus.

"Isn't this something you should be asking me later, in some dark interrogation room?" Myrra Dal was watching him with a great deal of focus, as if she was waiting to pounce. She glanced again at the stroller. Tobias took a step back, pulling the stroller with him. He leaned on it a little and concentrated all his strength on keeping the gun raised. The bleeding had to have stopped by now.

He should have repeated his order for her to get down on the floor, or he should have just tranqed her where she stood, but instead he asked, "Why did you tell the concierge that the world was ending?"

Myrra Dal's eyes widened a little. Her hands stayed raised. She was calculating, he could tell, whether to lie or tell the truth. It was a look he'd seen on a million faces in a million interrogation videos. "Just tell me the truth," he thought, no, said. He'd spoken the words out loud. He hadn't meant to.

Myrra Dal's face crumpled a little.

"I told him that because the world *is* ending," she said, her voice full of exhaustion. There was a fuzzy blackness coming in at the edges of his eyes.

"I don't believe you," he said.

"Good," she shot back. "Fine. Nobody fucking believes me. I'm not going to waste time trying to convince the person arresting me. Just get back to me in a month, and we'll see who's right."

Even through his haze, Tobias knew she was telling some kind of truth. He believed that she believed it. The cloudy blackness was closing in. He slapped his face again. He needed to detain her. Simpson would—

He let go of the stroller, stumbled, and jostled the baby—he'd been leaning against it more than he'd thought. A caterwauling sound rose up. The baby was crying. Myrra Dal flinched, looked pained. Tobias fought the urge to comfort the child. He couldn't handle the sound of a crying baby.

He fished a pair of handcuffs out from where they were hooked on his holster.

"You *are* prepared," she said when she saw the cuffs. Was that a joke?

"Get down on the ground, please," he said. Even as he said it, he saw his gun arm lower, even though his brain was shouting to keep it raised. His knees buckled, and he felt his body crumple. No control now.

He saw Myrra come toward him, through the pinhole of his vision, felt her catch him, a safe grip, one hand cradling the back of his neck, another firm and flat on the small of his back, lowering him down.

"Shhh..." Her voice was close, next to his ear. The voice was panicked, almost guilty. "I'm sorry I had to hit you—"

He felt the brush of her hand knocking the gun away, heard it distantly as it skittered across the stone floor.

Despite himself, he felt calm. Tobias let his mind swim. He thought, Let me not wake up. He thought of his little steel desk in the precinct and his little white apartment in the city. He appreciated the life he had. He thought of Barnes, and of all the chances he'd been given.

Let me not wake up, he thought again. I couldn't stand the disappointment.

19

MYRRA

The boat cut calmly through the waves of the Palmer Sea. It was dark outside, the water black and impenetrable when Myrra tried to look below the surface.

The ambient hum of the motor had helped to quiet Charlotte. Poor thing. She was so tired. Myrra had swaddled her again and tied Charlotte's body in a sling, tight against her torso. She'd stopped screaming, but she would still let out small sounds every few minutes. Myrra could feel the vibration of Charlotte crying against her sternum, as though it echoed back in her own heart.

She could have left Charlotte at the hotel—Security would have discovered the stroller before long next to their bloodied agent. She was no longer surprised that she'd kept her. Hauling Charlotte around was exhausting and inconvenient. The majority of the space in her bag was devoted to baby supplies. And yet.

When Myrra fell asleep at night, there was another being breathing beside her. Just like old times.

Myrra smoothed Charlotte's downy hair. Charlotte tilted her head up in response, reaching with her mouth until she found one of Myrra's fingers to suck on. They'd lost her pacifier somewhere along the way.

Myrra pushed hard on the wheel and realigned the nose of the boat with the highest peaks on the jagged horizon. The man had been right—fishing boats were a little unruly. But Myrra was getting the hang of it. The Kittimer Mountains. The peaks had a strange colorful glow. She'd heard that the glow came from all the stained glass. It was a sight to see.

Myrra's hands still shook a little from the adrenaline. The noise it made when she'd brought down the fire extinguisher on his head. She'd thought she'd killed him. It was surprising for her to discover her own ruthlessness, like a low snarling animal that had lived all this time inside her chest. Up until this point in her life, she'd survived mostly by lying, by manipulating, and by hiding. She'd endured violence plenty but had never really inflicted violence upon others. It was a shock to her system.

The smell of blood too, that unexpected smell of metal, the heat of it. Her senses had simultaneously overlaid the moment with the memory of the women of the laundry all ganging up on her after they'd caught her cheating at cards. She was beating a man and being beaten at the same time.

Even now, in placid water, far from another human being, Myrra was having flashes of fists coming down on her face. She would have to take new precautionary measures once she reached the opposite shore, but for now she needed to calm down. She at least had a head start.

She decided to take inventory of her surroundings. It was what she used to do when waking up from a nightmare as a child. Her mother had taught her that: When you wake up, and you don't know where you are, just start counting the objects in the room. What's above you? The ceiling with the light bulb and that corner of paint peeling down. What's below you? That old mattress that sags in the middle. What's to your right? The table and the clock. What's to your left? Me, sleeping beside you.

What was above her now? The sky, the stars. Myrra instinctively looked for cracks, to see if this was the night when everything broke apart. (How matter-of-fact she'd become, even through all the fear. The mind could really adapt to anything.) It was a futile gesture. Even if the cracks were there, she wouldn't be able to make them out. She had no idea how high the sky was above her, but the entire thing was bathed in an impenetrable blackness right now.

What was below her? The boat, with its top-of-the-line engine and a tiny cabin under Myrra's feet. And below that, black water, small silvery waves. The water was a little less crowded with objects now than it had been. After a few days, most of the detritus had sunk back down to the bottom of the ocean or ended up on a beach. But the occasional bottle or shard of furniture still floated around, butting up against the side of the boat as it cut through the current. Myrra pictured the skeleton of Palmer even farther below. An entire dead city was entombed underneath her. Even if everyone got out alive, something still died. She imagined Palmer haunted by unseen ghosts: the empty towers, silent streets, abandoned parks, irrelevant fountains. And when the world gives way, she thought, will everyone here live as ghosts in space and haunt the place we once occupied, among the shards of metal and debris?

Myrra shook off the image. What was ahead of her? Directly in front of her body was Charlotte, rubbing her face against Myrra's breast. Her moaning had stopped. She would be asleep in a minute. Myrra smiled. And distantly ahead were the mountains, getting taller as Myrra got closer. They were definitely glowing. One face of the central peak emitted a purple light; another point near the top was an incandescent orange. And parts of the mountains, too, didn't look like mountains at all but like a set of increasingly tall towers. Like a city stacked.

What was behind her? Nabat. Caves. Pillars. Stone. Sem. Fear. Waiting. Refugees and crowds. David—no, Tobias. Tobias Bendel. Prying agents. Running. Money. Luxury. New London. Imogene. Marcus. Antiques. Paper and wood. Work. Waiting. Mother. Factories. Contracts. Slavery.

Myrra thought about Security again, considering the situation as calmly as she could.

She could keep ahead of them; she just had to be smarter about this in future. She had already chucked the account card in Nabat after pulling as much cash as she could. Hopefully the ID could be altered again, or she could find a place where IDs were unnecessary. Kittimer was low tech, full of temples and religious sects, not security cameras.

She could keep ahead of them. Anyway, she thought morbidly, she wouldn't have to outwit them for long. Maybe Kittimer would end up being the perfect place to die.

20

KITTIMER

In mapping the world the ship, the design team originally conceived the interior to be a mirror of the natural world on Earth. Grasslands, tundra, jungles, mountains, deserts, as much flora and fauna as could fit on the food chain. In short, a full set of ecosystems. But as they moved forward with the process, the designers began to regard their adherence to nature as a wasted opportunity. Were there things about the Earth that could be altered, or bettered? Then they started thinking philosophically, about the nature of the natural world: What makes the sea the sea? Is a mountain still a mountain if it's not made of stone and earth?

When it came time to nail down the details of the Kittimer mountain range, designers started advocating for artistic augmentation. The mountains became half geology, half architecture. Instead of the usual gray and white, they wanted pops of color. They decided to incorporate stained glass in as many areas as they could. They looked to mountaintop monasteries for inspiration. If they were going to add stained glass, the mountains ought to be a place of meditation and spirituality.

When the mountain range city was completed, it looked at a distance like a classic picture postcard of the Alps or the Himalayas. Snow still dusted the peaks, jagged outcroppings of rock shot up toward the sky, and there was even a tree line. At other angles, however, you could see that some of those outcroppings were towers and buildings, stacked on top of each other in a pile. Urban roads peeked out here and there behind the rocks and snowdrifts. Under the drifting snow, panes of colored glass replaced stone bluffs, and rose windows replaced basalt columns.

And in this case, substance also followed style. Even after the designers and their purposes were long forgotten, the Kittimer Mountains evolved to become a region defined by spirituality. Kittimer has more mosques, churches, synagogues, and temples per capita than any other city in the world the ship. Not all who live in Kittimer believe in a higher power, but the entire area is tinted with belief nonetheless.

Kittimer is far enough from the epicenter of the quakes that the city is intact when the end comes.

When the world breaks apart, the citizens of Kittimer consider themselves ready for it. Anyone opting for panic has already left the city. Those who remain break into factions and retreat to favored houses of worship. Some pray cyclical hypnotizing prayers. Some light candles. Some meditate. Some just sit and think quietly on what the afterlife will be. If it will be. People touch each other, kiss, and hold hands. Many are smiling.

But it is hard to tell if the people of Kittimer are truly as ready as they claim. In the deafening crashing noise that comes before everyone dies, smiles stay on faces, but they're screwed a little tighter. The hands holding one another grip with a harder desperation. The cycles of prayer accelerate to a breakneck speed. Nobody is really ready for the unknown.

21

MYRRA

Myrra sat outside on a bridge uniting two mountains, supported by arches and pillars that descended deep into the ravines between the peaks. Snow was more abundant near the tops of the mountains, but down at this elevation the only cold was a slight crispness to the air. It was a blue-sky day, beautiful and cloudless. Myrra could see the landscape below with perfect clarity. In front of her, a considerable distance away, was the Palmer Sea. Behind her the mountain range diminished into foothills, vineyard valleys, and, eventually, a blue-green desert. Myrra was curious about the desert, but not curious enough to uproot Charlotte again.

They would need to buy new baby clothes soon; she was growing. There was still time for little milestones. Charlotte squatted down on the sidewalk in front of her. Each of her hands held tightly to Myrra's fingers, and she was pulling down on them, harder than usual. Myrra watched her. She squinted and her mouth puckered and pinched. Whatever she was trying to do, she was concentrating hard. She pulled down on Myrra's fingers again and rocked forward and backward. Myrra scrunched up her face to match Charlotte's and leaned closer to her.

"That's a very serious face," Myrra said to her, and laughed. Charlotte didn't giggle back at her, just kept up her determined expression and continued to rock back and forth. Then it dawned on her: Charlotte was trying to stand. She'd never done that before.

"Come on," Myrra said. "Pull up."

Charlotte squinched her forehead further.

"Come on. You can do it."

Charlotte leaned her body way back and rocked forward, this time using the momentum to pull her body up to stand. Myrra raised her fingers up with her, taking care that she didn't lose her grip. Charlotte's knees buckled for a second, but she held on.

"You did it!" Myrra cried out, her voice much higher pitched than usual.

Charlotte's eyes grew wide as saucers, as though she'd just given herself the shock of a lifetime. She held on harder to Myrra's fingers, a vise grip, and turned her head this way and that.

"You're OK," Myrra said, softening her voice this time.

At this moment Myrra was relieved to concentrate on something so simple. They'd been in Kittimer four days and no one had tracked them down. She'd been checking the news—trains and ferries were running again in Nabat. But no sign of Tobias. Myrra still woke in a panic at night, vacillated regularly between fear and calm and stress and acceptance. But here in this moment, she was content. It was startling to realize that she could be happy, after everything that had transpired. She wasn't sure she trusted the feeling.

Then Charlotte giggled again and bounced her knees, testing her balance and getting bolder. She looked at Myrra with great focus and let out a shout.

"Aaaaah!" she said. She worked her jaw up and down. "Aaaaauuuuaaaahh!"

Was she trying to talk as well? Suddenly all Myrra wanted in the world was to hear Charlotte's first word before everything collapsed.

Though she worried about getting her hopes up, Myrra couldn't help anticipating what Charlotte's first word might be. *Ma?* Wasn't *ma* the standard? Myrra remembered the parenting guides that Imogene had bought when Charlotte was first born—she had all the latest up-to-date parenting advice uploaded onto a separate tablet that she bought brand-new for the occasion. She called it her "Mommy Tablet." Imogene only got through one or two of the guides before hastily discarding the rest and tossing the tablet into a forgotten drawer.

"Waste of money...they all say the same thing," Imogene had said. One piece of advice that Imogene had taken to heart was Talk to Your Baby, as often as possible, and not in baby talk. Babbling baby talk was strictly forbidden.

"Talking to a baby in full, complete sentences helps the development of synapses," Imogene had said once while handing Charlotte to Myrra. She was on her way to a charity lunch.

Myrra remembered her focusing rather intensely on Charlotte after that, speaking directly at her.

"Charlotte," she said, in a tone that suggested calling a meeting to order in a boardroom. "Charlotte, I have to go meet with the Gorman Conservation Foundation." She overpronounced each word.

"I'll be back soon. I will miss you. I love you." Then she kissed the top of Charlotte's head and departed. In retrospect, Imogene hadn't been a terrible mother all the time. There just hadn't been much natural instinct, and never enough hours in the day.

Myrra had leafed through one of Imogene's abandoned parenting books later when she was alone. Partially as reading practice, and partially to understand this new, vulnerable being that was in the house.

"Infants tend to pay more attention and respond more eagerly to baby talk than to normal adult conversation," it had read. "The playfully exaggerated and high-pitched tone your voice takes lights up your little one's mind. But use full sentences as well! It is important for your baby to hear how normal conversation sounds. As your child develops and matures, so should the way you talk to her."

Myrra suspected that Imogene's real problem with baby talk had been that she didn't like sounding ridiculous. Still, in a small gesture to her ghost, Myrra tried to keep the extra-gooey baby talk to a minimum.

Myrra found herself softening to Imogene's memory as the days progressed. Maybe that always happened with the dead over time. But also, in a strange way, Myrra was thankful that Imogene had taken the time to tell her what was going on before jumping off the roof. The knowledge that everyone was going to die was a torturous burden, but it also allowed for choice. Without that knowledge, Myrra didn't think she would have felt the freedom to leave. Imogene hadn't needed to tell her—Myrra liked to think that her decision to do so was an impulse of kindness.

Myrra tried to talk to Charlotte as much as possible now that she saw her trying for words. First thing when they woke up each morning, Myrra started chanting, "Mamamamama" to her, over and over again. It echoed the chanting of the monks in the monastery up the hill. She heard them repeating foreign words in singsong tones, keeping time with the clamor of the bells at dawn, noon, and dusk.

Kittimer had no shortage of bells. Everywhere Myrra walked she heard bells, the sound traversing the roads that zigzagged up steep slopes, through pathways that circled and wound up towers and spires. All tones, high and low, fluttering soft tinkles and large bellowing clangs. Myrra collected their names in her head. Her tongue curled deliciously around the foreign words: *ghanta*, *rin*, *agogô*, *tubular*, *suzu*.

And then under the bells other sounds emerged, the chanting, the prayers, the mantras, drums, hymns, songs, and ululating cries. All blended together into a low hum, the white noise of the faithful. At first Myrra had worried that the noise would bother her or, worse, keep Charlotte awake. But after about twelve hours in Kittimer, it became clear that the sounds of religious services weren't all that different from the sounds of New London traffic.

Myrra and Charlotte had much more minimal accommodation now. Instead of a huge marble hotel suite there was a small simple room in a hostel, with plain cement floors and a shared bathroom and kitchenette. Instead of a cliffside view and a balcony, the hostel looked out on a steep side street. There was no window view from their room at all, though the outer wall, the one that faced the street, was composed of a thick pane of frosted pink glass, and it bathed the small room in a rosy light that made everything seem soft. Myrra was still having panic attacks at night, and she especially appreciated the calming effect that the color had on her anxiety-ridden mind. It was easier to calm herself down in this room than it had been in Nabat. Myrra had learned at this point that she felt safer and more at home in a simple, cramped space. It annoyed her that this vestige of contract work had stuck with her, but she accepted that there was nothing she could do to change it.

There was stained glass everywhere. Thick colored panels

replaced the walls in buildings, wedged between I beams and structural supports. Often they were simple slabs of color, as in their room at the hostel, but sometimes the designs would be more ornate, blending many colors into scenes and knots and patterns. Myrra loved wandering into certain temples and cathedrals to stare at the complex geometry of the rose windows, study how the tiny fragments of color all assembled together. None of this inspired in her the same religious devotion that others had, but the beauty still stirred something within. She worried if it was shallow or wrong to like the beauty of a church if she wasn't also practicing the faith that had inspired its artistry.

Myrra pulled a jar of mashed peas out of the hostel's communal fridge for Charlotte's lunch. When she looked up over the fridge door she saw a very old, pale woman hunched over Charlotte's stroller. Possessive alarm flared up in Myrra, but she fought to remain calm. The woman straightened up and tilted her face toward Myrra. "Is this your baby?"

What a question.

"Yes," Myrra said, and then, trying not to sound terse, she added, "Her name is Charlotte."

"Charlotte," the woman said, looking down at her. Her gaze was unfocused and her expression vacant. She smiled, and the wrinkles in her cheeks stretched and deepened as she did so. "What a lovely name."

Since Nabat, Myrra had become increasingly nervous about interacting with others. Even in the hostel's communal spaces, she tried her best to keep to herself and avoid questions. Every time they went out on an errand, she circled the odd block to check to see if anyone was following her. Myrra briefly worried about giving out Charlotte's real name to this woman, but it was a relatively common name, and anyway, this woman didn't seem altogether there.

The old woman bent forward over the stroller again. "Hello, Charlotte, hello, sweetheart."

Charlotte laughed and let out another loud "aaaaaughaaa-uuugh" sound, wagging her jaw up and down as she shouted out. She was getting so close to talking, Myrra could sense it.

Myrra sat down at a table next to Charlotte's stroller and stirred the peas in the jar. Without invitation, the woman sat down across from Myrra and watched as Myrra spooned peas into Charlotte's open mouth. She made Myrra uneasy, but then everything made her uneasy these days.

"I have a granddaughter who looks just like her," the woman said eventually. "At least she used to. I haven't seen her in some time."

Myrra softened. The woman had such a vulnerable look on her face.

"What's your granddaughter's name?"

"Grace," she said. Her voice sounded thin and far away. She kept looking at Charlotte, but her smile diminished.

"I haven't seen her in a long time," she said again. "She's in New London. I left New London because I didn't want to die in a hospital—I wanted to die here. But then I just kept living. And now I'm afraid if I leave, I'll get sick again."

Myrra didn't know what to do with this information. A plump dark-skinned woman entered the room and joined them. She looked down at the old woman with kind eyes.

"Annie," she said, "I thought you were going to tell me if you wanted to leave your room."

"I shouldn't have to ask permission," Annie said.

"Of course not, that's not what I meant," the woman said. "I was just worried about you."

The old woman, Annie, turned her focus back to Charlotte. The plump woman mouthed "Sorry" over Annie's head, looking at Myrra. Myrra smiled back at her and scooped another spoonful of pea mush, waving it at Charlotte's face. Charlotte ate the next bite happily, though drops of green oozed out of her mouth and dribbled down her chin. Myrra wiped her chin with a rag.

"This is Charlotte," Annie said to the woman. "Doesn't she look like Grace?"

The plump woman looked at Charlotte and nodded, keeping the smile on her face.

"Maybe a little bit," she said. "In the eyes."

Then she turned to Myrra. She held out her hand to shake. Myrra took it.

"I'm Rachel," she said. She gestured to the old woman. "And this is Annie."

"Nice to meet you," she replied, and then thought a minute before she remembered her new pseudonym: "I'm Karen."

"So," Rachel started, pulling a chair up next to Annie, "you on a pilgrimage?"

"No," Myrra said, laughing. It was the first question everyone asked here. "I just like the mountains."

Annie and Rachel had been in Kittimer, in the hostel, for a year and a half. As the conversation progressed, it was clear that Annie wasn't always completely cogent, but Rachel confirmed that she had been telling the truth about coming here to die.

"Pittock's disease," Rachel leaned in to tell her while Annie was distracted by Charlotte. Myrra nodded at her as if she knew what that was.

"But it was the craziest thing," she said. "Once we got here, her joint pain went away, her lungs cleared, it was as if the whole thing never happened. Unfortunately"—Rachel leaned in even farther—"some of the neurological damage stuck. Poor thing."

Myrra kept an eye on Charlotte as Rachel talked, wary of Annie trying to pick her up. A few times she heard Annie call Charlotte "Grace."

Rachel seemed excited to have someone to talk to who was below the age of ninety. She gossiped about the Palmer earthquake ("Awful, wasn't it? I can't believe it, we barely felt a shudder out here..."), she asked Myrra about Charlotte's father, eyeing the difference in their skin tones ("Is he still in the picture?"), and she levied cheerful complaints against the hostel's amenities ("I mean, I know we're all here to get back to a more pure life, but the bedding is *terrible*...").

That last one especially amused Myrra. Over the course of the past week, Myrra had come to realize that there were two distinct classes of people living in Kittimer: there were wealthy people who lived in lavish houses and apartments, and there were people who were still wealthy, but who lived in sparse dwellings designed to improve one's soul. Annie and Rachel, it seemed, belonged to the latter category. And as with most people in that category, the minimalism didn't seem to do much for Rachel's spirit, though it did cause her to complain.

There was also a third class of people, Myrra considered: those who lived in more limited dwellings because they actually did have limited means. But nobody in Kittimer bothered discussing that group of people, between all the church visits and chanting.

"Mamaaa... ma-maaaaa... ma-mamamamamaaaaaa..." Myrra sang on one note, softly, her face close to Charlotte's as they lay in bed. Charlotte's eyelids kept drooping as she fought sleep. Myrra loved Charlotte's eyelids, the waxy newness of the skin, the tiny feathery eyelashes poking out.

There was no bassinet now, and there were no porters to set one up. Charlotte slept against the wall so she wouldn't fall off the edge of the bed at night, and Myrra slept next to her. At first Myrra had been worried that she would roll over on her while sleeping, but her old childhood instincts were still there. Myrra kept still on her side and welcomed the weight of a warm body next to her, even one as small as Charlotte's.

The room was bathed in darkness, just the dim hint of a rosy light from the streetlamps outside. The sun had set hours ago, but Myrra could still hear the melodic chanting up the hill. Charlotte's eyes were almost closed.

"Ma-mamamaaaaa..." she sang again. Charlotte's eyes jumped open, and her nose squinched up in annoyance. Myrra smoothed her hair.

"Sorry," she whispered to her. "I'll leave it."

Charlotte's eyelids drifted closed again. Myrra let herself drift off after a few minutes, after she knew that Charlotte was really asleep. The song of *ma-mamamaaaa* continued to echo in her skull, even after her voice was silent and her eyes were closed.

22

TOBIAS

For what felt like the millionth time that day, Tobias was looking at Simpson, Simpson was looking disappointed, and Tobias was saying, "I'm sorry."

His stitches were bleeding again, and somehow he'd managed to stain Simpson's sleeve in the process. But that wasn't what he was apologizing about. Not really. He just found himself apologizing regularly now, about one thing or another. The apologies were all variations on a theme, all referencing his mistake without speaking of it. I'm sorry I let Myrra Dal go. I'm sorry I got injured. I'm sorry I messed up the case. I'm sorry I'm a terrible agent, a terrible partner.

Everyone said reassuring things to him regarding Dal's escape, but their tone never matched their words. Every word that came out of Simpson's mouth sounded like disappointment. And Barnes. Barnes was especially hard to think about.

They'd called to update Barnes that morning, at Simpson's insistence.

"You can't just avoid him, this is an official investigation,"

Simpson had said when Tobias advocated delaying the call. "This isn't like hiding your report card when you got a bad grade."

And in one sentence Simpson reduced him from a competent Security agent to an ashamed freshman. Tobias had felt like saying that he'd never received bad grades in school, but he realized that it was entirely beyond the point.

They'd called him, and Barnes maintained a calm, measured reaction. Lots of "Well, in the future you'll know..." and "It would have been better if..." eventually devolving to the classic "These things happen..." There was a pause before each of these phrases, as though Barnes didn't quite know what to say, fishing for meaningful conversation on the fly.

It would have been better if he'd yelled. If Tobias had been any other agent in the bureau, he would have yelled.

Then came the death blow.

"Under the circumstances, maybe it'd be best if you came back in. I could throw this one to Emerson—"

"No, we can handle it, we've got leads—" Tobias practically shouted into the speaker, just as he looked over and saw Simpson nodding in agreement at the words *came back in*. Simpson stopped mid-nod and glared at Tobias.

Barnes paused. Tobias could picture him in his office, behind that beautiful oak desk, twirling the edge of his mustache the way he sometimes did when he was mulling something over.

Simpson cut in, in the quiet. "Sir, I think it might be a good idea for Emerson to have a look. We can head back and give him what we've got so far—"

"What's your lead?" Barnes asked.

Tobias jumped in before Simpson had a chance to speak.

"She headed to Kittimer," he said. Simpson looked at him as if he had three heads.

"What makes you say that?"

Barnes sounded almost playful as he asked the question. Tobias knew he was asking about the lead for the same reason that he hadn't yelled. He knew that Barnes didn't entirely take him seriously. He didn't care. This was his shot, and if that meant grabbing on to the unfair advantage that Barnes had laid out, so be it.

"We know she took a boat," Tobias said.

"That doesn't mean she took it to Kittimer," Simpson interrupted. "She could have gone any number of places. She could have followed the coast, headed to Troy. She could have doubled back, just to throw us off. She's clever enough."

"Simpson has a point," Barnes said.

Tobias shook his head, then realized that Barnes wouldn't have registered the gesture. He pressed on.

"Troy's a tech hub. Most of the other towns on this side of the coast are. She's smart enough to avoid surveillance. Kittimer's so old-fashioned, you barely get a network signal."

He didn't say it, but he also knew that Myrra was looking for a place that would feel reassuring. He had seen the lights of Kittimer as a kid, when he was dragged along on a yacht party with David. The mountains' warm colorful light, like a cozy lit cabin on a cold night. As a person who believed she was waiting for the apocalypse, she'd follow that kind of warmth and comfort.

He also didn't say that she believed the world was ending. For some reason he couldn't bring himself to share that fact, even though it might have helped his case to clue them into her state of mind. He didn't want to say the words out loud. He mostly kept himself from wondering why.

A heavy sigh muddled the sound in their earpieces. Barnes always put his face too close to the speaker. He was used to the earlier generations of tech, with lower volume and more static.

"That's still not much to go on," Barnes said. "What—"

The feed cut out, and the screen went black. One moment Tobias could hear the background noises of the New London headquarters, and the next there was silence. Tobias picked up the tablet and started tapping at the screen.

"It got disconnected," he said, looking up at Simpson. Simpson looked as if he was about to smash the tablet over his head.

"No shit," Simpson replied. "What the hell do you think you're doing?"

He knew it was selfish, and he knew he was making Simpson furious, but he had to keep going anyhow.

"We need to stay on this," he pleaded.

"Why? We blew it. Emerson's capable—it won't take him too long to find her with the notes we give him. I would like to see my wife and kids. Don't you want to see Barnes? Make sure he's OK?"

"I can't. I can't go back to Barnes with this thing half-finished, he'll never look at me the same way again." Tobias looked down at his feet, counted to five. He didn't want to sound too aggressive, but there was an anger rising in him, at all the pushback he'd received every step of the way, when all he'd ever tried to do was a job well done.

"You don't get it," he continued, not looking up. "This is my one shot. I won't get another one. If I screw this up, everyone will either assume I'm an idiot criminal, or they'll assume I'm an idiot that Barnes just patronized."

Simpson let out a slow whistling breath. Tobias could tell he was trying to find the right words, ones that wouldn't be insulting.

"Look, Bendel, it's not your fault. This one is weird. Usually we have someone in custody within a week." He paused. "I don't even think her getting away was really your fault."

Tobias looked at him, trying to read his face. He wanted to

believe him. He couldn't tell if Simpson was telling him the truth or telling him what he wanted to hear.

"It doesn't matter," he said. "Nobody will give me the benefit of the doubt. Barnes was the only one who ever did."

Now it was Simpson's turn to look away. He looked a little manic, his eyes shining and darting around, as if he were searching for an exit.

"I want to get out of here," he told Tobias. It sounded like a religious confession. "Ever since the earthquake, something doesn't feel right. I want to get back to my kids. I think it might calm me down."

Tobias almost gave in at that. If he weren't so selfish, maybe he would have. Instead he asked, practically begged, "Can we just try Kittimer? If we don't find her there, then we can go home."

Simpson scratched at the back of his head with one hand, still looking around, not quite meeting Tobias's eyes.

"One week," Simpson said. Tobias could have hugged him, but settled for a handshake. Same as Barnes.

And Simpson backed him once they got Barnes back on the line.

"Sorry—" Barnes started. "Connection's been on the fritz ever since the quake. We've got IT working on it..."

Simpson cut in, his voice reluctant at first, but decisive. "Listen, I think the kid's got a good instinct on this one. It'll be worth it to check Kittimer for a few days. If nothing comes of it, then we'll come home. That work for you, sir?"

Barnes sounded surprised, but acquiesced. Tobias nearly melted from gratitude.

A lot of it had to do with his career, he knew that. He couldn't fathom leaving a case halfway through, like leaving a kitchen spill halfway cleaned, with the soggy rag still crumpled in a puddle on the counter.

But there was a feeling of possession there too. He knew Myrra Dal, and he wanted to finish the path they had started. He wanted to hear more of what she had to say. He still had questions.

These were things he didn't feel like sharing with Simpson. He was already having too much trouble being taken seriously.

They went back to their corner of the Nabat jail cell. Tobias waited his turn in line at the bathroom, then stood in front of the mirror and dutifully checked his head wound to note how it was healing. There were still spots of bleeding here and there, and the stitches were messy—the hospitals were overrun after Palmer. There would almost certainly be a scar. His first, come to think of it, at least where scars on the skin were concerned.

23

MYRRA

Rachel wanted to take Myrra to see the dervishes.

"I know you're not really here for a pilgrimage, but you don't have to be religious to enjoy it." Myrra gave her a skeptical look, but Rachel just doubled down on her suggestion. "I haven't had a chance to see the dervishes in *months*, come on—" She grabbed Myrra's wrist and tugged at it with both hands, like a small child pulling a parent toward an ice cream shop. Her energy was infectious.

Myrra thought they would be able to walk to the temple, but once they got to the corner Rachel flagged down a cab. Myrra peered in the back seat, wary of cameras. She couldn't find any and reluctantly climbed in.

"The best Sama ceremonies are a couple peaks over," Rachel explained, once they were all shoved together in the back seat. "Anything you find in our section is strictly for tourists...not authentic at all." Myrra liked the way Rachel leaned in and talked conspiratorially about this or that; it felt good to be someone's friend.

"Where are we going?" Annie asked.

"We're going to see the spinning men," Rachel told her. Annie hunched her shoulders in disdain. Myrra, who was nestled next to her with Charlotte on her lap, felt Annie's bony shoulders poke against her arms as she moved.

"No," Annie said, with authoritarian force. "We're going to go home. Take me home."

"We'll go home, right after this stop," Rachel replied, using a singsong voice usually reserved for children. "But Charlotte really, really wanted to see the dervishes; you don't want Charlotte to miss out, do you?"

This seemed to distract Annie. Myrra felt her frail body relax as the old woman turned and crooked a finger at Charlotte's face.

"Charlotte," she murmured. "Hello, sweetie, sweetheart... sweet Gracie girl."

Myrra pulled Charlotte back a little from Annie's looming finger. She didn't appreciate Rachel foisting Charlotte on Annie like some sort of toy. The taxi sped across the first tall bridge, where Myrra had helped Charlotte stand, then barreled downhill around the opposite peak. Trees, snowdrifts, rocks, towers, windows, and the occasional minaret all whooshed past Myrra's window view. Soon they were crossing another, lower bridge toward a third mountain peak, this one even deeper into the range. The taxi climbed again, making hairpin turns as it worked its way up the slope.

The cab stopped on a street that featured multiple mosques and synagogues. A sign next to their chosen temple advertised vodun fetishes that contained kosher and halal animal bones. Shrines made to order.

Rachel got out first and retrieved the walker and stroller from the trunk. She pulled a card out of Annie's purse and handed it to the cabbie.

Rachel beckoned to them to follow. "Come on, it's starting."

They walked into a large circular room, with seating for spectators in a ring around the outside. A small half wall of stone separated the audience from the main floor space. It was crowded, but with a little searching they found a few seats right up against the barrier. Myrra craned her neck up to see the dome above them and gripped Charlotte tighter on her lap. It felt as though her body were falling in space. The dome was composed entirely of metal and stained glass laid out in a mesmerizing geometric pattern, triangles, squares, and rectangles projecting bright rays of orange, yellow, red, and purple. She closed her eyes and could still feel her skin bathed in the color.

"Here they come," Rachel said, tugging on the fabric of her sleeve.

Myrra lowered her head to take in the room at eye level. A processional of figures in black robes and tall brown hats entered the center circle. She looked to her left at Rachel, who had her eyes fixed on them with rapt attention. Beyond her sat Annie, a little less interested. Charlotte sat on her lap sucking on her new pacifier, more entranced by the colorful ceiling above than by the people marching slowly in front of them.

The robed figures walked slowly and deliberately around the circle, bowing to each other at intervals. Somewhere a person had started singing an unearthly warbling song. Then one by one they shed their black robes to reveal white ones underneath. Charlotte reached forward, trying to touch the dervishes, but Myrra kept a tight grip on her.

"I guess the colors have different meanings for different sects, but I was always told that the white robes are meant to symbolize death, and the black robes are meant to symbolize a grave, and their hats are supposed to symbolize tombstones," Rachel whispered to her matter-of-factly.

"So it's a funeral procession?"

"No, they're trying to bring themselves closer to God."

The dervishes began to spin in place, allowing the momentum to unfurl their arms upward like flower petals toward the sun. The edges of their robes likewise billowed out in undulating waves. They lifted their faces toward the light of the dome, arms raised, and spun and spun till it seemed impossible that they were still standing. The light filtering down through the stained glass lit each figure with electric color.

The whole ritual was beautiful and hypnotic, but Myrra couldn't help feeling like an intruder who had walked in on something deeply personal and intimate. She looked over at Rachel. Her face was rapturous. There were tears in her eyes. It must be different to watch such a ceremony when you believed in it.

Religion was rampant among contract workers. She remembered the dorm in the factory, with an idol tacked above the head of each cot. Crosses, stars, little plastic cards with tiny painted deities. She remembered her mother's small blue figure, a man with a placid face and many arms. She kept it hidden in her pocket, would show it to Myrra as she tucked her in at night and say, "He protects the universe. He protects all of us."

As Myrra grew older, her mother's talks of religion grew more frequent. She would talk on and on about the wandering cycle of rebirth and redeath, and of the moral weight surrounding their every action. Near the end, it seemed every decision was something Myrra's mother weighed as if it were going to make or break their lives. She talked about their lives to come, after this one.

"We work hard, and we will be rewarded," she was known to repeat.

And later: "I work hard, and I will be rewarded."

It wasn't a religion anymore, not the way the others practiced it. She was picking out pieces of it, here and there, to suit her own logic. It was something broken and wrong. Myrra felt her mother slipping away from her by degrees.

Then there was the morning that Myrra woke up and her mother was not in their bed. The factory bosses told her that she had gotten sick and had to be taken to the hospital. When she didn't come back, Myrra briefly believed that her mother had done it, she had escaped that terrible wheel. She pictured her not dying, but receding into particles of light.

Now, with the benefit of age and hindsight, she knew different. Her beliefs had not saved her. Myrra didn't know where her mother was, but wherever she had gone, she hadn't bothered to take her daughter with her.

Myrra stared at the colorful bodies whirling in circles, faster and faster, and felt isolation instead of communion. It was an incredibly beautiful thing to witness, but it was not a source of solace against what was to come. She pictured the dome shattering and shards of glass floating upward. She imagined the dervishes lifting off the ground and spinning up and up, their faces terrified by the light above them.

Rachel waited until they were out of the temple to ask Myrra how she'd liked the show, and Myrra said with all honesty that it had been a beautiful display. Rachel was radiant; the tears on her cheeks had only halfway dried.

"It's been too long since I've visited this place," Rachel said, pressing the backs of her fingers against her face in an attempt to cool the blush on her cheeks. "I wish I could come every week."

"What stops you?" Myrra asked in a distracted way. She was half-focused on Rachel and half-focused on Charlotte, who was making a game of spitting her pacifier out into the basket of the stroller and then crying until Myrra retrieved it for her. Annie walked beside the stroller and cackled every time Charlotte spit it out again.

"Annie usually doesn't let me," Rachel replied. "She usually insists that I go to Mass with her."

Myrra, who was still bent over the stroller on a pacifier search, heard Rachel stop short at the last statement, as if she were trying to suck the words back into her lungs. And then she understood, instinctively, why.

Rachel was under contract.

She had managed to twist the situation to her advantage, but she was still technically owned by the senile woman shuffling along beside the stroller.

Immediately Rachel shifted in Myrra's esteem from a casual friend to a subject of great curiosity. She was the most lively and outgoing contract worker that Myrra had ever met. Had she always been that way, or had she evolved into a bolder person as Annie's health deteriorated? How long had she worked for Annie? Had she done anything to encourage Annie's illness?

She popped the pacifier back into Charlotte's mouth and rose to look at Rachel. Her mouth was parted a little, as if she were about to say something more. She looked like a video on pause. She knew she had said too much. She knew that Myrra had caught it.

Myrra stuffed down her curiosity for the moment and smiled at her. She kept her tone conversational.

"Well, I've never been to a Catholic Mass before, but that"—Myrra gestured back toward the temple—"was incredible."

Myrra saw Rachel's face and shoulders relax. Her eyes darted over Myrra's shoulder, and she took off in a run.

"I see a cab!" she shouted back. "Come on!"

Myrra took off after her, trying to maneuver the stroller as gracefully as possible, and also looking behind her to ensure that they weren't about to leave Annie behind. The old woman followed as fast as she could, the feet of her walker clacking furiously against the cement sidewalk.

"Where are we going now?" she cried out.

The next day, Myrra bought a bottle of wine and waited until nightfall. She yearned to hear about Rachel's experience; would there be emotions there to mirror her own? And a deeper wish was buried under this surface curiosity, one Myrra tried not to think about, a wish for someone to tell her story to, someone who might understand her own point of view. It was a dangerous temptation, one Myrra's logical brain told her to avoid.

She caught Rachel just as she was leaving Annie's room, after Myrra knew the old woman would be asleep.

"Care to join me?" She held the bottle up in front of Rachel's face with a smile. "I figure I owed you... You showed me some of Kittimer's culture, but I still haven't tried any genuine Kittimer wine. The guy at the store assured me it's the best red in the region."

Rachel looked a little reluctant. It was possible she was still unsure of Myrra after her slipup the day before. Myrra waggled her eyebrows, almost flirtatious. Rachel relented and laughed.

"Come on," Myrra said, walking down the hall with the bottle. "Don't make me drink alone." She heard Rachel's giggles and footsteps behind her.

"Where's the baby?" Rachel asked, half whispering. It was fairly late, and the hostel was full to capacity.

"She's just over here," Myrra said back, keeping her voice low until they got to the kitchen. Charlotte had fallen asleep in her stroller after a long day walking around town. While Rachel grabbed a seat in one of the mismatched chairs in the kitchen, Myrra searched the cupboards for clean glasses. She found one clean water glass and a chipped mug. Pouring a generous amount of wine into the water glass first, she handed it to Rachel. Then she poured a slightly lesser amount into her own mug. She sat down across from Rachel and held up the mug.

"Cheers," she said. Rachel looked dubiously at their shoddy cups but touched her glass to the ceramic side of Myrra's mug.

"This hostel is terrible," Rachel said, then took a long drink. Myrra sipped at her wine in turn. "When we first got here, we were staying in a fabulous hotel, up near the peak of the basilica? It was incredible. Silk sheets, gold handles on the doors. And the view! You could see the whole of the Palmer Sea from the window."

Rachel sighed. "But then Annie started getting even sicker, and her Catholic guilt kicked in, and she decided God was punishing her for having nice things."

Myrra laughed at Rachel's delivery of this information: very matter-of-fact, with little seeming care for Annie's health. But then, it was only fair. Annie certainly felt like a sympathetic case, here at the end of her life, all frail and confused. But only Rachel would know of Annie's previous sins, from her younger years when she'd had the upper hand.

"When did her mind start to go?" Myrra asked, taking another small sip of wine. As if in sympathetic response, Rachel took a long gulp. Myrra took the bottle and topped her off.

Rachel took a moment to think. "She was diagnosed about... three years ago? Yeah, that sounds right. This was back in New London... It was mostly just the physical symptoms at first, though, the joint pain, stuff like that. Her daughter started closing in at that point, anticipating the inheritance. She put her in a hospital the first chance they could get."

Myrra broke in. "Is that the one with the granddaughter, Grace?"

Rachel smiled and, almost as a reflex, looked over at Charlotte sleeping in the stroller. "Yeah. Gracie was a cutie." Her smile faded. "Her mother, though—what a vulture."

She took another long gulp of wine, and Myrra obligingly topped her off again.

"This is good," she said. "Anyway, after about a year of doctors poking at her, Annie could feel her mind starting to go. Her daughter had taken over the town house by then. I still remember Annie grabbing me one night. She kept repeating to me, 'I don't want to die here. I don't want to die here.' So, before her mind was completely gone, I helped her rearrange her bank accounts and we left town to come here. She said she wanted to spend some time with God before she died."

It didn't take much to get Rachel talking, even if she had been wary the day before. Part of it was the wine, Myrra knew, and part of it was Rachel's naturally outgoing personality. But part of it was the same impulse that Myrra shared—a desire to tell your story to someone and have them listen and understand.

Myrra was suspicious about Rachel helping to "rearrange" Annie's bank accounts, but she didn't judge her for it. After using Marcus's severed hand to open a safe, Myrra wasn't allowed to judge anyone.

"So now you live in Kittimer, indefinitely?" Myrra asked, nudging her on.

"I guess so," Rachel said, with a shrug and a smile. "I mean, Annie's definitely doing better. Her brain suffered some damage, but all the other symptoms vanished."

"She doesn't want to go back?" Myrra asked.

"Every now and again she does. She misses Gracie. She even

misses her daughter. But then I remind her that if she leaves, she'll probably get sick again, so we stay."

Myrra could now see Rachel's situation with full clarity. She was in control so long as Annie stayed estranged from her family. Of course she would keep Annie here.

"What happens if Annie dies?" Myrra asked, and then wished she hadn't. Up until this point they had skirted around the issue of Rachel's true job title. Rachel looked aghast, but she stayed in her chair.

"I don't know what will happen," she said first. She paused and looked to the side.

"No, I guess I do know," she said finally. "Her daughter will inherit my contract." A wince on her face as she said the word *contract*. "But I don't like to think about that."

"I'm so sorry." Myrra gave her a smile and touched her arm. On the bright side, Rachel would probably never have to worry about losing her autonomy again. Annie could last another few months at least. Rachel would die living her best life.

Rachel's eyes were pooling, but she held the tears back. She stared for a moment at Myrra, a little confused, a little searching.

"Thank you," she said. Her voice cracked slightly. "I have to say, this is not the way people usually respond when they find out about me."

"I just know what it's like not to be in charge of your own life," Myrra said, worried about revealing too much. She tried to pull the statement back and cap it off with a joke. "I had a bad husband once," she said, as a light explanation. "All men are scum."

Rachel let out a short bark of a laugh and then immediately cupped her hand over her mouth. They were going to wake people up.

They spent the rest of the night chatting about Myrra's fictional ex-husband, the rich blond father of Charlotte and all-around louse. All the salacious gossip that Rachel seemed to love. The lie was Myrra's gift to Rachel, for giving her the truth.

In Kittimer it was easy to be lulled into a sense of safety. With the bells and the mountain winds, the distant chanting and prayers, Myrra spent her days almost forgetting that the world was breaking apart, almost forgetting about Security. It was only at night it came back to her: she lay awake waiting for a cataclysmic sound, or for agents to break down her door. Waiting for the anvil to drop on their heads.

She wondered if she was being foolish, to stay in one place for so many days, but it was so calm here, and Charlotte was growing and changing, and didn't they deserve this for a little while? A place to feel safe? Just safe, for a little while.

The anvil took another few days to land. It was another lovely summery day, and she was just coming back from a shopping run—just the essentials, now that money was tight. Mashed peas and apricots for Charlotte, and sandwich supplies for herself.

The hostel's common area was empty. Myrra went about finding room in the cupboards for her food, leaving Charlotte in her stroller by the table. Everything was blissfully quiet; even the bells had stopped ringing for the moment.

She didn't immediately see Rachel enter the kitchen. She appeared right behind Myrra's shoulder, causing Myrra to jump straight out of her skin and drop the loaf of bread she'd been holding. Rachel wasn't usually that quiet.

"Oh! I'm sorry—" Rachel said, and bent to pick it up for her. "Didn't mean to startle you."

"Oh, it's nothing, I just didn't see you there," Myrra replied, taking the bread from Rachel's outstretched hand.

"Everything OK? You seem a little edgy." Rachel cocked her head in concern.

"It's nothing. Just haven't been sleeping well."

"Poor thing. The mattresses here really are a nightmare."

Myrra nodded in assent, but didn't add anything further to the conversation. Something was off with the way Rachel was acting. Her face held the same expression it always did, but today it seemed tightly fastened down, as if she were cheerful by force.

"Where's Annie?" Myrra asked her, trying to suss out the situation.

"Oh, she's in her room sleeping." Rachel waved generally in the direction of the bedroom. "Thought I'd take the opportunity to roam." She laughed a little to herself. The laugh felt forced too.

Myrra wedged the last jar of baby food onto the packed shelf and shut the cupboard door.

"That sounds nice," she said, and backed away toward Charlotte's stroller. Nothing was strictly *wrong*, but there were alarm bells going off somewhere in her chest, and Myrra trusted her instincts enough to leave. Her cash was in her pockets. That's all they'd need to disappear. If they needed to disappear.

"We'll leave you to your roaming..." she said, trying to keep her tone light. "We've got somewhere to be, actually." She gripped Charlotte's stroller and pushed her way to the door, keeping her eyes on Rachel the whole time.

The cheerful mask slipped off Rachel's face, and before Myrra could get very far, she ran at Myrra and lunged.

Rachel's hands closed on Myrra's left ankle and pulled, dragging her roughly to the floor. Myrra heard a crashing noise; Charlotte's stroller was sideways on the ground, and the baby was screaming.

Rachel grunted and panted behind her as her hands climbed, from her ankles up to her calf, clawing at her knees and bunching around her skirts. Myrra kicked at her, her foot connecting once with Rachel's cheek and again with her shoulder. But Rachel was used to pain, and she was at least fifty pounds larger than Myrra.

Myrra flailed at her with her fists as Rachel threw her body weight on top of her. Desperately Myrra's hands clawed and scratched at her attacker's face, leaving streaks of blood across her cheeks. Rachel bit Myrra's hand, drawing blood of her own. She held on to Myrra's fingers with her teeth, a wild look in her eye, and for a moment Myrra was convinced that Rachel was going to bite her fingers off. Instead she spit out Myrra's hand and seized both her wrists, pinning them down to the ground above her head. Rachel had her now, and spit in her face to prove it.

This was different from squaring off against Security. Contract workers knew how to fight.

From her spot atop Myrra, Rachel gripped Myrra's wrists in one hand, then turned behind her and reached out across the floor with the other, searching for something—what?

Myrra didn't want to find out. Taking advantage of Rachel's distraction, Myrra squirmed and wriggled out from under her, crawling toward Charlotte's overturned stroller. Every move she made left bloody handprints on the floor.

"Hey!" Rachel shouted behind her. Myrra looked back and saw Rachel standing over her, swinging something glassy and dark—a wine bottle?—toward her face. She felt something hard and cold connect with her temple; a crunch; then the world went hazy.

Myrra woke with her cheek leaning against a cement wall. Her head was pounding. It was too dark to see. When she tried to move, her arms knocked into something long and rigid. A broom handle? She reached out again, and a whole tangle of brooms and mops tumbled down on her. A closet. She was in a closet.

Myrra felt around for a doorknob; she was frustrated but not surprised when the door turned out to be locked. She rattled the door against its frame; this was a low-rent place; perhaps the hinges were weak. Perhaps the lock was cheap. There was always a way. Myrra remembered the stroller lying sideways on the floor, the sound of Charlotte crying. She didn't hear Charlotte crying now.

She slammed her body into the door, ramming it as hard as she could. It was difficult to get any momentum in such a cramped space, but she gave it her all. Even after her shoulder had gone numb with pain, and it felt as if all the bells of Kittimer were clanging in her skull, the door didn't give. She kept hitting it anyway.

"Just stop." She heard Rachel shout on the other side. "You're not going to break down that door."

"Rachel, what's going on? Let me out!" She knew what was probably going on. But she wanted to hear Rachel explain it.

She heard footsteps draw closer to the door. For a foolish, hopeful moment, Myrra thought maybe Rachel actually was going to unlock the door. Instead she spoke in a low trembling voice through the crack in the door.

"Do you think I'm stupid?" she asked. "I knew something was going on. That baby looks nothing like you. You talk to me, pretend to be my friend, get me to tell you all sorts of shit about my life and Annie and my contract..." Her voice broke.

"Where's Charlotte?" Myrra interrupted.

"I'm not going to tell you. Just to spite you, I'm not going to tell you."

Myrra threw her body against the door again, and Rachel smacked the door with something heavy in response. It made a huge noise in the closet, causing the pain in Myrra's head to ratchet up even further.

"Stop it!" Rachel hit the door one more time for good measure.

"You got me to tell you everything, and all this time, you weren't any better than me. Just thought I'd be stupid enough to swallow what you told me. You, with all your airs, swanning about with all your free time and your baby, visiting churches, wandering the town." She sniffed. "I could have done that too, if I'd killed my boss."

Rachel went quiet. Myrra felt the pressure of her body as she leaned against the outside of the door. She considered denying Rachel's accusations, sticking by her fake name and fake life, but somehow she couldn't bring herself to do it.

"I didn't pretend to be your friend," Myrra said instead. "I was your friend."

"I was your private joke."

"That's not true—"

"Shut up." The rage had left her voice, replaced by a sad tiredness. "Security will be here soon, so just stop trying to break down the door."

Security. Again, she was not surprised, but it still hit her hard. She started scrambling on the floor for something sharp. There was a chance she could fight her way out when they opened the door, if they didn't tranq her right away.

She needed to keep Rachel talking as she searched. "How did you figure it out?"

Had there been bulletins in Kittimer she hadn't seen? She pictured plastic flyers littering the streets, with just her face and the word *DANGEROUS* printed above it.

Rachel sighed, and Myrra felt it through the door. Such a thin metal surface, it was maddening she couldn't break through. Her fingers scrabbled along the dusty floor. The best she could come up with was a broken-off plastic broom handle. At least it had a sharp point on one side.

"You've got a couple scars on the insides of your arms," Rachel replied. "You worked in a laundry, right?"

"Yeah."

"My grandma had scars like that. From the heat presses."

Myrra looked down at her own forearms, though it was impossible to see anything in the dark. Still, she knew the scars that Rachel was talking about. They were so thin and faded at this point that Myrra barely remembered they were there. But Rachel had noticed them. Of course she had.

"So you figure out who I am, and your first move is to call Security. That takes a certain kind of person."

Myrra had known lots of people willing to stomp on each other to appease authority. As early as when she was working in the factory with her mother, Myrra had noticed the foremen doling out favors to workers willing to report on their fellows—strikes, stolen merchandise, even laziness on the job could be quelled with the promise of a few extra helpings in the dinner line. Myrra understood the mechanics behind it: keep the rats eating each other and they won't overtake the kitchen. But she'd thought Rachel was smarter than that.

"You never respected me, why should I treat you any better? You got out, but you were OK watching me struggle? Just so you could pretend to have some wine-and-girlfriends time with me? That takes a certain kind of person too." Rachel pushed away from the door, and Myrra felt it jostle. She heard the tap-tap of Rachel's footsteps as she walked back a few paces. "And anyway, it's a way out. Annie's not going to live much longer, and I refuse to go back to New London."

Myrra let out a small breath. She'd cut a deal. Rachel was getting out of her contract. It barely seemed possible.

She wanted to believe that even with freedom dangled in front of her, she wouldn't do what Rachel had done. But she wasn't so sure. It wasn't that long ago that Myrra had been willing to spend the rest of her life lying to a man in order to get free. This life could drive you to extremes.

But knowing what she knew now, she couldn't fathom compromising like that. Imogene had bestowed upon her a terrible gift, but a gift nonetheless. She would never do such a thing now, but who's to say she wouldn't have a month earlier, if the bribe had been just right and she had still been ignorant of her own expiration date?

So she could understand Rachel's decision. But she was still enraged by it.

"Well, I hope you enjoy your freedom. You'll be dead in weeks," she spit into the door.

The footsteps stopped.

"What—" Rachel said, but never got to finish her sentence.

Myrra heard a distant door open, the heavy authoritative steps of a Security officer, and the distinctive click of a tranq gun. Myrra gripped her broken broom handle and waited for the door to open.

24

TOBIAS

Kittimer was a huge amount of ground to cover. They had picked a hotel that they thought was in a central location, but it turned out Myrra Dal was living on the edge of town, three whole mountain peaks away. They grabbed their cuffs and guns, piled into their rental car, and were parked in front of the hostel, Myrra Dal's new hideaway, in just under an hour.

Tobias had forgotten how large Kittimer was. He'd only visited a couple of times, when he was a kid, never with Barnes. Barnes was a devout Christian, but he viewed a visit to Kittimer as being disloyal to his own local church. And he wasn't all that fond of the other things Kittimer had to offer, skiing and hiking and wine tasting, all things that had the potential to make him look foolish. But Ingrid had taken him to Kittimer once, shortly after a particularly loud fight with David. Tobias remembered hearing the crystal highball glasses they'd swiped from the hotel as they shattered against a wall. He couldn't remember what the fight had been about, or what the last straw for Ingrid had been, but she left David briefly that time, and she took Tobias to Kittimer, where she vowed that they were going to lead a more moral life. But then she'd gotten bored a couple of weeks in, and pretty soon after that they were back with David, Ingrid laughing and drunk, as if nothing had ever happened. Ingrid was good at forgetting, and as a kid, Tobias had tried to follow her example. Now all Tobias could remember about the situation was that it had seemed startlingly normal at the time.

Tobias had visited Kittimer alone once, after his parents were detained. At that time Tobias had come to Kittimer for the same reason so many did: to see if he could find his faith. His family was technically Jewish. When he suggested the trip to Barnes, his adoptive father had been supportive, telling him that a man needed to stand on his own and seek out his own identity. So he toured different synagogues, attended different services, and, after a week in the mountains, went home happy, but uncertain about the experience. Anything he did to explore his heritage strengthened his bond to David and Ingrid. And when he returned to Barnes's apartment to see the usual grilled cheese and eggs waiting for him at the dinner table (Barnes wasn't much of a cook), he ultimately decided it was fine enough to have faith in a person instead of in a gospel.

Now, with Myrra Dal so close, Tobias was looking forward to restoring Barnes's faith in him. All would be forgotten if he managed to finish the job, if he saw it through to the end.

Simpson parked them at a curb just around the corner from the hostel entrance. The building was situated on a steep switchback road, like so many buildings in Kittimer. Sometimes it felt as if the roads were nothing but turns and corners.

"How many exits?" Simpson asked as they got out of the car.

"Two," Tobias replied, happy to be reliable for information. He'd done as much research as he could on the way over. "The front door and another side exit off the kitchen, by the dumpsters."

"Got it." They rounded the corner, and Simpson took an

appraising look at the front door. "Why don't you hang back and cover the rear door. I'll handle stuff on the inside."

Tobias's face fell. He'd lost Simpson's respect entirely.

"Don't give me that look," Simpson said in response, and Tobias kicked himself again, this time for being so emotionally transparent. "Myrra Dal has seen you, she hasn't seen me. Just in case she happens to be hanging around the common space, I don't want her making a break for it."

"OK," Tobias said, feeling a little placated. He hid around the corner by the dumpsters and waited. He comforted himself thinking about future cases, future successes. He was a rookie, after all. These things happened. Perhaps he'd end up head of a bureau one day, on a different squad in a different city, out of Barnes's shadow. By that point maybe Barnes would be retired. Maybe he'd be living with Tobias, and Tobias would be taking care of him instead of vice versa.

He walked a little closer to the door. It was quiet inside. He pictured Myrra in her room cradling the baby, Simpson shattering the whole picture when he came crashing in with tranq guns and handcuffs. He forced himself to push past the sympathy; this was a society, and she had broken the law. Multiple laws. She'd cut off a dead man's hand. She'd nearly killed him with a fire extinguisher. This case was almost over, then everything could return to normal. He could return home, professional and proud. If he could just get through this case, he would still be seen as competent.

A crash inside interrupted his daydreaming. The distinctive pop-pop of a tranq gun going off. Somewhere, muffled behind the door, he heard Simpson swearing.

Tobias unholstered his gun and positioned himself flush against the wall next to the door. He waited. Inside he heard more crashes. A woman shouting. Footsteps running. A baby crying.

The door swung open in one violent motion, and Tobias found himself looking at Myrra again, which was just as surreal as the first time in Nabat. She was holding on to Charlotte with a tight, instinctive grip. She hadn't seen him yet.

"Hold it," Tobias said, with his gun leveled at her. At first she looked confused, then her face fell. In the span of two seconds her face went from vengeful to exhausted. She took a step toward him and he took a step back. Kept his gun raised.

"Please," she said. "Please."

In that moment, Tobias wasn't certain he could say why, he almost lowered his weapon, almost let her run. Something in her tone. The simplicity of it. It was her last play, he knew.

But a second later, Simpson came crashing through the door behind her, sporting a shoulder wound and carrying a blood-covered broken stick. Simpson leveled his gaze at Tobias, almost as if to say, *Well, go on.*

He pulled the trigger.

25

MYRRA

Myrra sat on the floor in another utility closet, this one at the agents' hotel, hands cuffed around the rail of a heavy set of shelves. She had been sitting in this position for hours now, and her shoulders and hips were starting to feel stiff. A single naked light bulb hummed above her, harsh and cold. They'd cleared out the shelves around her. Nothing left that she could reach for and weaponize. She didn't know where Charlotte was, and that thought stabbed through her. Her arms felt too light without the weight of her.

Myrra heard the scrape of a key in the lock on the other side of the closet door. The lock turned, and the blond agent emerged from the other side. He had a blue mug in his hand with a hotel logo on the front: "Kittimer Heights Inn." The letters arced over a white illustration of a mountain with lines shooting out from behind the mountain on all sides, like radiating light. There was a slight bulge under his blue button-up shirt, at the shoulder. A bandage, Myrra imagined. She smiled, thinking about the scratch she'd given him with the broom handle. She'd found Charlotte.

She'd made it out the back door. And that look on Bendel's face—she'd seen him waver.

She'd almost made it. Almost.

"Sorry about the accommodations here," the blond agent said, clicking the door behind him. "We'll try and find you a cushion or something if we have to wait here much longer . . . Transportation schedules are still a little disorganized after the quake."

"It doesn't matter."

He bent down in front of her and placed the mug in her hands.

"Have some water," he said, putting on a kind face. She didn't trust it, but she took the water, bending her head toward her cuffed hands and greedily downing the contents of the mug.

"I'm Agent Simpson, by the way," she heard, while her tongue lapped up the last drops of moisture. She didn't know how long she'd been here, but it felt like years. She handed the mug back to Simpson. He stood and put it on a far shelf, out of reach.

"Where's Charlotte?" she asked.

"Charlotte's safe," he replied. He almost smiled. Smug, she thought. She wanted to scream in his face, rattle the shelf till it fell over and smashed their heads in. But instead she kept quiet, almost submissive. Survive, she thought. Then she laughed at herself for thinking it, knowing what was coming.

"What's so funny?" Simpson asked.

"Nothing."

"Nothing, huh?" Simpson searched around and pulled out a folding chair that was wedged between a shelf and the wall. This must be some janitor's private hideaway, Myrra thought. Simpson unfolded the chair and placed it in the center of the floor space. He sat, leaning forward so he could loom over her. Myrra sat up a little straighter.

He looked like an aging movie star. She could tell that he had once been very fit, but in the intervening years he'd allowed his belly to grow a little slack, let the skin under his jaw sag. But he still had a perfect sweep of blond hair, still had some heft in his arms. He didn't scare her. He seemed the definition of the once-successful middle-aged male.

He didn't speak for a moment. His blue eyes scanned her, sizing her up.

"You didn't kill the Carlyles," he said.

"What, you think I'm not strong enough to pull it off?" This response would not help her case, but Myrra didn't like being underestimated. And what did it really matter in the long term?

"No, I believe you could do it. I saw what you did to Bendel's head. What you did to my shoulder. But Bendel said that you'd be too smart to snap and kill your employers. Now that I see you, I agree with him." Simpson sat up and leaned back, stretching his arms up and interlacing his fingers at the back of his head. The picture of confidence.

"I'd like to see Charlotte, please." She stared into his smug face and focused all her anger on him like a laser. She tried her best not to blink.

What time was it? Was Charlotte asleep? Had they been playing with her, feeding her at the right times? She hoped that someone had thought to hold her and soothe her, and simultaneously she hated the thought of either Tobias or Simpson bonding with her.

"Charlotte's OK, I promise you," Simpson said. "I've got kids myself, I know how to take care of a baby." He was throwing Myrra crumbs of information about himself, trying to gain her trust. He was still playing the good guy, but she knew: once they were in New London, he'd toss her in a dark cell, incinerate her, do whatever they did to contract workers who misbehaved, and Simpson would never look back.

"How old are your kids?" Let's play friendly. See where that goes. She imagined his kids had the same blond hair and blue eyes. She imagined he had a matching blonde wife.

"Let's see..." Simpson raised his eyes to the ceiling and let out a short whistle, thinking. "Brandon is six, and Julie is ten."

He pulled a tablet out of his bag, tapped and swiped the screen, and flipped it around to show Myrra a picture of his family. She'd had it wrong. His wife was shorter, with dark skin and a muscular build. Her black hair was cropped close to her head. The kids had their mother's face, skin, and hair, maybe a little lighter, but definitely not blond. They both had blue eyes like their dad. All three of them were sitting on a bench in a garden—Myrra recognized it as Sakura Park.

"They're cute."

Simpson flipped the tablet back around and stared at the image on the screen. He smiled, and this time Myrra could tell it was genuine. "Yeah, they take after their mother, that's why."

"I like that park," Myrra offered. "I used to find excuses to walk that way every time the trees were in bloom. I used to take Charlotte there, when Imogene needed her out of the house."

"Yeah, I haven't seen the cherry blossoms in a while. Always too much to do," Simpson said. He pushed a button on the tablet and the screen went black. He stowed it back in his bag. "I haven't seen my kids in a while either. And that's because of you."

His face went stern. Now it was Simpson's turn to stare daggers at her. He put his head in his hands for a moment and scrubbed his fingers through his hair in a gesture of frustration and absolute fatigue. When his head rose up again, he was wearing the good-guy mask again. He smiled at her. Not genuine.

"How about this: you tell me what happened to Imogene and Marcus Carlyle, in your own words, and I'll bring Charlotte in here so you can see her, make sure she's OK."

Myrra wanted immediately to say yes. But he was a practiced agent—he'd know if she lied, but she also knew he wouldn't believe the truth. And he wouldn't let her see Charlotte; she could never take him at his word. That false kindness, the by-the-book ways he'd tried to connect.

"I don't think I can trust you on that," Myrra said.

"Why is that?"

"I don't think you see me as anything but a report to file."

His expression faltered a little. "Listen, Myrra, I want to help you—"

"I don't blame you. These are stressful times. You want to get back to your kids," she said. The mask dropped. Now she'd hit on something. "Have you even talked to them, since the earthquake?"

Simpson didn't say anything. He wasn't smiling anymore.

"I'm just the same as you. I've separated you from your kids. And you," she said, "now you're separating me from Charlotte."

Simpson looked angrier, trying to hold it together. "That's fine," he said, standing up and pushing the chair back. The chair's metal feet scraped against the cement floor, a sudden unpleasant sound to end the standoff. "I thought we could take care of your statement now, to pass the time until we can get a train out of here, but if you don't want to cooperate, we'll just wait till we're back in New London. At that point, Charlotte will be miles away, with her next of kin or placed in the system for adoption."

He folded up the chair and walked back to the door. Myrra felt a swell of panic. This was a misstep. She couldn't go back to New London. Whatever was left of her life would be over if they managed to transport her back. She needed to stay here, where it was easier to escape, where Charlotte was still within arm's reach. Charlotte couldn't be more than a few rooms away. These guys didn't have any backup. They were glorified bounty hunters.

She needed to stay where she was until she could find her next escape route. A dropped key, an open door, maybe an ally. Tobias Bendel might take her seriously. She'd assaulted him, but she had also seen the worried look on his face. He was halfway to believing her. If she could convince him all the way, maybe he'd see how futile all this was. Maybe he'd let her go.

Simpson was halfway out the door.

"I'll give a statement," Myrra shouted after him. Simpson stopped, his hand on the doorknob. "But I'll only give it to your partner. Agent Bendel."

She could tell from the look in Simpson's eyes that this rankled him, but he nodded. She felt some pleasure in his annoyance. She'd seen enough on the ride from the hostel to understand the power dynamics at play between them. Simpson was the mentor, Tobias was the rookie. Maybe she could use that to her advantage as well.

Simpson shut the door. She was alone again with her sore body, the cold empty shelves, and the buzzing of the light bulb. Myrra thought again of Charlotte, hoped she wasn't too upset without her. She pictured Charlotte sleeping, the way her eyes darted under her eyelids when she dreamed. She focused on this thought and used it to try to keep calm. She waited.

It might have been five minutes, it might have been an hour, but eventually the closet door opened again, and Tobias Bendel was on the other side. He unfolded the same folding chair and sat down in front of her, but much more simply than Simpson. No swagger, no intimidation. He sat up very straight in his chair.

"Hi," Tobias said. "Tobias" fit him. He didn't seem like an Agent Bendel. He didn't seem like a David. The left side of his forehead was swollen and mottled with purple and green. There was a scab peeking out from his hairline. He caught her looking at his forehead and, almost as if it were a reflex, he mussed his hair to hide the bruise.

She'd really hit him hard. She was able to get a good look at him now, now that she wasn't being pushed around in handcuffs, now that she wasn't desperately trying to keep Charlotte in her sights. Charlotte was gone now. A wave of emotion burst forth at the thought, but she forced herself to suppress it. Stay in the moment, see what it can get you. There was always a way out. She would get Charlotte back.

"Sorry again, about hitting you." She jerked her hand to point at his bruise. There was a limited range of motion with these cuffs, but he seemed to understand. The bruise was so vivid and bright on his skin, it reminded her of Imogene's watercolors. Myrra liked bruises. She'd had many in her life. She had a few now, on her arms, after her last encounter with Rachel. She suspected she'd end up with some on her wrists from these handcuffs. The way the colors shifted from yellow to green to purple to blue, markers of time and healing. Bruises were proof that the blood was still pumping. They were proof that she was still alive.

"I don't think we should talk about that," Tobias said.

"Are you afraid of me now?"

"Not any more than I was before," he said.

"That's an honest answer."

He was still sitting so straight in the chair, as though his spine were fused to a metal pole. He struck her as the type of person who didn't often relax. That metal chair couldn't be comfortable, she thought, but then again, it was better than a cement floor. She remembered the feeling she'd had with him when they first met, that understanding, the feeling that, in his own way, he'd also lived a hard life.

"I think if I lied, you'd know it," he said. She smiled at that. Here was a person who did not underestimate her.

"I would," she said. "I knew you were lying from the start."

"You did?" He seemed surprised and a little humbled.

"I didn't know you were an agent, but I knew your name wasn't David."

"David's my father's name." There was a way that he said that, a different tone when he said the word *father.* There was bad blood there.

"Why did you choose it?" she asked.

"You know, I don't know. It was the first name to come into my head."

"Do you think you will know it if I lie?" she asked. He didn't answer right away, just looked at her face and thought about it. He was much calmer than he had been the last time they'd met—maybe it was just the fact that she was handcuffed now, and he had the upper hand. But there was something else: this whole conversation felt surreal, more like old friends meeting than an interrogation. She wondered if there had been some real damage done when she'd gone at him with that fire extinguisher.

"I think I would," he said finally. She thought so too.

"Do you believe me, then, that the world is going to end?" She ventured to hope.

"I believe that you believe it." He was almost willfully stoic in his response. A willful denial. There was something behind it, feelings of confusion and fear, feelings he was tamping down.

He stood up. "One minute—" he said. He stood on the chair and reached up to screw the light bulb a little tighter. The humming stopped. Myrra felt more at ease almost immediately.

"That was driving me crazy," he said. He sat back down, reached into his bag, and pulled out a tablet, let it rest on his thigh.

"I thought maybe you guys did that as some sort of on-the-fly interrogation technique."

Tobias craned his neck up to consider the bulb. "That would have been clever, but no."

He relaxed a little in his chair, finally, leaning his elbows against his knees. He seemed to be focusing himself. He reached for the tablet in his lap and pressed a button on the screen that she couldn't see.

"Myrra Dal, you've agreed to give a statement concerning the deaths of Imogene Carlyle and Marcus Carlyle. Your statement will be recorded for legal purposes. Please speak loudly and clearly." Suddenly his tone was all business. Myrra straightened herself involuntarily on her spot on the floor, in response to the shift in the conversation. She noticed he hadn't recorded the start of their conversation. That, apparently, had been different.

"Please begin by telling us, in your own words, what transpired on the night of July fifth..."

Myrra did her best to leave nothing out. Not because she wanted to help Tobias in any way, but because she hoped that the more detail she gave, the more likely it was that Tobias would empathize with her and, most importantly, that he'd believe her. If he believed they were all going to die soon, there would be no reason to bring her in. There'd be no reward for him, no light at the end of the tunnel.

There were stretches of time now when Myrra forgot that she was going to die (that everyone was going to die). Maybe it was impossible to hold on to that kind of information for any length of time before the brain tried to process it as something else. It was too much carnage for one mind to stand.

In Kittimer, especially, she had been able to forget. Instead of thinking about the sky cracking open, she would get distracted by

Charlotte's laugh or a new sound she was trying to make. Instead of remembering the way Imogene's body had hovered in space for a moment before falling, she would get caught up in the intricacies of a stained glass window or the carved rib-like arches of a cathedral.

But then the feeling would return—just walking down the street, or midway through feeding Charlotte, with the spoon poised midway between a baby food jar and Charlotte's mouth, Myrra would remember how fleeting all this was, the thought would strike her like a lightning bolt to the chest. An electric, adrenaline-fueled anxiety would return, she would feel her breath quicken and her muscles tense. Her life, Charlotte's life, everyone's life was stacked on the end of a burning matchstick.

She was feeling that anxiety now as she tried to explain to Tobias what she'd experienced in the past weeks. It was all ratcheting up in her, every fear was flooding back. And Myrra felt her senses sharpen as they had before—the gleam of the light off the metal shelves suddenly grew brighter. Every individual nerve in her wrists pricked against the abrasion of the handcuffs, in pain, but singing: I am alive. Of the drab cement of the floor and walls, Myrra could suddenly make out every shifting shade of gray, every grain of pulverized rock that made the paste that had hardened into the surface before her. And she was grateful for each sensation, she found it all beautiful, even as the tension in her body wound tighter.

Where was Charlotte? She wished she could see Charlotte.

Tobias listened to the story with a dispassionate look—difficult to make out what he thought—asking the occasional question for clarification or to spur the narrative along. When she mentioned the emails she'd read on Marcus's tablet, Tobias's face perked up in recognition. Had he read them too?

It hurt her to relive all this. Myrra was acutely aware she was breathing too fast and that her voice was getting higher. In a distant, disaffected part of her brain, she heard herself thinking that she must be on the edge of a panic attack. She tried to focus. She had to get ahold of herself. This conversation needed to go a certain way, she needed to get Tobias on her side, and she wasn't going to be able to do that if she couldn't keep control of her own emotions.

Tobias held up a hand, a signal to her to stop talking. He tapped a button on his tablet, pausing the recording.

"Are you all right?" Tobias asked. He looked concerned. "Do you want some more water?"

"No—" Her voice broke a little as she said it. She wished she had the range of motion to slap her own face. Get it under control. She took a breath, a consciously deep, drawn-out breath. "Charlotte. I'd like to see Charlotte, please."

"I can't do that yet, we need to finish this statement first. Take a moment, if you need, to breathe and calm down." He sounded sympathetic but professional. Myrra's heart fell. She hadn't yet managed to get him. She could tell by the tone of his voice, his body language, that he remained detached.

"Do you believe me?" she asked. There was a desperation in her voice that she wished weren't there.

"I believe you've told me the truth about everything that's happened to you."

"Do you believe what I've told you, that the world's going to break apart?"

Tobias sighed and shifted in his chair. He looked down at his hands, thinking. In some ways, she knew, Tobias was trying to draw her to his side the same way she was trying to draw him to hers. He had an investigation to wrap up. He had people he wanted to impress.

"I understand what you saw, and what you were told, but I can't believe it."

"But I saw the schematics—"

"I'm sure you did. But just because something was broken doesn't mean they didn't find a way to fix it," he said, looking up again. "I've read through your family's file—" Myrra jolted up, thinking he meant her mother, then realized he was referring to the Carlyles.

"They were wealthy, but they were also tense, troubled—Marcus Carlyle could have easily fallen prey to paranoia. We've traveled through space for over a hundred years. I'm sure the world's been cracked, dented, impaled, any number of things. But it still keeps going. We're not going to know about every little chink in the world's armor; information like that is what causes people to panic and riot."

Myrra searched his face. He seemed adamant, stubborn, even. "I appreciate that you believe it, and I appreciate that everything that you've gone through up until this point would mess with a person's head enough—where you would end up believing in something so catastrophic. I—" He paused again, looked into his hands again, as though searching for the next thought.

"It's not— I shouldn't really say—" Tobias pursed his lips, gathered his words. He looked at her directly and tried again. "I like you. You're smart. You know how to handle yourself." He gestured, with a half smile, to the bruise on his forehead. "I know too much about you at this point not to like you. And I can tell what you're trying to do. But I'm not going to let you go."

He had seen through her. Myrra's hope sank and fell, the image of her and Charlotte together crumbling away to ash. She felt, she felt, and she didn't want to feel. There was a heat behind her eyes, she could feel the tears coming on, and she hated herself for them.

She wouldn't cry, not in front of Security, not in front of someone so petty. She wanted to shout at him or convince him another way, but she knew if she spoke the tears would come. She had to calm down.

Tobias at least looked upset at her reaction. Almost a little guilty.

"I believe in the system," he said. He was speaking in a level, rational tone of voice. "Not that the system is perfect, but I believe that there must always be a system in place. There are people in my life whom I respect, who count on me—it matters, how we behave in a situation like this. There's a lot of things that happened to you that are unfair, but you've broken the law now too, and I have to do my job. That's how it works. Cause and consequence."

It was unbelievably frustrating. There was no convincing someone so dogmatic. Myrra breathed in and out a few times till she knew her voice would come out even. She felt the tears recede.

"Does the system matter," she asked, "if it ceases to exist in a couple weeks?"

"I don't believe it will, but yes, hypothetically, it still does."

Myrra was readying herself for another rejoinder when she heard a loud noise, somewhere outside, out of the room, out of the building, somewhere off on a distant horizon. It sounded like a screaming metal animal.

Out of nowhere, her stomach felt as if it were rising up into her chest. Her anxiety and stress must have reached a point of nausea.

But then she looked over at Tobias and realized there was something wrong with him as well. One hand clutched at his chest, and the other was gripping the seat of his chair hard. He looked confused. He looked scared. She watched him, through her own discomfort, with her heart in her throat. His chest was heaving. At first his eyes searched around the room for a cause, then finally they rested on her. He locked on to her with a questioning look, as though she might be causing this.

"What—" he said, and fell silent.

Her body felt buoyant, as if she'd been dropped in a pool of water, and her head felt lighter on her neck. A tendril of her black hair floated in front of her face, a waveform bobbing up and down in the air in front of her. She gasped in surprise as her body lifted off the cement floor and rose into the air. She thought, briefly, that it was a relief after sitting on that hard surface for so long.

She looked over at Tobias. Tobias was still staring at her, a look of shock on his face. His body hovered lightly above his chair, and the chair too was now hovering above the floor, slightly askew in the air. His hair was rippling above his head, shining brunet waves catching the light here and there. It was uncanny and beautiful. His glasses started floating away from his face. Myrra watched as he brought his arm up to catch them, and she saw how that motion propelled his body sideways. He continued to stare at her. She felt as if he was using her as his anchor.

"How—?" he asked.

"I don't know," she said, and after that they were past the point of talking. They just looked around in awe.

Myrra, at this point, was upside down. She looked down at Tobias (well, up; he was drifting above the bottoms of her feet) and felt a little jealous. Her body was now floating in space, but she was still shackled to the shelves, which were fused to the wall. He was free to move about the room; she was stuck on a short chain. Her head was a short distance away from the floor, and if she stretched her arms and legs to their full lengths, she could almost touch the gray ceiling with the tips of her toes.

Tobias's head drifted toward one of her feet, and she shoved him lightly sideways, sending his body spinning in the opposite direction.

"Hey—" he shouted in surprise. Myrra let out a short laugh, and she didn't know why. She was afraid, of course she was afraid. Tobias laughed too and then also looked confused. Something very wrong was happening. Myrra thought this was probably the end of everything. The sky would tear apart, and then everything would be sucked out into—where? Myrra wasn't even sure she knew what the universe looked like, outside their contained little world. She'd read books and seen pictures. It was all a lot of black. Just black. And instead of clutching Charlotte close at the end, as she'd planned, she was floating through the air with a man she didn't know. But through all that fear and confusion, they were, at the same time, *floating in the air.* There was wonder in that. What could she do but laugh?

Random objects were floating out of Tobias's bag, which was still bobbing close to the floor, just a few centimeters off the cement. His glasses case hovered near the ceiling. A spare pair of socks, folded into a ball, bounced off the side of Myrra's shoulder. Tobias's tablet floated between them, momentarily blocking his face from view. He looked like a body with a black rectangle for a head. Then it bobbed away toward a wall, and she could see his face again.

Then a plastic bag lifted itself up past the lip of his bag, as though it were rising in an elevator. Inside the bag was a tiny lump of blue plastic, a figurine of a man with many arms. Her mother's totem. The bag floated, and the statue floated, independent, inside it. It drifted up between their faces, as the tablet had. Tobias's face blurred and warped through the plastic.

"Where did you get that?" Myrra asked. It felt like a violation. That was a secret part of herself that he'd been carrying around next to case notes and spare socks.

"It's evidence," he said, by way of explanation. The words were rational, but he sounded like a kid who'd just been caught stealing gum.

"Why do you have it in your bag?" she asked.

Tobias tapped the edge of a shelf with his foot, pushing himself farther away from Myrra. She was still stuck upside down, seeing him upside down.

"It just seemed important to keep close," he said.

More evidence bags floated out of his satchel—she recognized a bundle of her letters to Jake. And one more, containing her book. She'd been missing these things. He wasn't supposed to have them. They looked clinical, wrapped in plastic, sealed and catalogued. Despite their terrible wrappings, though, she was happy to see them again. Her throat caught at the nostalgia of them, even though it hadn't been that long since she was sleeping on a mattress, storing these things in the mattress stuffing. So much had happened. She looked at the cover of the book through the plastic.

"The world is round," she said.

"And it goes around and around," Tobias replied.

He must have read it. Her eyes narrowed—that didn't sound like Security procedure. She was about to question him further when another lurching roar sounded off in the distance. This was it. She squeezed her eyes shut. She thought of her mother and the wild look she'd had near the end of her life. She thought of Charlotte's rosy cheeks and the warmth of her body. She thought of the shades of gray on the walls in this room, and the smooth stone of Nabat's grand chambers, and the calm pattern of waves in the Palmer Sea, and the sea of people who cycled through New London from day to day, and how beautiful and terrible it all was at the same time, how human cruelty and love could exist all at once.

She was prepared, she thought, maybe, to die. Then no, no she wasn't, and she screamed.

She thought of Tobias next to her, and thought maybe he wasn't so bad; if you had to die next to someone, he seemed at least like a person who understood her. But Charlotte, she wanted Charlotte. She wanted her mother to be here, she even wanted, in an odd way, to see Jake and Marcus and Imogene again. She hoped Sem was OK, hoped he was with his father. She hoped even Rachel was safe. She hoped someone was holding Charlotte right now, even if she couldn't be there to touch her.

And suddenly everything dropped again. She heard the folding chair clang to the floor and heard the softer *thunk* of a body—Tobias—hitting the floor as well. Myrra landed on the side of her shoulder and cried out in pain, and then cried at the thought that she was, at least, feeling pain. She was alive. She lay on her side and continued to cry, keeping her eyes closed, her arms still extended above at an odd angle to where the handcuffs kept her attached to the shelf. She pulled her knees awkwardly in to her chest and let her body shake.

Tobias groaned, somewhere away from her, on the cement. Myrra craned her neck to look at him. He was lying on his side, his back to her. The chair had landed sideways on the floor. Tobias took in a sharp breath and sat straight up, like a person waking to a harsh alarm.

"What was that?" he asked.

Myrra didn't respond. She'd said it all before. She watched him, her body twisted on the floor, her gaze partially obscured by her armpit. She was too tired to try to sit up. He clutched his side, where he'd landed, and winced.

"Are you all right?" he asked. "Can you move?"

"You have my things," she said, looking over at the scattered evidence bags on the floor.

"It's procedure," he said, in a voice so shaky it sounded as if he wasn't even convincing himself. She stared at him silently, just long enough to convey that she didn't believe him. He didn't speak.

The door of the closet whipped open, and Simpson was in the room now, looking panicked, and—thank God—holding Charlotte. Charlotte saw Myrra and started immediately squirming in Simpson's grip, reaching out for her. Myrra leaned toward her outspread arms without thinking and felt another stab of pain as the handcuffs hindered her and cut into her skin.

Simpson held on to Charlotte tighter and looked down at Tobias. "Is everyone OK?" he asked.

Myrra sat up. Her shoulder joints screamed in pain at the movement, but she could move. Nothing seemed to be broken. She nodded at Tobias, then looked back at Charlotte.

"Is she OK?" she asked Simpson. "Did she fall?"

Simpson regarded Charlotte with a frown, looking more like a concerned father than a Security agent. "She's all right. I kept hold of her the whole time."

"Thank you," Myrra said. Simpson turned his head to look at her, surprised.

Simpson adjusted Charlotte to the side of his hip, just as Myrra would have done. Charlotte continued to wriggle and thrash, but he held firm. He offered his free arm to Tobias, who took it and slowly wrenched his body up. He moved like a man of eighty rather than a young man in his prime. Maybe he was injured in the earthquake, Myrra thought. Then again, there was also the injury he'd sustained from his run-in with her. She couldn't help but be proud of that.

"Can I hold Charlotte?" she asked, even though she knew the answer. "She's upset."

Simpson and Tobias looked down at her.

"Maybe later," Simpson said. Strangely, he sounded sincere. Everyone was thrown off their usual rhythms now.

Simpson turned back to Tobias as though Myrra were no longer in the room. He looked wary, as if he was still waiting for another knockout blow to come. "We need to call in to headquarters—they'll have news."

"Uh-huh," Tobias said. He turned his head slowly toward Myrra as he spoke. He had a peculiar look on his face. He wasn't quite calm, but he did seem as if he was trying to put puzzle pieces together as he stared at her face. It wasn't a look of calm, she realized. It was a look of recognition.

"Yes," she said.

"Yes what?" Simpson asked. Tobias didn't respond to him, but as he gathered the scattered objects back into his bag, he approached Myrra with the book and the small figure, both still wrapped in their plastic sheaths. He didn't say anything to her, just handed the objects over in silence. Simpson, in a haze of confusion and trauma, disregarded the gesture entirely and pulled Tobias toward the door. Tobias never took his eyes off Myrra, even when the last visible crack in the doorway was just a sliver of his face.

Now you believe me, she thought.

26

TOBIAS

Simpson kept staring at walls. It was good he had the baby to hold, otherwise it seemed to Tobias that Simpson's body might abandon gravity again, and he would just float out the window and up through the sky.

Tobias stood in Simpson's hotel room next to the minibar and waited for the travel-size espresso machine to finish its slow drip-drip of liquid into Tobias's waiting cup. They weren't able to get through to headquarters. All the lines were tied up, and no amount of Security clout could untie them right now. They had to wait.

Myrra was right. She was right. He understood that, even though he still couldn't grasp the full cosmic consequence. It was impossible to see it all at once. His brain took it in in pieces. First he thought of the mechanics of the thing—it was something solid and mathematical to grab on to. She said there was a rupture in the hull, was that right? It wasn't something he could see—not on the sky, or the ground, or the walls of the horizon. Ipso facto, it was something on the outer shell of the world, somewhere past the walls and gears and insulation. He realized he didn't even know what existed between the inner and outer walls of the world—was it gears? He'd always imagined an impossibly dense thicket of wires, belts, and gears.

He had a fundamental knowledge of how it was all put together; they'd taught a basic summary in elementary school. He'd been made to memorize certain phrases: *outer hull*, *inner hull*, *solar sail*, *rotary axle*. Why had he never endeavored to learn what these things meant, beyond the names and their placements on a diagram?

Next his brain started calculating how long it had been, when the crack had first manifested. Myrra said the problem had been discovered over a year ago. When had the earthquakes started? The uncountable tiny earthquakes, so common in the past year that they'd begun to feel normal, like just something to adjust to. Six months ago, Tobias had taken the time to reinforce the floating shelves on his wall. It was amazing what people could excuse away.

These were all logical thoughts. The scarier ones, the more emotional ones, would come soon enough, Tobias knew. For now he stuck with what he was good at: detecting.

How long did they have left? Hard to tell.

How would it happen? No, don't go there yet.

He couldn't picture himself dying, or anyone he knew dying, but he pictured other, small things dying. He pictured the world absent grasshoppers or house cats. He pictured other, less frightening things careening through space; tablets, straws, a New London lamppost, a street cart. The hotel espresso machine, still processing coffee in the vacuum of space, so that each little droplet came out as a perfect sphere and floated away on its own through the darkness. Barnes's wood desk, still pristine, almost emitting its own light as it drifted farther and farther away from the world. The paintings that had once belonged to his family, ones that he'd never seen and now never would see, spinning through the black, never losing momentum. He thought again of the Roman Opałka painting, the one that was just numbers counting to infinity. He didn't know why he was thinking about these things.

Official-sounding chatter came blaring through the speakers bolted to the hotel wall, and the bright-blue light of the television suddenly assaulted Tobias's eyes. Simpson had turned on the news.

"The news is just coming in, regarding the, uh, phenomenon that we've all experienced. We're receiving an announcement from Parliament now—" The newscaster was doing his best to sound as if he had it together. This is it, Tobias thought. The announcement. Tobias had gotten to know the secret ahead of everyone else, but only by half an hour. It felt like a lifetime.

Tobias sat down on the bed next to Simpson and Charlotte, who was bouncing on his knee. They both watched the screen and waited.

There were a lot of diagrams. That was when the newscaster's voice sounded the strongest, when he was able to explain the minutiae of a diagram. Other times, when he was using words like *cataclysm*, *future*, and *inevitable*, his voice wavered. Tobias noticed that all the talking heads were dancing around certain words and phrases. *Apocalypse* and *end of the world* were never said.

The newscaster rambled on for over an hour with charts and statistics and interviews with experts. His eyes looked glassy. Tobias could see he was slowly winding down—he had started to repeat himself and stumble over numbers and population percentages.

"Those are the facts as we have them, currently, but stay tuned"—the man looked bewildered at what he was saying—"stay tuned for further updates. This has been Gary Meacham for News Four."

He made an odd noise after the canned speech, something between a squeal and a cough, then added, "Good luck."

The broadcast then cut to a pretaped segment on the results of the Troy football final. Simpson raised the remote in his hand and shut off the screen. He didn't speak for a long time.

"There must be shuttles, or escape pods..." he said.

"You don't bother with escape pods when there's nothing to escape to. Telos is still fifty years away," Tobias said.

"So they never even built them?"

"I guess not." It seemed strange to Tobias that they hadn't, but he also recognized the term *escape pod* for what it was: a perfectly useless security blanket.

"Can't they send an engineering team out to fix it—?"

"That's what they've been trying to do for the last year or so," he said, thinking back to Myrra describing Marcus's correspondence.

Simpson had been bobbing Charlotte up and down on his knee to keep her quiet. Tobias noticed his knee moving a little faster now, the movement becoming more of a nervous tic than a parenting tactic. The baby was starting to look perturbed.

"You're taking this very calmly," Simpson said.

"I'm not. I just don't feel like screaming." Tobias added, "Yet."

"Yet," Simpson said, parroting him.

They stayed where they were, on the edge of the hotel bed. They were very still, save for Simpson's frenetic knee. Charlotte Carlyle, as if sensing the heaviness in the air, kept quiet and looked at them both, uneasily, from one face to the other.

"We need to go home," Simpson said finally. He stood and handed Charlotte to Tobias. He walked over to his bag, pulled his tablet and earpiece out of a pocket, and began searching for numbers on the touch screen. There was no way he'd get a call through to the bureau, Tobias thought—now, after the news broadcast, it was only going to be more difficult to get in touch with New London Security.

"Hello, my love; no, I'm OK—" Simpson made a beeline for the bathroom and closed the door behind him.

Of course. Only Tobias the Automaton would assume that a person would call headquarters at a time like this. Tobias considered whether he could call Barnes at home, but no, he would be working right now. Probably mapping out plans for crowd control, bracing for the ensuing panic. He couldn't call Barnes at headquarters, and suddenly he desperately wanted to hear his voice.

Tobias held Charlotte up in the air, gripping her under her armpits. This was the first time he'd held her. Her feet dangled and swayed. She looked back at his face and reached out, trying to grab his nose. She hooked a single finger into his nostril and tugged at his face, like a fisherman reeling in a catch. Tobias cried out in surprise, and in pain; Charlotte was much stronger than he'd expected her to be. Were all babies this strong? He always felt as if he needed to treat babies the same way one would treat fine bone china, as if they were apt to shatter at the slightest gesture. But Charlotte had heft to her; she'd grown considerably since the last picture he'd seen, the family portrait that Barnes had brought up on his tablet. Babies grow fast, he thought. He'd never spent much time around kids.

He lowered Charlotte so her feet balanced on his knees. Charlotte took her finger out of his nose and waved her arms around, trying to balance upright on her own. Her eyes were wide and black in the dim room. Tobias still had both hands around her torso, but now he pulled them back and let them hover just a millimeter away from her on all sides, just close enough to catch her, but far enough that she had the freedom to balance if she was able. She teetered one way, and Tobias's left hand bolstered her. She teetered slightly the other way, and she was saved by Tobias's right hand. Then she swayed, cautiously upright, in the middle.

Tobias smiled at Charlotte and nodded at her to give her a physical gesture, to let her know how well she was doing. He counted the seconds, how long she stood on her own: one—two—three—four—five—six—

Her left knee buckled, and Tobias caught her and held her tight. His first incongruous thought was, I'll have to tell Myrra. Myrra will be so excited.

He stood up, raised Charlotte above his head, and spun, just as he'd seen Myrra do. Charlotte giggled and laughed. Tobias laughed too. This wasn't what he should be doing, but it was all he wanted to do. He knew, logically, that his senses weren't reliable right now, that he was probably in a panic state, but from where he stood, it looked as if Charlotte's face was glowing.

He flopped back onto the bed, still holding the radiant Charlotte in the air, her feet dangling above his face. He kept laughing, and then all at once he was crying at the same time. Crying and laughing and crying, until he could barely breathe.

He wondered how many people had heard the news and how many were still ignorant. Everyone would know in the cities, and, thanks to gossip, everyone in smaller towns would know within an hour or two. Tobias wondered if there was anyone out there more isolated, someone who might just wake up one morning, and, without warning, end up sucked up into the sky. What if someone was on a long camping trip right now—somewhere in the outer Kittimer range, or in that big forest park between Troy and New London? Could it be possible to go on not knowing, right up until the end? Would that be preferable?

Charlotte pointed one of her toes and kicked him in the chin, as if to say, Pay attention to me, you doofus. Tobias smiled a half smile and looked up at the soles of her feet, and the tiny creases in her skin between the ball and arch of each foot. Her skin would never wrinkle or age. Then he thought of himself in the same way: he would never get wrinkled, would never get fat, would never go bald or gray.

The tears subsided; Tobias took deeper breaths and felt a little calmer. Charlotte kicked him in the chin again.

"Hey," Tobias said, feigning annoyance. He lowered her until she was sitting on his chest. She rose up with every inhalation and down with every exhalation. Charlotte pursed her lips and pushed them out, almost as if she were getting ready to blow a smoke ring.

"Whoooooooooooo," she said, letting out a high-pitched singsong tone. She seemed satisfied with the result.

"Are you an owl?" Tobias asked her. He wondered if Myrra had ever taken her to the zoo, back when she still served the family.

"Whoooooo!" she sang out again, much louder this time. This girl had pipes. She would have made a good singer, Tobias thought.

The bathroom door opened again and Simpson came out in a rush.

"We need to charge up the rental car and head out before anybody gets the idea to steal it. There's no way we're going to be able to get back to New London by train." Simpson had a fistful of toiletries in his hand from the bathroom, a toothbrush, a miniature tube of toothpaste, a comb, and a razor. He chucked them all into the open bag, along with his tablet.

"How is Ruth?" Tobias asked in a small voice. For some reason Simpson's tone sounded angry, demanded submissiveness.

"She's scared," Simpson said. "Everybody's scared."

"How are the kids?" he asked.

"They don't really understand. They're scared because Mom's

scared." Simpson's face was crumbling. Tobias wanted to fix it. He sat up, readjusting Charlotte on his lap.

"OK—OK, we'll take the rental and just drive it back. We'll go now, like you said, while everyone's still in a panic haze, and get out before any riots start. We'll pack Myrra and Charlotte in the back seat, and—"

"Why would we take them with us?" Simpson interrupted with an incredulous look.

"What?" Tobias wished he had a more coherent response. He hadn't thought of a scenario where they wouldn't be bringing Myrra Dal back with them.

"As far as I'm concerned, whatever trouble she was in—she's cleared. With what's going on, we've all got bigger things to worry about now. She wants us to let her go, she wants to take the baby—I say we let her. They'll just slow us down on the way back."

"But—" Tobias was searching for words. He suddenly felt very frustrated. "No. We still have a job to do."

Simpson looked at him as if he were absolutely insane. Tobias knew, in some part of his brain, that what he was saying made no sense. But something made him say it anyway. He wasn't sure if it was stubbornness, or if he still felt the specter of Barnes's disappointment—but surely Barnes wouldn't be disappointed in him now, not with mortality looming in front of them all, inescapable. He didn't want to investigate why, he just knew that he didn't want Myrra Dal and Charlotte to leave.

He said none of this to Simpson, just let his absurd protestation hang in the air between them.

Simpson zipped up his bag and reached out for Charlotte. Tobias held on to her a little tighter and didn't move.

"We can talk about this later," Simpson said. "Right now, go back to your room and pack. We'll give the baby to Myrra Dal to take care of. I have to go see if there's any available charging ports in the hotel's garage—that rental's fairly new, a full battery should get us back home in one go."

Simpson stood over Tobias and waited, his arms outstretched, to take Charlotte. He was lying, Tobias could tell. He wasn't just going to give Charlotte back; he was going to let them go. Tobias had officially lost Simpson's trust with his crazy argument—Simpson was going to act on his own now. Tobias wanted to punch him, wanted to run with the baby, wanted so many things. He wanted to talk to Barnes. He wanted the world to make sense.

Instead he deposited Charlotte into Simpson's waiting arms.

"OK," he said.

"I'll be coming back here once it's charged. Pack. Get whatever supplies you think you'll need. Meet me back here in an hour," Simpson said. Tobias wondered if he could believe him on that at least. He sounded sincere.

"OK," he said again, and headed toward his own hotel room to pack a bag, already wishing that Simpson would return, not wanting to be left alone with his own thoughts.

Inside the hotel there had been a cocoon of quiet, but outside, the world was officially ending: people wandered the streets crying and shouting, every other second a car horn honked or tires screeched as families sped out of town. To go where?

Lots and lots of bells, coming from the various temples and places of prayer. Hopefully spiritual leaders could keep the town relatively calm. Riots had broken out in New London; Tobias had made the mistake of checking his tablet for the news. Barnes was out there.

He had a vague notion that he should buy water bottles.

The walk to the convenience store down the street shouldn't have felt dangerous, but on the way he had to dodge two cars that hopped the curb in a vain attempt to escape traffic. A woman in a gray business suit knelt weeping a few feet from the store door.

The shelves of the store had mostly been ransacked. There were only a dozen or so bottles of water left. Tobias opened the empty backpack he'd brought and swept the remaining stock into his bag. There was still an untouched box of protein bars at the sales counter. Tobias loaded them into his bag as well.

Improbably, there was still a cashier in the store. He didn't pay attention to the empty shelves at all, or to the people running in and out the door with merchandise in their arms. Instead his eyes were glued to a news broadcast playing on a screen above the register. Tobias heard the name "Nabat" and stopped to listen.

"Due to a combination of quakes and the world's recent state of weightlessness, the small tourist town of Nabat has suffered a devastating cave-in. Nabat, a cavern community situated in the cliffs just off the coast of the Palmer Sea, had incurred a considerable amount of structural damage in the wake of recent quakes. The collapse occurred just minutes before the hull breach was announced—" The newscaster's voice sounded high and tense, like that of someone desperately clinging to an official script in order to keep together.

Tobias tuned out the rest of the broadcast. He didn't want to hear any more. He said a prayer for the beautiful collapsed pillars and carved walls, for the people living in the catacombs and the refugees sleeping on floors, washed up from Palmer. How many people had been in Nabat when it collapsed?

More haunting still was that Tobias knew he'd never find out. They'd all be dead before an account of the bodies could be made. It was possible there weren't even enough resources to try for rescue or cleanup. With everything collapsing at once, authorities might have to leave them all entombed in the cliffs.

The cashier gave him a blank look when he handed over his account card.

"What's the point?" he asked.

Tobias didn't know a logical response to this, but he couldn't fathom not paying.

"Call it courtesy," Tobias said, and forced the card into the man's hand. He charged it with a short humorless laugh.

Back on the street, Tobias felt his tablet buzz in his bag, and he scrambled to reach it underneath the box of protein bars. The call was coming through from New London Security Bureau Headquarters.

"Barnes?" Tobias waited to hear his gruff voice, maybe the crunch of him eating biscuits in the background. Only Barnes would bother to call him in these times. He'd been friendly with the other guys on the force, but he'd never made any real friends. No one who would call him in a crisis. It was hard for Tobias to know what he ought to do with himself, now that he was facing down the end of everything. He felt like an actor who had been thrown onstage to improvise a scene with no context. The world was ending: What should he do next? What should he do with his hands?

But Barnes felt like a good answer to all those questions. It was what people did, in times of crisis. They stayed with their families. They supported one another. Simpson was right. It was time to head home.

The voice on the phone was not Barnes's voice. A young voice, as young as his own, maybe younger, responded. "Agent Bendel?"

"Yes, this is Agent Bendel."

"I'm afraid I have some terrible news." The young agent seemed shaken and eager to stick to the official bureau script. It was something to hang on to, in uncertain times. Tobias knew that as well as anyone. Tobias waited on his end of the call, allowing silence to be his response. He was too worried about what came next, too worried to say anything that would coax the conversation along. The young agent waited for a few more wordless seconds. Tobias could feel his uncertainty.

"Um," the agent continued, finally. "I'm so sorry to be the one to tell you this, but we just got word—Director Barnes was discovered dead an hour ago, on the sidewalk. He was found under a pile of rubble after a building collapsed. A number of New London structures have suffered partial collapse; they were structurally weakened during the quake, and now rioters have been running in and out where they shouldn't—"

"Stop," Tobias interrupted. The agent stammered but fell silent. "That can't be right—he should be in the office right now."

"Director Barnes was actually off duty at the time," the agent said. His voice was measured; he was worried about getting cut off again. "Near as we can tell, he went out on his own to help with crowd control. We think he followed a group of people into an unstable building, and shortly thereafter the walls and second floor collapsed."

This was absurd. Barnes couldn't die on the same day that Tobias learned the world was ending. Everything was accelerating and spinning out of control as if he were strapped in on a broken carnival ride; he couldn't get off. He shook his head and tried to concentrate. Barnes was dead. Were there others in the rubble? What was the state of his body? The agent hadn't said. It didn't matter. Died in a riot, died pleasantly in his sleep, whether it was a quick surprise or slow and expected, whether it was violent or peaceful, it was wrong, because Barnes had died without Tobias by his side. Tobias had failed him. Barnes had died, and Tobias hadn't been there.

There on the sidewalk in Kittimer, with people moaning and crying all around him, Tobias felt his knees collapse under him. He crouched against a wall outside the entrance to the hotel. He opened his mouth, but no sound came out. Tears coursed down his face. He was now one with the crowd in its collective mourning.

"Hello? Hello?" The agent was still on the line. Tobias didn't respond, just listened to the agent's confused voice through the speaker, unwilling to let the moment pass. He couldn't think of a thing to say.

27

MYRRA

Myrra sat on the cement floor, still shackled to a shelf, and still feeling the absence of Charlotte, but the pain was a little duller with a book in her hand. At least her mind had someplace else to go.

She turned the page and relished the matte pulp feel of real paper in her hand, the way the pages faded from white to brown at the edges. It was a totem she could touch and hold and feel the weight of.

Her mother's old totem was also back with her, now resting snug in her dress pocket. Myrra was less sure about its return than she was about the book's. Something about what she'd been through, the knowledge of her—well, everyone's—impending death, the shock of having Charlotte taken away from her, it had made all her old wounds reopen and bleed afresh. Every time she cried, she was crying about not just one pain but every pain and frustration she'd ever experienced. Myrra took the totem out of her pocket and examined it. Its placid, smiling face was laughing at her. She hated her mother anew. Life had been tough for her;

Myrra knew that firsthand. So life was painful, but what else was there to do except fight through it? If her mother had been unable to fight for herself, Myrra thought she could have at least fought for the sake of her daughter, fought to protect her.

That morning as a child when she woke up and her mother wasn't there, the factory foreman had still tried to rouse her to work a shift—the littlest children were often tapped to sweep the metal shavings off the floors and do bits of spot cleaning. Instead of going along willingly, she gripped her mother's pillow, screamed, and kicked at the foreman's arms, getting more and more violent until finally the man gave up and decided it wasn't worth the trouble. Then she stayed in the dorm bed all day and cried so hard she gave herself stomach cramps. She did the same thing the next day, fighting off the foreman again, this time the foreman getting more irate but still unwilling to injure himself handling a little girl.

On the evening of that second day, another worker passed by the bed and stared down at her. She had just finished a shift on the floor; her tan uniform was covered in iron filings. Her face was covered in the same metallic gray; there was a circle of clean skin around her nose, mouth, and eyes where her goggles and face mask had been. Myrra had cried herself down to a shaky husk; all she could do was look up at the woman from her spot curled up on the bed and sniffle.

"The foreman's going to sell you soon if you don't get out of bed, and it won't be to anyplace good."

Myrra didn't offer any sort of response, just glared back and got ready to kick if this woman tried to drag her out of her spot the way the foreman had. But the woman didn't make a move to touch her. Instead she crouched down next to the bed so she was at eye level with Myrra.

"Today you mourned her," she said. "Now what are you going to do tomorrow?"

Then she stood and walked away toward the dorm bathrooms, presumably to rinse the metal off her skin.

The next week, that same woman shoved Myrra out of a food line in order to get the last piece of bread on the tray. People give and people take. But Myrra absorbed the lesson that her mother had never learned, and with every new chapter of survival in Myrra's life, there was more resentment for the woman who had seemingly given up.

But she had hung on to her mother's deity this long, and she didn't know why; moving from place to place, always making room for it in a little pocket in the mattress. Maybe one could value an object out of both love and spite; she kept the figure because she missed her mother, and she kept it as a reminder of her mother's failings.

Maybe the loss of gravity meant that the end was coming soon. Maybe it was just another hiccup in a long parade of problems the world would experience before it finally gave up and broke apart. But it was not worth it to stay crying on the floor. She would push and kick her way forward until the sky split apart above her. What else was there to do? She tried to think of the next possible solution. Maybe she could escape in transit. The trick would be getting Charlotte and keeping her safe during the escape.

The shunting sound of the door's dead bolt rang out in the empty room, made Myrra jump. The door swung open, and Agent Simpson stood before her, holding Charlotte. It was as if, by thinking of Charlotte, Myrra had summoned her. Why was he bringing her in here? A few scattered hopes and scenarios ran through Myrra's head, but she waited silently for the explanation before getting too ahead of herself.

Charlotte fussed and wriggled in Simpson's grasp, as she had before when he'd brought her in.

"There's something wrong with the ship. It's all over the news. Everyone's going to die," Simpson said, keeping an iron grip on the struggling baby.

"Yes, I know."

"I thought you might," he said. He let out a short exhalation that might have been a laugh. It was hard to tell. He wasn't smiling. "Is that why you ran?"

"Yes."

He sounded too calm, too matter-of-fact. It sent surges of worry through Myrra. She had flashes of Imogene holding Charlotte on the edge of the roof deck. She readied herself to talk Simpson down off some similar ledge.

Instead he fished a key ring out of his pocket and knelt down to unlock Myrra's handcuffs. Then he handed Charlotte to her.

"This is not what I want to be doing in the last days of my life," he said.

Myrra immediately started crying again, relief flowing through her and gushing out of her. All she could think to say was, "Thank you."

Simpson's eyes were welling up as well. "So maybe I'm not such a bad guy, after all."

Myrra could see he needed the reassurance. If he was willing to give her Charlotte, she was more than willing to do him a good turn.

"You're a good person. And a good father," she said. "And you should go home to your kids."

"Yeah," Simpson said, and wiped his running nose with the back of his hand. "Yeah."

He stood up and made for the door.

"Good luck," she heard him say, though he didn't turn back to look at her.

"You too," she shouted back to the closing door. Then she turned her attention to Charlotte, nuzzling her face, kissing her hair, smelling the top of her head. She stood up, and her joints seized with pain after being in the same position for so long. Myrra ignored it and ran out the door: she would need to get a bag and as many supplies as she could steal as quickly as possible, and then they needed to leave the city. There were too many people in Kittimer—maybe their fear would manifest in more temple services and more prayer, but Myrra couldn't take that risk. There was always the chance that people would go the other route and turn violent. Myrra didn't want to be here when the chaos erupted.

Everything in Kittimer was chaos, which made it especially hard to find a spare vehicle. But when she did finally find a scooter charging in a back alley, that did make it all that much easier to steal. She packed it full of as much water, diapers, and energy bars as she could carry. The people of Kittimer weren't rioting, per se: there were no smashed windows, no fights breaking out. There was noise: as Myrra drifted in and out of different buildings seeking supplies, every shop had its screen tuned in to the news, its brightness assaulting Myrra, the chatter on one screen overlapping with the chatter of another in a different room so it sounded as if the newscasters were having some kind of escalating argument.

Most people were just trying to get out of town, and if they weren't locked in traffic, they were wandering the streets with vacant looks on their faces, veering one way and then another, as if they were unsure of their direction. Bells clanged at all different pitches from every mosque, temple, church, and cathedral, another noise to join in the argument with the news reports.

Traffic was gridlocked. Myrra thanked her luck that it was a scooter she'd found to steal. She wove between lanes, around and through honking cars, and sometimes on sidewalks if it felt safe enough. The roads twirled downward around the spires of the mountains, zigzagging on hairpin turns through increasingly steep switchback slopes. Here and there cars smashed into each other in the traffic, but nobody got out and shouted, everyone stayed in their cars and did their best to just keep moving. There was more to worry about now than a dented bumper.

A flower cart had been overturned on a sidewalk—in an effort to go around an especially wide box truck, Myrra turned the scooter up onto the sidewalk, the front wheel plowing over piles of spilled roses and chrysanthemums, causing petals of yellow, orange, red, and pink to explode into the air around them. Charlotte laughed and reached out to try to catch them, but Myrra had wrapped Charlotte too tightly against her body to allow for much movement. The flowers were beautiful. Charlotte's laugh was beautiful. The feeling of air on the skin of her wrists, instead of steel cutting in and bruising, was beautiful.

Where was everybody going? Maybe some sought out family; Myrra thought of Simpson and said a small prayer that he'd get back to his wife and kids. What sort of family did Tobias have? He seemed more adrift. A pedestrian ran in front of her scooter, so close that Myrra nearly hit her, then continued on down an alley, on her way to—somewhere. Maybe some people just wanted to visit one last beautiful place, a place they held dear in their memory. Myrra didn't know why people's automatic reaction to an apocalypse was to think they needed to move, needed to leave their current location, wherever that happened to be. She couldn't judge; it had been the same for her. When she was told that the world was ending, with no single goal to grab on to, Myrra's first impulse had been to run. And she was running now, again, maybe to get away from the crowds, or maybe just to keep from standing still.

And where was she headed? Out of instinct she'd stolen a vehicle, but past that she had no real aim. No one was chasing her now; she didn't even need to leave, but she knew she didn't want to stay.

She stopped the scooter and idled at the corner, realizing that the street to her left looked familiar. She had walked down that sidewalk with Charlotte, on the way back from buying bread. It dawned on her: without meaning to (or maybe she had, in some part of her brain), she had directed them back to the hostel. It was only a few blocks away from this corner.

Myrra laughed to herself. It wasn't a bad idea to stop back in; there could be more food there worth taking, and some of her clothes and luggage had been left behind in the room. She turned the scooter left, weaving around a throng of people sitting down in the middle of the street, obsessively praying, and through the cars that honked around them.

Inside the hostel it was dark. Had someone cut the power?

"Ah! Ah!" Charlotte shouted out suddenly in the dark space, eager to hear an echo.

"Shhh..." Myrra said, smoothing her hair and kissing the warm skin of her forehead. It wouldn't do to make too much noise.

Myrra dragged the scooter inside with her, wary of leaving it on the street. Someone would do to her what she had done; she felt a brief flash of guilt at her theft, but as soon as it rose up she shoved the feeling away. This was the end of the world. The rules were different.

They walked into the hostel's common rooms and rifled through the kitchen cupboards. The food had mostly been picked clean, though Myrra found a half-full bottle of cooking sherry in one of the back corners and shoved it down into the limited space in her bag. Anything alcoholic or flammable was worth taking, though her backpack was getting so full the seams were threatening to burst.

Someone had ransacked her room as well, though she found some of her clothes on the floor. They must not have been the right size, Myrra thought. She struggled to stuff what she could into the side pocket of her pack.

"Did you escape, or did they let you out?"

Myrra rose up, full of adrenaline. Rachel was standing in the doorway.

She looked a little worse for the wear. A bruise bloomed across her cheek where Myrra had kicked her; long streaks of scabs made their way across her face and neck from Myrra's nails. Rachel didn't make a move to come in.

"They let me go."

"I'm not sure I believe you," Rachel said in a strange lofty way. It almost sounded as if she was joking. It definitely sounded as if she was drunk. Myrra remembered there had been a lot of wine bottles in the kitchen last time she'd been here.

"It doesn't really matter much if you do or don't." Myrra stood with her pack. With the supplies on her back and Charlotte swaddled against her front, it almost balanced out.

"Look at you, you're like one of those ants who carries a million times its own..." Rachel let out a derisive laugh and didn't finish her thought.

"Right before they arrested you, you told me I was going to die. And here I am—I'm going to die. I don't know how you knew."

The smile slipped off her face. She leaned against the doorjamb with a bitter, exhausted expression that mirrored the darker feelings in Myrra's own heart.

Myrra didn't respond. She truly didn't think Rachel wanted her to.

Rachel didn't feel like a threat anymore. But Myrra still wished she would get out of the doorway so she and Charlotte could leave.

Leave—to go where? a small voice inside taunted her. She had been running away from plenty, but she had nowhere to run to. Oh, what did it matter? Anywhere they went, she was no better than the people wandering outside. They would run and run in circles till doomsday.

"In any case, maybe I should thank you," Rachel said. "Because of all this, I've finally left Annie."

"You make it sound like I'm causing the world to break apart."

"It feels like you are." Rachel's eyes hardened on her. Maybe there was still a threat there. Myrra took a reflexive step back.

"It's so fucked up, the things you think you have to do. I never had to stay. I should have left ages ago. Or maybe I should have just shoved Annie off a roof, like you did."

Myrra didn't refute the implied accusation. There is no refuting drunken logic.

"What have you done with Annie?" she asked. Annie might have been a terrible employer in earlier days, Myrra didn't know. It still seemed cruel to kill her now, when she was mindless and vulnerable.

Rachel let out another barking laugh at the look of concern on Myrra's face. "Relax. I'm not you. I sedated her and left her in the room. Her daughter will send someone to fetch her."

"You spoke to Annie's daughter?" Myrra wondered privately of the chances of anyone being able to transport Annie back to New London in all this chaos.

Rachel shoved herself off the doorjamb, struggling to stand upright. She backed into the hall and wandered in the direction of her own rooms. Myrra was grateful to not be penned in by her any longer, but still kept an eye out as Rachel wandered down the abandoned corridor, a black silhouette against the pink light pouring in through the stained glass.

Rachel's silhouette spoke, her voice steeped in sarcasm.

"Of course. She told me not to worry. Their family knows the right people. They qualify for Escape."

"Escape? What escape?" Myrra asked, the word lighting up her mind like a match in a dark room.

"Who cares? I didn't ask the specifics. It's not meant for the likes of you or me. The rich will always be taken care of a little better than the rest of us. They even die better than we do."

The silhouette wandered farther down the hall, stumbled over something on the floor, possibly a bottle, and, with all coordination gone, fell down with a great heaviness, the heaviness of giving up. Despite her wariness, there was still enough friendly feeling left in Myrra for her to walk over and check that Rachel was OK.

Rachel lay prostrate on the ground, her thick black hair sticking out at all angles. Myrra stood over her, unsure if she was there to help or just to witness the spectacle. Rachel's nose was bleeding. The muscles in her stomach were seizing and shaking her body; Myrra couldn't tell if she was laughing or crying. She pinched her arm, trying to get her attention.

"What did you mean, escape? Are they dying better, or surviving better?"

"Don't kid yourself. We're all dying." It was definitely laughter. Rachel's body was shaking with morbid laughter. "Look what they make us do. I betrayed you. I shouldn't have betrayed you," she said. "But you betrayed me too. You should have told me… We're the same. You should have told me."

The features of her face bunched up and contorted, full of anger and irony.

"I feel like breaking things. I think that's what I'll do with the rest of my life. Break things." Rachel stared up at Myrra with an intensity that made Myrra think she'd suddenly gone sober. "And if you don't leave soon, I'm going to start with you."

28

TOBIAS

Tobias was ten when David and Ingrid were detained. It was in New London. They had left him in the apartment that morning, an apartment Tobias now recognized had been a squat. David and Ingrid had taken over the luxe high-rise apartment of some well-to-do family who were summering elsewhere. David had ruffled his hair and said, "We'll be back later, kiddo," and Ingrid had been too busy looking through her purse for a missing lipstick to say anything to him at all. Then they were out the door. It was the last time Tobias had ever seen them in person.

He'd waited all day in the apartment and late into the night. It wasn't unusual for his parents to be gone longer than they'd claimed, so he went about his day as usual, cooking noodles on the stovetop for lunch, finding bread in the cupboards for a peanut butter sandwich dinner. He watched all the late-night comedy shows, brushed his teeth, and then stumbled into bed. The next morning, he was still alone. A little rarer, but not unheard of. He scrambled himself an egg and watched the morning news. Around noon there was a knock on the door. Ingrid and David had instructed him to never answer the door when they weren't there. He turned off the TV screen, avoided creaks in the floors, and let the person knock. They were persistent. Usually people stopped after three and went away. This person knocked five, six, eight times. Finally a deep masculine voice called through the door: "Tobias? Tobias—your mom and dad sent me. Can you open up the door?"

Tobias still didn't answer, but he was getting scared now. Once a loan shark had tried that tactic on him, looking for collateral to make sure David paid his debts. He stood silent and stared at the doorknob, wishing he were tall enough to reach the peephole. The person on the other end made a grumbling noise, and soon there was a scratching sound near the doorknob. He remembered wondering if the person had a key or was picking the lock. The door opened, and Tobias could tell immediately that the man wasn't a loan shark. The agent's badge was the dead giveaway, of course, but there was also something honest and solid about him. He had both feet planted firmly on the ground. Even back then, Barnes had sported his mustache and same haircut, though at that time his hair was more brown than gray. He had a barrel chest that, even in those days, you could foresee migrating lower and becoming a potbelly.

He strolled up to Tobias and held out his hand to shake. Tobias, leery of the situation but not especially afraid of the man in front of him, took it.

"I'm Agent Barnes," he said. "I've come to collect you."

"Where are David and Ingrid?" he remembered asking.

"Is that what you call them?" Barnes had been surprised.

"They don't like me calling them Mom and Dad," Tobias said. "It makes them feel old."

"Age is inevitable," Barnes said matter-of-factly. "They should let you call them Mom and Dad." He wandered through the apartment toward the kitchen.

"You must be hungry," he said.

"I made myself breakfast," Tobias responded, following him. "Can you tell me where David and Ingrid are, please?"

Barnes stood in the kitchen door, took in the washed-up pots and pans, the half-finished plate of scrambled eggs, the spatula, and the empty juice glass. He turned to look at Tobias, his eyes widened in appreciation.

"You really did cook," he said.

Tobias nodded.

"You do this a lot?" he asked.

Tobias nodded again.

Barnes put his hands on his hips, assessing the situation, looking back and forth between the kitchen and Tobias.

"You're a bit different from your parents, aren't you?" he asked then. Tobias remembered that Barnes had had a way of speaking to him even then, talking to him like a rational adult instead of a kid, never talking down. He'd liked that from the start.

Barnes guided him over to the apartment's breakfast nook, sat him down in one chair while he sat down in another, so that for the first time they were facing each other eye-to-eye.

"Your folks were detained yesterday afternoon on charges of credit card fraud," Barnes said. "Do you know what that means?"

Tobias shook his head. He was getting a little scared now, but didn't want to show it in front of the Security agent.

"It's OK if you don't," Barnes said. He leaned back in his chair and didn't speak for a couple of minutes. He was looking at Tobias as if he was trying to figure him out, with a certain level of appreciation. It reminded Tobias of the way David would look at paintings he really liked.

"Here's what I'm going to do," Barnes said finally. "I'm going to take you out for a milkshake. Whether you're hungry or not, everyone's always got room for a milkshake. And you can ask me all the questions you want about David and Ingrid, and what happened to them, and I promise to tell you the truth. I will not lie to you." He bent forward and enunciated each word in that last sentence, as if it was especially important.

He held out his hand to shake, as if they were closing a deal. Tobias took it. He was still scared, but he appreciated anyone who took the truth that seriously.

They'd gone out for a milkshake down the street, and Tobias had asked a lot of questions, and, true to his word, Barnes took the time to answer every one, with as much clarity and detail as he could muster. The conversation ended up taking hours, and they went through two milkshakes, a plate of chicken, and two plates of fries. Barnes never showed any trace of impatience.

And a couple of weeks later, after the paperwork had been pushed through the proper channels, Tobias was living with Barnes. It was the safest he'd ever felt.

Alone now.

Tobias walked past the hotel's front doors. He was due to meet Simpson but couldn't go inside yet. To go inside meant moving on to the next thing. He couldn't move on just yet. The shock of grief had muffled the sounds around him, but now as he walked he observed his surroundings again and felt the cacophony of sound. Everywhere he went he bumped into people making noise, sometimes crying, but sometimes just emitting long sustained sounds. Sounds that he couldn't fathom coming from human voices. And the bells, everywhere the bells—where in New London there would be sirens and Security protocols blaring out of speakers fixed over the streets, here the community answer to public panic came in the form of bells. They clanged at all octaves, hummed in different areas of his bones; the higher tones buzzed in the top of his skull, deeper ones in his hips. If he concentrated, he could pick out the peal of bells that resonated in his chest, thrummed at the same frequency as his sadness. He walked in the direction of those bells.

Blocks away from the hotel—five, six, who was counting?—Tobias entered a temple, squeezed past other mourners, some panicked and loud, some still. They were mourning the world, Tobias was mourning Barnes. And the world. Everything. Tobias was mourning everything. The chiming of the bells—his bells—came from somewhere high above him and resonated down the walls, through the floors, through his shoes.

The walls were bare granite, but farther in, near the center of the temple space, a crowd of people had gathered in a pool of colorful light. Every person had their neck craned up toward the ceiling. Tobias followed them and looked up too.

A huge stained glass dome hovered several floors above him, shining color down upon his face. He scanned the fragments of color without focus until his eyes rested on one particular panel: a man with a paintbrush dripping with red, poised in front of a doorway. Tobias recognized the scene from his father's barely used Haggadah. The lamb's blood, painted above the door, would spare the Israelites from God's plague. In light of what was happening, it was a terrifying image. Despite this, despite all he knew, Tobias felt his eyes well up with tears, just as the walls and floor welled up with sound. He felt acutely aware of his own body, of every nerve pricking through his skin. The color was unbearably intense. He'd never felt such an intense reaction to color before, not even with any of the paintings David had shown him.

It wasn't right, the beauty of it. Everything should be in

monochrome now. There were studies, Tobias remembered—when people suffered from depression, apparently colors actually appeared duller. These colors were hitting his eyes with such saturated intensity, it was as if he were experiencing color for the first time. It didn't feel right.

The crowd shifted and shoved him, and Tobias stumbled into a pure patch of blue. He raised a hand in front of his face. In the light, his skin was blue. The most brilliant blue he'd ever seen. And if he smiled, his teeth would be blue. And if he opened his mouth, the blue would shoot down inside him, filling him up from the soles of his feet, overtaking his body. Maybe he could find Barnes again here, in this blue. Maybe that was why he felt this way; maybe Barnes was part of the blue.

Even as he thought it, the logical part of his brain shut him down. Barnes is dead. The feelings you feel are just heightened chemical reactions due to grief. You can never find Barnes again, certainly not in a temple, under some bits of stained glass.

And just like that, the blue was back to being a color once more. The world dulled around him. Even the bells quieted, stopped humming just for him. Tobias was abandoned; even in the throngs of people around him, he was completely and utterly isolated.

He thought of Barnes, alone and bleeding out under rubble. What would they do with his body? Tobias wasn't there to make arrangements. Would anyone even think to hold a funeral, in all this mess? More likely Tobias would never get to see Barnes's body, would never get to see Barnes, in any form, again.

His life felt half-lived, unreal. He trudged out of the church, back toward the hotel.

Simpson stood in the hall outside Tobias's room, looking wired.

"It's getting bad out there," Simpson said. "Nobody outright tried to steal the car, but everyone was trying to steal my charging connection—had to wave my tranq gun around four, five times—"

Tobias unlocked the door to his room, staring in wonder at Simpson's energy. Didn't he know that Barnes was dead? But no, of course he didn't.

"Are you packed?" Simpson barged in ahead of him, and Tobias let him. "I've got the car hidden for now, but we shouldn't leave it for long..."

"Barnes is dead," Tobias said simply, cutting into Simpson's train of thought. He barely recognized his own voice as he spoke.

"What?" Simpson stared back at him, looking almost angry at the suggestion.

"He's dead."

Simpson's whole body slumped.

"What happened?"

"There were some people panicking, running into evacuated structures, Barnes went after them and a building collapsed—I don't—" Tobias sighed. It took a monumental amount of energy to repeat this. "I don't really know the details. Security didn't really know the details."

"Oh." The noise came from somewhere deep in Simpson's belly.

He reached out an arm to Tobias, looked on the verge of pulling him in for a hug, but stopped short. Instead his arm just dangled out in space, his fingertips inches away from Tobias's shoulder. At a loss.

"You can stay with Ruth and me, if you want. You shouldn't be alone." He must have known that Tobias had nowhere else to go.

Simpson dropped his arm and started to pace, though Tobias couldn't figure out why. Maybe he just needed to move. Tobias felt a wave of self-pity. How broken must he look right now, for

Simpson to offer him a place with his family? Simpson, who only tolerated him at best?

"I let Myrra Dal go," Simpson said midstride. He said it like it was an afterthought. After the news of Barnes, Tobias had almost forgotten how important this case had been to him just hours before. So Myrra was gone. His chest ached at the thought, though he couldn't place why. It wasn't the case. His career might as well be ash in a fire after all that had happened. No, it just felt like another person to miss. Odd as it was to think, Myrra felt like his last remaining friend.

"It was the right thing to do," Simpson added.

Tobias nodded. He knew Simpson was right, but he felt the loss all the same.

They wove the car down the mountain, inching through traffic, driving up on the sidewalks when necessary. Bells were replaced by the noise of honking.

Every few minutes someone would bang on their windows, asking for a ride. One man flashed a wallet full of account cards at them. He wore an expensive-looking gray suit that had become rumpled with the dust of the street.

Simpson kept the doors firmly locked. He was on the phone with his wife, offering reassurances as they squeezed through the cars.

"My love, we're leaving now. I'll take the back roads, I promise—"

Tobias sat in the back seat, trying to give him privacy. There was no one he could call, he thought, indulging in his sadness.

Though that wasn't strictly true. He felt like an orphan, carrying Barnes's death like a cinder block weighing down his body. But he wasn't entirely without family. David and Ingrid were alive and well and sitting in a New London jail.

They weren't the people he wanted to talk to. He wanted to talk to Barnes, to see him one more time behind that wood desk, giving him tough love and advice. But these were terrifying times. This was what one did in times like these—reached out to family. Maybe, he thought, this could all culminate in one last moment of connection for him. Maybe things happened for a reason.

Simpson was still chattering away with Ruth in the front seat. If Simpson was getting a connection, Tobias should be fine. He dialed the New London Security Bureau. It rang for a long time before finally connecting. Tobias was patient.

"Hello?" a young voice answered. Tobias was pretty sure it was the same agent he'd spoken with before. He wondered if the bureau was working with a skeleton crew. Maybe there were only a handful of agents left who were willing to stay on the job.

"Hello—this is Agent Tobias Bendel." There was static in the connection, making it difficult to hear clearly. "I believe you spoke to me before, to inform me about Director Barnes?"

"What—? Oh...yes." The agent sounded distracted. "Sorry. Yes, that was me."

There was an awkward silence.

"I was wondering if you could help me—"

"Sorry...the connection is a bit weak—" the agent shouted on the other end. The static was building in the background. The network must be overloaded with calls right now.

"I wanted to know if you could help me," Tobias shouted louder, hoping he wasn't disturbing Simpson's call too much. Simpson was having his own shouting match in the front seat. "I need to get connected to the New London Prison. There are two prisoners there that I wish to speak to, one on the women's side and one on the men's. I know it's a big favor, but I was hoping, since I'm an agent, maybe something could be arranged—"

The agent cut in. "Usually you'd need to set up a formal request, arrange an appointment—" There was a pause on the other end. The agent sighed into the receiver. When he spoke again, his tone was much less formal. "Fuck it. In the wake of what's happened, what difference does it make? There's only three of us left here at the bureau, and most of the prison guards have bailed. There's comm boxes in the prisoners' cells. If you've got their codes I can probably connect you."

Tobias searched the documents on his tablet, fishing for the prisoner ID codes that had been given to him long ago, never to be used.

"I think I've got them here—"

"OK, read it out slowly—the connection is terrible—"

Tobias furnished him with all the information he could. The line clicked out. Some ironically cheerful hold music took its place. Digital tones, a tinny sound, hard to place the song. Beethoven? Maybe.

Doubt settled into his stomach. He hadn't spoken to his parents in well over a decade. What was he supposed to say to them? Tobias almost hung up the phone then and there. The bile that he'd felt for them most of his life rose up again in force. These people, these irresponsible, entitled people, who had the gall to continue living when Barnes was not. These people who were so incapable of raising him, who should have never had a child. He should never have been born. It would have been better, that sort of oblivion, than the pain he was feeling now.

He stayed on the line anyway. His parents were not good people. Though if he thought about it, with the stark lens through which he viewed his own life, now, here at the end of it: Was he a good person? Was Barnes? What made someone worthy of regard?

An especially pitchy Muzak high note was cut off midwhine.

Tobias heard a voice through his earpiece, a voice that sounded familiar, but older and thinner and sadder. It was a voice he had not heard in over a decade.

"Hello?" David said.

His heart swelled for a moment, an old childish instinct, one that he didn't fully trust.

"Toby?"

Only Barnes calls me Toby was his first thought, but then he remembered that David, once upon a time, had called him Toby too.

"I'm here," he said. "Is Ingrid there too?"

"Toby?" Ingrid's voice, a little more overlaid with static than David's.

"How—how are you?" Tobias asked. The question felt entirely casual and wrong, but what else was there to say, really? Too much could be said that was honest, but also hurtful.

"It's been awful..." Ingrid said. "I've wasted away in here. It's good you can't see me."

"Nonsense, you still light up a room," David said, and Ingrid sighed in response. David always knew just what to say.

Tobias heard a screech and felt his body shift and slam into the door of the car. Simpson had swerved to avoid a truck that had desperately wedged itself into the traffic. He'd hung up with Ruth and now his concentration was completely focused on the road. Maybe they'd survive the drive at least, Tobias thought.

"Sorry—" Simpson called back to Tobias. "Everyone's crazy out here—"

Tobias waved at Simpson's face in the rearview mirror and righted his body. David was chattering away in his earpiece, dimly muffled by static.

"Not much to say," David said. "Prison isn't pleasant. The

mattresses are lumpy and the sheets scratch. But we get by. These years would have been nicer, maybe, if our son had visited from time to time."

David spoke lightly, but Tobias felt the stab of his words nonetheless.

"David, not now, not when we've finally got him on the phone—"

"You're right, dear, you're right," David said, glossing over all. "Toby, how are you? How have the years been for you?"

There was still an edge to what he said, an edge that Tobias desperately wished to smooth out. Ingrid seemed about the same, frailer, but still herself. But this David was harsher than he remembered, quicker to the fight. He supposed seventeen years in prison would do that to a man.

He stared out the car window as Simpson sped forward ten meters, hopping up on the sidewalk and knocking over a souvenir cart as he went. Wooden prayer beads flew off their red string bracelets and scattered across the pavement.

"I'm sorry, I—" How to phrase his intentions? He barely knew them himself. "I just wanted to call you, see how you were, given everything that's going on—"

He noticed he kept hearing vague phrases like that: *what's going on*, *the terrible news*, *times like these*. How had the agent put it on the phone—"in the wake of what's happened"? It was an awful lot of words for *apocalypse*, but no one wanted to say it outright.

"You're not telling me you believe what they're spewing on the news, are you?" David said.

Another ill-timed stop by Simpson sent Tobias flying off the seat and onto the car floor. Tobias struggled to sit up again, and only after he was properly upright again did the absurdity of his father's words sink in.

"You don't?"

An awkward pause hung in the air around his question.

"Of course not. The world won't break apart," David said. "I'm not a fool."

"You don't understand, Toby." Ingrid's voice came into the mix, sounding so much more distant than David's, the occasional syllable dropping away midsentence. The static was getting worse. "They tell us all sorts of things in here that aren't true, mostly to keep the prisoners in line. We didn't know it before, but now, being in here as long as we have, it's easier to see just how much the government lies to us."

There was a version of what she was saying that was true. Tobias was sure the government had lied plenty of times over the course of his life. But there were so many other reasons to believe it.

"But the sheer number of quakes—I've watched cities crumble to the ground. I've felt my body rise up into the air. I was in Palmer, when it—" The trauma of memory came back to him, and he couldn't finish the sentence. And Myrra, he thought, as a final reason. I believe Myrra.

The car bumped back over the curb again. Simpson stole a look back at him, must have heard the distress in his voice. "Who are you talking to?"

Tobias shook his head. He couldn't explain right now. Simpson turned back around, jerked the steering wheel just in time to avoid a panicked woman running across the road.

"I'm not saying that disturbing things haven't happened—" David cut in. "But the government's using these disasters, exaggerating them in the media to keep us all in line. That's what they do."

"You were in Palmer, Tobias? I hope you didn't get hurt..." Ingrid cut in. Was her line on a delay?

"I'm fine, Ingrid."

Of course he should have expected that there would be people out there who would deny all this; wherever there was bad news, there were always people willing to forcibly turn away from it. He just hadn't expected that his mother and father would be in their numbers.

He thought of a million arguments to convince them of the truth of it. But there simply wasn't time. He could hear the crackling on the line, not just on Ingrid's side now but on David's too. The network was going to go down soon.

"I never thought you'd grow up to be so gullible, Toby," David said.

"It got him on the phone, anyway—" his mother chimed in.

"I'm sorry I haven't talked to you before now," he said, only half meaning it. He was aware that the apology would never be reciprocated on their end.

There was a short silence, and then David spoke.

"We appreciate the apology," he said, his voice sounding far away. As expected, no apologies were offered in return. Tobias felt suddenly very tired.

"Anyways, whether the world is ending or not—"

"Oh, don't be a rube, son—" David argued.

"—I just wanted to call and talk to you again." He almost threw in an *I love you*, but he knew that it would also be a half-truth. He loved his parents in that chemical way that was without choice or logic. But he hated them too. He did not love them as he loved Barnes.

Ingrid broke in. "Will you visit? I'd love to see how you've grown up. Though again—you'll have to pardon my appearance these days."

"Nonsense," David said again. "You look beautiful."

It was like a record repeating.

"Sure, I'd love to visit." He knew he would never visit, never see them again. There had been a moment, in some unspoken corner of his mind, when he'd entertained the idea of being with them at the end, feeling the closeness he'd never felt as a child, feeling at home in this world. But he was sure now that his place was not with them.

"Our Toby, all grown up. Do you look like me, or do you look like your mother?" David asked. Static was eating at the fiber of his voice, like ants overwhelming a plate of food.

"I look like you."

David shouted, celebrating his genetic prowess.

Ingrid laughed. "Oh, Toby, when you come, could you bring us some chocolate—"

Her voice cut off midsentence. The call had dropped. Tobias jumped at the sudden silence, the way one would normally jump at a loud noise. He tried the line again but couldn't get the agent back. Couldn't get any signal at all.

That, he thought, was the last conversation I will have with my parents. He had hoped it would bring him comfort, or at least a sense of closure. It brought none. The world owes me nothing, he thought, certainly not a perfect ending. He hurt for his mother and father, for the shock and confusion they would feel at the end. Wouldn't it have been better for them to acknowledge the truth, to be able to talk to their son about something real for once? There was no connection there, none at all. But maybe it was better to pretend. They wouldn't see death coming, and it would come fast. Tobias pictured it: the prison would go dark, and then they would go dark. In a blink.

Maybe they would be all right. It helped him to imagine it so.

"Who was that on the phone?" Simpson asked again.

"No one," Tobias said. Simpson looked doubtful, but let it go.

He should have known better than to chase comfort with people he barely knew anymore, family or no. Barnes knew him. But he was gone. He leaned forward and put his head between his knees. He could fall asleep for a million years.

"Everything still good with your family?" Tobias asked. He half expected Simpson to tell him that they were dead too, considering how abruptly Barnes had been torn away.

"Ruth seems calmer. The kids are playing a board game. They're staying inside until we can get there. They've got plenty of food." Everything was still fine on Simpson's side. Tobias felt happy and jealous all at once.

"I grabbed a map..." Simpson brandished a folded plastic brochure. Tobias climbed into the front seat again and took a look.

"It'll be important to take back roads once we get out of Kittimer. No major cities. We'll curve around the Palmer Sea, avoid Troy. It's less direct, but I think ultimately it'll still be the fastest way home..."

Simpson continued to explain the game plan as they drove. They were about halfway down the mountain now, inching toward one of the bridges between peaks. Tobias let him talk and didn't pay attention. He was thinking about Myrra. She felt like the most natural thing to think about—it was almost like working with muscle memory. He'd been concentrating on her so much over the past few weeks.

Where was Myrra likely to go, now that she was free from the chase? Forward. She wouldn't want to stay in Kittimer; after this she would want to keep moving. And she wouldn't want to go back to the Palmer Sea. Where did that leave her? He worried for her, and especially for Charlotte, even though he knew he shouldn't. Myrra was a survivor, and anyway, everyone was dying soon.

It was a horrible thing to think, a casual toss-off: everyone was dying soon.

He thought of their last conversation. They understood one another. He looked at Simpson, staring ahead with a viselike grip on the steering wheel. He was trying to remember Simpson's kids' names, but he couldn't think of them. What an ass he'd been.

They were nearly to the bridge. He thought of Imogene Carlyle. Tobias hoped they wouldn't see anyone trying to jump.

Even yesterday (such a short time ago), when everything had still been calm and everyone had still been alive, there had been so few people whom he really knew, who really knew him. Tobias had always wanted a small life, he had contented himself with the idea that it was the quality of his connections, not the quantity, that mattered. Now Barnes was gone, and there was no one who knew him. Simpson cared, but he had a whole other life that took precedence. Myrra Dal, somehow, was the next-closest person.

The bridge opened up before them, and the car crept over the soft slope of it. Tobias marveled at the landscape that unfolded around them. He scanned every zigzagging road going down the mountain face. The roads themselves looked like flowing rivers with all the people who walked down each path. The lines of each street grew finer and finer the farther they descended, the people shrinking to minuscule dots. On one side, off in the distance, past the bodies of people walking alongside their car, he saw the Palmer Sea glittering in the afternoon light. On the other side, past the mountains, he saw the cresting sandy hills of the Border Desert, colors moving in waves from blue to green. It looked for all the world like a twin sea to Palmer, a sea of sand. It stretched far out into the distance, past the horizon, past comprehension.

Tobias sat up in his seat and craned his neck to get a better look. He'd never come this way through Kittimer and never had a chance to see the desert in person.

"Wow," Tobias said. Even Simpson tore his eyes from the road to have a look.

The car stopped again. Traffic had bottlenecked on the bridge.

"Hey—there's somebody down there..." Simpson said, squinting through the window at the blue waves of sand.

"Where?" Tobias squinted along with him.

"Down there on the road, just past the base of the mountains." Simpson pointed, and Tobias's eyes followed.

Out near the base of a mountain, so far down that it barely looked like a trickle of water weaving between the dunes, Tobias spotted the road. A vehicle was moving down its path, so far away that all he could really see was a glint of metal reflecting the sun, moving away from the mountains and toward the horizon.

"Who would be stupid enough to drive out into that? There's nothing out there."

"There must be something," Tobias replied.

And then it hit him like a jolt.

"It's Myrra," he said. He knew it deep, in the soles of his feet. It was Myrra. He didn't know what she was chasing, but he knew she'd found something to chase.

"You can't know that," Simpson said. But even he sounded unsure. "Oh—" he said, and resumed his grip on the wheel. Traffic was moving again, mind-bendingly slowly, but it was moving.

Tobias could not take his eyes off the tiny speck of light in the distance. He followed it until it was barely visible, until it disappeared into the hills past the bounds of his vision, and even then he kept his eyes glued to the spot where it had disappeared.

He thought about the stone of the bridge, worn smooth by a thousand tires and shoes that had passed over its surface. This bridge will stay the same when everyone is dead, Tobias thought. A ruin in space. If the world were to break apart right now, this is where our bodies would rise, mine and Simpson's, up into the atmosphere, a car for a tomb.

He reached out and grabbed the handle of the car door. Unlocked it.

"Don't unlock the door, Bendel. Someone could break in," Simpson said, a worried look on his face. It sounded like he was trying to shake Tobias out of a haze. Maybe he thinks I'm going into shock, Tobias thought. Maybe I am going into shock. Maybe that is a reasonable response right here, right now.

Tobias thought about where he wanted to be when the atmosphere got sucked out of the world, when the water got sucked out of the Palmer Sea with the last of the fish and the sharks, when the air got funneled out through the sky, and trees, saplings maybe, were lifted out of the ground shaking soil off their roots as they spun into the air—where did he want to be when all of that went down, when the world went down? There wasn't a quick answer to that question, no easy flash-bang-in-the-brain epiphany. There was no particular place that left him feeling sentimental. Depressingly, the place that came closest was the desk pool at the Security Bureau. But that lost its luster without Barnes sitting there behind his warm wooden door. All of New London lost its luster without Barnes.

Some things were becoming clear, though: even if Simpson was volunteering to adopt him out of genuine care, it was not where he wanted to be. He would die watching a family cling together while he, inevitably, would be outside looking in. Even if they were holding him close, he would not be a part of them.

Tobias had once interviewed a convict who was describing a murder he'd committed. The convict had told him, almost as an excuse for his crime, that everyone dies badly, and everyone dies alone. Tobias wasn't sure he believed that, but he did believe that it was possible to die surrounded by people and still feel alone, if they weren't your people, the people who understood you.

All this flashed through his head in the seconds after Simpson gestured to him to lock the door, to stay in the car that would whisk him to a safe, known place. Not the place he wanted to be.

"Stop the car," Tobias said. "I want to get out."

"What?" Simpson shouted back with unexpected anger. He braked reflexively, and the truck behind them immediately honked a horn. Simpson shifted his feet on the pedals, and the car resumed its crawl.

Tobias understood: he wasn't operating from a place of logic, in fact he'd abandoned rationality hours ago, and he was sure it was exasperating for someone as levelheaded as Simpson. Simpson turned to face him, a look of confusion on his face. He leaned past Tobias and relocked the door.

"I'm not going to change my mind. I need to get out," Tobias said. He raised his hands in front of him in defense, as if at any moment Simpson might leap at him.

"Bendel, just come with me," he said through gritted teeth.

"I want you to know how much I appreciate your offer. But if I go with you—" Tobias searched for the right way to say this. "It's where you should be; it's not where I should be."

He reached out and put a hand on Simpson's shoulder. Simpson's tension eased, just a little bit.

"Where else are you gonna go?" Simpson asked. It might have been Tobias's imagination, but it sounded as if his voice was breaking. "Do you have family somewhere?"

"I've got nobody." Tobias let out a small laugh as he said it. It was absurd. "But I don't think it's going to help if you try and take me in like a stray cat."

That had been the wrong thing to say. Simpson faced front again, sheepish. "It wouldn't be like that—"

"No, no—I know. I shouldn't have put it that way. I really appreciate it. I just can't."

There was a pause between them while Simpson took a few deep breaths, trying to keep himself composed. For the first time, Tobias considered that maybe Simpson had wanted him there for the journey at least, someone to talk to on the road back to New London, to help him stay sane.

"What are you gonna do, then? Stay in Kittimer?"

"I'm going to follow Myrra Dal," Tobias said. He hadn't even been sure that that was his decision until he said it out loud, but there it was.

Simpson looked at him in disappointment.

"It's not like that—" Tobias said. "I just feel like I know her now. I think she'll need someone around, someone to talk to. You already have your people. Maybe I can be her people." Tobias shrugged, almost to acknowledge the presumptuousness of that. Maybe she wouldn't want someone else around. "And if not, it's something to do, at least."

Simpson's eyes welled up. Tobias had meant the last bit as a joke, but it came out sounding especially sad. Nothing he could do about that. It was life.

Simpson put the car in park, and an explosion of car horns offered its response. Tobias still had his hand on Simpson's shoulder. He pulled Simpson into a hug, which Simpson allowed. The hug was stiff and unnatural, but Tobias held on anyway, because Simpson was someone he could touch, might be the last person he touched, ever, in his life. Simpson heaved a deep sigh that Tobias could tell was meant to keep tears at bay. He pulled away from Tobias, gripped him by both shoulders, and looked him in the eye.

"Take care, kid." He gave Tobias a sad smile. Tobias pulled his bag from the back seat, unlocked the door, and swiftly exited the car before any bystanders had a chance to jump in. He watched Simpson relock it promptly and continue driving away. He kept his eyes on the portion of Simpson's face he could see in the rear-view until it too got lost in the crowd.

29

THE BORDER DESERT

When creating an artificial world, it is important to hide all wires and scaffolds, to tuck the seams behind the backdrops. It was important, especially for that first generation who left the old world behind, that this place should really feel like an open-air landscape and not a tin can people were trapped in. To prevent the potential claustrophobia, the designers of the world (the ship) created the Border Desert, which, as the name suggests, borders the landscape of the world on all sides and puts an inhospitable environment between the population of the world and the walls of the horizon. This way the horizon would feel ever distant, the way it was meant to be.

The desert itself is simply sand. Lots and lots of sand. Due to the natural weather patterns that have formed in the ship (the world), these outer regions also experience high wind levels and low precipitation. It is a harsh place. Though it is meant to keep people out, a few scattered, stubborn people do homestead among the dunes. One thing that is true about humanity: there will always be those who push the limits of stability and survival just to say they can. They scale the unscalable mountains, they dive to the impenetrable depths, they love the unlovable person, they will live in the unlivable desert.

The dunes themselves are something of a draw for the occasional survivalist tourist. Each hill and crest, formed in a wavelike shape by the turning winds, is built upon sands of blue, green, white, and brown. Thus the desert itself, at a distance, actually looks more like waves on a sea than mounds of sand. There is a very utilitarian reason for the unusual colors: when designers were tasked with producing miles and miles of sand, the most practical and economic way to do it was to grind up glass. Billions of wine, beer, soda, and water bottles, not to mention the occasional discarded car window or mirror, were transformed into grains of sand, which forever altered the glass from something with sharp and slicing edges to something pillowy and soft. Different-colored pieces of glass often have different masses, so, over time, with the spinning of the ship and the winds that roiled around, the different grains of sand started separating and clustering into different colors on their own, forming monochrome dunes.

When the world gives way, not many people will die in this desert, because not many people live here. The grains of sand, however, will lift into the air and form funnels that swirl toward the sky. Once the atmosphere is gone completely, what sand is left inside the shell of the world will cluster into clouds; ice will crystallize and form around each grain. If you were to stand in the center of the desert at this time it would appear as if all around you, millions of snowflakes were swirling and falling upward in reverse.

Let's examine that concept of reverse, because while the death of everything is in some ways tragic, there's a magnificent feat we can bear witness to if we reverse the entropy of this moment and play time backward to the origin of an object. Take this thing floating around in the deadness of space, this tiny speck that looks like a snowflake. Twist back the hours, and the crystals of ice shrink backward toward a core, the core grain of sand drifts back toward the shell of the ship. The ship mends itself, which is something too, but let's keep our eye on the sand. The grain of sand rests itself back on the tip of a mighty green dune, and over a century the dune collapses and the grain of sand sifts back in with a multitude of other grains, until the sand has traveled back through space and is back on the old world, the single grain rises in an arc back into a landscaping truck, which reverses back to a recycling factory where the grain was once ground up. The grain meets its brothers and, speck by speck, reassembles into a beer bottle, which in turn refills and returns to a bar somewhere outside Cincinnati and is redeposited into the hands of a woman breaking up with her lover. And that is the miracle of time, how a bottle of Rolling Rock can travel from a dive in Cincinnati through space, through light years, through forms and functions, to one day become a snowflake in a distant galaxy.

30

MYRRA

Myrra raced away from the hostel and Rachel's bloody, angry face, her mind alight with desperate possibility. Rachel had mentioned a word: *escape*. It was easy enough to jump from there to the notion that there was a way off this world. A shuttle, perhaps? Cryogenic freezing of bodies?

Sure, nobody had ever made the freezing thing work; Marcus used to laugh at the sci-fi shows she watched while cleaning and show her hard data, calling her stupid. But maybe they'd worked something out, now that the world was on the line.

And sure, Rachel had then said that everyone was going to die, but what did she know, really? A petty woman, stewing in anger and self-loathing. She could just as easily be wrong as be right.

And sure, Myrra also thought about Imogene and Marcus. If there had been any hope of escape, any chance of them buying their way to survival, why would they have jumped? But there was always the chance that this was a survival plan that had been concocted after they died. A chance.

There would be no escape for her, she knew. But Charlotte belonged to the rarified classes. She was the heir of the Carlyles, the richest of the rich. If Annie qualified for whatever this was, surely Charlotte did. Then even if Myrra died, at least her death would have been for good. At least Charlotte could go on and on.

She knew believing in this was all wrong. It was crazy. But Kittimer was falling apart; she had nowhere left to go where she wouldn't be surrounded by desperate, panicked people. She needed something to chase. Myrra hung her hopes on something thin as string, fragile as a fly wing. She hung her hopes on a word. *Escape.*

If there was any chance that people were leaving the world, they would have to head toward the hull of the ship. Myrra didn't know the geography of the world in great detail, but she knew that to get to the edge of the world, you had to go through the Border Desert.

The dunes started small at first, then increased in size until there were some as tall as a three-story building. Myrra followed narrower and narrower roads out of Kittimer until eventually the only road left was a hard dirt path labeled "Service Road," which wove in and out between the dunes, deeper into the desert beyond.

The road curved constantly, surrounding her with hills of sand so tall it was impossible to see what was beyond each turn. Gusts of wind came at them from one side and then the other, constantly changing direction. An hour into the drive, Charlotte fell asleep with the sound of the motor; Myrra could feel the vibrations of her snores against her chest, even if she couldn't hear them over the din of the scooter and the howling wind. Hours and hours of driving, and all she saw was more crests of barren sand, in alternating shades of blue, green, brown, and white. She'd never seen such sand. It was a landscape to get lost in.

Day stretched out longer when the surroundings were as repetitive as this. It might have been wishful thinking, but the sun looked a little lower in the sky. Myrra was starting to doubt her decision to come out here. The desert hadn't seemed this big from the top of the mountains. Maybe the road had curved sideways; Myrra's aim had been to drive directly away from Kittimer toward the horizon, but the road could have turned somewhere, maybe she was traveling parallel to the mountains; there was no way to tell. But this was the only road she'd found. So she continued.

A motor sounded out in the distance, ahead of her somewhere, getting louder and closer. Myrra stopped the scooter and felt around for the knife she had stashed in her bag just as a truck emerged from behind the nearest dune. It was a utility vehicle of some kind with a canvas roof. Just one man inside, wearing denim coveralls, a wild, panicked look in his eye. He didn't even stop as he passed, but yelled out the window, "We're all fucked! What're you going that way for?"

The truck disappeared behind her, and she stayed still, listening to the sound of the engine as it grew softer and softer, dissipating until it blended into the sound of the wind. On one hand, she was relieved that the man had kept driving—she didn't want trouble. But on the other, he could have offered her some guidance, told her what to expect, how long the road was at the very least. And if she was honest with herself, she would have liked a little conversation to break up the monotony.

The sun was definitely getting lower now. And as Myrra turned another corner, a surprise: just ahead, a tall metal structure, gleaming impossibly in the sun. It was simple enough, just two thick metal poles, each about ten meters tall, propping up a catwalk that passed over the road. Myrra stopped at the base of one of the poles and stared up at it as though it were an alien being. She couldn't discern its purpose. A sign hung off the edge of the catwalk on one side. It read "Checkpoint 4." Myrra wondered where she could find Checkpoints 1, 2, and 3.

She found a ladder on the opposite side. Leaving her bag and the scooter behind, and checking to make sure Charlotte was still safely tied tightly around her, she climbed up until she emerged on top of the catwalk. From up here, she understood. This must have been a watch post.

Up here the desert unfurled before her with layers and layers of color, blues, greens, hints of white and brown, each dune cresting behind another like a wave on a sea. Myrra imagined a boat cutting through the sand, sending up showers of white like sea foam. It wasn't a boat she'd ever seen in person, but rather one she'd seen in a painting Marcus kept in his office. Instead of an engine on the back, the boat had sheets tied to it, stretched out on three tall poles that towered up from its decks.

Marcus had caught her staring at the painting one day when she was supposed to be dusting. "Do you know what that is?"

"No," she answered truthfully.

"It's a very old type of boat, from the old world; it's called a frigate. This was a ship in the British navy seven hundred years ago."

Myrra rolled the word over in her head: *frigate*. It sounded like machinery.

He pointed over her shoulder at the blotch of black paint that was meant to be the boat: "The ships themselves were made of wood, and these"—he raised his finger to gesture to the squares of white—"these are the sails."

Marcus was in professor mode. Myrra ventured a question.

"What are the sails for?" she asked. They were such a dominant part of the thing. The ship seemed more sail than anything else.

"They catch the wind," he said. Myrra couldn't fathom how that would be useful to a ship. Marcus walked around to stand beside her, pushing his face close to the painting, his eyes poring over the brushstrokes. This was about a year and a half before his suicide, so he was still calm and collected, no sweat soaking through his shirts.

He glanced sideways at Myrra, and she must have looked confused, because he elaborated: "The sails catch the wind the way a kite would—you've seen the ones in the park before?"

Myrra nodded.

"Well, they catch the wind, and the wind pushes them forward, like a kite, and then the sailors angled the sails so that the wind pushed them in the direction they wanted to go." He nodded and smiled at her, satisfied in his own knowledge.

"That sounds like a lot of work."

"It was." Marcus's eyes turned and rested once more on the ship. "It must have been a glorious time to be alive."

Myrra nodded, though she privately disagreed. Marcus often expounded on the glories of the past, but it seemed to Myrra that the past involved a lot of tasks that took longer and involved a lot more complications than in the present. In Myrra's experience, working harder for a thing didn't necessarily make it more rewarding. A pie wasn't better baked if she'd had to spend half a day making the dough from scratch. She'd take a boat with a motor any day.

Charlotte cried out and wriggled against her, breaking Myrra's train of thought. She was squinting, and she kept turning her head this way and that—the wind was much harsher up high than it was down near the ground.

"Shhh...I'm sorry, sweetie," Myrra cooed, and she adjusted the scarf to hide Charlotte's face. Then she climbed back down, leaving the imaginary boat on its imaginary sea.

Later, as the scooter puttered along and the sky grew darker, Myrra kept thinking about sails. She remembered the diagram on Marcus's computer: in all the bits of terminology, Myrra remembered seeing the phrase *solar sails*. Myrra couldn't begin to imagine how those sails worked in space, but she did like the comparison. Her world was a frigate too, just like the one in the painting, bobbing up and down in an uncertain sea.

Myrra came across three bodies on the side of the road, two men and a woman. Stopping to investigate, she saw that the sand was overtaking two of them, only their shoulders and heads visible. Their clothes were in tatters, covered in grease stains, and their skin looked so sallow that Myrra immediately imagined the smell of rotten milk. They were unnaturally thin—Myrra could see their bones protruding—and their skin flaked away on their lips. Must have died of thirst, Myrra thought.

Their arms reached out down the road, toward Kittimer. They had been traveling in the opposite direction, she realized. Wherever she was headed, that's where they'd escaped from. It was possible her destination was just as dangerous as what she'd left.

Myrra looked ahead on the uncertain road and then looked down again at the bodies, at the pale skin on their faces. They must have looked dead even when they were alive.

She got back on the scooter and kept driving. If there was an escape plan, where were all the others heading to the hull? Possibly there were other roads.

Thoughts like this terrified her, but whatever awaited them, Myrra felt it was inevitable now, as if her path were on rails: no alternate routes, no reversing course.

There were places where the road grew treacherously narrow, where the slopes of sand on either side encroached and threatened to swallow the path completely. It felt to Myrra like a smaller version of what was happening with the hull of the world: slowly and inevitably, the universe was seeping in.

Near sunset, Myrra felt another earthquake shudder under the wheels of the scooter. The quake was small and didn't last long, but Myrra was astonished to see a dune she passed collapse on one side, the sand cascading down in a tiny stream at first, and the stream then getting larger and wider, falling faster as it barreled toward the bottom. By the time everything settled it had taken out a third of the road behind them. The dunes were magnificent, but they were lying in wait to swallow her up.

It was getting cold, and it was getting dark. The wind felt especially wicked. Myrra decided to make camp by the side of the road, in a small wedge of space between two hills, where the wind felt a little lighter. She sat Charlotte down on the ground next to the scooter and dug into the bag, looking for diapers.

Charlotte began shivering the second Myrra sat her down. She didn't have Myrra's body keeping her warm; they needed something to battle the cold. They needed a fire. She had a lighter, but nothing flammable. It hadn't really occurred to her before, but it was probably deliberate on the part of the government, to keep wood and paper scarce. If the world was one big closed system, large fires could be disastrous.

Myrra looked around her for a twig, dried leaf, anything, but all she saw was sand. She rifled through her backpack: some of the clothes she'd stolen from Imogene might do, silk would probably burn, and the wool sweaters. From the outside pocket she pulled out her Gertrude Stein book, and she felt a stab through her heart at the thought of burning it. But Charlotte was shaking, and the temperature was only going to drop more as the night wore on.

She would just burn part of the book, for survival's sake. Each page tearing felt like a death, and she couldn't tell if her eyes burned from the wind or her grief or both, but no one was around to see her cry anyway. There would be no one around to judge.

The flames caught, and with the scooter propped up to provide a little shelter, the fire kept burning. She fed in a couple of Imogene's sweaters, for more fuel. Myrra pulled out the thick green blanket she'd stolen back in Kittimer and wrapped it around her and Charlotte. She was asleep within seconds.

The fire only lasted half an hour before the wind changed. Myrra woke to Charlotte crying—grains of sand pelted her face like a swarm of stinging insects; it was impossible to see. Myrra felt around for Charlotte and realized she was still lying next to her. She held her close and tried to shield her face from the worst of the storm around them, tucking her into her shirt. Myrra raised the blanket—it nearly flew out of her hands as it caught the wind, but she held on tight—tied two of the corners to spokes on the scooter, and weighed down the other corners with bottles of water, whatever she had that was heavy, trying to create a tent. Charlotte screamed against her shoulder, the sand assaulting them from all sides. She let go of the blanket and sat back to see if it would hold; the fabric billowed and bucked against the wind, but the knots held firm. Then, dumping whatever clothes she had onto the ground under the blanket, she climbed in, pulling Charlotte inside with her. It was the tiniest pocket of shelter, but it kept the wind out and a little heat in. Myrra thought of their little fire, now reduced to ash buried in the sand. That was half of her book, gone. And for what?

She pulled Charlotte close against her chest with her little head just under her chin and mounded piles of clothes on top of them to keep warm. Charlotte fell asleep right away, but Myrra lay there for hours worrying. The wind howled outside, buffeting the blanket like a violent intruder trying to break into a house.

The next day, Myrra woke partially submerged in white and blue sand. Her eyes flew open in panic and she looked down to make sure Charlotte wasn't drowning. All she could see of Charlotte was her right shoulder, her neck, and her head, but the important thing was that she was getting air. Charlotte was still sleeping. Myrra wasn't surprised; they were exhausted enough that it didn't matter if they were buried.

The wind was calm again. Myrra lifted her head to get a better look at the morning, but took care not to rouse Charlotte in the process. Her arm disappeared just below her right shoulder. Most of Myrra's body was buried, with small outcroppings emerging here and there: an elbow, a shoulder, the curve of her hip. They were islands in a blue sand sea.

Somewhere underneath the surface, her arm was still cradling Charlotte's sleeping body. She could feel the sand rustle and move whenever Charlotte took an especially big breath. Myrra rested her head back down on the divot of sand where her face had lain when she'd been asleep, and she waited for Charlotte to wake.

She wondered if it was possible to count how many grains of sand were in the desert. Maybe it would be like counting sheep. Maybe she could drift back to sleep for a little while. She was still so tired.

Jake used to try to explain his physics homework to her. He

told her once that there were more atoms in the human body than there were stars in the known universe.

"What do you mean by 'the known universe'?" she had asked him at the time. Instead of sand, she felt the memory of holding his hand.

"Well, supposedly the universe is infinite. There aren't any walls. It just sort of goes on and on in all directions." They were lying on a hill in Sakura Park, Jake beside her, staring up at the sky as he talked. "So we can't see it all; we haven't figured out how to map it all yet."

She wondered where Jake was now. Would they keep the grocery store open if the world was ending? People still needed food. Would he and his parents leave for the countryside? It seemed as if the first instinct for a lot of people was to move, was to travel to wherever they were not. She hoped that Jake was safe, for now anyway.

Her mouth felt dry. Saliva was no longer wet; instead it formed a sort of paste on her tongue. But Charlotte still slept, so Myrra stayed still.

She could never get a handle on what Jake meant by *atoms*. He'd tried to explain it a couple of times.

"Well, they're the building blocks of all matter," he'd say. Myrra would understand this academically, but she couldn't picture it and that frustrated her. It frustrated her, deep down, that she always seemed to know less than everyone else around her.

Jake would try again. "There are these things called cells. And cells are very, very, very small. So small you can't see them with the naked eye—you need a microscope. Smaller than that are molecules, and even smaller than that are atoms. And atoms are in everything. They make up everything in the universe."

Did that mean there were atoms in the air of an empty room?

Were there atoms making up the not-air that filled up outer space? If so, that meant that wherever the hull of the world ripped apart, it wouldn't be a hole at all; it would still be filled with something.

Some time later (was it an hour, was it five minutes?) Charlotte stirred, popped open her eyes, and immediately started crying.

Myrra sat up, lifted Charlotte up above her. The sand shifted and avalanched around them, like some geological cataclysm happening in miniature. Myrra took them both out of the tent and set Charlotte down in front of her in the open air so she could move freely. Then she stood up and dusted herself off. She let Charlotte cry; the girl needed a chance to express herself.

Myrra felt dirty everywhere; there were grains of sand in the corners of her eyes and her lips, inside her shoes, in between her toes, in the fold of skin under her breasts, around the edges of her nostrils, embedded in the caverns of her ears. Her skin looked a pale dusty blue; Charlotte's did too. When she bent over and shook out her hair, a blue granular waterfall rained out of it.

For the second time that morning, Myrra realized how thirsty she was. Then she realized how thirsty Charlotte must be. She found their water bottles buried near the edges of the blanket, still roughly in the place she'd put them last night. The scooter was also half-submerged. The dune had migrated in the night and now covered most of the road.

After feeding Charlotte and giving her a few long drinks of water—as slowly as she could, to keep Charlotte from getting sick—Myrra started working to dig out the scooter from under the sand. While she dug, moving scoops of sand away with both hands, she took mental stock of their supplies. They still had plenty of water and food. The desert had to end soon. Or the world had to end. This road seemed less and less like a good idea. She hadn't understood what this place would be like. She'd only seen it at a distance and heard stories. The desert had seemed calm enough from her spot in the mountains.

She watched Charlotte, gratefully sipping her water, confused and clutching Myrra's shirt. Charlotte had no idea what was going on. She couldn't know why they'd left the penthouse, let alone why they were now covered in sand, wasting away in a desert. But she held on to Myrra. She trusted Myrra.

Maybe they should have stayed in Kittimer. Maybe they should have stayed in Nabat. Maybe Charlotte should have stayed in New London, left alone in the penthouse, or abandoned by Myrra on some hospital steps.

Shoulds get you nowhere, she tried to tell herself, though every bone in her body felt heavy. She'd dragged Charlotte this far. And if there was even a chance that Charlotte might get out of this alive, Myrra would survive long enough to take her the rest of the way. She slapped herself in the face, trying to wake up, get focused. She remembered Tobias doing that after she'd hit him in the head. It hadn't worked well for him.

Once she'd cleared away most of the sand, she tried to turn over the motor on the scooter. It made a loud ratchety clicking sound but didn't start. Myrra tried again, turning the key more forcefully. More clicking. Once more. This time there was no sound at all. The battery was completely dead. Myrra wasn't sure if sand had gotten into the wiring or the motor was just never meant to hold a charge that long, but it didn't matter. The scooter was useless now, just a big hunk of metal.

Myrra collapsed in the sand next to this inert thing and sank her dusty face into her dusty hands. She and Charlotte had polished off two water bottles, but she was still thirsty. The energy bars she'd stolen tasted like sawdust, and she had a hard time swallowing them with so little saliva. They'd driven half the day yesterday, and the desert still seemed to go on and on. Charlotte continued crying in the sand a few feet away from her. Myrra started crying too. This had been a stupid decision, yet it was hard to imagine making a different one. The universe was taunting her.

They would have to continue on foot. She'd done it before, out of New London. She would do it again. Still crying, Myrra rose to her feet and started counting out which supplies she could carry while also carrying Charlotte. What was most important.

The water, of course. And food. Diapers. The blanket had proven invaluable. Myrra kept a couple of scarves that she could wrap around their faces should another sandstorm kick up, and dumped the rest of their clothes. She kept *The World Is Round*, rationalizing that it might be useful for future fires, but also knowing it would break her to give up any more of its pages. She tried to toss her mother's blue figure into the sand but ultimately lowered her arm right before the throw and slipped it back into her pocket.

She wrapped Charlotte back up around her in the scarf. Charlotte's tears streaked down her cheeks, cleaning the blue away in stripes down her skin. Myrra kept crying too, they were crying in conversation. You are crying now, she thought to herself, but what are you going to do after that?

"I know, I know," she said to Charlotte, and gently rustled some of the sand out of her hair. "But we've got to keep going."

Myrra slipped her arms through the straps of her backpack. It was unbearably heavy. Already she could feel grains of sand trapped under the straps, trapped between the fabric and her skin. They would rub her skin raw by the end of the day. So be it.

Another tremor shook the ground under her feet. Myrra bent her knees to keep her balance. Charlotte cried out in surprise, another loud scream. The dune that had engulfed the scooter collapsed on its side. Within seconds the sand had buried it up to the handlebars. They needed to get away from this part of the road. The shaking of the earth hadn't fully stopped, but Myrra started walking anyway. The road stayed narrow, but at least there was still a road there.

31

TOBIAS

He stole a car. It shocked him, how easy it was. He found a particularly vulnerable-looking couple, flashed his badge, bullied them until they gave in, didn't give them time to think before he took the keys and drove away, out of Kittimer and into the desert. He wasn't proud of himself—everyone now had an important place to go, everyone had an equal right to the term *emergency*. In another place, in another time, if Tobias had needed to commandeer a car as a Security agent, it would have been the right thing to do. But none of this was fair. Wherever that couple was going, their journey was equally important to them as his was to him. But he took their car anyway, and he knew, even after all this contemplation, that he would do it again if he needed to. He could picture David smirking at him, giving him an I-told-you-so look. When the chips were down, he was his father's son.

There was only one service road leading out of this part of Kittimer. He drove for hours. When he wasn't thinking about the couple that he'd stranded, he was thinking about the absurdity of what he was doing, that there was only a minimal chance that

Myrra Dal had taken this road. He was following this path on a hunch, and he wasn't sure he was in a stable enough state of mind to be acting on hunches. Despite this, he kept driving.

The desert terrified him, though not for the normal reasons. There was no water or food and the sandstorms were intense, but he had planned for all that, and Tobias generally wasn't scared of things so long as they fit a plan. What scared him was the sheer endlessness of it all, dune after dune, the same landscape, the infinite twisting road.

The desert appeared to go on forever, but it had to stop eventually. And he'd stolen a good car at least: it was small, but it had a full charge and a cyclical engine, so Tobias estimated it would last him a couple of days. And there was good traction on the tires, which was important; the farther he went, the narrower the road became, with hills of sand cutting in closer and closer and obscuring the path. Tobias assumed that there were usually workers to maintain it and to keep the sand from swallowing it up. He also assumed that those workers had heard the news and abandoned their posts.

He was trying his best not to think of anything except the road in front of him, but he kept picturing Barnes, half-buried by brick on a sidewalk, the legs of the anonymous crowd stepping over his body. He wondered if the bureau would even have the time or energy to give him a memorial. Maybe Tobias should have gone back; maybe he was a terrible person for not going back to take care of Barnes's affairs. A guilty part of him wondered if he was chasing this ludicrous idea as a way to distract himself, the more inane the plan the better. But Barnes wasn't there anymore, just his body. He didn't know what Barnes would have made of his decision; Barnes had never been much for the pomp and circumstance of a funeral, but then again, he had also held courtesy in high esteem. Making arrangements for a loved one was a courtesy, one that Tobias had abandoned. He knew for sure that Barnes would not have approved of him stealing the car. Tobias couldn't tell anymore if his actions were selfish or just human. Maybe there was no difference.

He'd been driving through the desert for most of a day when a flash of something along the side of the road nearly blinded him. It was a handlebar poking out of the sand. Tobias got out of the car and dug to excavate it: it was an electric scooter, battery sapped and caked in blue dust. A pile of objects, mostly clothes, lay abandoned next to the tires. He picked up the clothing one article at a time, letting grains of blue fall away as he did so. He held up one item, and his memory surged with recognition: a green dress, something Myrra had worn in Nabat. He hadn't been so foolish after all—they were here.

He looked around, almost expecting to see Myrra and Charlotte appear over the nearest hill, but he was alone.

If they'd lost their scooter, Myrra would have bailed out all nonessential supplies and continued on foot. Tobias walked up the road a few paces, looking for footprints. The wind wiped away most everything out here, but Tobias thought he could see a few divots in the sand that could have been footprints. They were still following the road.

Tobias took some of the more practical clothing items out of the pile and threw them in the car; he had the space to store them, and if he did find Myrra and Charlotte, they might want them back. If he didn't find them—the thought came with a pang of loneliness—then at least the clothes would make good fuel for a fire.

The ground shook again—another small quake, and before his eyes the scooter was half-buried in falling sand once more. Nature swallows everything up.

⋆ ⋆ ⋆

He didn't have long to wait before finding them. An hour later he rounded his millionth curve and nearly ran over Charlotte crawling across the road. He braked and then sat there for a moment in disbelief, watching Charlotte go. She was getting fast—she'd already reached the opposite side. Tobias looked around. He didn't see Myrra. Worry budded and bloomed in his brain—she could be buried under falling sand, having collapsed after too little water or too much heat. She wouldn't normally let Charlotte out of her sight.

He looked back at Charlotte. She was making a beeline for the nearest hill. Tobias jumped out of the car and scooped her up before she could disturb the sand. The ground shuddered under his feet. The tremors stayed small, but they were getting more and more frequent.

Charlotte reached her hands out, trying to touch the colorful sand. Tobias adjusted the way he held her, propping her up on his side so she straddled his hip, the way he'd seen parents holding their kids at the train station. It felt all right. Charlotte didn't seem too upset, or, to be more accurate, she was upset that she hadn't reached the dune, but she didn't seem to be uncomfortable with the way he was holding her.

She furrowed her brow at him in consternation and made a short frustrated noise that sounded like "eh."

"I know," Tobias said back to her. "I'm no fun."

Charlotte stuck her lower lip out but didn't cry. Tobias looked around the dunes again. No sign of Myrra.

"Where's your mother?" he asked Charlotte, and then he realized his mistake. He knew where her mother was: in a refrigerated morgue drawer back in New London. Or maybe they'd cremated her by now. As with Barnes, he wondered if Imogene

Carlyle had received a proper funeral before everything had gone to hell. Probably no one was bothering with funerals now.

Wait. There was a sound, barely audible, in the distance—someone was crying. It was hard to make out, the wind was picking up again, but the sound came from farther ahead, behind a huge white tower of sand in front of them. Keeping a good hold on Charlotte, he jogged around the bend in the road.

Myrra was at the foot of the dune, frantically digging, her face streaked with tears. Her pack was on its side a meter away, sand already overtaking it. It looked as if the dune had recently caved in on that side. She was scooping white sand up by the armful, heaving it behind her, sobbing with each breath. She hadn't noticed Tobias yet.

"Hey—" Tobias called out to her, trying to shout over the wind. He held Charlotte with one arm, and with the other he waved at Myrra. He jogged closer. "Hey!" he shouted again.

Myrra turned and looked at him, and her face collapsed in relief and sadness. "Oh!" she cried out, and she ran toward them. Tobias gave Charlotte to her immediately. Myrra grabbed for her in a rush of panic, like someone grabbing at a life preserver as they were drowning. She clutched at Charlotte until Tobias worried that she would hurt her from squeezing her so hard.

"I thought—" she said between gasps. "The sand collapsed, and I thought she'd..." She didn't finish the thought. Another sob rose out of her.

"She was just around the corner," Tobias said, gesturing behind him. "Crawling across the road."

Myrra sighed and looked up at the sky. Charlotte's face was nestled in the crook of her neck.

"I think I'm going crazy out here. Fuck." She shoved a stray clump of hair out of her face with her spare arm. She looked around in a sort of scattered way, as if she was trying to get her bearings. "She's gotten so fast—just a few weeks ago, she'd sit wherever I put her—"

"That's what I thought, that she'd gotten really fast," Tobias said, commiserating. He remembered helping Myrra in Nabat, how she'd plonked Charlotte down in the corner of the bathroom and she'd stayed there the whole time. Babies grew fast.

Myrra looked up at him and blinked as though waking up from a dream, and suddenly she took a few steps back, full of suspicion. She shot a quick look behind her at her pack.

"What are you doing here?" she asked him. She sounded exhausted, that particular brand of exhaustion where only the survival instincts were left. The desert had beaten her up: the skin around her lips was starting to peel, her skin was covered in blue and green dust. She looked delirious.

He stayed quiet, unsure how to begin.

"It doesn't look like you have any backup out here," she said, going for her pack and pulling out a knife. "I can take you down. I've done it before."

She glared at him. He felt, reflexively, for the bump on his head. It was mostly healed now.

"I'm not here to bring you in," he said. "That would be absurd, at this point."

"OK," she said, and then she gave him a look that invited him to explain himself. She didn't put down the knife.

"I don't quite know how to—" He stopped himself, tried again. "I couldn't think of anywhere else to go. So I followed you."

That wasn't quite an explanation, but he was getting there.

"What about your partner?" Myrra asked.

"Simpson went back home to be with his family," Tobias said.

"Don't you have family? Friends?"

Tobias shrugged and then felt surprised at his own casual gesture.

"No," he said, laughing a little at himself, because he could either do that or cry, and he didn't want to cry just yet. "I've led such a stupid, focused, isolated life that now, at the end of it, the person I know best is the person I've been investigating."

Myrra stared at him with what he hoped was some understanding.

Cut to the chase, he thought.

"I was wondering if I could come with you, wherever you're going."

The expression on Myrra's face changed from suspicion to something else. Pity? He hoped not. Empathy? Maybe. She tilted her head a little and looked up, as if she was considering an argument.

"OK," she said.

"Really?" Tobias asked. He sounded like a kid at Christmas. He realized he was feeling each new emotion with more intensity than usual, as if the events of the past two days had stripped away all his psychological filters. Maybe this was how it felt to approach death. Or maybe it was just how it felt to be grieving.

"You seem sincere," she said. "And I can tell when you lie."

She hitched Charlotte up higher on her hip and went to get her pack.

"I have a car, if that helps." He pointed back the way he'd come. She immediately turned and walked past him, headed in that direction.

"You should have led with that," she called over her shoulder. "I would have followed you anywhere to get out of this wind."

As if the wind were pleased at the mention, another gust of green sand kicked up behind Myrra, splashing at her back. The color blossomed around her on all sides, it looked like a halo, an aura, surrounding her body. She was radiating green, threatening and alive at the same time.

32

MYRRA & TOBIAS

This was a mistake. She should have known better than to make decisions when she was desperate. *Desperate* didn't even cover it: she was dehydrated, half-starved, and sleep deprived, and up until twenty minutes ago she'd been sure that Charlotte was suffocating under a mound of sand. Her nerves were sharp as razor wire.

Tobias was only a few feet away, in the driver's seat. Charlotte was too far out of arm's reach, strapped into the back seat. This car had locks. Just two days ago, he'd put her in handcuffs. He looked over at her, one hand on the steering wheel and one hand on the ignition; there was blue sand embedded in the rims of his glasses. When he turned the key over, the electric motor hummed, just audible under the ignition.

"Seat belt?" Tobias asked.

"No," Myrra responded. She didn't want to be any more strapped in than she already was.

Silence filled the car. She didn't know what to say to him. What did he expect this arrangement to be? Was he expecting sex? A picture of Sem popped into her mind, a whiskey glass in his hand, a look of anticipation on his face. Or Jake, taking the time to teach her, but always with a hand on the small of her back. And more, many more, before that. She'd used that tool when she had to; she didn't want to use it anymore. Myrra didn't want any more turmoil. She just wanted to feel safe.

And Charlotte. She wanted Charlotte to be safe.

"Where are we headed?" Tobias asked, both hands now on the steering wheel. He looked at her with an open expression. Open and transparent.

Myrra sighed. Her plan to save Charlotte was an outlandish one. Hard to buy into, hard to believe. She considered lying to him. It would be easy. She'd doled out lies to everyone her whole life, especially in the last few weeks. But as easy as they tasted, those same falsehoods were turning slightly poisonous on her tongue, one after the other like too much whiskey. She was getting a hangover from all this lying.

Ironically, the person she'd lied to the least was Tobias. She remembered the look on his face after the gravity cut out. He believed her now. And she needed to trust someone. This wasn't working alone.

"Are you OK?" Tobias asked. She must have looked tense.

"I'm fine. I'm thinking."

Tobias watched her, worried. "If you don't want me here, that's fine—I understand." His face fell as he said it, but he turned off the ignition and moved his hand to the door handle. "You can keep the car. I owe you that much."

Myrra reached out and laid a hand on his arm to stop him. "That's not it. I just—I have a plan. But it might be crazy. It might be completely pointless...I'm just worried you won't believe me."

Tobias let out a rueful laugh and shook his head. His hand fell away from the door. "I'm not allowed to *not* believe you anymore."

So Myrra started to explain, and, to her utter surprise, Tobias listened.

"I'm not sure I fully understand what escape is," Tobias said after she laid it out. He took great pains to keep his tone trusting and optimistic.

"I don't really know what escape is either," Myrra said. "All I know is what I got from Rachel—it's a program for the rich. And it's some sort of apocalypse avoidance."

"Wait—" A memory fluttered in Tobias's head. "I think I saw something about this, in Marcus Carlyle's correspondence history..." He reached for his bag, now tucked next to Charlotte in the back seat. Charlotte waved and grabbed for his wrists. He found his tablet and began rifling through the downloaded documents, noting with slight despair that his battery was down to 10 percent. They wouldn't be able to lean on technology much longer.

He found the folder with Marcus's correspondence. The "Escape Protocol" email was near the top, having been sent to his inbox shortly after he died. Myrra peered over his shoulder, reading with great interest. Phrases jumped out to Tobias that had previously seemed mundane—*life-planning program*, *limited-capacity offer*, *discretion*.

"'Escape' could mean nothing... but look at this message. This sounds like something, right?" Myrra said, turning to him. Her face was full of fear and hope. He desperately wanted to be the one to keep that hope alive. But...

"It does sound like something..." he started.

"Like maybe they have a shuttle, or some kind of hypersleep program—"

Hypersleep? He'd never heard of that working outside of science fiction, but he stopped himself from arguing. A shuttle or smaller craft seemed plausible. Especially paired with the phrase *limited capacity*. It made sense that Marcus Carlyle might be among the chosen few.

"The problem is, even if some sort of shuttle did exist, we would never be let on board. Are you trying to hijack it, force your way into whatever this is?" Tobias cringed at the thought. After seeing all the panic in Kittimer, after Barnes, after everything, he didn't want to face more conflict.

"No—" Myrra said, reaching out to touch his arm again in a comforting gesture, almost as if she'd read his mind. "No, you misunderstand. I don't think we can save ourselves. I think we might be able to save Charlotte."

Oh.

Tobias settled into this thought. It should have upset him, being presented with a chance to keep living only to have it yanked away. Instead it energized him. He was so incredibly tired, wading through thick murky grief. The thought of trying to fight for his own life, on top of everything else, frankly exhausted him. But fighting for Charlotte's life seemed easier, purer, somehow.

Myrra was still talking. "And I just think, if any sort of escape vehicle exists, it's bound to be in the hull, right? It's the only way out, to get to the edge of the world. So that's why I think we have to keep going through the desert..."

Tobias interrupted with one more question. "And you think they'd be willing to take Charlotte?"

"If they offered a spot to Marcus, right? They ought to take Charlotte. She's a Carlyle."

"Maybe."

It was still a thin premise. The logic was thin all the way through. But it made a kind of sense.

Myrra was staring resolutely out the windshield, her eyes a little glassy but focused. Sand was collecting on top of the windshield wipers.

"Imogene was a terrible mother, but she tried. I think her best act of motherhood might have been not taking Charlotte with her when she jumped." Myrra sniffed and wiped her nose on the back of her hand. "She left her with me for protection. I'm supposed to protect her. That's what parents are supposed to do."

There was a long silence as Myrra continued to stare through the glass, unblinking. Tobias knew there was more to this, could feel the layers of raw emotion stacked up, providing the foundations of Myrra's logic. He knew Myrra's file inside and out. Her mother had been gone by the time Myrra was five. Her father never even met her.

"That sounds nice, what you want to give to Charlotte. Protection." Tobias looked down at the palms of his hands, contemplating his fingerprints, all the tiny strands of genetic material. "My parents were pretty terrible too. I don't know if you could say they tried. Barnes"—his voice cracked a little at the mention of the name. "My adopted father, Barnes, he wasn't perfect either, but with him I felt safe. He did his best. All we can do is our best, I guess."

Myrra finally blinked and looked at him.

"When did he die?" she asked. The past tense must have tipped her off.

"He died a few hours after they announced on the news that it was the end of the world," he said, as if that weren't a completely ridiculous sentence. It felt so empty to say it.

She took his hand. Her skin felt dry but warm. "I'm sorry."

Their plan was a doomed one, Tobias was almost certain. But it felt right, to break the chain of hurt that David and Ingrid had passed down, to salve the wounds that Barnes's death had left behind, to chase protection for another, to focus on something outside of himself. All they could do was their best.

"I like your plan," Tobias said to Myrra, still holding her rough, cracked hand. "I think we should go for it."

Myrra smiled, and Tobias felt a little lighter. It was small, but it was something.

Tobias turned the ignition, and the engine whirred to life again. They drove slowly onward, over the flat road when it was wide enough, and sometimes over the sides of the dunes when it narrowed. Myrra worried once or twice that the car's tires would get stuck, but they kept on. Charlotte fell asleep to the sound of the motor after thirty minutes.

"How much longer do you think the car will go?" Myrra asked. Tobias jumped at the break in the quiet.

"I think it's got another day in it," he said. "Hopefully we can reach the wall by then, but if not, we'll be pretty close."

"Do you know anything about the wall, do you know if there's a way we can get into the hull from there?"

"Yeah, there should be. Engineers built in access doors." He gave her a strange look. "You didn't know that?"

"Not everyone gets to go to school to learn this stuff." She didn't like his tone. And she was sick of feeling stupid, sick of having to ask people how the world worked.

"How much school did they give you?" Tobias asked, a little hesitant.

"I got lessons one day a week until I was eight."

"They're supposed to keep you in school till you're sixteen, aren't they?" Tobias ventured.

"They don't really check. And anyway, I think it's easier for them if they keep us stupid." It was freeing to talk about this stuff openly, to let the anger in. Tobias didn't speak right away. Myrra hoped he was stewing in guilt.

"I'm sorry that's the way it was," he said. It sounded genuine enough. He kept his eyes on the road—what was visible beyond all that sand. "I don't know if you've heard how it usually goes when workers break contract. This was my first case in the field, but Simpson told me how in his experience they usually catch folks in about twenty-four to forty-eight hours. You had us on the run for weeks. So I don't know if it's any consolation, but even without the geography lessons, I'd say you're one of the smartest people I've ever met."

Myrra smiled. It was a smile fueled by anger and the satisfaction of disrupting people's expectations. She found a button on the side of the seat and reclined a few inches.

"What kinds of schools did you go to? How high did you go—all the way up?" she asked, knowing it would poke at his guilt.

"I got through university, if that's what you mean." He raised his eyebrows and half smiled. "But actually, I didn't have any regular schooling till I was about eleven. I had to take a ton of tests just to qualify for public, once Barnes tried to enroll me."

"So what happened to your birth parents? How did you end up with Barnes?" she asked, not caring to sugarcoat the question. She had a feeling Tobias would appreciate the directness.

Tobias didn't know how to begin. To explain his parents, he'd have to explain his upbringing. He wasn't sure Myrra really wanted to hear it. Nobody was really sincere when asking personal questions. When someone asked you how you were doing, they were looking for a fifteen-second answer at most. He stole a glance at her.

She seemed genuinely interested. She gave him a little shrug in response, as if to say, We have time.

In the end he let it all out. Tobias kept his composure and kept his eyes on the road, but he let loose his burden like a bucket dumping out water. And in talking he realized, possibly for the first time, how distant he felt from the rest of the world. He'd acclimated to loneliness from a young age, like a fish surviving in the shallowest of puddles, and as he grew, he'd enforced that loneliness in his adult life, refashioned his perspective on it as if it were some kind of strength of character.

Myrra stayed quiet except for an occasional *mm-hmm* of agreement or quick, soft "I'm sorry." He couldn't be sure, but it felt as if some of the tension was unwinding out of her. It hadn't been his intention to tell his sob story as a way to get her trust. Her life had been infinitely harder. More than anything, he didn't want her to feel as if he were trying to manipulate the situation. But if trust was the one silver lining to all this, he would take it.

The car hit a bump in the road, jostling Charlotte awake. She was crying before she even opened her eyes.

"Sorry," Tobias said as Myrra climbed into the back seat to comfort her.

"It's fine," Myrra responded. "She always wakes up like this."

He watched her in the rearview mirror. Myrra puffed up her cheeks, brought her face close to Charlotte's, and then dipped her head down and blew her cheeks out on Charlotte's belly. Charlotte hiccupped. Myrra blew another puff of air over her belly button, and this time Charlotte relented and giggled.

"Hello, little girl!" Myrra tickled her sides. "Hello!"

Myrra settled herself into the seat next to Charlotte and started up a round of peekaboo. She caught Tobias's eye in the rearview, and he shifted his eyes back to the road.

"You haven't spent much time around children, have you?"

Tobias shook his head. He was embarrassed but couldn't quite tell why.

The sky started acting strange. Myrra was leaning her cheek against the window, looking straight up, following a single cloud with her eyes. She noticed the color of the sky behind the cloud steadily change. Shade by shade it shifted from light blue to greenish blue to yellow to orange in the span of five minutes. According to the clock in the car, it was around three in the afternoon.

"Do you see—?" Myrra didn't finish the sentence. She couldn't think of an easy way to describe it.

She could tell that Tobias hadn't noticed; he was too busy concentrating on the road. Myrra gestured up at the sky through the window—it grew darker before their eyes, the colors dimming into a deeper orange, rosy along the edges of the horizon, like a ripe peach. It was a sped-up sunset.

"What's going on?" Tobias asked, though Myrra didn't know if he expected her to give an answer. He stopped the car and got out to get a better look. Myrra followed him.

"Do you suppose certain things are just glitching now, now that the world's breaking down?" Tobias asked.

"Could be," Myrra said. The sky was a deep violet now, as sensuous as one of Imogene's velvet cushions—stars winked on in the dark expanse. "Or, if there's someone who usually programs this stuff, maybe they just decided to fuck off and now the system's going haywire."

Myrra stared straight up and counted the stars as they appeared. She turned to look at Tobias beside her: his mouth was wide open, his eyes big as saucers. Myrra laughed.

"What?" Tobias asked.

"You're so serious," she said.

"These are serious times," Tobias replied.

"Serious and absurd."

A glaring orange light caught Myrra full in the face. Behind them, like a band coming back for an encore, the sun started to rise.

They stopped for the night, though night was a relative concept now. The sun had risen and set five times in the last five hours. Tobias pinched blankets and shirts in the cracks between the windows and the doors to get it as dark as possible. Even with the improvised shades, he wasn't sure he'd be able to sleep.

Myrra read to Charlotte in the back of the car. "'All around the sun was shining and the bell was ringing and the woods were thinning and the green was shining.'" Charlotte's eyes were drooping. Her little head sank down into the pile of scarves Myrra had set up for her as a pillow.

Tobias listened, leaning against the side door and staring at the empty passenger seat. It was soothing to listen to Myrra read, but something about the words made Tobias feel incredibly vulnerable. They were such delicate beings, trapped in such a harsh place. The wind raged again. All around them there were small little pinging noises as the sand hit the windows and the sides of the car. A chorus of sand.

"'It made her feel a little lonesome, until then she had been busy climbing but now she was beginning beginning hearing everything and it was a little lonesome.'"

Myrra slowed down on the last words, let her voice diminish in volume, looked over the top of the book to watch Charlotte. The baby let out a small snore. Closing the book and bunching up the corner of her sleeve, Myrra delicately wiped away the snot that was dripping out of Charlotte's nose.

Myrra leaned her head back against the leather headrest and regarded Tobias. He looked back at her, but both kept quiet. *Quiet* was a relative term—Charlotte was still snoring, and sand was still pelting the plexiglass. But it still felt quiet.

"That's an odd story, isn't it? I don't remember reading anything like that when I was a kid." He kept his voice soft, glancing over at Charlotte asleep.

"I like it," Myrra said. "It has simple words. I used to borrow books from Marcus's collection, but they were always harder to get through."

He looked down at the book in her hand. Such a rare thing; he'd handled only one or two books in his entire life. He held out a hand.

"May I?"

Myrra handed it over to him gently. There were pages torn out; he shuddered as though he were looking at an amputated limb. Tobias leafed through its browning pages, turning each over gingerly between two fingers.

"Jake gave you this, right?" he asked while examining an illustration of a boy and a lion.

"Yes." Myrra sounded surprised, and Tobias realized his faux pas. It was an awkward reminder that he'd studied her and that only a few days prior he'd been hunting her.

"How much do you know about me, exactly?" she asked.

Tobias was too tired for quick thinking, though he desperately wished he could soften the situation with a few white lies.

"I know a lot about you. More than I should," he said finally. "Part of the job. I'm sorry."

Through a crack in the blankets, the orange light of a sunset filtered through. Or maybe it was a sunrise. He'd lost track. Tobias reclined his seat, enough to lean back but not enough to squish

Charlotte, asleep on the seat behind him. He stretched out on his side and watched Myrra. She looked regretful but not suspicious.

"Did you guys talk to Jake?" Myrra asked.

"Yeah, we talked to him," Tobias said.

Myrra winced at the thought.

"I treated him badly," she admitted. "I led him on. I didn't love him."

Tobias thought back to the interview, how much he'd judged Jake at the time. He'd felt so much older, so much smarter, but in the end he wasn't above anyone. Cosmically, he was just as clueless as the next person.

"I'm sorry about that," Myrra continued. Her eyelids were drooping. "It's strange, I didn't think I would be, but I am. He offered me friendship, and I used him."

"He'll be fine," he said, trying to sound reassuring. There was nothing else to say. They would never see Jake again. "As fine as any of us can be."

Myrra couldn't get it out of her head, how much Tobias knew about her. She knew he felt bad about it, and that on some level it was part of his job; that's what agents did, investigated people. He was trying his best to play it down; on the long drive, he listened to her tell stories of her life, acted interested in them, even if she had a sneaking suspicion that he knew some of the details already.

"I need a distraction," she said. This was partially true—Tobias had been quiet for the past few hours, and she was tired of talking. "Tell me something about yourself, something I don't know."

"Um. OK," he replied, grinning uncomfortably. It was fun to throw him off balance. He thought for a minute, then slowed the car down and pulled out his tablet, clicked on a photo album, and handed it to her. Then he resumed driving. Safety first, Myrra thought.

The album was a series of paintings; Myrra could tell by the variations in style that they had been painted by a number of different artists. They were stranger, moodier, less classical than the pieces that Marcus had collected and shown on his walls. She sifted through the photos, holding for a few seconds on each one.

"My family once had a great art collection, back on the old world. They sold half of it off to buy passage to Telos. David never shut up about it, and it was the only story of his that I actually liked hearing." Tobias mostly kept his eyes on the road, but she noticed he couldn't help stealing glances down at the tablet in her hands to see which one she was looking at. He peered down as her hand hovered over a nude portrait. "That's Lucian Freud—he's great—"

They were beautiful pieces—some of them looked familiar, as if maybe Myrra had seen them in a book or on the walls of an art collector's penthouse. She'd gone along to enough meetings and dinner parties at the Carlyles' behest; she'd seen plenty.

"So now," Tobias continued, "anytime I visit a museum, or end up at a fancy party, I look around at the art on the walls, to see if any of it once belonged to my family. I've never found one, though." She shifted to another painting, and when Tobias caught the one she was looking at, he touched her hand to stop her from shifting to the next image. "This one's my favorite. The painter was trying to count to infinity—"

It was a simple gray painting with lines of white-painted numbers scrolling across the canvas. Of course, Myrra thought. Of course this was his favorite painting. It was the most orderly thing she'd ever seen. Then a jolt of familiarity hit, and she realized; she sat up and turned to him. "I've seen this!"

"You're joking." Tobias's eyes widened. "Where?"

She felt giddy, as if they were two strangers meeting at a bar, shocked to have the same friend in common, or to find out that they had both grown up in the same small town.

"It was at Senator Davis's house, in his entryway. Imogene used to loan me out to their kitchen staff whenever she visited for a dinner party." Myrra leaned closer, her eyes wide, her body alive with a sudden surge of energy. "It confused me; I didn't really understand what all the numbers meant. I thought maybe it was a painting of a receipt, or computer code."

"Nope," Tobias said. "It was infinity all along."

"Do you know how high he got, before he died?"

Tobias furrowed his brow. "Actually, I don't."

Charlotte was in the back seat, playing with a set of keys that Tobias had found in the bottom of his knapsack. "They're to my apartment. So they're pretty useless, at this point," he'd said upon handing them over, not without amusement.

Charlotte had come up with a game where she'd drop the keys on the floor, shout, "Uh-oh" (her new favorite sound), and wait for Myrra to retrieve them. The repetition was starting to get to Myrra. She was up front with Tobias, looking warily at the charge display on the car's dashboard. The battery was getting low. To keep her eyes off the battery light on the dash, Myrra tried looking out the window instead. The sun continued to rise and set at a maddening pace, but what was more concerning was the clouds clustering in lumps above them. Up until this point the sky had been clear, with only the occasional wisp of white passing by.

"It's not usual for there to be this many clouds out here, is it?" she asked. It seemed like the type of thing Tobias would know.

Tobias followed her eyes and looked up at the mass above them. "No. It's probably due to messed-up daylight patterns."

The next time the sun rose, Myrra marked the color of them—they were no longer white. Now they were swollen and gray, big bellied with rain. Within ten minutes, fat water droplets were splatting against the windshield. Here and there at first, and then more and more until sheets of water cascaded against the glass. Through the sound of water pounding against metal, Myrra heard a telltale jangling noise from the back seat. Charlotte had dropped the keys again.

"Uh-oh!" she shouted.

"Shit," Tobias mumbled. Myrra watched as he toggled the windshield wipers to their fastest setting. The dunes outside swam together through a watery filter, watercolor sweeps of blue and brown and green and white. Now Myrra truly felt as though they were at sea.

Tobias sat forward in the driver's seat, pushing his face closer to the windshield. Charlotte started to fuss, and Myrra reached around on the floor behind the seats, searching for the keys she'd dropped. "OK, sweetie, OK..."

"Deserts aren't meant to have this much rain," she heard Tobias say. He sounded apprehensive. "It's going to flood."

Myrra felt the jagged edge of cold metal deep under Tobias's seat. How the keys had wandered that far in such a short time was a mystery. She deposited them back in Charlotte's hands.

"Uh-oh," Charlotte said again.

"Uh-oh," Myrra parroted back. "You dropped the keys! Hang on to them this time, OK?"

"Oh," Charlotte replied. She wove her fingers in between the bits of metal, entranced.

"Will we be OK?" Myrra asked Tobias, settling back into her seat.

"I don't know," Tobias mumbled, squinting to try to see.

And then, ten minutes into another nightfall, there was another earthquake. Myrra heard the rumble of the ground and what sounded like the rumble of sand being displaced in the dunes. It was impossible to see anything outside. The car stopped with a sudden jolt. As slowly as they were going, Myrra was still flung forward, ending up half in her seat and half on the floor. She craned her neck back from her jostled position to check the back seat. Charlotte was safely strapped in.

"Battery dead?" Myrra asked, pulling herself back up. No—the wipers were still going full tilt. Tobias pushed on the accelerator; Myrra heard the whir of tires spinning underneath them, but felt no motion.

"I think we're stuck in mud," Tobias said. He unbuckled his seat belt. "I'm going to go see how bad it is."

He shook his shoulders a little, steeling himself, then opened the door and rushed out, slamming it shut before too much rain could get in. It was as though he'd disappeared completely; the water flowed so thickly down the windows, it was impossible to make out his shape outside. Myrra waited a few minutes. She cupped her hands against the window, pushed her face close to the glass; nothing. Myrra looked back at Charlotte—she was swinging the keys around and around the metal circle of the ring, mesmerized. She would be fine for a few minutes. Myrra counted to ten, then jumped out of the car to find Tobias.

Her feet were immediately submerged up to the ankles in loose wet sand. She hadn't even had a chance to look around the car for Tobias before her clothes were soaked through. She found him on his hands and knees at the front driver's-side tire, digging away the sand that had piled in front of it.

"Here—" she shouted, getting down on all fours next to him to assist. Tobias looked at her through the water beading on his glasses. She could tell he was on the verge of protesting and telling her to get back in the car, but then he seemed to think better of it and continued digging.

She sank her arms in up to her elbows and flung mud behind her, but it was no use; more mud just poured down to replace it.

"Let's get back in," Tobias eventually shouted to her over the din of the rain. "We won't be able to do anything until the rain lets up."

She nodded at him, and they raced back to their respective car doors. The moment the doors clicked shut, Myrra noticed the difference in sound; it wasn't quiet per se, but everything was suddenly muffled. Charlotte still twirled her keys, enviously dry. They were trapped in a bubble under the sea, their own miniature Palmer. She sat and stared ahead at the windshield in shock, completely drenched. Water dripped off her hair onto the car seat. Pat. Pat. Pat.

She turned to Tobias. Myrra couldn't see his eyes through all the condensation that had formed on his glasses. His dark-brown hair had gone black with wet and was plastered in curls to his forehead. Clothing was merely a film clinging to their bodies at this point. Tobias pulled off his glasses and, in a futile attempt, tried to wipe them down on the sopping corner of his shirt.

"Do you have towels packed somewhere around here?" Myrra asked. She looked over the top of the back seat—clothes and bags were piled in small mountains in the hatchback trunk.

"No," Tobias said, his shoulders slumping. "Towels would have been useful."

They dried themselves off with diapers instead. Myrra counted out how many they had left. There should still be enough for Charlotte to last until they died. Her spine tingled underneath her wet clothing. It was unsettling to consider death in such practical terms.

Tobias hung his head upside down beside the dash and rubbed the inside of a diaper back and forth against his hair.

"This works surprisingly well," he said, rubbing the edge of the diaper around his ears.

"The best brand for absorbing moisture," she said, holding up the package. She'd wrapped two diapers around her own hair, but her clothes were soaked through. Tobias's clothes were dripping as well.

Tobias caught her eye. "I snagged some of the clothes you dumped, if you want to change."

Myrra glanced around the confines of the car.

"I won't look if you won't," he added.

She climbed back and rifled through Tobias's supplies, tossing him a gray button-down shirt followed by jeans, boxers, and a pair of thick socks. Searching through the odds and ends, she found a serviceable blue dress for herself. Leggings. Bra. Underwear. All wonderfully dry. She changed, keeping her body facing the rear of the car, patting down the last bits of sopping skin. Her feet were still bare.

"Can I steal a pair of your socks?" she called up, and out of instinct she turned to look at Tobias. He was only halfway into his shirt, contorted, trying to pull his jeans up over his boxers. It was an endearing pose; he looked like a teenager hurrying back into his clothes after a midnight tryst, just about to sneak out his girlfriend's window. Tobias blushed, and she hurriedly turned back around.

"Sorry—" she shouted over her shoulder.

"Oh, no—it's fine," he said. "And sure, take the socks."

She slipped on a thick gray pair and wiggled her toes happily in the enveloping dry warmth. The gray matched Tobias's shirt. He was fastidious enough; no doubt that was on purpose.

"OK, dressed," he shouted from the front.

Myrra took one of the half-damp diapers and wiped off the front seat before climbing over and sitting back down next to him. She heard the keys clang to the floor behind her.

"Uh-oh!" Charlotte cried out, clearly thrilled with herself.

Myrra retrieved them, then Tobias took a turn, then Myrra again, while they listened to the rain subside and waited for the sand to dry out. The earth shook again, a tiny quake. The sun set and rose.

33

MYRRA & TOBIAS

Tobias had hoped that being around Myrra and Charlotte would keep him calm, but that wasn't strictly true. Myrra did not fix his mental state—in fact she complicated it. Just his having to regularly interact with a person meant that Tobias's emotions were more present on the surface—anxieties that he'd usually try to ignore were now mirrored in Myrra. In many ways he felt closer to a breakdown now than he had in Kittimer. But it didn't matter. It was good to have her around. No, *good* was too simple—nothing about life was good right now. Myrra was neither good nor bad, Charlotte was neither good nor bad. But they were necessary. It was necessary to have someone there to fret over, to consider when making choices, to react to, to argue with, to talk to, to remind him that he was alive. In all his ball of pain, it was necessary to remember that he was still alive.

The car didn't last very long past the rainstorm. Steadily, incrementally, it slowed and puttered until it stopped moving altogether.

Myrra, who'd had her eyes glued to the charge display on the dash for the past hour, let out a sigh.

"That's that," she said, sounding frustrated but also resigned.

Tobias slumped forward and let his forehead come to rest on the steering wheel. He closed his eyes and tried not to feel hopeless. They'd been driving for two days and they were still surrounded by sand. It was hard to hold on to the feeling that not too long ago, he'd looked around and considered this sand beautiful and majestic, all the blues and greens. Things could change from majestic to monotonous in no time at all.

He heard the sound of the car door wrenching and squelching open—the machinery was still a little waterlogged. He raised his head back up. Myrra was walking down the road, peering ahead with her hand shading her face, examining the way forward. Myrra was always pushing forward. It was awe inspiring.

"Tobias," she called out. He liked that she hadn't yet tried to call him Toby, but that he wasn't Bendel to her either, as his coworkers always called him.

"Yeah?" he answered back.

"Come out here a minute—does the sky look strange to you?"

He braced himself for another rainstorm, or lightning, or a tornado—who knew what the universe would throw at them next? He climbed out of the car and stretched his arms and legs, trying to wrench the frustration from his body. From her spot in the back seat, Charlotte watched Tobias and started crying the second he closed the car door.

"Charlotte's crying," Tobias said. Myrra cocked an ear toward the sound, as though trying to suss out a foreign language.

"She wants you to pick her up," Myrra said.

"Me?" Tobias asked. He pointed a finger at his own chest and then felt like an idiot. As if to confirm this, Myrra laughed at him.

"Yeah, you. She didn't mind when I got out of the car." Tobias looked at Myrra, then at Charlotte, then back at Myrra again, unsure of what to do. Myrra laughed again.

"Go pick her up." She waved a hand at him, shooing him toward Charlotte.

He opened the door to the back seat, bent down, and unstrapped Charlotte from her seat. She stopped crying immediately and raised her arms to him. He lifted her and held her against the side of his torso with her chubby little legs straddling his waist. She relaxed and leaned her head against his shoulder. Tobias stopped moving and just watched her, awestruck at her trust.

"Come over here," Myrra said. "Take a look at the sky."

He walked over and stood next to her. The sky did look strange: a little too bright, a little too flat. Not like vast space. More like a wall. Tobias smiled in relief.

"We're close," he said.

Myrra laid a reassuring hand on his arm, then combed the sand out of Charlotte's hair. Tobias like the gesture; it felt familiar, as if Myrra had brushed her hand over his arm before, as if they'd known each other for years rather than weeks.

They packed bags with essentials and abandoned the car. Myrra let Tobias keep Charlotte, surprising herself with how little she minded Tobias holding her. "I have a scarf that I use as a sling when I want my hands free," she offered, but Tobias refused. Myrra caught his small smile when Charlotte nestled her head deeper into his shoulder, and she understood.

As they walked, the road straightened out and the dunes got smaller. Myrra had imagined that the wall of the horizon would be painted, like the traditional scene paintings displayed in the Carlyles' entryway. But as they approached the wall, she saw that it was actually a massive glowing projection screen. It made sense—the way the colors of the sky changed and shifted with the time of day, the horizon couldn't exist as a single flat landscape.

The closer they got, the brighter the screen became, until they were just feet away from the wall and it was a wall of undecipherable light. Even now, as the colors of the sky shifted toward dusk, it was oppressively bright when you stood this close. Myrra squinted, trying to adjust her eyes—so this was the edge of the world, the start of the sky. She'd never felt so small. Even if it was just technology and engineering, it felt as though she were staring into the face of the gods.

"Did they teach you about this in school?" Myrra asked. Her voice came out hushed.

"No," Tobias replied, also keeping his tone reverently quiet. Charlotte moaned and tried to bury her face in Tobias's shirt.

Myrra's eyes were starting to hurt. They needed to focus: a road as long as this didn't just end in a spot of nowhere against a wall. There had to be something. She tried to make out any discernible shapes through the glare, and—there. A few meters away, there was a large steel door embedded in the screen.

"Over here—" She ran toward it.

The door was heavy, but with the two of them pulling at the handle, it opened. Tobias looked at her with uncertainty. On the other side was a long dark corridor; the walls, ceiling, and floor were entirely made of metal. It reminded Myrra of the machinery in the factory where she and her mother had once worked. It was impossible to see very far inside. Somewhere deep in the blackness, Myrra heard a rhythmic thumping. It hummed in the bones of her chest.

The hall was shadowed and black and wet, with water or hydraulic oil, Myrra couldn't be sure. Not at all like a place where the rich might escape. "They even die better than we do," Rachel had said. Whatever this was, it wasn't *better.* It seemed less and less likely that there would be anything here that could save Charlotte. Myrra felt the cloud of this knowledge, this suspicion, descend upon her like fog on a mountain. But we are here now, she thought. We are here now, with nowhere else to go. Her thin string of hope was going to snap at any minute, the invisible line that had pulled her along this far. But it wasn't gone yet. And she had to see this through. She couldn't die with a maybe.

Myrra felt Tobias's hand on her shoulder.

"Forward?" he asked.

"Forward," she replied, putting on a resolute face.

They crossed the threshold of the door, closing it behind them.

It wasn't as dark as it had initially looked. Once they were away from the blinding light of the horizon wall, Tobias could start to make out his surroundings. The dim hallway became clearer: pipes and valves overhead, metal grating under their feet. Lamps with metal shades swung from naked wires attached to the ceiling. Compared to the light they had just seen, these gave out only the barest pinpricks of illumination. This must be the inside of the hull.

Charlotte let out a high-pitched scream, then giggled when she heard her own voice bounce off the metal walls. He wished she wouldn't; they didn't know who was around to hear. "Shhhh..." Tobias whispered, bouncing her in his arms.

There was a distant sound reverberating through the pipes as they walked—Tobias listened and tried to make it out. At first it sounded to him like a heartbeat, and a sudden panicked thought ran through him, that they had entered through the mouth of some beast and were now traveling through his innards, hearing his blood pulse, while they waited to be digested.

"It's music," Myrra said suddenly, as if reading his thoughts. Music? He listened closer. The heartbeat turned into a bass line. Tobias was reminded of electronica clubs in New London, speakers thumping out bass beats so hard they shook the floor. He'd had to sit through one too many deafening nights like that in training, when Barnes had assigned him to shadow the Narcotics Division.

At one point Tobias tripped over something soft. He looked down: it was a leg. Peering closer, he realized it was a young man leaned against the wall. A girl about his age lay beside him, her arms entwined around his shoulders. Both were pale, with dirt and oil smeared on their skins; their clothes might at one time have had defining color but were now a faded gray-brown. They were so still, it was hard to tell if they were dead or sleeping. Tobias crouched down and pulled an empty bottle out of the girl's hand. The bottle looked as if it had once contained cleaning solvent. That would put someone to sleep, he thought. He looked closer. It was shallow, but they were breathing.

"Tobias?" he heard Myrra whisper somewhere ahead of him. He stood and jogged to catch up.

The hallway ended with another metal door, this one with a tiny porthole window. Myrra was craning her neck up to get a look—she wasn't quite tall enough. Tobias peered through, over her head, but couldn't make out more than some railings and pipes.

"Forward," he said, and they heaved the door open with its large metal handle. The music instantly got louder, blaring out of some unseen speakers, bouncing off the metal walls.

"Look..." Myrra tugged on his sleeve and pointed above them. Scaffolding and metal staircases rose and unfolded above them, flight after flight, level after level, into a distance that was too high to see and too vast to comprehend. Everything was lit with the same metal lamps, casting harsh blue industrial light that threw shadows onto every surface. At the levels nearest to them, Tobias could make out the lines of the stairs and stair rails and grated walkways, but the farther they rose, the more each piece just tangled into an indiscernible thicket of lines and darkness. Now that he was properly taking in his surroundings, Tobias noticed that there was near-infinite space to their right and their left as well. The distance from the door they had just walked through to the metal wall in front of them looked to be about ten meters, but the distances above them and to either side swept on forever. It made the skyscrapers of New London look like a child's building blocks by comparison.

There were people clustered in groups here and there, sprawled out on the floor and on the walkways above them. The stench of sweat and medicinal alcohol filled the air. They moved forward, looking for signs or any sort of guidepost that could tell them where they were. They walked past stairs and railings, ducking under beams and wiring. Tobias looked up through a grate directly above them only to see a man and woman, naked and emaciated, fucking and grunting in the open air. Myrra grabbed his hand and hurried them forward.

Once they were clear, Myrra stopped and looked at Charlotte, as if checking to make sure she was still there. Her eyes had that wild animal look again, same as in Nabat. Tobias handed Charlotte to her, hoping that would help. She clutched Charlotte and looked at Tobias gratefully. He wished he could hug her, but knew better than to try.

This place felt like the dorms in her worst moments, it felt like factory machinery, it felt like every claustrophobic place where Myrra had been stowed, all her life, in between bouts of working. She could feel cold sweat pouring off her skin. She looked over at

Tobias: he looked scared too. Somehow that helped; it wasn't just she who felt crazy here. It wasn't just her own paranoia seeping in. Charlotte clutched at her side and sucked on the fabric of her dress—she didn't like it here either.

At one point a woman shouted at them, sitting up from her spot on a staircase.

"Where the hell did you come from?" Her hair hung in mats from the side of her head. She gaped at them, openmouthed: half her teeth were gone, and the teeth that remained were blackened and rotting away.

"What is this place?" Myrra asked.

"I asked you first," the woman said. She was slurring her words a little.

"We came in from the desert," Tobias said. Myrra noticed that he was trying to make his voice sound deeper. "Where are we now?"

"You are in between the inner and outer hull. And this"—she threw her arms out haphazardly—"is our end-of-the-world party!" She let out a cackle that sounded like a motor dying.

"How the heck did you get here from the desert?" she asked.

"We had a car."

"It still work?"

"No," Tobias said. "The battery died about a kilometer away from the wall."

The woman rose up on unsteady knees. Myrra noticed a pipe in her hand, something fashioned out of a bottle cap, tape, and some metal tubing. Something black, oily, and acrid was crumpled in the bowl of the pipe. On reflex, she turned and pulled Charlotte away from the cloud of smoke.

"I'll tell the boys," she said. "They might want to go salvage the battery acid."

"For what?" Myrra asked, then immediately regretted it.

"There's all sorts of fun things you can make with battery acid," the woman said, flashing a hollow black-toothed grin. She wandered up the staircase, out of sight.

"Fuck," Myrra mumbled, stroking Charlotte's hair. It was as though they'd crossed the threshold into hell.

Myrra remembered the stories from her childhood, talk of workers being thrown into sewers when they were bad, or getting processed into dog food. Myrra thought of Cora, her legs flailing as she squeezed through a window, the sound of tranq darts, the fear and bile that had filled her as a child. And she knew, as suddenly as an electric shock, that this was where Cora had gone.

"Who are all these people?" Tobias asked.

"I'm pretty sure they're contract workers. Runaways," Myrra said.

"How can you tell?"

"I just know."

She absorbed that thought, let it sink in, how her identity had been shaped, how thin the border was between who she was and livestock. She thought of her mother, whose mind had slipped too far, whose hands had lost their grip on that imaginary thread of sanity.

She looked at Tobias. Already a fine layer of grime was accumulating on his cheeks. He had looked so sheepish when he revealed how much he knew about her background. Would he know? Had he known, all along?

"When my mother left..." she started, choosing to say "left" instead of "was taken" because it had always felt like a choice to Myrra, that her mother had walked out on her rather than been dragged, as unfair as that might be. "Before she left, she wasn't...

well. She'd given up, in a sense. Do you know what happened to her?"

It drained her, just to ask the question. It felt like jumping off a building. She hoped she could survive the answer.

Tobias stared past her, into the tangled metal around them, as if trying to work out his own memories.

"Ami Dal got put into a mental hospital on suicide watch," he said.

This was it, she thought. She steeled herself, picturing how it must have happened, almost in the same ways she'd been picturing her own death most nights, over and over. When it came to her mother's fate, a million horrible scenarios had run in a maddening cycle through Myrra's head since childhood. All the ways she could have done it, some outlandish, some mundane. At least here maybe that cycle would stop.

"But eventually, after a number of escape attempts and disturbances, she got labeled a problem patient and was transferred to an alternate facility."

Myrra snapped back in. That wasn't the answer she'd been expecting. "What? Where?"

"I don't know. The file didn't say anything more."

"Escape attempts." "Disturbances." That sounded like a woman fighting, not one who had given up, after all. Something, Myrra would probably never know what, had kept her from taking the plunge. There are so many of us tempted to let death in, she thought, imagining Imogene on the terrace wall and remembering herself not too long ago, panicked and gripping the rail of a cliffside balcony. Who knows what small thing did it for her, what keeps us from letting death in. Even now, when death waits at the threshold for the whole world.

Her mother had been a troublesome patient. Tobias's eyes widened. Something clicked.

Myrra guessed his train of thought.

"She was sent here."

Even with the proof laid out in front of him, Tobias's mind went into denial on reflex. No. He'd been told, in training, what happened to escaped contract workers—there was some sort of rehabilitation program they were sent to. All systematic, all objective. Agents tracked down workers who broke contract, took evidence into account, gave them their fair trial.

But. Had he ever seen with his own eyes what happened to workers after their conviction? They just loaded them into transfer vans. He remembered Barnes explaining it to him—it was a separate government department. His heart sank with the realization. He had never thought about it, any of it.

Had Barnes known? Probably not—Barnes took bureaucracy at face value. But not questioning it was just as great a sin as knowing in the first place. He thought back to the beliefs he had learned from Barnes: it wasn't a fair system, but it was what they had to work with, and they couldn't change it at this point.

There came another rush of guilt. What did it mean to mourn a man you loved and at the same time be rudely awakened to his flaws? Tobias didn't know how to hold both those feelings at once. All he knew was that he was drowning in sorrow.

He looked at Myrra and wondered why she tolerated his presence at all. Myrra was stroking Charlotte's hair with a far-off look. Was her mother alive somewhere here? Maybe his whole purpose in the end would be to reunite them and then go die somewhere alone. Maybe with an act like that he could be absolved.

"They used to tell us such horror stories of what would happen if we ran off," she said. There was a long silence afterward. Tobias couldn't tell if there was more to the story.

"I'm so sorry," he started, and then couldn't think of what to apologize for first. For his complicity? For handcuffing her? For her entire life? He couldn't find a way to finish, so his "sorry" just hung in the air, dangling like a loose shoelace.

"Tell me what you're thinking," he asked.

"I'm thinking we need to find whoever's in charge." She didn't look like she hated him.

Tobias shifted gears, jumped into problem-solving mode. If he couldn't apologize for the problems of the world, he could at least fix the problem at hand.

Tobias looked around at all the levels above them. If this really was the space between the inner and outer hull, then it was enormous. Unfathomably enormous. Finding any one particular person in this place would be like trying to find a single grain of sand on a beach.

Don't think of the big picture, he thought. Just like in any other investigation, just take the most logical path, step by step, and the big picture will find you.

"Let's find the source of this music," he said, gesturing to the thumping beats reverberating through the pipes and the walls. "Whoever set this up is bound to know something."

"You're right." She stayed where she was, standing tall, holding Charlotte in a secure embrace. But her expression faltered, just a little. Almost imperceptibly, the corners of her mouth turned downward.

"Forward," he said, and took her hand.

It was harder, almost, to imagine her mother sane. To imagine her continuing and fighting against her circumstances. She'd repeated to herself over and over, as she grew, as she moved from one demeaning job to the next: I will not be like her. I will not give up. There is always a way out. I will fight. I will not be like her. Sadness over her loss had curdled into anger long ago, and she'd built the foundations of her identity on that anger. It had driven her forward. What would drive her now?

Charlotte reached up and tugged on a lock of her hair. There was Charlotte. There was always Charlotte.

She looked around at the endless thicket of metal and shadows surrounding them. The sane part of her brain warned her: There is no escape here. No escape for anyone, no matter how rich or highborn. But the insane part of her still held on—there was still a maybe there. There was still a door that hadn't yet closed.

She didn't hold on to the idea because it made any sort of sense. She held on because she needed a reason to keep going. Now, in the absence of anger, this was all she had.

34

IN BETWEEN

It's hard to know the best way to build a world, just as it's hard to know the best way to tell a story. One very important question faced the designers of the world the ship: Would they build it to reflect the actual circumstances of its surroundings, or would they keep the world an insulated closed system? To put it another way: Would they build windows?

Their first instinct was for windows, just as someone telling a story initially thinks that the best course is to tell the bare, unvarnished truth. But as anyone knows who has lived in the shifting, complicated realm of humanity, truth is not a singular thing. Facts are something else; facts are finite and unchanging, but truth is different from fact, and there are as many versions of the truth as there are people to consider it. It was a fact that these architects and engineers were designing a ship whose purpose was to propel itself through space for a period of centuries, until it reached the new home world. But this would also be a place where people would be born, grow, and die without ever knowing the ship's origin point or its destination. In fact, it was a ship, but in truth, it would be the world to the people living inside it.

In the end they opted to keep it an enclosed space. It is not for us to say if that was a wrong or right choice, but it was a choice made by people chasing the spirit of the truth. They hid any especially unsightly scenery between two layers: the outside hull and the walls of the inner world. Inside this narrow space is a world of gears and grease and machinery, rusted spots patched with tar on the walls, and wires in bundles following mazelike patterns along the ceilings and the walls and underneath the grates in the floors. A lot of moving parts go into making a world work. It is a monstrous, exquisite machine, and it takes a lot of people to maintain and operate it.

At first workers tasked with the job were paid engineers and mechanics, but their morale started breaking as they worked between the walls. Eventually the government opted to keep a small staff of mechanics on the job to oversee operations, well paid and rotated out weekly for sanity's sake. All grunt jobs were taken over by runaway contract workers, placed in a new work detail by the government's penal system. There was less worry for these workers' psychological well-being: they were all half-insane already.

The workers in the hull were the first to know that something had gone wrong with the ship. They knew on instinct, they knew it without knowing, based on the sounds of the creaking metal, the change in the vibrations of the engines, the static in the air. They knew before the engineers checked in, before word was relayed to politicians, before the public was alerted and consumed in despair. That was their privilege.

It is also their privilege to see the space outside; unlike the inner confines of the world, the outer hull does have windows. They were installed for practical purposes, but the workers in this part of the world regard them with deific adoration. After a lifetime encased in narrow, dark machinery, most workers do not wish to go back into the aesthetically designed world. They look out at the stars through these windows and comfort themselves with the knowledge that they are seeing the universe as it really is. This is their truth.

When the world finally cracks open, the workers in this in-between place will all be sucked out into the black. Being so close to the outer layers of the ship, they will be the first to go. And for them, as it is for all, death will be confusing and terrifying. But they will have spent their lives looking out at space through a pane of reinforced plexiglass, with their faces pressed against it, feeling the cold, mere centimeters away from oblivion. They have been waiting for oblivion; it has always stood right outside their door. There will be relief in finally meeting it, mixed in with all the pain, like pulling out a loose tooth—the soreness, the uncertainty, then a pop, a sting, a bleed, and: done.

35

MYRRA & TOBIAS

They kept walking, occasionally stopping to talk to people clustered together in underfed groups, when they looked sober enough to speak. There was a lot of interest in Charlotte, people reaching out to her with waggling fingers, big smiles on their faces. Myrra responded with smiles of her own, but kept a tight hold on Charlotte. Some folks seemed normal enough: pale and thin, but able to laugh and hold a conversation. Others seemed as if their sanity was on a knife's edge.

One woman, old, but hard to tell how old, since everyone here had skin that sagged and cracked around the eyes, asked Myrra about their previous lives and occupations. Myrra told the truth about herself: being a contract worker here meant solidarity, that she was to be trusted.

Before Tobias had a chance to open his mouth, Myrra also cut in on his behalf. "He's a journalist," she said, shooting Tobias a look. "He wrote obituaries for the *New London Times*."

Tobias nodded, agreeing to the lie. Being a Security agent wouldn't go over well here.

"That's nice," the old woman said. "Did you ever write one for Beverly Moss? She was my employer; died about ten years ago from liver failure."

Tobias looked slightly confused but played along.

"No," he said. "That was before my time."

"No matter. I certainly didn't mourn her." The woman shrugged and chewed on something absently in the back of her jaw.

Through the bits and pieces of half-drunk conversation, they finally figured out that the hull was divided into ten giant vertical sectors. They were in Sector Nine.

"We're lucky—Sector Eight is where the breach is. Could have been us," the old woman said. "They've had that sector vacuum-sealed for over a year, trying to make repairs."

Myrra pictured the diagram of the world again, a tin can cylinder. In its interior, one flat circle was the ground, and the other the sky. Thinking of these sectors, she pictured them separating in tall vertical stripes along the sides of the cylinder.

"Does that sound right?" she asked him, trying to convey the visual she'd imagined. Tobias had been to university, surely he would know.

He looked apologetic. "I honestly don't know. They kind of glossed over the mechanics of the hull—I'm not sure the teachers really understood it."

The music was getting louder. They must be getting closer. They asked directions from a young couple raiding a utility closet; according to them, the person running the DJ booth was named Tom. The young woman pointed to her right. "If you walk three levels up on the stairs, it's an hour's walk that way."

Her companion had one bony arm gripped around her waist, and the other arm was filled with boxes of food and bottles of drain cleaner. His pupils were wide and black, his eyes bloodshot, but his smile was warm. So many of the younger workers were paired up, huddled together, flirting. Maybe the end of the world was just more tolerable that way. He pulled two energy bars from one of his boxes and pressed them into Myrra's hands.

"Give these to him when you see him," he added. "Say hi from Lin and Maya." Then the two scurried off, giggling, clutching their loot.

In the distance a crowd formed around a raised metal platform next to an elevator shaft that ran up through the scaffolding, literally sky-high, like an infinitely long pneumatic tube. Tobias noticed that, unlike the rest of the darker, greasier metal surfaces in this place, the elevator was outfitted in polished chrome. It practically glowed, even from this far away. As a person who valued cleanliness, Tobias regarded it like a shining beacon. Everywhere they walked, he tried to protect his clothes from all the grimy soot-laden surfaces, but it was in vain—streaks of black grease ran down his pant legs, he could feel soot accumulating in his pores.

More than anything, Tobias felt tired, and he was having trouble remembering the last time he'd felt awake. Time had become unmoored, like a ball of yarn unraveled and left tangled on the floor. The sped-up carousel of sunrises and sunsets in the desert, and now here in this world with no light, it was impossible to tell... Was it evening? Was it morning? Was it the middle of the night? He looked down at his watch, wiping soot off the glass screen.

"What time is it?" Myrra appeared over his shoulder, making him jump. Had she been that close the entire time? Her hand was on his arm.

"It's four in the morning."

The absurdity registered on Myrra's face and she let out a sound, halfway between a moan and a laugh. It occurred to him that she was still carrying Charlotte. If he was tired, she must be exhausted.

"You want to stop and rest for a while?" he asked. He watched her consider it, nearly give in to temptation.

"No—"

"Want me to take Charlotte?"

Myrra put a protective arm around the baby nestled asleep in her scarf.

"It'll be OK," Tobias said, sensing her hesitation. He knew she could use a break, but she needed to be the one to decide. As far as he was concerned, she was entitled to make all the decisions from here on out. She nodded and unwound the scarf, cradling Charlotte gently. Somehow, even with music pounding around them, Charlotte was asleep. Tobias couldn't help but feel a little jealous. Myrra leaned into Tobias so that they were face-to-face, almost touching, transferring Charlotte into his arms. She tied the scarf around him so that Charlotte could curl against his chest. A lock of Myrra's hair caught in his glasses. She smiled and reached up to untangle it.

"I'll walk ahead, so you can keep an eye on us," Tobias said. He wasn't sure she heard. The music was getting louder the closer they got to the elevator platform. Tobias pulled an old shirt out of his bag and wrapped it awkwardly around Charlotte's head, trying to muffle her ears. She cried out, her eyes still closed and her face scrunched together, but then fell back asleep again in minutes. Poor thing—to sleep through any of this noise, Charlotte must be completely spent.

The closer they got the denser the crowd became, everyone moving in unison, eyes closed, dancing with a kind of ecstatic oblivion. They wove through throngs of people until they reached the platform. The air was filled with the salt of sweat.

They both looked around, craning their necks over the dancing bodies. Tobias noticed a small glass-paneled room off to the side of the elevator shaft. Inside, a dark-skinned man was adjusting sliders on a control panel, a set of headphones halfway over his ears. He was shirtless, sweating and smiling, bobbing along to waves of music pouring out of the speakers. It had been a long time since he had seen sun, and a long time since his hair had met with a pair of scissors. It hung in dreadlocks down his back, his beard a tangled mess in the front.

Myrra leaned in close to Tobias so that he could hear her over the music. "I think that's Tom," she shouted in his ear. Tobias grabbed her hand and pushed through the throng of people until they reached the glass room. They rapped loudly on the door, trying to get his attention over the noise. Eventually the man noticed them, nodding and smiling beatifically. He cracked open the door and poked his head out.

"Requests?" he asked. He was older than he'd looked at a distance. A blue workman's shirt hung over the back of his chair. Someone had drawn a flower on the front of his chest in black marker with a smiling face in the middle. Tobias examined his eyes. He seemed sober.

"No," Tobias said. "We're looking for Tom."

The man threw his arms up in the air in an ecstatic wave.

"You found him!" He smiled even wider at the two of them.

"We need information!" Myrra shouted. Tobias could barely hear her. He noticed she was shifting her expression to match his energy, smiling, leaning in. Tobias stepped back, full of admiration, and let her work her magic. Myrra and Tom spoke back and forth, all smiles, but Tobias couldn't make out what they were saying. Eventually Tom sat up and nodded at her, giving them both a goofy grin. Myrra turned back to Tobias and shouted in his ear.

"Come on," she said. "He's taking us someplace where we can talk."

Tom hopped out into the crowd, pulled off his headphones, and tossed them at one of the dancing bodies near the door.

"Ryan, you're deejaying," he shouted at him, then gestured to Myrra and Tobias. "Follow me."

The interior of the elevator carriage was more brushed chrome, large enough to lie down in, larger even than the penthouse elevator at Atlas Tower. With all the noise and the dark outside, it took her a second to adjust to such a calm, well-lit environment.

"Have a seat." Tom waved at the bench in the back, and Myrra and Tobias collapsed onto the cushions. Tom had put his workman's shirt back on but left it unbuttoned, the blue fabric flapping against the skin of his chest.

It felt good to sit, as though her body were floating and her legs had vanished completely. Tobias lowered Charlotte onto his lap and leaned against Myrra's shoulder. She could feel the warmth of his skin through the fabric of her dress. She felt the vibration of his breathing, and under that the breathing of Charlotte, who had slumped down and now lay half in each of their laps.

Tom gave them a quizzical look, as though seeing them for the first time. His eyes roamed over their clothes and shoes, their hair. "Where did you two come in from?"

"We followed the road from Kittimer," Tobias said. His voice sounded hoarse. Myrra dug into her bag and handed him a water bottle. He looked at her gratefully, as though she'd just presented him with a chest of gold, and took a long drink. After a moment of consideration, Tobias passed the bottle to Tom, who gulped down the rest.

Tom's eyes grew even wider. "Through the desert? Why did you head here?"

Myrra paused. She worried about asking questions, the desperation of it, and she worried about the answers.

"I heard that there might be some sort of escape plan in place—shuttles, or pods, or something..." Myrra was rambling. She wished she had something more concrete to go on.

Tom laughed at her, not entirely cruelly, just in shock and disbelief. "Does it look like anyone's got an escape plan?"

"Well, not for us, but we'd heard there might be some sort of program that the rich were buying into. Charlotte"—Myrra stuck out a finger and let Charlotte wrap her tiny fingers around—"is the daughter of one of the richest families in New London—the world, really. We figured she would qualify for special treatment."

Myrra could feel, even as she spoke, that she was grasping at straws. She felt Tobias's hand rest on her knee, a preemptive gesture of comfort. Tom looked down at her, his eyes softening with sympathy.

"No, there's nothing like that here. Not in the hull, anyway." He spoke with incredible gentleness, but it still felt like knives stabbing through her. "Honestly, I don't think anyone's conceived of a shuttle that could keep people alive long enough to get them to Telos. It's just not technologically possible. We put all our engineering into this one ship. If this ship can't do it, then nothing can."

He crouched down and rested his eyes on the baby, reaching out a large hand and placing it softly on Charlotte's knee. "I'm sorry," he said.

Her thin string of hope snapped.

You knew this, she thought. You knew this was too good to be true.

But she mourned anyway. She would die. She'd come to terms with that. But she'd hoped, if she forced pure will onto the universe, she'd hoped that she could save Charlotte. Now in the image of her frozen and drifting through space, she was also holding a small frozen child.

She would hold her till the end—she wouldn't let go of her, she wouldn't—

Her body hunched and shook from sobs. She wanted to fold in on herself, layer by layer, until she was as small and compact as a marble. Another part of her brain kept chiding her for her reaction. Why couldn't she stop crying? Why couldn't she calm down?

Myrra felt warm arms wrap around her body. She looked up and realized Tobias was hugging her, with Charlotte squished in between them. It didn't make her sadness go away, but it felt better. She leaned into it and kept crying.

Tobias kept hugging her, rocking her back and forth. Charlotte reached up and touched her hand to Myrra's cheek. She looked confused.

"What do you need? What can I do?" Tobias whispered to her with gentle curiosity. Nobody'd ever asked her that before.

"I don't know," she answered honestly. She wasn't used to answering such a question. But she was deeply moved that he'd asked.

Tobias held on to Myrra as she shook and cried. She bent herself around Charlotte, as if her body alone could act as a buffer against the universe. He wished he could help her more. He wished he could know what she needed.

A part of him had known it wouldn't work. But he'd still hoped, for Myrra's sake. For Charlotte's sake. But he'd been so happy to be a part of their little unit, to have a shared purpose. Maybe he should have spoken up.

But would it have mattered?

"This might be too much," she said, her face muffled in her own lap. "This might be too much for me."

He just wanted to fix everything. He clenched his fist. In his hand he imagined a million long silver strings, reaching out through the hull, back into the world, attaching themselves to the ground and the horizon and the sky. If he could just hold on to those strings tight enough, if he could twist and pull hard enough, maybe he could hold the universe together.

Tobias rubbed Myrra's back and shoulders and felt the muscles relax a tiny bit. That was something, he thought. He could fix that. Just a tiny bit.

"It was always going to be too much, at some point," he said.

Minutes later, a million years later, Myrra came up for air. She felt numb and impossibly sad, but her body still felt relief in sitting up and taking fuller breaths. Instinct always dominates, in the end.

Tom was still with them in the elevator, but he stayed politely silent. Myrra was grateful.

"Thanks for talking to us," she said when she was composed enough to speak.

Tom nodded at her. "I'm actually really grateful you guys asked for my help. I was getting a little tired of the DJ booth."

"That sound setup is impressive," Tobias said. "Do you do a lot of the tech work around here?"

Myrra almost laughed at Tobias, talking about mechanics and engineering at a time like this.

"Technically I'm not supposed to. They've got paid guys they rotate in for that kind of work. But you pick up things, the longer you stay in here. And I've been here awhile."

Tom reached into his pocket and produced a small tin full of something sticky and herbal. He pinched a fingerful out of the tin and stuck it inside his cheek to chew. "The last of the paid guys and managers left about a week ago. Some were saying they had an in on this suicide program, designer drugs, I guess, make you feel like you're floating up on a cloud instead of dying. The fools. There are good and bad ways to die, but none of them have to do with what drugs you're taking."

Myrra focused on his words, the puzzle pieces falling into place. "Was the program called Escape?"

"Sounds right, I don't know."

Tobias looked at her.

Myrra laughed, filled with morbid humor, thinking of the morning that she'd chopped the hand off his bloodied corpse. "Too bad Marcus got word too late. Would have been an easier way to go."

"So there's no one left here, overseeing the workers," Tobias observed.

"We outnumber them by quite a bit. Once word got out that the hull wasn't going to get fixed, even the guys that wanted to stay, we let them know they weren't welcome." Tom flashed a devilish smile, showing off the remaining teeth he had. "If we're going out, we'll go out dancing instead of working."

Myrra considered the dark greasy world they'd wandered through. "And everyone stayed here?"

"Folks were exploring a bit at first, but all the kitchens and mess halls are on the first ten levels, so eventually they all just settled in here."

"Nobody left and went into the desert?"

"Not many. It's essentially suicide without a car," he said. "Plus, most folks end up preferring it here, over time."

"Really?" Tobias asked, gently incredulous.

"It's true," Tom insisted. "You two haven't seen a window yet?"

"A window to what?" Tobias asked.

Tom's face settled into a knowing expression. Myrra couldn't quite make him out. He seemed unnaturally calm and attentive, as though every moment were a religious experience. He would have fit as the follower of a guru somewhere in Kittimer, but it was difficult to make sense of him here.

"You guys feel like taking a ride?" he said, gesturing to the elevator buttons.

"Where does the elevator go?" Myrra asked. She didn't much feel like going anywhere. She'd failed at every goal she'd tried to attain these past few weeks. She was tired of wandering. In some ways, she wanted life to just be done with, instead of this terrible waiting and the need to fill up the time.

"There's elevators that go all the way up to the sky." Tom made a long vertical gesture with his hands. "But the best window's at the halfway point, just before the gravity shift."

Myrra didn't fully understand that, but was too tired to ask about it.

Tobias squeezed her shoulder and gave her a worried look.

"Let's check it out," he said casually, as if he were offering up a posh place for lunch. It was all so pointless. Myrra stared at him, not willing to say yes or no. He offered her a careworn smile. "It'll be a distraction, at least."

They didn't have much left besides distractions. And one more question, Myrra realized, though one she was almost too afraid to ask. Every previous answer had been a bad one.

Tom was busying himself entering a code into the elevator's keypad.

"Hey, Tom," Myrra asked, trying to keep her voice even. "Have you ever run into anyone out here named Ami Dal?"

Tom shook his head. "Doesn't ring a bell, but the hull is very big. There's a worker placement manifest on the mid-deck where we're heading; I can check for you if you want. Who is Ami Dal?"

"She's my mother."

Tom nodded with understanding but didn't say anything more. He finished entering the key code; the elevator jerked once or twice, then started to rise.

"Oh—" Tobias reached into the top of his bag and pulled out two energy bars. He tossed them to Tom. "Lin and Maya say hi."

Tom took them and examined the packaging, his eyes glistening.

"Aw..." he said. "Those two kids..."

He tucked both away into his pocket. He looked at Myrra and Tobias, gesturing to an empty spot on the corner of the bench. "May I?"

They nodded, he sat.

"Thanks. It's a long ride." His jaw rolled the chew around in his mouth lazily.

"I'm so tired," Tom said. "I've been playing for days. Everyone's afraid to stop dancing, afraid to be apart in case the end comes. But I'm glad for the rest."

The four of them fell into silence. Tom leaned against the side wall of the elevator. His chin bobbed down once, twice, then fell lightly against his chest, cushioned partly on the pillow of his own beard. A bit of brown drool trickled out of his mouth.

Without him noticing it, Myrra had fallen asleep against Tobias's shoulder. Charlotte, too, lay snoring between their laps. Tobias himself was exhausted, but tried his best to stay still for their sakes.

Far from feeling lonely, being the only one awake, Tobias pictured himself as some sort of sentinel, keeping watch while the others rested. It was all he could offer for protection.

He passed the time thinking about Barnes, and what the measure was for a good man. What the measure was for a good life. Would Barnes have been proud of him? Did that matter, when Barnes had proved to be so wrong about so many things? With all this new knowledge roiling inside him, Tobias did not think of himself as a particularly good man, or that he'd led a particularly honorable life. But that couldn't matter less now. Nothing could change it. All he could do was be the best person he could be for however much time was left, and hope that the entirety of a life well lived could fit into the span of a few days, or a few hours. How much longer would it be?

The elevator slowed smoothly to a halt, jolting Tobias out of his half-conscious daze. He checked the time. They'd been ascending for half an hour.

"Are we here?" Myrra asked sleepily, raising her head. She looked over at Tobias as if he might know. He laughed. Her hair was sticking up at odd angles.

"You're halfway," Tom said, rising groggily.

There was a pleasant dinging noise as the elevator doors parted. The doors led out into a wide metal room with solid walls, ceilings, floors, and Tobias was relieved to see no scaffolding. It was quiet and deserted. Every footfall they made in the room reverberated and carried.

Charlotte rubbed her eyes and started crying in Tobias's arms. Myrra perked up at the noise.

"Is she just tired?" he asked, trying to rock her.

"No, I think she needs changing, here—" Myrra took her and laid her down on the floor.

Tom looked fondly at them while Myrra changed the diaper. He leaned in to Tobias and said, "You make a nice family."

Tobias didn't know what to say to that, but it gave him a glimmer of happiness.

Two women wearing headscarves wandered in from a door at the opposite end of the room, walking amicably, hand in hand. They had the same underfed look as the other contract workers but seemed content nonetheless. They cried out and rushed over when they saw Charlotte. "Oh! A baby!"

"Hello, sweet one." One of the women leaned down a little too close, and Tobias noticed Myrra's shoulders hunch defensively.

"What have you two been up to?" Tom asked. He seemed to know everyone. The women shifted their focus from the baby and walked over to Tom, but Myrra's shoulders stayed tense.

Tobias sat down beside her. "You OK?"

"Yeah, just a reflex." Myrra laid a hand down on Charlotte's stomach. Charlotte batted it away, then rolled over and started crawling across the room.

"Oh, no you don't..." Tobias got up and chased after her.

"We could use a ride back down now—we've run out of food—" The two women fell into discussion with Tom about what food was left in the kitchens.

Tobias scooped Charlotte off the floor, and the ground started to shake. His knees buckled and he fought to stay upright, keeping a tight grip on Charlotte as he looked over his shoulder at Myrra; she was on her hands and knees, trying to stay steady.

"Charlotte—" she cried.

"I've got her—" Tobias answered.

It was a short quake but even more violent than the others before, and with metal surrounding them on all sides, the walls and ceilings shrieked like some primitive death omen. Tobias couldn't help but think, This is it. He didn't feel ready—he clutched Charlotte and sought out Myrra with his eyes. She looked back at him—he didn't feel ready at all.

Then the shaking stopped. Everyone fell silent at the reminder of what was to come.

Myrra crawled toward Charlotte and Tobias—he ran over and met her halfway, collapsed down next to her. She reached out for Charlotte, grabbed Tobias by the arms, held the both of them close, so tight her arms ached.

"Not long now," Tom said in a quiet mumble. Nobody responded.

"Wait—I was going to look up your mother," Tom said, hurrying toward a screen embedded in the metal wall. Tom continued talking, as if the sound of his own voice soothed him. He'd lost his knowing repose. His movements had a nervous energy.

"Sana, you ever come across a woman named Ami Dal?" he asked one of the women, punching buttons.

"No—" Sana said, helping her friend up off the floor. "Should I?"

"I s'pose not..." Tom said distractedly, scrolling through the lines of names on the screen. He mouthed each one to himself as he ran through. Myrra left Tobias and Charlotte to stand behind his shoulder, unable to contain her curiosity.

"Here she is—" Tom said. Myrra's mind went anxiously still, waiting and hoping. Tom pressed a finger against the screen, then streaked it horizontally across the surface, leaving a fingerprint smudge as he traced the line of data.

"Says here..." He squinted. "She was assigned to Sector Ten when she arrived..."

His face fell. "She died two years ago. I'm sorry."

Myrra mourned all over again, a heavy aching grief, like stones sewn into her stomach. But it was a funny thing—so much had fallen apart in so short a period that her body didn't allow another complete collapse. She couldn't go any lower; it just added to the texture of the floor of grief that was already there. The texture felt like acceptance. She had to accept what was, and what was to come. She breathed it in, like a blue, heady smoke.

Tom was still talking, seemingly afraid of silence. "She actually lived a long life here, all things considered. People don't usually last that long..."

"You say Sector Ten?" Sana piped up from a few feet away. She was looking at Myrra with an immense amount of sympathy.

"Yeah."

"There are some folks here who used to work Sector Ten. They came to visit the window." Sana laid a hand on her friend's arm and jogged toward the doorway where they'd entered. "One second, let me just see—"

She disappeared through the door. Myrra could hear her distantly, her voice echoing off the metal walls. "Any of you here ever meet Ami Dal?"

A chatter of garbled speech echoed forth in response, but Myrra couldn't make any of it out. She felt a hand on her elbow. Tobias was standing beside her, holding Charlotte. She hadn't noticed him walk up.

"You OK?" he asked. He was trying to be serious, but at the same time, Charlotte kept reaching up to try to snatch his glasses. Myrra allowed a small smile to break through and caught her raised hand, encircling her pale fist in her cracked brown fingers.

"I'm fine," she said, which was true and not true: Of course she wasn't fine. Who could be fine right now? But it was all relative.

And relatively speaking, she was doing better than she should have been. Her mind and her soul were still treading water.

"Hey," Sana said, emerging with four other workers, dragging one of them by the hand. She waved excitedly at Myrra, jangling the old woman's arm in her grasp. "Luce here knew Ami Dal!"

The old woman—Luce—was a head shorter than Sana, though it was hard to tell exactly how tall she was from the way she hunched. Her skin had the same dark pallor as Tom's. Sana pulled her across the room and presented her proudly to Myrra, letting go only when they were standing right in front of her. Luce, for her part, glared disapprovingly at Sana, clearly unappreciative of being jerked around like a rag doll. Despite her squat stature, she had an air of dignity about her, and a look that practically screamed, *Respect your elders.*

Luce abandoned her disapproval and turned to look at Myrra, taking in her face with a pair of sharp gray eyes.

"You look like her," she said in a voice that reminded Myrra of a dry broom sweeping across a stone floor. "You Myrra?"

She nodded.

Her mother had talked about her. For some reason she'd assumed Ami had wiped her right out of her mind. Myrra stood there, completely dumb, imagining what her mother could have possibly said about her, until finally Luce piped up again and asked, "So, what is it you want to know about her?"

What a thing, to come up with a specific question about a person that might fill in the gaps of two decades of missing history.

"I-I don't know—" Myrra stammered. "What was she like while she was here? Was she happy?"

Luce tilted her head and gave her a sidelong glance that made Myrra realize how stupid her question was. "Nobody's exactly happy here."

"Of course—"

"But she liked to talk. She talked a lot. It got her into trouble with the engineers, sometimes." Luce let out a dry cackle. "She talked about you. Told us how much she missed you. Most of us have people we've left behind. It's one of the most frequent topics of conversation around here, speculating on the lives of people we can't see."

Myrra glanced around and saw a few faces, Tom's among them, nod with knowing.

"She liked to say she missed you, but that she didn't worry about you. She said you were a survivor."

Myrra felt a warmth in her chest, like a light turning on in a dark room. Luce wrinkled her forehead and peered at Myrra.

"Where'd you come in from? You don't look like you've spent much time here."

"We came in from the desert. And Kittimer before that."

Luce's eyes widened and her head reared back slightly in her surprise. "You came in from the desert? Then Ami must've been right about you."

The light inside her grew. She'd been a survivor even back then, even as a child with no loss or anger at all. She hadn't thought of herself that way. And her mother had been a survivor too. Or more of a survivor than Myrra had thought, in any case. But she still needed to know.

"How did she die?" she asked.

"Cancer, I think."

Nothing violent. Nothing self-destructive. Myrra felt anxiety peel away from her like a shed layer of skin. She was still sad, but the sadness was fresh and new and healthy. Her emotions could breathe.

"But I wasn't there. That's just what I heard from others. I got transferred five years ago. We only worked together for a few years, on an electrical shift up on the sky."

"The sky?" It was Tobias who piped up behind her shoulder, asking the question.

"Well, of course you have folks up there operating the sky, how else would it work?" Luce seemed to enjoy knowing more than Tobias. Myrra could understand. He had that look of someone who ought to know everything. "Of course, there's no one left up there now. Everyone migrated further down to where the kitchens are."

"Is that why the days have been changing so fast?" he asked.

"Have they? I wouldn't know."

"There's been a sunrise or sunset every half hour," Myrra confirmed.

Luce looked amused. "It could be. They left the schedule to run automated, but things degrade."

"Can we go up and see the sky?" She directed her question to Tom, who seemed to know the ins and outs best. She suddenly had the urge to stand where her mother had stood.

"Technically you go down; there's a gravity shift." Tom laughed at their confused looks. "It's to do with the way the world spins. It's hard to explain, but I'll show you if you want."

"It's actually quite lovely up there," Luce added. "You can see the whole world, humming along above you."

Tom put an excited hand on Myrra's shoulder. "But before you do that, you've got to check out the window. To see that again for the first time, that would be my wish if I could make it happen."

Tom gave her an eager push toward the door at the opposite end of the room. Myrra looked back at him, and he gave her a small gleeful nod, then fell into a conversation with the group of workers about possible changes to the stereo.

Tobias looked dubious as well but followed behind, holding Charlotte and bouncing her a little as they walked. How quickly he's gotten the hang of it, she thought. How quickly things change.

They walked over to the doorway at the end of the room, where Sana and Luce and the others had emerged. The room on the other side was smaller and very dark. There were a string of embedded desks in the center, with tablets and instruments attached that Tobias couldn't make out. All desks pointed toward the wall of the outer hull. Tobias turned to look and had to steady himself against the desk.

"Oh my God..." he said.

It was a window, about four meters wide, three meters high, and it looked out at the stars. The real stars. Stars the likes of which Tobias had never seen. Both of them stumbled toward the desks and sat on one of them, never taking their eyes off the view. Somewhere on the way, Myrra took his hand and held it, tight. Tobias sat and gaped—he thought of color, of the stained glass in Kittimer and the paintings he had seen with his father, the boundless depths of the reds and blues and purples that a good painter could achieve, the layers and complexity to be found in a good shade of black. Nothing he'd seen could beat this black.

The whole world was so small compared with the vastness that extended beyond this window, and what a thin layer of material it was that kept them from all that black outside. It was a deeply humbling thing, to stand in front of the universe. How could he hope to stand here and think of himself, of his feelings, his hopes, and claim any right, any need for them to exist?

Myrra was holding his hand. It felt like a tether; he was a balloon, she was the string, keeping him from floating away and popping when the weather got rough. Myrra held on to his hand, and

Charlotte weighed him down at his side, and he knew for certain that if they had not been there to ground him, his molecules would have separated and dispersed into thin air.

He was going to die. It hit him again, as it had over and over that past week. He would die soon, and when he did, that was where his body would go, out past that window, stiffly turning over and over in darkness, drifting between stars. The thought broke his heart in two, but it wasn't a panicked thought. For the first time since he'd learned their fates, his mind wasn't trying to fight the feeling of it.

For Myrra it was impossible to understand the dimensions of what she saw. It wasn't like the dunes of the desert, which up until now had seemed to go on forever, or like the catacombs of Nabat, which had receded into deeper and deeper darkness. This was darker; this was something really and truly endless. There was no horizon.

She compared the stars, in her mind's eye, to the stars as she'd known them, the ones she'd seen every night growing up in New London. They'd felt so far away; now they seemed flat by comparison. And here there were so many! Here, in front of her, was a multitude of stars, a storm of stars, dancing into the great beyond.

Her heart filled—it was hard to express the feeling this view gave her. There was such grace to what she was seeing—light and fire, movement and life. Memories flashed in her brain, of similar moments that had elicited the same feeling. The time Imogene had permitted her to come along to the ballet so she could hold her furs. She'd stood at the back of the theater and watched as the dancer moved with absolute fluidity, her limbs flicking and floating like ribbons in the wind. It had filled her with something—she couldn't call it happiness, it wasn't as simple as that, it was something rounder, more all-consuming. What else had done that?

Charlotte's delicate blonde eyelashes, closing and opening, when she'd first laid her head on Myrra's chest. Her own mother when she was young, her eyes too, the dark-brown depth of them, as alive and deep as the darkness before her, looking out at her with a desperate and confused love.

And Myrra knew all at once, in this place, that she had forgiven her mother completely, and it was not a forgiveness based on exhaustion or giving up; she had forgiven her because in the greatness of what was before her, the loss of one person was a small thing, a single action in a multitude of actions stretching out in all directions. They were alone in an infinite black space, about to die, and so every action was full of meaning and insignificant, all at the same time.

There was the sound of a man clearing his throat. Tobias heard him, but didn't let his eyes leave the window.

"This is why folks don't leave," Tom said. "You understand now?"

"I understand," he said.

With great reluctance Tobias tore his eyes away and looked over at Tom. His serene energy was faltering; he seemed edgy now, standing in the doorway. He shifted his weight from one foot to the other, watching them.

"I think it's going to happen soon," Tom said. "I can feel it, in the walls."

Myrra turned her head to look at Tom as well. She squeezed Tobias's hand tighter.

"This is the halfway point, like I said," Tom continued. "So I was wondering, do you guys want to go all the way up, or are you happy here? I want to get back downstairs and be with everyone when it—" He stopped himself, changing tacks. "But I wanted to check on you guys before I did."

Myrra looked at Tobias.

"What do you want to do?" she asked him.

What a thing to ask. The truth was, Tobias's world had turned so completely around that he had no sense of direction left. It was clear to him now that he'd spent his life chasing all the wrong things, and now, at the end of it, he didn't want to chase after anything anymore. They were so close to death now, and he'd come so close to it being an empty death, a lonely death. Everyone dies alone, a man had told him years ago, and even then, at his most unsentimental, Tobias hadn't believed that was true. But you needed to find your people. He didn't care where he died, or what they did next, so long as they stayed together.

"I'm happy with you," he said. "I'll want what you want."

He smiled. She was still holding his hand.

"I'm so glad I've seen this," she said to Tobias, "but I think I'd like to keep going. If we're saying goodbye soon, I want to stand where my mother stood, and see our world one more time."

Tom opened a wide round hatch in the ceiling by the elevator bay and extended a ladder down from inside. Myrra looked up. The ladder rose up through a long wide tunnel above them, long enough that it was difficult to see the end. But it didn't feel infinite now, not after she'd seen the stars.

"So because of the way this world spins, this is sort of the last room where your feet are going to stay firmly on the ground," Tom explained. "Just climb up this ladder—it's going to go on for a while, I'd say about twenty-five, thirty meters. Keep a good grip, and about halfway through you're going to feel your weight start to shift. Just go with it, and you'll end up climbing down the ladder the rest of the way. Then you take another elevator at the end, and that'll lead you down to the sky."

Myrra looked over at Tobias, to see if he understood. Tobias looked as confused as Myrra felt.

"It'll make sense once you see it in action," Tom added. "I can't go with you that far. Like I said, I'd like to be down with everyone else for the rest of the time that's left." His voice broke halfway through his last sentence.

"The elevator on the other side has a button marked 'S,' for the sky floor. Just press that, and you should be good," he said. "Good luck."

He gave a small nod and started back toward his elevator, where Sana and Luce and a number of other workers were waiting. Myrra ran over impulsively and gave a long hug to Luce. She held her tight, feeling the woman's bones through her skin.

"Careful, you're going to break me!" she said, her words muffled in Myrra's shoulder. For a moment Myrra was worried that she'd hurt her, but when she pulled back, Luce was laughing. Tears streamed down Myrra's cheeks.

"Thank you for telling me about her."

The elevator doors opened, and they all filed in. Everyone was crying. They were so close to the end that now every touch, every interaction, felt momentous.

"Happy to meet you," Tom said. Luce nodded in agreement, sniffing a little.

"We are beholden to you," Myrra said. The words felt right for the occasion.

Tom gave a nod of his chin, tears welling up in his eyes. He raised a hand, and the chrome doors closed before him.

They climbed. The ladder was made of rough metal, same as the walls and floors. There was a faint dripping coming from somewhere, though Myrra couldn't see where. The tunnel surrounding the ladder was wide enough inside to keep it from feeling claustrophobic. Lamps protruded from the walls every few meters, giving them just enough light to keep going.

Myrra had Charlotte wrapped tightly around her body in the scarf, to keep her hands free. She went up the hatch first and heard Tobias clamber up behind her, rung by rung.

Her body became more buoyant the higher they climbed.

"Are you feeling this?" she called down to Tobias, wanting to make sure it wasn't hallucination or exhaustion.

"Yes—" he called out. He sounded nervous. "My shoes are barely touching the ladder."

Her feet became feathers, skimming along each rung. She followed Tom's advice and kept a firm grip with her hands.

"Oh—" She let out an involuntary noise. Her feet left the ladder entirely and her body floated sideways, perpendicular to the ladder, bobbing and drifting as if it were on an ocean current. She looked down at Tobias and laughed. He floated as well, one hand gripping the ladder and one hand trying to wrangle his glasses, which were floating off his head.

"This reminds me of your botched interrogation," she said. He laughed along with her but looked a little guilty, and suddenly she wished she hadn't brought it up.

Charlotte was chattering away in unintelligible sounds, lots of "oohs" and "aaahs," very excited by her sudden weightlessness. She wriggled against Myrra's chest, wrapped tight—she was getting too big for that scarf.

"Aaagah," she said, patting Myrra's neck, trying to get her attention.

"That's right," Myrra responded. She tentatively released one hand from the ladder, then the other, and hovered with Charlotte in midair. She looked below her—or was it above her?—and shouted to Tobias, "Try it!"

Tobias followed suit, lifting his hands just a few centimeters off the rung, his fingers curved as though he were still gripping it. He could only let go for a few seconds before he rushed to grab hold again. "You're better at this than me," he called back.

Charlotte was still making sounds and smacking at the sides of Myrra's face, evidently frustrated that she wasn't paying attention.

"Ohhh..." she said. "Uh-oh."

Her too-loud voice, the voice of someone still testing how loud she could get, rang through the metal tunnel. "Mmmm..." she said. She tugged on a strand of Myrra's hair.

"Mmma," Myrra repeated back. "Mamamaaa..."

She looked down at Tobias. "I've been trying to get her to say her first word," she explained. Myrra reached out a hand and pushed on the side of the ladder, sending her and Charlotte into a twirl. Charlotte squealed with delight. They were dancing.

"Mmmaa," Charlotte said. Myrra held her breath and let their bodies slow down and drift. She was so close to saying it. One more milestone... one more, please, before it was all over.

"Maammaa," Myrra said again, guiding Charlotte, testing the waters. She held her lips closed forcibly on the *M*s, exaggerating them.

"Mama," Charlotte replied, as if it were the easiest thing in the world.

"Ha!" Myrra erupted in one loud clear laugh.

Charlotte responded to the joy on Myrra's face and said it again, louder. "Maamaa!"

"That's her first word?" Tobias asked.

"Yes!" Myrra shouted.

Charlotte kept shouting, first "Mama," then "Maa-maaa," then just shouting long "aaahhhhs" out through space, caterwauling up and down the tunnel.

"I wish Imogene could see this," she said, staring at Charlotte's happy face. Myrra sent out a prayer to Imogene, dead on a slab in the morgue, shattered on a sidewalk. She had birthed Charlotte, named her. Those things were important, even if she hadn't had much of a chance to raise her.

Myrra swam back with Charlotte toward the ladder and grabbed hold again. Tobias hadn't wanted to say anything, but he let out a sigh of relief. Though he logically understood the physics of the situation, thinking back to classrooms and centrifugal force, he didn't completely trust it. Myrra didn't notice his worrying anyway; she was too busy watching Charlotte in awe. He didn't want to ruin their moment. The three of them proceeded, using just their hands to move along the ladder, their feet still stuck out in midair. They kept moving up—down? Tobias couldn't tell, and anyway, there didn't seem to be an easy up or down, now that he'd seen all the infinite directions of space. They kept going in the direction that they were going.

At some point Tobias felt his feet pulling up above his head. They kept moving, and his feet kept pulling in the opposite direction from the one they had been pulling in before, until his body had completely reversed direction. Up was officially down. It was very unsettling. Tobias held on to the ladder for dear life. There was some awkwardness once his feet settled back onto the cold metal rungs—due to his previous position, his body was now facing out, away from the ladder. With great care and a hefty dose of fear, he turned his body to reorient himself. It was funny how afraid he was of falling off a ladder, when he knew that he was unlikely to live out the day.

Was it even day? He checked his watch. The screen was black, with just a small frowning-face icon in the middle. Battery dead.

He looked down at Myrra, who was now below him when just minutes ago she had been above.

"You OK?" he asked.

"Yeah," she said, though she sounded somewhat breathless.

Another small tremor shook the walls around them. Both kept a tight grip on the ladder and waited for it to pass. What if the world ended right now; what if we died right here? Tobias wondered. Would that be so bad?

The quake passed. Tobias heard the soft clanking sound of Myrra's shoes descending the rungs. He followed.

His body felt heavier the farther down he went. He remembered a teacher in his seventh grade science class explaining how the world spun, how it kept everyone's feet on the ground. He was a wiry slip of a man, with thick glasses and a thin mustache. He had all sorts of diagrams, showing what the world looked like at a distance, animations to show the motion of it. He was very passionate about the subject, but not very articulate. Tobias had dutifully taken down notes on everything the teacher described, memorized all the terminology: *exterior axle*, *centrifugal force*, *path of inertia*. He'd copied down the distance from the ground to the sky, the circumference of the world on the ground. Tobias had been a very good student. He'd gotten an A on his exams, but it had meant nothing to him. He'd never really understood how the whole thing worked until now.

The elevator on the other side was the same shining chrome as the first, with the same cushioned bench inside. It made Myrra miss all the warm wood of Marcus's office and the textured stone of Nabat. They pressed the down button and sat down next to each other.

Myrra felt as if she were asleep and dreaming; everything had a slow-motion quality, even the way she unwrapped Charlotte from her scarf, her hands moving in lazy, wide circles. Charlotte, by contrast, was a ball of energy. She shook off the scarf and scrambled to have Myrra put her down on the floor, then crawled back and forth, back and forth, as if she were doing wind sprints. Myrra realized, a little guiltily, that they hadn't really let her move around since going inside the hull. There had always been a protective arm, a sling to keep her close. Charlotte rolled her body across the floor, kicking her legs out with abandon.

"At least she learned her first word, before everything ended," Myrra said to Tobias. She was suddenly very aware of their legs touching, of his finger on her wrist.

"I don't know, I think her first word might have been *uh-oh*," Tobias replied. Myrra let out a short laugh.

What if we died here on the elevator, on the way to the sky? Myrra wondered. Would that be so bad? She thought back to the ladder and their bodies floating, dancing through the air. Maybe they should have stayed there. Maybe that was the place to die.

"So do you understand the gravity shift, what happened on the ladder?" She hated being the dumb one, but she couldn't quite picture how the physics worked, and she was desperately curious.

"Kind of..." Tobias wavered. "Have you ever been on a spinning carnival ride—?"

She gave him a look. That was a stupid question, and he knew it. "Of course not."

"OK, try this." He held his hand up, palm flat, then grabbed her hand and pressed her palm against his.

"So the world is spinning, right? End over end, ground over sky. And the ground spins fast enough that—" He pushed hard against her hand, and on instinct she pushed hard back. "Objects, people, boats, cars, they all press against it. So by that same logic, the sky is spinning too—"

"So we can walk on the sky," she said, finishing his thought. She pushed harder against his hand and smiled. It felt like a contest now.

"Right. And since the world is shaped like a cylinder, if you travel up the side, between those two outer points, where the spinning is the fastest—"

"The gravity goes away, and we float," she finished.

"Well, not technically gravity, it's centrifugal..." Tobias stopped himself. She was still pushing forcefully against his hand, and he was looking at her, trying to suss her out. She liked it when he looked confused, when she made him a little uncomfortable. His strength faltered, and she fell forward against him, her face against his neck. She looked up at him. He looked terrified.

Well, why not? She pulled his head down and kissed him, because it felt good, because she chose to, because it was the end of the world and she liked his glasses and Charlotte had said her first word, and her mother loved her after all and when she was sad he had asked her what she needed. Tobias leaned into her too, caressed the back of her neck with his hand. She'd never kissed someone without an ulterior motive—she'd never kissed someone just to kiss them.

Then she pulled back and their faces parted, and she could feel energy crackling in the space between them.

"I'm glad you're here," she said.

"Me too." And he didn't lean in or try to push the moment; he simply laid a hand on her knee. Myrra liked that too.

36

MYRRA & TOBIAS

When the elevator doors opened, Myrra and Tobias were met with another vast tract of space. There was a metal floor, and there was a metal ceiling, but aside from the wall directly behind them, Tobias could see no boundary. The space was dimly lit, as Sector Nine had been, just enough light to make out the surroundings and not trip over anything on the floor. They wandered forward, hand in hand, Myrra holding Charlotte against her hip.

Ten minutes into the walk, a brilliant white light suddenly turned on in front of them, nearly blinding them.

"What—?" Myrra exclaimed, and tried to shade Charlotte's eyes. Tobias waited for his vision to adjust. It was a giant projection lamp, pointing upward toward a hole in the ceiling. Looking around, he could see countless more lamps dispersed in the distance.

"They're stars," he said. "The sky must have switched to nightfall." The sky, as it turned out, was nothing more than a great sheet of metal with holes poked into it.

"They'll probably stay lit for the next half hour or so," he surmised. Tobias thought back to the desert, how quickly the sun had set and risen. Presumably that aspect of the world was still broken.

The holes were rough and forcibly punched through. They reminded Tobias of holes punched in the lid of a jar with a screwdriver. Barnes had taken him hiking once or twice, when Tobias first came to live with him. He remembered finding a praying mantis in a grass field. It was a small green thing, and yet somehow it had a menace to it. Much like Myrra. Barnes scooped it up in a jar he'd kept in his bag, with air holes already punched into the top. They put in some grass, and a few ants they found along the way, for food. Tobias took it home and kept it on his windowsill. He thought he would make a pet of it, but the mantis died within days. He remembered feeling more guilty than sad. Guilt and grief washed over him again at the thought of Barnes, settling deep inside him like a lingering stomachache.

Myrra had no such memories of catching bugs in jars. When she looked up at the sky, she was mostly surprised that the engineers had done such a rough job of it. She'd expected clean-cut holes in the metal. Everything else in this world was so elegant. Then again, stars were only meant to be seen at a distance. Maybe this was where they'd skimped.

They walked for a long time, too long to measure, especially since Tobias's watch was broken. Myrra noted with amusement when he occasionally raised his wrist to check it, then stopped halfway through the motion and dropped his hand again. For someone like him it must be maddening not to know the time. To Myrra it felt as if there were no time, as if time had abandoned ship days ago, a coward who didn't want to see the end of everything and so had jumped overboard.

Occasionally the floor shuddered beneath their feet. When this happened, Charlotte let out a loud screech, trying to match the volume of the creaking metal around them. She seemed completely unafraid. Myrra wished she could say the same. She was jumpy as hell. At least the stars had turned on—it felt better walking around when there was more light.

"What's that?" Tobias asked, peering into the dark. Myrra followed his gaze. Off in the distance a long piece of metal hung down from the ceiling. They walked closer—it was another ladder, leading up to a circular hatch above them. Tobias walked forward, climbed up one rung, shook it, testing its weight. He held out a hand.

"Want to go sit among the stars?" he asked, his tone forcefully light and jaunty, as though they were on some adventure in a storybook and not preparing to die. He was trying to distract her, and she was grateful.

Tobias turned the handle on the hatch and popped it open. Light flooded down on top of them. Once Tobias climbed through, Myrra handed Charlotte up to him, then followed behind.

It was dusk outside; the starlight streamed out of the holes in the floor like spotlights, and the walls of the horizon projected a gradient of dusky purple. They wandered away from the nearest artificial star; the light was too bright to stand too close. Birds' nests littered the ground: pigeons roosted around them everywhere, ruffling their feathers as if they were unused to the company. No other signs of life besides the birds. Tobias had trouble comprehending how pigeons had come to roost up here at all, and he felt suddenly obsessed with the mechanics of the thing.

"Do you suppose they're able to fly through the midpoint of the atmosphere, when everything goes weightless, and come out on the other side?" he asked.

"I don't know," Myrra replied. She was concentrating on the floor, her feet dodging droppings.

"Do bird wings work in weightlessness?" he muttered to himself. It suddenly seemed so important.

Myrra stopped walking completely, and Tobias turned to her. She was staring upward, pointing. "Look," she said.

He looked up above their heads and saw the entire expanse of the world above them, skyscrapers, trees and mountains clinging to the ceiling like stalactites. The whole world was reaching toward them with fingers of human progress, with each building and tower usurping its predecessor, reaching ever closer.

They found the patch of sky where the floor seemed cleanest and sat, Tobias and Myrra leaning against each other, forming their own architecture. At first they let Charlotte roam free in front of them, but she kept crawling away, trying to chase the pigeons, so finally Myrra just pulled her onto her lap instead. At first Charlotte fussed and wriggled, but when another tremor shook the sky for a few seconds, she changed her tune and clung to Myrra's knee. Maybe even Charlotte is sensing it now, Myrra thought.

She could picture her mother sitting here years ago on the same sky, on a break from labor, looking up at the world. And maybe she was thinking of me, she thought, maybe she tried to pinpoint which city I was in, which building. Maybe she squinted in the same illogical way that I'm squinting now, trying to spot me on the ground.

Another quake shook. From where they were sitting, they could properly see that it was the whole world that was shaking; the sky, the walls of the horizon, and the mountains and cities and towns and seas and rivers above them. It was a marvelous picture—they were lucky to have a clear view, not a cloud in the sky. Leagues above them, mountains loomed with their snowy cragged peaks, flanked by the mirror surface of the Palmer Sea, which was fixed improbably upside down over their heads, not a drop of water spilled.

Tobias thought, similar to what he had thought before: What if we died here, sitting on the sky? And Tobias knew, even as he asked the question, that this was where it would end. He stole a glance at Myrra, who was busy staring overhead. There was no one around them. No one else had found this place. They had the most exclusive spot to sit and watch the end of the world. He looked around, looked above him. It was a beautiful place to die.

His father's voice entered his head: young Tobias, looking at the image of Cape Cod, saying to his father, "It's a beach," and his father snapping back, "Yes, but it's the right beach."

There was no right place to die.

Myrra reached out to grab Tobias's hand and pulled Charlotte closer. She was full of feelings: sadness, fear, happiness, anticipation, anxiety, anger, exultation. She brushed her calloused fingertips over Tobias's knuckles and felt the warm softness of Charlotte leaning into her. This had to be enough.

Without any one reason why (it was all reasons), Myrra's eyes welled up again and tears coursed quietly down her cheeks. As a way to calm down, Myrra focused on Tobias's face and told him a story.

"I remember the first time I ever tasted sugar," she started. "When I'd worked with my mother in the factory, they'd just served us eggs and porridge and bread: necessity food. But then I got transferred to the bakery. It was the only good part of my mother going away, that I ended up transferring out of the factory.

The baker who ran it was much kinder. And one day, after I'd done an especially thorough job sweeping, he gave me an éclair. The filling got all over my hands. I got so sticky. I tasted sugar on my fingers for weeks afterward. At least, that's what it felt like."

The story had no purpose. Myrra just needed to talk. Maybe she just wanted to share one last part of her life, before it went away. Her memories felt like marbles dropped on the floor, and she needed to catch as many as she could before they all rolled away.

Tobias smiled, soaking in the sound of her talking, as though Myrra's voice were permeating the pores of his skin. The words alone, the hum of a voice talking to him, regarding him, reminding him he was still here, was important.

Charlotte pushed off Myrra's lap and tried to stand. Tobias and Myrra both held out their hands, giving Charlotte something to grab on to. He heard a crack above them. Overhead, he watched a mountain crumbling. It was uncanny to see boulders rolling upward.

Myrra and Tobias looked out onto the projected walls. The horizon was shifting into night, turning a deeper and deeper blue. Tobias felt a thrill to his senses; this blue struck him hard, the same as it had in Kittimer, it was filling him up inside, it was sensuous and new and vibrant. It was a blue of loneliness. It was a blue of endings.

He wanted to say to Myrra: My life is remarkable now, for having seen all this with you. Instead he held on to Myrra's hand tighter. He felt that he must be hallucinating. Her face was glowing. Tobias dipped his head down and kissed Myrra lightly on the mouth. There was no other way to fully express his gratitude that she had agreed to share even a tiny sliver of time with him.

★ ★ ★

Myrra touched his cheek, felt the bristle of it; Tobias hadn't shaved in a few days. The world shook again. Charlotte's knees buckled, and Myrra swooped her back into her lap before she had a chance to fall down. She wrapped an arm around Tobias and held on until she felt as if the three of them might meld together. Tears carved pathways down her cheeks.

She wanted to say so many things. She wanted to have epiphanies. She wanted to ask all life's questions and feel the answers instinctively in her bones. At this point, after facing so much, she knew she was supposed to be wise and accepting of what came next, but she couldn't be. She turned to Tobias.

"I want..." she said, and couldn't finish the sentence.

He looked at her. He was crying too.

"Me too."

She could hear the pigeons cooing and ruffling their feathers. The birds were agitated.

From her lap Charlotte reached up and tugged on her ear, murmuring unintelligible sounds. Myrra kissed her on top of her head and stared off into the field of spotlights.

"Does it even matter, how we die?" She spoke softly to herself. Tobias heard it anyway, even though the world was shaking again.

"It matters, I think, when it's all that's left."

They held each other, and they waited. It was hard to discern lengths of time. They stayed there for minutes. They stayed there for days. They stayed there for a lifetime. And the world kept going, round and round and round, until it couldn't go round anymore.

ACKNOWLEDGMENTS

Thank you to Sarah Bedingfield for looking at a plot map on a blackboard and saying yes to it, and for all your guidance thereafter. Thanks also to the rest of the LGR team.

Thank you to my editor, Angeline Rodriguez, for seeing what I wanted this book to be and helping to make it a reality. To the rest of the team at Orbit and Hachette: I also owe you a huge debt of gratitude, specifically Tim Holman, Rachel Goldstein, Lisa Marie Pompilio, Lauren Panepinto, and S. B. Kleinman.

Thank you to everyone at Stony Brook MFA, especially Susan Scarf Merrell with her genius story brain and Paul Harding with his genius prose brain.

There are many people who helped me early in this process, who provided a crucial leg up: thank you to Emma Straub for always readily saying yes in the midst of a busy life, to Julia Fierro for those Sackett Street Writers' Workshop discounts, to Amelia Kahaney for all the advice over coffee. Thank you to every teacher I've ever had. Thank you to Marian Mitchell Donahue for the kitchen table craft chats with glasses of whiskey. Thank you to Kristie Stevens for reading all my terrible fan fiction when we were young.

To my parents, Larry Levien and Denise Kramer-Levien: thank

you for framing that kindergarten story I wrote (the one with all the aliens and entrails) rather than sending me to therapy.

And thank you to Michael del Castillo, my handsome genius of a husband, for the boundless support. I will love you past the end of the world.

SOUTHERN NEW HAMPSHIRE UNIVERSITY
3 4676 00198 9018